BEATITUDES & WOES

A Speculative Fiction Anthology

Edited by Travis Perry

Featuring stories by CW Briar, Parker J. Cole, RJ Conte, Hillari DeSchane, Lelia Rose Foreman, Gen Gavel, AT Hamlet, Rachel Kimberly Hastings, JL Ender, Rebekah Loper, Andra Marquardt, Steve Rzasa, and Randy Streu

Contents

Foreword by Parker J Cole

One day, about several months ago, in a Facebook group not so far away, an author posted this:

... I think it would be cool if someone organized a speculative anthology where each story is based on one of the 9 Beatitudes in Matthew or one of the 4 woes of Luke. 13 authors, each assigned/choosing one of those verses, expressing it in fantastical story form...

That author, CW Briar, had created a firestorm.

Immediately, interest piqued. Christian authors and readers jumped on the bandwagon on this wonderful idea. Of course! Why hadn't many of us thought of it before? General online excitement ensued as authors clamored for a chance to be one of the ones selected for this project. After all, most of us could recite them forwards and backwards.

But had we ever had a chance to explore them in a deeper context? What better way to do that than through the universal language of story?

When Jesus spoke to the crowds, He spoke to them by stories. Most of us can remember the parables because in fact, they are stories. The Sower and the Seed; The Rich Man and Lazarus, The Parable of the Prodigal Son. These parables have been passed down for millennia, spread along through the saving grace of the Gospel.

So, for a group of Christian authors and readers, utilizing

the element of story, we thought it was the best idea since sliced bread. For though the Beatitudes and Woes are simply spoken, within those few words, are great knowledge and understanding.

When Jesus said, "Blessed are those who mourn, for they shall be comforted," what did He mean? Commentaries of learned men and women abound but what if RJ Conte's "The Tears of the Emperor," a wonderful, richly styled story can help us understand better?

When Jesus said, "Blessed are the poor in spirit, for theirs is the kingdom of heaven," the struggles of the protagonist of Andra Marquardt's "The Promise," may illustrate how that *feels* better than understanding all the words Jesus used in their historical context.

Those are just two of stories told in this unique collection. Also, in that post not so long ago, CW Briar went on to say... *I'm not about to be the editor for this (at least not on my own), but if one of you wants to run with this, let me know.*

Authors, being imaginative, God-gifted people, need discipline. Not just in the written word but in bringing an idea of this scope together. When Jesus calls us His sheep, it's not a compliment. Sheep are hard-headed creatures. They need a shepherd to care for them.

And herding authors? Getting a group of starry-eyed, space nebula-seeking writers together? Keep them accountable and on track to make this project go from idea to published work?

You're going to need more than luck. You're going to need prayer and military discipline for that. And who better than that a military officer to whip us into shape? Each story has been painstakingly edited by our commander and handpicked for its quality and enjoyment.

Fortunately, Bear Publications, headed by Travis Perry, fits the bill perfectly. A member of the US Armed Forces (Army Reserve), Travis Perry is also a multi-talented writer, editor, and publisher of great speculative fiction stories. His company has published a number of anthologies unique to Christian publishing. *Mythic Orbits, Vol. 1 & 2*; *Medieval Mars*; *Victorian Venus* and a few more.

So, prepare to see these well-loved verses like you've never envisioned them before. These thirteen tales will keep you on the edge of your seat and perhaps give context to Biblical truths in ways you've never comprehended before.

Enter into the realm of Beatitudes and Woes.

Acknowledgement

Though not listed on the front cover as an author or editor, Cindy Koepp was an essential part of producing this book, assisting with editing, organizing, and marketing. Mary Campagna Findley did an excellent job on the front cover design, while Tabatha Catalan Guerrero, my wife, is producing ads and promotional pieces.

Thank you, each of you, for your invaluable contributions to this project!

Travis Perry, July 2019 Wichita Falls, Texas

The Promise

Cantis watched the dark clouds roiling toward him. Lightning flashed over the red-stone mountains making them look like lava-covered volcanoes. He mentally calculated the distance from home and the speed of the storm. He needed to leave now if he wanted to avoid getting caught in the deluge.

He started his All-T, and the engine rumbled through his bones. He always liked that sensation.

Halfway home, large droplets pounded his chest and helmet. He could barely see through his goggles and no amount of wiping helped. He removed them and endured the sting of the rain until his face went numb.

The storm passed by the time he reached the house, and the blue-green gas giant this dreary world orbited filled the sky. From the ash-filled rain when the Giant didn't block the sun's heat to the unrelenting cold when it did, Tellain was the most hostile planet Cantis had ever lived on. Due to the incessant earthquakes and volcanic eruptions, in a few hundred years, it would be unlivable. Most inhabitants had already moved to more stable worlds.

He and his twin, Cathrin, would have to leave soon, too. But go where? Their parents had brought them here because the local genetic and immunology hospital supposedly had a cure for Cathrin, But after two years of tests and too many medications to count, she hadn't improved.

Cantis shut off the All-T's engine the moment he entered the garage and stared at the door to the house. With their parents now dead, the decision was his. A more populated Federate system to look for a cure, or give up on finding a cure and watch Cathrin die a slow death? Considering his promise to his parents and to Cathrin that he would always take care of her, he had no choice.

He hung his dirty goggles on the handlebars and worked the stiffness out of his fingers. If no answers came to him out in the hills, none would come to him in the garage.

After he changed clothes, he went to check on Cathrin. Betti, one of Cathrin's nurses, approached carrying a small load of laundry. She smiled at him and said, "Doctor Helmers left you a message."

He nodded and gritted his teeth. Probably another so-called miracle drug that promised to cure all of Cathrin's ills.

The smell of dusty leather lingered in the small, dark den where his father spent most of his time. The only light came from the small window which deepened the cold, almost abandoned feeling to the room.

The last time his father sat behind the desk, it had been covered in medical books and pamphlets, and a holographic display glowed with floating files of potential cures sent over interstellar link.

Cantis had understood little of it. He wasn't a doctor, nor did he ever want to be. It was bad enough watching his sister slowly deteriorate. Why would he want to subject himself to trying and failing to help others?

He shook away the thoughts as he turned on the computer inlayed into the desk.

A single unopened message icon blinked at him.

His finger hovered over the screen as he debated yet again if continuing to search for a cure was worth the cost, the time, and the pain.

"A promise is a promise," he whispered as he touched it.

Dr. Helmers message read, *This may be a long shot, but I found a researcher who's developed a remedy for a disease similar to Cathrin's. I've contacted her about Cathrin, and she's hoping you'll contact her. Her name is Dr. Lyllith Mahest.*

Cantis wrote down the contact information. He'd never heard of Dr. Mayhest's world, so he linked to the Federate Library to research it.

The planet was called Verl, and was located just outside Federate territory.

Surprising. Most advanced research and new technologies were developed in what everyone called Federate Central since they had easier access to… well… everything. It didn't orbit a gas giant, so he wouldn't have to worry about earthquakes or volcanoes. At least he hoped not. Then again, it was twice as far as most other inhabited systems from Tellain, so the trip would take a minimum of a month. Was Cathrin healthy enough to survive a long trip, and could they even find a ship that would take them and all her equipment? To find out, he'd have to go to Xylus City. Driving to Xylus City would take almost a day, and possibly another two or three days to get everything ready.

He frowned. He'd have to leave Cathrin in the care of the nurses for a minimum of two days. It's not that he didn't trust them, but he'd never spent that much time away from her.

He shut off the computer and stood. Like it or not, he had to keep his promise to take care of her, and staying on Tellain was no longer a good option. Leaving for two days to purchase transportation to Verl wasn't much of a sacrifice if Dr. Mahest indeed had a cure.

Cathrin sat in her wheelchair in front of her table, her attention completely focused on her drawing. This time she used chalk, which left a brownish residue all over her fingers. She even had a pinkish smudge on her cheek.

The muscles in his shoulders unbunched as he sat next to her. His beautiful, forever innocent twin never failed to relax him by her mere presence. She saw only the good and beauty of the world and the people in it. In many ways he envied her, because he tended to see only the ugly and the dark. She kept him grounded while he did his best to keep her safe and happy.

She looked up at him and grinned. "What are you drawing?"

She covered it up with her hands, and said, "Not done."

"Do you want me to read to you while you finish?"

She studied him and her expression fell. "You're sad." He never could hide anything from her.

"I am." He paused. "I have to leave for a few days. Dr. Helmers found someone who might be able help you. I'll have to leave in the morning to get everything ready."
Large tears filled her eyes and dripped on her arms.

He held her close and said, "I'll be back as soon as I can, and I'll holo you as soon as I get there."
She pulled away and wiped her face. "Okay."

He kissed her forehead and said, "I'll be back later to see your drawing. And I'll read to you before bed."

She beamed at him before returning to her drawing with her usual vigor.

The next morning, he sat next to Cathrin's bed and watched her sleep in the pre-dawn light.

4

The only sound was the soft, rhythmic whooshing of the respirator since Cathrin didn't have the strength to breath on her own while she slept.

Betti would soon arrive to wake her and get her ready, but he wanted this moment, just the two of them.

He kissed her cool cheek.

She wrinkled her face and opened her eyes. She grinned at him and pointed at her mask.

He gently removed it.

"Hi!"

"Good morning, Cat. I know it's early, but I wanted to say goodbye before I left."

"So soon?"

"Yeah."

She held out her thin arms so he gently leaned over her and let her hug him. Odd how comforting and safe he felt in her embrace. It wasn't her arms, he realized, but her love for him that surrounded and warmed him.

I don't deserve you, but I thank God for you.

She gave him a kiss on the cheek and said, "Love you."

"I love you, too, Cat. I'll holo you as soon as I can."

* * *

An hour after sunset, he could see the lights of Xylus City and the spaceport illuminating the low-lying clouds in a grayish-yellow glow.

Most of the taller buildings were dark silhouettes, but the spaceport was abuzz with ships of all sizes taking off and landing—a chaotic dance of white, red, and green lights. A luxury liner headed toward him. It blocked out the sky as it passed over his head. The hair on his neck and arms stood on end from the power of her engines and shielding.

He envied the captain of the liner. He had hoped to become a pilot one day, and even started lessons, but their parents died before he could finish.

Because he hadn't earned his license, he would have to hire a pilot as well. Many pilots owned their own ship, so finding both in one shot should be easy. The big question was cost. He had received a decent inheritance, but he wanted to use that for more education—once he figured out what job he could train for that wouldn't take him away from Cathrin. This trip could deplete it all, and he'd have to find a job that would pay well enough for him and Cathrin.

At least he didn't have to worry about her medical expenses. Their parents had set up a separate trust, and any money that remained after she died would go for more research into a cure. The traffic thickened when he reached the boundary of Xylus City and what he anticipated would take an hour took almost three. He resolved that wherever they moved to, it wouldn't be a big city like this. Too stressful watching out for other drivers, and he couldn't go as fast as he wanted to.

When he finally found a parking spot in the massive lot, he took a deep breath and stretched his stiffened neck until it cracked. He was not looking forward to the drive home.

He entered the spaceport and quickly found the information desk.

"Where can I rent a ship?"

"Just follow the instructions." The older man pointed at one of the three touchscreens in front of him. "Choose your requirements, and it'll give you a list of prospects. Once you choose one, it'll inform the owner and they'll come get you."

"Do some come with their own crews?"

The man quirked an eyebrow at him. Probably wondering why someone as young as Cantis would request a crewed ship, let alone be able to afford one.

He shrugged a second later and said, "If that's what you require."

"Thanks."

Unfamiliar with the system, he had to start over three times before he found a ship that could work. Except no cost was listed. He'd have to negotiate with the owner, something he'd never done before. He didn't want to pay too much, but he also didn't want to counter so low the owner would say no.

A small robot with six wheels and a roundish face with two black eyes scooted up to him. "Cantis Greer?" it said in a female voice.

"Um, yeah." "Follow me, please."

Cantis followed it through the bustling concourse filled with almost as many robots as people. Some rolled on four wheels, some walked on tiny legs while others hovered a meter or so above the ground.

Maybe he could study robotics...

They entered a large bay that held small atmospheric shuttles as well as ships bigger than their house.

The robot stopped in front of a blue ship about twenty meters long with delta-shaped wings and a sharp nose. It had one engine in the rear and two smaller ones on each wing. An LVS, if Cantis remembered right. It was one of the more luxurious private ships one could get, and this one looked brand new.

This is going to be expensive.

The robot disappeared underneath the ship and a minute

7

later a tall, thin man with gray hair appeared from the hatch near the middle of the ship.

He studied Cantis as he stepped down the ramp. Cantis tried not to look away from his intense stare.

"You must be Cantis Greer," he said in a deep voice. "Yes, sir. Anton Martinetti?"

He nodded. "You're younger than I expected."

And you're older than I expected. He bit his lip to prevent the thought from escaping. He couldn't afford to insult the man.

"I'm old enough," he said instead.

Anton chuckled and said, "Come on in. I'll give you a tour."

The ship looked as new on the inside. It even had that astringent and oily new-ship smell.

Anton led down a narrow corridor and he pointed out the kitchen, the three guest cabins, and the bridge. In the center of the oval-shaped bridge sat a console with a pilot and copilot's chair.

Cantis shoved his hands in his coat pockets to fight the urge to plop into the pilot's seat and study the controls.

Anton took the seat and said, "Your app said you need to go to Verl with two other passengers."

"Yes. Myself, my sister, and her nurse."

"Nurse?"

"My sister suffers from a degenerative disease which requires constant care. I'll also need to bring some medical equipment, but it won't take up much room. Her wheelchair and a respirator to help her breathe at night. We're going to Verl to see a doctor who might be able to help her. Don't worry, though. She's healthy enough to travel as long as all the medical equipment functions."

"Power requirements?"

"Standard outlets work just fine."

Anton tapped the arm of the chair as he seemed to think.

"You realize the trip will take us through both Federate and non-Federate territory, and the trip will take a standard month."

"Yes, sir."

"I'll also keep tally of any extra power, food, and water consumption, and will charge extra if I think you're using too much."

"Of course."

"Twenty thousand."

Cantis almost choked. Twenty thousand? "You need to think about it?"

Sure he could afford it, but twenty thousand! Then again, LVS's were faster than most, and it looked big and comfortable enough for a month-long trip.

"I don't suppose I could talk you down some? I did take some pilot lessons, I can cook, and am decent at fixing things in case your engineer needs a hand."

Anton's eyes narrowed and he chewed on the inside of his cheek. "How's this: I'll take two thousand off now, and if I like your cooking and you help out when I need it without question or delay, I'll consider taking off another two."

A total of eighteen with a possibility of sixteen if he worked hard enough.

"Yeah. I can do that."

Anton stood and held out his hand.

As Cantis shook it, Anton said, "I'll draw up the contract and link it to you. When do you want to leave?"

"We should be ready in about three days."

"Three days it is, then."

9

* * *

Cantis leaned up against the bulkhead behind the bridge and watched Cathrin.

Anton allowed Cathrin to sit next to the pilot's console as he and Nathan, the copilot and Anton's older brother, performed their pre-flights. She hadn't stopped grinning since he offered. "What do you think, Cathrin?" Nathan asked. His voice was as deep Anton's, but gravelly. They also looked a lot alike, except Nathan was a bit rounder in the middle. Cathrin's grin widened.

"We'll be in the air in an hour. Unfortunately, you can't stay here when we do. You'll have to buckle down in your quarters."

"I'll take you," Cantis said.

"Thank you!" Cathrin waved as Cantis pushed her wheelchair out of the bridge.

"I like them," Cathrin said when they reached her quarters. Betti was already preparing the straps that hooked Cathrin's chair to the floor.

"Me too," Cantis said. Mostly he was pleased how well they treated Cathrin. Like a person and not a cripple or an idiot. Then again, they were paid to treat all of them well. He shook his head. He needed to keep his cynicism in check. Neither one of them gave him any indication they were anything but sincere.

* * *

Cantis wiped grease on his coveralls and studied the pump to make sure he reassembled it correctly.

"I'm done," he said.

10

Nathan sat next to him and took the pump. He studied every centimeter and manually pushed the pumping mechanism.

"Nice job. It's getting on sleep time, so go hit your pillow. You'll need the rest because we're leaving Federate territory in a few hours. We all need to keep an extra eye out."

"Why?"

"You mean you don't—you never heard of the Marauders?"

"Sure, but— I guess I didn't think about them coming after us. I thought they only went after larger liners or merchant ships."

"That's true, mostly. Smaller ships like ours aren't normally worth the effort. We still like to stay vigilant, though. If you decide to become a pilot, you'll need to cognize where and when Marauders tend to hit, avoid those areas when possible, and keep eyes open when you can't."

"And where we're going—"

"Is one such area."

"Thanks for telling me." Nathan nodded as he left the bench to reinstall the pump. *And thanks for making sure I won't get any sleep tonight.*

He entered his and Cathrin's quarters. She was sitting up in bed and doodling on a tablet. With limited space in their room, they couldn't bring any of her art supplies. So they settled on a sketch tablet. She didn't like it as much as her pencils and paints, but it was better than nothing.

Betti stood from the couch and said, "Everything is set. Just put on her mask when she's ready to go to sleep. It'll turn on automatically."

"Thanks, Betti. Good night."

Betti yawned as she left.

"What are you drawing?" Cantis asked as he sat next to her bed.

11

"Writing."

"What are you writing?"

Cathrin turned the tablet toward him. Her scrawling was hard to read at first, but he soon recognized what she wrote. It was one of their mom's favorite scriptural passages.

"Blessed are the poor in spirit—"

"For theirs is the kingdom of heaven." Cathrin finished.

"What made you think of that?"

She shrugged.

"You miss them, don't you?"

A solitary tear slid down her cheek and glinted yellow from the light above her. He gently wiped it away. "I miss them, too, Cat."

She shook her head. "Not that."

"What, then?"

She looked at him. Something in her gaze made him catch his breath. It wasn't sadness or fear, but something different. Something deeper.

He stroked her cheek. "What's wrong?"

She shrugged and said, "I'm sleepy."

Either she didn't want to tell him, or she didn't have the words. He learned a long time ago not to push. She could be stubborn when she wanted to.

He helped her lay down. When he grabbed respirator her mask, she grasped his other arm and said, "Pray with me."

"Pray?"

She hadn't asked him to pray with her in years. She mostly prayed with Dad. It was their own nightly ritual. She *was* thinking of them, but why would she lie about it? Unless she was thinking of them and something else?

"Okay. What do you want to pray about?"

"You."

"Me?"

Her grip on his arm increased. "God wants you to know. He's always with you, will always be with you. Never forget."

Cantis gaped at her and his skin tingled. That might have been the longest sentence she'd ever spoken, and her voice never sounded so strong.

He removed her hand from his arm and said, "I know, Cat."

Did he, though? Truth was, although he believed in God and did pray, his prayers tended to sound more like a friendly conversation than worshipful. Sometimes. More often than not, he whined and complained when something didn't go his way. He often feared he took God for granted and his anemic prayers reflected that. Maybe Cathrin sensed it and wanted him to do better, too.

But why now?

Between what Nathan just told him and Cathrin wanting to pray for him, did this mean something terrible was going to happen?

He suddenly felt a strong desire to pray. Even if it was out of fear, he didn't care as long as it helped alleviate that fear.

* * *

Cantis stared out at the murky gray of hyperspace from the pilot's seat.

After five days, nothing bad had happened. He relaxed some, but still felt a tension from Anton and Nathan. He supposed they wouldn't relax until they entered safer territory. Then again, the closer they came to safer territory, the lesser their chances of an ambush.

He hoped so, anyway.

"Ready for a break?" Anton said.

"Sure." He stood so Anton could take over. "Everything's nominal, although the engine temp is fluctuating more than usual."

Anton sat and checked the gauges. "Not enough for concern. The engine's still new, so the fluctuation's not a surprise. Still, we'll give her a thorough check at our next stop."

"When's that?"

"Two more hours. Have you ever seen a deep-space research ship?"

"No. I've read about them, though." They were often two to three kilometers long, and could stay in deep space for years at a time.

"You could be in for a treat then. This outpost services them sometimes."

"Do you mind if I stay?"

"No. I like the company. There's only so much one can do when flying on autopilot."

"How long have you been a pilot?"

Anton smiled. "Since about your age. Started with transporting freight, and been doing that for the last thirty-odd years. Bought this beauty just a few weeks ago. You're our first passengers."

"Why not continue transporting freight?"

"Boredom. Flying the same routes to the same systems month after month got tedious. People tend to travel to more interesting places."

"So now you get to travel everywhere, and get paid for it."

Anton laughed. "That's the hope."

Cantis barraged him with more questions about the LVS,

piloting and navigation, and places Anton had seen. Until the ship's nav buzzed to indicate they neared their destination.

Anton disengaged the autopilot, and the gray of hyperspace disappeared. It looked like they exited a thick fog.

They flew toward what looked like a massive, spoked wheel. A supernova behind it glowed blue and orange. Too bad they were on a schedule, because Cantis would have loved to explore the station. As big as it was, a tour would take weeks, easy. He instead leaned forward to look for a deep-space vessel. "I don't see—"

A new alarm sounded and the ship jerked to the port followed by a loud thump. More alarms sounded and lights flashed all over the console.

"What—?"

Anton swore at the same time Nathan ran in. "Marauders!"

"I know. Get them to the kitchen."

Nathan grabbed Cantis's arm and dragged him off the bridge. "Get your sister and Betti to the mess as quickly as possible."

He paused. "Do you know how to use a pulse?"

"Yes."

"You'll find them in the cabinet by the door—"

Something exploded in the engine room, and an acrid smoke filled the corridor.

"Move!"

The scrubbers kicked in the moment he took off running, and by the time he reached their room, most of the smoke had cleared. Still, his throat burned and his eyes stung, but he tried not to think about it. He had to get Cathrin and Betti to safety.

The door slid open. Betti stood in front of Cathrin, her face pale and eyes wide.

"Go to the kitchen. I'll take care of Cathrin."

"What's going on?"

"Marauders."

Betti ran into the corridor.

Cathrin held her tablet to her chest, and looked as pale as Betti.

"Cantis?"

He kissed her forehead and said, "Everything will be okay, Cat. Don't be scared."

"Okay," she said in a small voice.

When he pushed her into the corridor, something banged from above. He paused, but only for a second. He didn't want to get caught in the corridor if that sound above came from a Maurader ship attaching to the hull.

Betti stood in the middle of the room with her arms wrapped around her chest.

"Take Cathrin and hide," he said.

When they disappeared behind the counter, he locked the door and opened the cabinet Nathan told him about. Inside, he found three small pulse pistols and extra power cartridges.

He took one and loaded a cartridge. It glowed green, indicating a full charge. He pointed it at the door with shaky, frigid hands. He reminded himself to keep his finger off the trigger like his Dad had taught him. He didn't want to accidentally shoot Anton or Nathan.

A loud clang like something thick and heavy falling to the floor came from the hallway. Voices spoke, but he couldn't discern what they said.

Someone yelled and multiple shots of pulse rifles echoed from the other side of the door. A few pinged against the door itself, and he backed away. He was far too exposed, so he crouched behind the counter with the others.

Betti sat with her back against the counter, her eyes closed and her arms wrapped around her knees. Cathrin still clutched her tablet, but she no longer looked scared. Confused, maybe? More yelling. More shots. Someone screamed.

Silence.

Sweat trickled down Cantis's back and down the side of his face. He gripped the pistol even harder. Someone would come through that door eventually, so he closed his eyes and prayed it would be Anton or Nathan.

Voices on the other side of the door. Angry, frustrated voices, and a small scraping. Not Anton or Nathan, because they knew the combination to the door. That meant they were incapacitated or dead.

Cantis took a deep breath and tried to keep his hands steady.

"They'll kill you," Cathrin whispered.

He slid to the floor and stared at the pistol. He believed he could shoot anyone who tried to harm them, but belief wasn't enough. He wasn't trained, and he was but one man. They'd kill him the moment they saw the pistol, and what good was he to Cathrin and Betti then?

They had to surrender.

As the scraping increased, Cathrin held out her tablet and said, "Don't forget. God is with you. Will always be with you."

"Everything's going to be okay, Cathrin." *Liar.*

She continued to hold it out to him. He took it, but only because her arm shook with the effort.

The door swished open and multiple feet ran in.

For a few seconds, all Cantis could hear was his ragged breathing and blood whooshing through his ears. He stuffed the tablet in the back of his pants so they wouldn't think it was

17

a weapon.

A pair of black boots stood in front of him. He looked up into the barrel of a pulse rifle.

"What's this?" someone on the other side of the counter said. "A cripple?"

"Hands where we can see them," another said, "and stand up." Keeping his hands up, he stood, with Betti following suit.

Two other Marauders stood near the entry, their weapons pointed at them.

"We can't use the cripple," the tallest one standing closest to Cantis said. "What should we do with her?"

"Plank her," said the one standing next to Betti. A woman.

"No!" Cantis stepped in front of Cathrin. The tall one hit him
over the head with the butt of his rifle so hard Cantis fell to his knees, his eyes swimming.

"Another move like that and you'll go with her."

Cantis touched the side of his head. It stung, but he didn't feel any blood. He looked up at Cathrin when he could focus again.

"Don't fight," she whispered.

He shook his head. He would rather die with her.

"Please, Cantis. I'm going home. No one can hurt me there." Tears filled his eyes as he used the counter to help him stand.

"I can't."

He spotted the pistol less than a meter in front of him. If he dove for it, maybe...

The tall Marauder followed his gaze, laughed and picked it up. "Too slow."

"What can you do?" the female Marauder asked Betti.

Betti stared at the floor and said, "I'm—I'm a nurse."

"We can definitely use you. Vince, take her to the ship."

Vince pushed her out of the room. She didn't look back. "And what of you?" the woman asked. "Do we plank you, too, or do you want to live?"

How could he choose to live? Cathrin was everything to him—and everything he wasn't. Kind, generous, hopeful, his light when everything else seemed so dark.

He also couldn't deny her anything, and she wanted him to live, no matter what. Yet how could he stand by while they killed her? What kind of choice was that?

"Don't hurt her," he said. "She can't hurt you, and I have no skills you'd find useful. Leave us here, drop us off at the outpost. I don't care, just don't kill us."

The tall Marauder chuckled and the woman smirked.

"The ship's worth quite a bit of shell, but so are you, skills or no skills. No one will buy a cripple—"

"Stop calling her that," he said through gritted teeth. "She's my sister, her name is Cathrin, and she's far more important to me than anything else." He paused to swallow. "I will do whatever you say for however long you say as long as you let her go."

"You will do all that whether I let her live or not." She nodded at the tall Marauder who slid his rifle over his shoulder and approached Cathrin.

Cantis stepped between them and said, "No."

The tall Marauder stopped and raised his eyebrows at him. Cathrin took Cantis's hand and pulled.

He looked at her and said, "I can't, Cathrin."

The woman sighed and said, "Enough of this. Tranq him." Something sharp pierced the back of his neck, and a numbness spread from his neck all the way down his body.

"Love you," Cathrin whispered before everything went dark.

* * *

Cantis woke to a pounding pain in his head and a strange poking in his back. He sat up, and his eyes wobbled along with his stomach. He held his head in his hands and breathed deep until the nausea subsided. It did, but a dull, throbbing pain remained. Cathrin was gone. Tossed into space like garbage. He didn't see it happen, but he didn't need to. The cold, empty place in his heart told him. He dropped his hands and looked around. He sat on a slab bolted to a gray wall. There were no windows except for one no bigger than his face in the door. In the other corner, was a sink and a small toilet. A brig. If he judged the deep rumbling of the engines correctly, the Marauder's ship was big. Maybe as big as the luxury liner that flew over his head back in Xylus City.

As if any of that mattered.

Where were the Marauders taking him, and what did they plan to do with him and Betti?

His heart, on the other hand, didn't care. That part of him preferred to be floating out in the cold vacuum of space with Cathrin.

He lay back down and winced as something once again poked his back. He reached behind him and pulled out Cathrin's tablet. Some protector he was. The Marauders didn't see him as enough of a threat to even search him.

He stared at the darkened screen. If he turned it on and looked at her drawings, he would weep and never stop. Even now, tears threatened to pool, and the pain in his stomach grew so intense he doubled over with a groan.

The tablet dropped onto the floor on its edge and the screen flickered on.

"Never forget," his sister's voice whispered inside his mind.

On the screen was written the verse she had been practicing before they left, only the penmanship had greatly improved.

"Blessed are the poor in spirit," he read aloud. "Poor" was right. Too much grief. No hope. No future, either. That's not what the verse meant, but that's how he felt.

He kicked the tablet underneath the bed. Where was God when the Marauders attacked, spaced his sister, and kidnapped him and Betti—wherever she was now?

Cantis wanted to scream. So many thoughts paraded through his mind. Everything Cathrin told him about God being with him, how she never let her pain or lack of ability to do certain things—including breathing—get her down, or weaken her faith.

Something in the room changed. The air warmed and it no longer smelled like grease with a touch of mold. Instead it smelled fresh, like when he took Cathrin to the local greenhouses.

His image of her frozen body floating alone in infinite darkness disappeared, replaced with the memory of the greenhouse filling with her giggles, and her wide eyes full of wonder when she caressed the blooming flowers.

He finally wept, but it wasn't with despair. At least not entirely. It felt more like release.

He remembered his promise to always take care of her, and although he couldn't take care of her body anymore, he could take care of her memory. What better way to do that then to be the person she always wanted him to be? To believe, to let go and allow God's spirit to strengthen his own, and let him be a part of the kingdom Cathrin had always belonged to and forever would?

21

As footsteps approached his cell, he closed his eyes and whispered, "I'm all yours. Whatever happens next, I'm yours."

Blessed are the poor in spirit
For theirs is the kingdom of heaven.

Andra Marquardt

Andra, author of "The Promise," writes both science fiction and fantasy and is an associate editor for Havok Magazine (goHavok.com). Her day job is as a registered professional land surveyor in North Dakota. She's been happily married for 25 years and counting, and they have a son who loves to keep them on their toes. They also own a yellow lab named Ruckus who suits her name perfectly.

The Tears of the Emperor

Laki only remembered crying one time in his entire life. The emperor swished his way down the corridor, the end of his purple robe brushing against the dark veins in the milky smooth marble. Every step of his padded sandals echoed like a whispered drumbeat inside his chest.

It's almost time… It's almost time… It's almost time…

Laki's neck tensed, his fingers quaking at his sides. He refrained from bunching up the folds of the lavish silk he wore, cursing its endless rustling against the floor. Why must he wear this robe? Why must he wear the twisted golden crown of palms on his forehead? Why must he be emperor?

Even now, his trained response to fear was to clench his jaw and contain it all, stuffing it deep down into an imaginary compartment inside the recesses of his lungs, his labored breathing easing as it was safely suppressed.

But for the first time in his life, the air whistling in and out of his nostrils didn't slow, and his muscles screamed for mercy. This time containing the sorrow wasn't enough. They were telling him he had to let go soon – to cry.

But he wasn't ready. He would never be ready. Not while Lei slept underneath an evil man's roof instead of her gauzy hammock inside the palace walls. Yet to refuse would be to go against the will of God, which was unthinkable.

* * *

Talia waited for him by the small bamboo table. She always waited for him by that table, out on the veranda that kissed the sea. The marble steps led down into the ocean that surrounded their island like a mother's vast arms. An ocean that could be tempestuous when angry. An ocean used by God to demand strict obedience from the one He made emperor.

Laki's father and mother slept down beneath that peaceful expanse. The golden blue-tipped waves bowed to their new, young emperor's feet over and over again each day as they swept across the lowest steps of the veranda attached to his palace, reminding him that they were his to command.

The palace was nearly empty of life, a room here and there for servants and advisors, people to whom Laki wished he could unburden himself. But only Talia treated him like family.

Family. Laki's family now consisted only of one younger sister, the Princess Lei. She with black hair as soft as a raven's feather and brown sugar skin. She who learned to play the tambourines and dance from the moment she could walk. Lei with her wave-foam white teeth and easy smile.

The last time he had laid eyes on her, she had been frowning, furrows in her brow deeper than the sea floor, all her youth and beauty soured into one dark glare. She had thrown her golden palm bangles on the floor at their father's feet, and forever after Laki had associated the sound of a broken heart with the noise of metal striking marble.

His father, gentle, kind, and aged, having seen his wife's body to a watery grave only eighteen months before, bowed his own knees to his daughter, his white beard brushing her manicured toenails. "Lei! Do not do this." His voice had sounded like gravel, his fingernails scraping against

26

the vein lines of the floor. "Our God forbids you bedding with a man of this kind of evil. He will use and break you. Look at the bruises that line your arms already! Lei, my daughter, please stay!"

She had not even looked down. With a quivering chin, she yanked her foot out from under his face, her golden sandal squeaking. Whirling on her heels, knuckles balled into pale fists, she strode soundlessly and proudly from the room, the swish of her flouncy silk sarong like a death sentence murmured for the whole room to hear.

Laki had stood in stunned stillness, rooted to the marble, heart stopping within his chest. Ever after, he hated himself for not having run after her, knocked her senseless, and carried her unconscious body back to lock her in her bedroom until she became sane again–became the little sister he knew.

The little sister who pulled on his dark curls until he had a headache, who kicked white sand onto his belly when he was too tired to play anymore, and who had begged him to tell her the same story repeatedly about the monkey and the biggest coconut in the tallest palm tree. He had grown tired of the story very quickly, but his mother had told him the time when Lei would beg him for stories would be but a single wave in his life – coming into tide and out again. Blink and it would be gone.

And so he had told her the story until he could recite it half- asleep, huddled next to her in her silk and tasseled hammock, her rag dolls piled around both of them, itching his face. The mosquito canopy always remained open against her parents' will, dancing in the ocean breeze that visited her through her wide, open window looking out to the sea. Her heart had always been wild and free, and she used to warble with birdlike singing whenever they held festivals to God, as if her joy could not be contained on their island.

It had taken one evil man to harpoon her soul to the shore and smother it inside his dingy hut. A man who smoked the addictive reeds he gathered along the far bank, and had enslaved her body to its hallucinogenic powers and his promises of love. Laki had stood there that day, his feet melted into the floor, knees watery like overripe melon, until his father broke the silence. The elderly emperor had sobbed into the marble, wetting his wispy beard, and even though Laki knew his tears held no magical property this time, the sight still took his breath
away in sudden terror.

Now, as he faltered out the open bamboo doors towards the veranda, panic squeezed Laki's throat, burning his mind with visions of his sister washed out to sea, drowning in the wrathful waves of God, waves brought on by his future tears. The thought almost brought him to his knees in pain, but he was arrested by a soft hand on his arm. Only Talia dared touch him, and on days like today he was starved for human touch. He had refused to marry, afraid of the moment he would be called upon to shed at least a single tear, afraid of what it would mean for a wife and children.

"My emperor, you look unwell." Talia's gentle voice was low and rich, older than her years. She wore a simple white linen tunic, draped across her chest, one shoulder uncovered, a turquoise necklace with heavy beads nestled against her collarbone.

"They've told me the time is coming soon. The priests showed me the signs and miracles God has demonstrated to them." Laki took a deep breath, his chest rattling with the heaviness of what he had never wanted to say. "They dream the same dreams. Their crops multiply on their own, their cows give birth to two-headed calves, and the water has changed to blood in their jars. They do not lie."

He was grateful Talia did not gasp. But her back stiffened, and she left her hand on his arm. "Be seated, my emperor. Please relieve your mind and talk to me."

As he lowered himself into his seaside gold-edged bamboo chair, he reached for the glass of coconut milk tea she always had waiting for him, a single lemon slice perched on the rim for him to add tang to the sweetness. "There is nothing new to say." He covered his face with one hand, the other holding the drink momentarily still. Then he sipped at it, barely able to taste the refreshing liquid, lifting his gaze to meet hers.

Talia's brown eyes scanned his face sharply, her skin milky, whiter than most of his people, testament to how much time she spent indoors helping run his political affairs. He had the offhand thought to give her a leave of absence before the end – just in case. But he knew their God would never count Talia with the evil.

"How much time?" she murmured. Her heart may have been as strong as the largest palm in a tropical storm, but he could tell she, too, was afraid.

"A week or two at most. And then somehow, when I've never been allowed to before, I must cry." Laki stared back into her steady gaze, wondering if he should kiss her before the end, and if she, the noble servant and advisor, would hate him for doing so. Would she ever consider becoming his queen? He could not live without her, and he knew that if the worst happened to his people because of him, only she would understand the true depths of torment he would endure.

All emperors of the island were of a single descendance that possessed a magical gift unique to them, and it had been passed down from father to son for generations. This gift – or curse - enabled that when officially and symbolically inaugurated to the throne, the first time the emperor cried, his tears would "cleanse the land of evil." After that, his tears would be like any normal man's.

In the past, this "cleansing" had produced everything from wars begun overnight, to a neighboring islander arriving by canoe with a sacred text, to an epidemic that saw many bodies offered to the sea. One could never be sure if the emperor's tears, when the land was deemed by God to need cleansing, would change hearts or stop them from beating.

In his father's day, Laki had only been a child of five, and Lei not even born, when the emperor had been called upon to shed tears for the land. The worst flood in their people's history drowned everything but the palace, resulting in a third of their people's deaths. The promise had been that only those who were evil had been swept to sea, but God's list of evil had surprised many. It was no discriminator of persons, snuffing out lives of adults as well as children, even infants who could not possibly have chosen a wicked path. The priests had said that God knew what their hearts would be, and that man was born evil from the start. That with God's help, they could actually
choose good, and not vice versa. Laki was aghast that they would be so sure, and wondered at their staunch confidence in their interpretations of the sacred texts.

In the meantime, his stomach stretched tighter and tighter every day since he had ascended the throne upon his father's passing three years ago – his funeral attended by as many people who could crowd the beach to bring him honor, the dark tops of their heads extending back into the trees until Laki lost sight of them. Yet the funeral had not been attended by the one person his eyes kept watch for: the emperor's own daughter.

And now Laki was on the throne, and his pent-up tears were waiting for the day when it was his turn to cleanse the island. He wished he could simply die instead. How he cursed the role that had been given to him.

His whole life, his mother and nursemaids had trained him to stifle his cries. Even in babyhood, he had received a sharp sting on the wrist from a thorny bramblebush stem whenever he cried. He had instead attempted, in small boyhood, to express his pent-up sorrows, pains, and frustrations with violence, at one point crushing all of his mother's precious gem-studded leis by throwing them to the floor and stomping on them with his sandal. Shards of the rock-hard flowers had stuck him through the thin shoes, piercing his feet until he bled, but he hadn't even felt the pain. Not until he heard his mother's cries, watching her weep with the tears he was never allowed to shed, had he been filled with regret. He realized then that hurting a loved one pained him far more than bloody feet. He had cried with her, and she had miraculously allowed him to do so, making him promise it would be the very last time he did. That when he was on the throne, his tears held power and must be held back to wait for the priests' command.

He had vowed to never do it again, but he hadn't only meant crying. He had meant hurting others to comfort himself, and had then turned to reading of sacred texts and meditation to assuage his neglected emotions.

Still, burning on his mind, waking him up most nights to toss and turn in dread, was the thought that when the priests read the signs and called upon him, he would be expected to dredge up tears he had never been allowed to shed, and that the blessed relief that had always been denied him could cause his people immense suffering.

And then there was his sister. Lei was most undoubtedly counted among the evil at this point. It was likely she would die.

God must hate them all.

But he had no heir, and suicide was the greatest affront to his people, who would be left floundering without an emperor and spiritual leader. Yet, he was almost cowardly enough to attempt it anyway, but for Talia. Talia with her attentive eyes and never-wavering faith in his righteous heart. Talia who would be completely alone, and who had given her life to work by his side.

No, at least he could not do that to Talia.

* * *

"It is time, sir." The head priest, his long black hair cleanly knotted at the back of his neck, stood as still as a felled palm, his red robe coarse but pristine. His steely grey eyes seemed to see beyond Laki's throne room, as if used to gazing into the depths of the afterlife itself. Back straight, chin raised, he gazed above Laki's face to the small window over the throne that was perpetually open to the sea breezes. Laki liked to feel the wind whisper in his hair, even locked inside the room where he answered petitions from his people, a secret nod to his beloved only sister.

"When?" Laki whispered, his hands trembling at his sides. Careless of decorum at that moment, he did not try to hide their quavering.

"Tomorrow." The priest's low voice was like a deep gong. Laki felt a sudden revulsion for the man. The holy man was only doing his job, speaking for all the priests' thoughts, carrying God's messages to their island nation – or so Laki was told. But the priest didn't waver and the corners of his mouth didn't turn down. His hands never twitched, and his face seemed more solid than the marble under his feet.

Couldn't they show the slightest compassion for the task ahead? Did the priests not fear for their people? Maybe living in the temple had stricken them of basic human emotions. Maybe they were as grief-starved as Laki himself. Maybe they only cried when their emperor showed them how by example. Softening at the thought, Laki bowed his head slightly, and waved his hand dismissively at the man of God.

The priest turned stiffly without a word, the coarse crackle of thick red fabric signaling his exit. Laki remained with his head bowed, staring at the perfectly hewn square marble blocks lying side by side in their tight, compact sequence. Would blood stain these floors? Injured, dying people rushing in to mourn with him? Would the nation dissolve into more tears than the ocean waves themselves after he managed to squeeze out the one drop demanded of him? Would he then cry and never cease, to make up for the years when he could not? Would he die from crying, his heart broken?

The tiny amount of starfruit and mahi mahi in his stomach rose at the thought. He had barely eaten for days, spending time personally gifting extra gold coins to guards who had served him his whole life, as well as advisors and friends under him who had never steered him wrong. Every spare moment he spent with Talia, rewriting laws to make sure his uncle or then his second cousin would become Emperor if he were to die in the aftermath of some atrocity, divvying up palace treasures and wealth ahead of time so that there would be no contention about what went where if his people were left without him or in need. And he listened to the reading of the sacred texts to calm his devastated, racing heart. Talia had begun laying a hand on his shoulder while she read, her thumb stroking the top of his shoulder blade over the thin silk, and it settled him with bittersweet comfort.

Now that he had a single day left, he threw off his grand silks and pulled on a simple servant's white wraparound skirt, leaving his chest bare. Removing his crown, he held its weight in his hands, staring at the interlacing design of palm leaves all the way around. Once a week, a servant rubbed it in coconut oil until it sparkled. It was the symbol of his highest authority but it had always felt like a curse on his head, adding invisible weight that bowed his young, thin shoulders.

Now he was glad to be rid of it. He set it on the seat of the throne, nodding to his surprised guards on either side of the room.

The younger one lowered his seven-foot spear, ready for action, his chest and back covered in laced-up bamboo armor. He stepped forward. "My emperor-"

Talia stepped into the room through the plush purple curtain to the left. She bowed low, her turquoise necklace tapping her chin. "The emperor will return safely, I promise. He will be with me today."

The young guard gave Laki a sad, obedient look. Returning his spear to the upright position against his side, he stood at attention once more.

Laki felt a kinship with the man in a way he had never felt with his own head priest who was supposed to care about sharing God's words with his people. "Please help yourselves to a feast. The cook has laid one out for everyone here." Laki waved a hand generously the men. "We don't know what tomorrow may bring, so please eat and enjoy

34

yourselves." His voice broke, but his eyes stayed dry. They had forgotten how to cry.

The young guards, even at the temptation of rich, delicious food, did not cheer or smile. Instead, they bowed with their faces to the ground, laying their spears next to them, clanking on the marble. When they stood up again, they slammed their fists over their hearts. "Long live the emperor!" they cried in unison. Their faces full of warm reverence and compassion, they exited the throne room silently, the older guiding the younger guard with a hand clasped onto his shoulder.

"Your kingdom loves you, my emperor," Talia murmured, then dropped her eyes modestly to the palm frond-woven pack at her side, fiddling with its strap. She handed it to him.

Automatically, like always, Laki swallowed the sick feeling in his windpipe. "They may not after tomorrow," he whispered. Checking inside the pack for the sleeping vapors he usually carried with him deep in the folds of his royal robes, he satisfied himself that the vial was full of fresh liquid.

He had only once needed to use the foul-smelling drug - the first night he had been inaugurated as emperor. His father had been fresh in his watery grave only a few hours when they had pronounced Laki as ruler in his stead. Once he had escaped the ceremony, he had flung himself into his silk hammock and had been so overwhelmed with his loss, grief, and the task ahead, that he had felt those terrifying tears burning behind his eyelids. Clutching in his palm the one thing along with the crown they had given him that day when he ascended the throne, he had opened it under his nose to put himself under before a tear could dare appear. He fainted in an instant, spilling the remainder all over himself. The servants had to enter with ocean-water soaked rags covering their noses and mouths, and his clothing and hammock had to be burned. The room had been scrubbed three times before the smell disappeared into his nightmares.

Now, he stroked the vial under his fingers inside the delicate pack, its presence more security than any human being he had ever known. Then he held a hand out to Talia.

She stopped short, staring at his hand in confusion.

"Please," he begged, his voice weak. "Please for today, can I just be Laki?"

"I… I'm not comfortable with that, my emperor." But she reached for his hand anyway, and her grip was a strong as a clam's shell.

Her strength settled him once again, and he shook his head, relieved to be free of the crown. "Let us now go find my sister."

* * *

Laki had known there was absolutely no hope. Nothing had convinced his sister to repent yet. He knew he couldn't force her to turn back to God before the island was cleansed.

At first he hadn't even wanted to try. Seeing her face one last time, only to have her last words be rejection, would make what he had to do a thousand times worse. He had hoped to ignore her up to the end, forgetting the memory of her smile, the squeeze of her thin arms around his waist, and the sound of her laughter like the loud calls of the toucans at sunrise.

Yet, try as he might, he could not, and he realized, with one day left to judgment, if he did not go find her – if he did not try – he would despise himself all the way into the afterlife. If he must see her face once more, look at those eyes gone cold with the nauseous poison of the smoked reed, at least to satisfy himself that he had done all he could…

then so be it. And if his tears were to cause her death – to cause God to extend mercy to her no more–then he wanted her face to be seared in his mind as punishment, his burden to bear for the rest of his life. The island was a bit too large for a man and woman on foot to traverse in a single day. He should have given himself more time. He should have brought one of the palace beasts. But he had not wished to call attention to himself.

Keeping his head down, in case his face was recognized, he skirted around the edges of the marketplace, avoiding the main roadway. Passing braying donkeys carrying palm baskets and shiny sea glass bottles, monkeys dancing in corners begging for spare figs, and jostling families laughing merrily, Laki stared at his people for perhaps the first time. Ages had passed since he had left the palace walls, and then he had been carried on a tasseled carpet litter, peeking out occasionally from bamboo-armored hanging curtains, his family seated next to him chattering in his ears. It has been nothing like what he and Talia did now–mingling with the villagers like they were one of them.

Men wore sarongs of palm prints in sea greens and blues, dowels in their earlobes swinging freely, chests bare. The women's wraps were pinks, yellows, and lavenders, draped over their curvy, brown frames. Bangles up and down their arms completed their bright, rainbow-colored attire, their black hair gathered into plump knots on top of their heads. Everyone avoided the heavy, dark, royalty colors, and the pastel shades felt jubilant and joyful in comparison to the rich blood shades he usually wore. Thickly thatched roofs blanketed stalls bursting with bananas, papayas, fish, octopus, and squid. White sand speckled the weathered wooden walkways, lining the thin

spaces in between the slats, soft and grainy under his sandals. Musicians sat around in a circle at one end, cheerful reedy flutes whistling exuberant tunes over the brisk, light tapping of multiple coconut drums. A woman yipped and danced in front of them, her arms high above her head, her crooked teeth
flashing in an ear-to-ear grin.

How could Laki do this to his people? How could he bring any ounce of sorrow to their peaceful, happy villages? He clutched at the bag holding the sleeping vapors as his chest ached with the heavy weight of his dread.

They stepped off the boardwalk into the fern-covered under- brush beneath towering palm trees, the noise of the village lingering behind them. Passing large full-family huts and log cabin homes on either side, they walked under the lush forest, chickens and pigs braying for attention in small twine enclosures, smoke wisping out of blackened stone chimneys. Laki finally released Talia's hand once the last notes of the flutes had receded completely, plunging them into an eerie calm.

The last he had heard, by sending palace servants out as spies, his sister Lei lived in a dingy village by the opposite seashore. The noxious reeds she smoked once grew in abundance on that bank. Lei had taken up with the leader of a group of troublemakers who sold the weed at exorbitant prices to those dependent on the drug. His father had outlawed the reeds after Lei left, but it hadn't halted all secret production, as people also grew them in secret inside their inner courtyard gardens.

Hours later, as the forest thinned, and the sound of lapping waves could be heard, they neared the thin island's opposite bank. All Laki's planned speech flew from his head, and his hands dampened with sweat. He dropped his chin to his chest, panic rising in his throat. What would he do if there was a confrontation with the lawless leader who was bedding his sister? How could he look such a man in the eye and not want to destroy him? Or maybe he could simply let the drugged brute murder him before he had to shed a tear and ruin his nation. The anger and fight dissipated from his shoulders in an instant.

He lifted his head again and took in a deep breath of his favorite scent: salty sea air. The waves on this side looked lonelier, the beach empty, no beautiful bamboo and marble palace seated at its tip. Driftwood sat abandoned where the reed plants had been yanked up. Seagulls pecked at the rocks surrounding the shore. The horizon was a greying blue, announcing that a sunset would be upon them within the hour. There was so little time.

Shacks and shanties lay to Laki's right. Weathered wood held up flimsy tiny frames, and he wondered how human beings could live in such poverty. He knew these could not be the homes of the law-breakers, their pockets lined with gold coins from selling the drug. They were probably hiding out deep in a northeast area of the forest off the beaten path. But he didn't know which direction to take.

Laki motioned to Talia without a word. No need to break the pregnant silence yet. He knew that when words would be necessary, the object of their mission would then be upon him, and he felt deep dread down to the soles of his sandaled feet – feet which ached, unaccustomed to so much walking through cluttered forest paths. He pulled one off his tired foot, sharp pains sparking under his toes. Shuffling forward in the soft smooth sand, he slipped off the other shoe, heading for the first shanty. White linen servant's garment, shoeless, a single woman by his side… would anyone listen to him or answer his questions?

Breeze ruffled Talia's hair, and it streamed around her cheeks and chin as she reached forward to take the sweaty, gritty sandals from his hand. "Let me carry these for you... Laki." She eyed him shyly under her lashes, and he saw warmth and respect in her eyes.

Her intimate use of his name provided the boost of courage he needed. It mattered not if he didn't look like an emperor. He came as a brother, nothing else.

Laki heard the call of the gulls flying over the ocean behind his back, and the whistling of the wind around the cove cliff beyond them, the seashore rising sharply. Shacks sat on the ledge of the cliff wall, uphill from the beach below, their lonely beautiful view of the ocean in sharp contrast to the bustling village he left hours ago outside his palace. He rapped his knuckles on the peeling wood of the first door.

It swung open to a bald man standing barefoot on a wooden floor, his skirt tattered but clean. Against the back wall, a woman in a grass skirt and plain, coarse brown wrap turned a fish every few seconds over a fire on a spit. Caution and nervousness filled the man's dark brown eyes at first, but then his expression turned to confusion, small wrinkles setting in on his forehead. "Servants of the palace?"

Laki sighed. Even in plain white linen, his thin legs and soft- skinned hands gave him away as having lived a pampered life. "We are looking for Princess Lei, sister to the emperor. Do you know where she could be?"

The furrows in the man's forehead deepened. He coughed heartily and clung to the edge of the door, sliding his body behind it. The woman roasting the fish fixed wide, concerned eyes on them. "We know nothing!" they said in unison.

Laki's shoulders slumped.

"If you could just point us in the right direction." Talia's voice was firm and commanding, yet kind.

The man let his hand drop reluctantly from the door down to his side. "I really don't know. If you ask farther up the coast, I think you might meet some of Saua's relatives. But I would not take up with such a man. He's violent and dangerous."

Saua. The first time Laki had heard the cursed name, it had passed from his sister's lips like a prayer.

"Thank you," Talia said with a small bow of her head. "Enjoy your meal."

The man nodded, his face grim. Laki knew, if pressed, he probably could have given them more information, but he didn't feel right insisting further. The man obviously worried for the safety of his wife, although by this time tomorrow most likely no one would be thinking of Saua at all any more. Laki shivered again, the late afternoon sea breeze hitting his bare back like the cold breath of an angry God.

He and Talia continued on, knocking on every shack, always receiving confused or fearful glances. Finally, they came to the last place, a well-built cabin, set back into the shade of the forest, cozy, with smoke dancing out of the chimney, the smell of roasted vegetables filling their noses. Laki's stomach growled, and he reached inside his pack for the dried squid he had stashed next to the sleeping vapors. After this last house, he would share the simple dinner with Talia and then turn back, the evening light casting dark shadows all throughout the tree branches. It would be night by the time they arrived home, the market silent and covered in blankets, the twinkling of galaxies in the sky bright to shine their way.

Frustrated, a deep ache of disappointment settling in his chest,

41

he knocked. There was the sound of many voices scuffling, laughing, and talking. A pang added to the ache in his chest as Laki instantly recognized the joy and warm friendship in the voices. This was a happy family.

A small child opened the door, and four adults, all varying ages, sat on cushions beside a luxurious dinner of potatoes, ham, and browned carrots. Their hearth was decorated in bright beads and tassels, and large, succulent flowers were propped up in bamboo pots over every surface.

"Come in, friend! From where do you hail?" bellowed a stout man at the head of the table, his flowing blue robe cheery in the light of the candles propped up in front of him. A woman his age with gray streaked through her black hair gave them a wide smile, instantly setting two extra wooden plates down at the end. Two younger adults dished out food equally on each plate.

"We do not mean to intrude. You do not have to feed us." Laki held up a hand, moved by their friendliness and generosity.

"You are welcome just the same to join us!" The man waved them in, and his jovial, booming voice seemed to draw Laki in by force, his feet moving against his will.

The little girl scampered back to her spot next to the older woman, her thumb in her mouth, her other hand clutching a ragged monkey doll made from bright red linen with black beads for eyes.

Laki gingerly sank down onto a pillow on the floor gratefully, crossing his legs to hide his bare sandy feet. Talia timidly knelt beside him, sending him uncomfortable glances. She clearly was not pleased that her emperor was partaking of a meal with strangers.

"I can contribute dried squid." Laki pulled the strips out of his pack and laid them on the table next to the ham.

"Thank you kindly!" The man tore great chunks of ham with his large teeth, the giant grin never leaving his massive face.

The older woman, presumably his wife, kept refilling everyone's hollowed-out coconuts with more fresh water, and the small child, coconut milk. The young adults chattered with each other in soft voices, occasionally smiling at Laki and Talia. They referred to the older man as their father.

Finally, the man set down his water and fixed his eyes on Laki. "I do not recognize the looks of you. Where are you from?"

Laki chewed his ham and carrots, watching Talia who ate tiny portions, her jaw moving nervously, ready at a moment's notice in case of danger. He reached for her hand under the low table, and she clutched it fiercely. Finally, when Laki knew he had drawn out answering the man for a lengthy enough span of time to make things awkward, he swallowed his last bite of food. "We are from the palace looking for Princess Lei. We must be on our way to return home before nightfall."

A hush passed around the room, bodies stilling. Every eye in the cabin turned to Laki.

The child leaped up, holding her monkey to her chest. "Mama!"

Talia drew in a sharp breath, dropping Laki's hand. "Mama?" he breathed.

His gaze flew to the girl, and he stared at her for the first time. Her hair was a soft deep brown, and her eyes sparkled, large and bright. Her forehead was high, her hair in short braids. She was clothed in a sandy gray dress shirt. Her lips were full and rosy, and they were parted in surprise.

The man slammed the table with the palms of his hands, startling everyone, especially Talia who gave a little yelp. "What does the palace want with her?"

His wife slung an arm around the child pulling her close.

Laki sat up straighter, shock jumbling his thoughts. "I am your Emperor Laki. I have been told by the priests I must shed tears tomorrow, and I have come to find my sister before it is too late."

Everyone gasped with Talia this time. The young adults' jaws dropped, and they bowed with their foreheads to the ground, their toenails scraping against the floor as they scuttled into position.

But the man of the house looked Laki in the eyes. "The emperor at my dinner table..." he murmured. "I thought I recognized your face. You look just like your father, Loa, our God rest his soul. Your father saw much death, but loved his people." His meaty hands clasped together, and he finally bowed his head over the tops of them, slowly and reverentially.

"You may all rise," Laki said, his voice weak. When they did so, he set his brow firmly. "I am very thankful for the dinner and hospitality, but I must be on my way. Tell me what you know of my sister."

"She's gone!" squeaked out the worried voice of the older woman, pulling the little girl into her lap, running a bony hand over the child's braids.

Her husband sighed, a groan rumbling in his chest. "This conversation is not good for little ears. Atali'i and Afa'fine," he motioned to his adult children, "take Tagi to play in the barn. Feed and water the animals for the night."

Laki's breath fled. "Tagi..." Lei had named the child for their mother. The name meant "weep." For the first time, he wondered if his sister's rebellion actually had something to do with losing her mother so young.

44

Sending nervous glances Laki's way, Atali'i and Afa'fine bowed and walked backwards out of the room, hefting the little girl out of the older woman's lap as they went.

The man, whose name Laki still did not know, raised his hands to his fat ponytail, running a hand through the hair that lay plastered to the top of his head. "Lei left."

Sagging against yet more shocking news, Laki leaned forward, placing both hands on the table. "What do you mean? And who is the child?"

The woman glanced sharply at her husband, but stayed silent and began to clear the table.

"That is her daughter, little Tagi," he said. "Named for my mother..." Laki breathed.

He nodded. "Lei had taken up with Saua and his band, and they led a wild life, drugged on the reeds your father tried to help us be rid of."

Laki closed his eyes. This he knew.

"But occasionally, we would see her, thin and unhappy, when she came down to the beach to let the child play. On those days, her eyes were clear but she looked ill. My wife took to bringing bits of our supper to them, suspecting the lonely youth was our very own princess. She felt especially for the child, raised in an environment of violence and debauchery. They've stayed in our home at times when they needed refuge.

"And then two days ago she came to our home in the dead of night. Atali'i heard the pounding on the door before anyone else, and let her in."

"Was she hurt?" Laki's heartrate rose, picturing his sister fleeing with only stars to light her way. He turned to look at Talia, seeking comfort in her gaze, but her face was pained, her mouth a thin line.

45

"Not that we could see," the older woman reassured gently. She turned from where she was rinsing the wooden plates in a large bucket of water in the corner.

The man leaned back, his fingers laced over his large belly. "She brought Tagi to us, though, and asked us if we would watch over her in secret. She said she had somewhere to go, somewhere she didn't want the child's father to know about. We agreed, of course. Then she left."

Laki growled in frustration. Where had she gone? To see him? Not possible. It would only have taken her a few hours to reach the palace, and this had occurred two days ago. "How did she look?" he demanded. "Did she seem afraid?"

The man squinted one small eye. "Nervous, yes, but also excited. Like she was on an adventure, but didn't want to be discovered."

Curious. What had happened to his sister?

"My emperor," Talia murmured, "we must be on our way. The night draws near."

Laki stood, smoothing out his linen sarong, lifting his bag. "We will take my niece with me."

The man and his wife's mouths dropped open as if to protest, but then they exchanged glances and seemed to think better of it. "Your wish is my command, my emperor," the man bowed, rising to his feet with a groan.

His wife hurried to his side, eyes wide. "You will take care of the little girl? She feels like my own!"

Talia rose to her feet and bowed low to the couple. "Emperor Laki is the most gentle man I know. He will care for her like she is his own."

A rush of gratitude soothed his churning stomach, and Laki softened his frown. "God's cleansing will hit this island in some form tomorrow. I fear..." His voice cracked, but he managed to steady himself. "I fear for the princess. Tagi will be safe with me, and I also hope her presence will draw my sister back home."

The man lowered his head, new respect in his look. "We will pray to our God with you, our emperor."

Tears sparkled in the woman's eyes, and she nodded her head rapidly. Fear and jealousy made Laki catch his breath for a second at the sudden emotion she so freely displayed, but he reminded himself that her tears were safe. "How old is she?" he asked softly.

"Tagi is three years old. Born on the day your father passed from this world." The man's booming voice softened to a quiet hush when he spoke the last few words.

Laki bit his lip. It seemed there had been another reason why his sister had not attended the funeral. "Talia, please go retrieve my niece."

* * *

They rode back on mules, given to them by the man and his wife. The sky was like a lid over the island – sealed in blackness, but with starry pinpricks of light, letting Laki know there was something beyond the smothering veil of thick darkness. Maybe God was watching their island through the holes made by the stars, checking to make sure Laki arrived back home to do his duty tomorrow. His stomach sank as they rode, the night air breezy and uncomfortable.

Talia had offered to carry the child on her own mule, but Laki had refused. This precious girl, named for his mother, owning eyes he remembered on his own little sister, should not leave his sight. They had not found his sister, but where God led them was a tiny slice of hope. Moonlight reflected in the child's eyes as they rode towards the forest, and she was full of questions. She had questions about everything. Why did the mules have large ears? Why did the trees have leaves? Why was he her uncle? Laki answered everything gladly, her small voice filling the return trip with something beautiful instead of the same old silence.

He had been shocked when she came willingly. All their hosts said was, "Tagi, this is your uncle. He wants to take you to see the palace. Your mother will come get you there," and she had held out her arms to Talia, smiling shyly at him with that rosy little mouth. What kind of life had she led to change hands once again willingly? Was she so used to being thrown on strangers' mercy that being told she had a long-lost uncle was nothing? Or was it the innocent babyhood of a three-year-old who has an intuition for kind people? Laki prayed it was the latter.

Before they left, the men had clasped their hands around each other's forearms like equals. "You have done us a great honor by your meal, your hospitality, and your protection of the tiny princess. Please never bow again to me," Laki pleaded.

The man looked him straight in the eyes, his towering frame bent to do so. "We are loyal to our emperor – but also loyal to our God. We know He does all things well, and we trust His will. We all lost loved ones in the flood that happened two and twenty years ago, but we did not blame your father. The burden he bore was a heavy one, but it was the will of God. We will see our loved ones again – not all who were washed away were evil. Some believed in God. This cleansing is something none of us really understand, not with the extent of our sacred texts. And I believe that someday it will make more sense to us.

Do not give up faith, my emperor. We all stand behind you."

Fumbling with his pack, Laki had clutched the sleeping vapors. Only by turning on his heels without a word had he narrowly escaped tearing up throughout the moving farewell. Now, as they approached the quiet marketplace, his niece Tagi slept, her body heavily slumped against his right arm, which held her fast. His bicep trembled with the exertion, but he welcomed the pain, a deep protective love for her blossoming in his heart. As they rode, he bent and kissed the top of her head, her hair cold from the wind. Even as she slept, she clutched her cloth monkey. He wondered if Lei had made it for her. The thought made his knees tremble.

When they arrived back home, Laki rode straight to the palace door and handed Tagi off to an anxious, waiting servant. "My emperor! We were worried!" the older woman exclaimed. Her white linen tunic was wrinkled as if she had slept in it. "Who is this?"

"My niece." As the woman gasped, he rubbed a hand over his face. "Keep it a secret for now. I will explain to the servants soon. See that she is placed in Lei's bedroom." No one had slept there for four years, but it was kept dusted, cleaned, and provided with fresh silk tunics for the day his sister might return.

As the servant carried the sleeping little girl inside, Talia took the reins of his donkey, her lower eyelids dark from exhaustion. "I will take the animals to the stable."

Laki's muscles groaned, stiff from the day's journey. "See that the stablehand waters and feeds them, and have someone take them back to the man's cabin at first light tomorrow. Send them with dates, dried fish, and five gold coins in thanks."

"I will, my emp... Laki..." she stuttered, her gaze flitting nervously around the courtyard.

No one knew what tomorrow would bring. And meanwhile, the best woman he had known stood in front of him. Her tired eyes and windswept hair were more precious to him than all of the marble in his hallways, than all the fish in his seas, than all the gold in his vaults.

Laki's weariness and lightheadedness overtook his senses. In two steps, he strode around the donkeys and cupped her face in his hands. Ignoring the sudden startled look in her eyes, he lowered his mouth to hers and kissed her long and gently. At first, she froze under his mouth, but then she dropped the reins and raised her hands to cover his own. She melted against him, her lips parting.

When he pulled away, her eyes flew open in horror, and she covered her mouth with the hand that had just warmly enveloped his.

Laki smiled sadly. "Just in case," he whispered, and turned to trudge up the marble steps. Hefting open the heavy doors, he stole one last glance back out at the beach, the huts, the distant horizon, and his nation. Today was no more. Tomorrow was upon him.

* * *

Laki slept fitfully, but he was surprised he slept at all. The activity of the previous day must have forced his mind into unconsciousness in spite of his dread.

The priests stood at his door the instant he awoke, solemn blood red robes ominously conveying a sense of dread in the throne room.

Laki could not eat. The first bite turned to sand in his throat.

Instead, he changed into his simplest purple tunic, and placed the palm leaf crown back on his head. He sat hunched on his throne and tried to conjure up the emotions of the previous day. The bustling marketplace... the disappointment of not finding his sister... the large man's words of faith and support... Nothing worked. His eyes were bone dry, and he trembled.

The priests stood in silence in a row a spear's throw away from him, their solemn, piercing eyes trained on his face. He could not breathe. Suffocating, his lungs felt paralyzed in his chest.

Talia had assumed personal charge of his niece, and was seeing to her bath, fresh garments, and breakfast. Laki stayed away, afraid to be in the child's presence on this fateful morning, hating himself for the demanded tears and what they might cause to happen to her mother.

But after an hour of forced rumination on every sorrowful thing that had happened in his life to no avail, with the priests still standing in front of him like unmoving planks of wood, Laki felt like running away back to the shore and hiding on his belly underneath the kind man's table.

The pressure built in his chest, and he had just begun to pace the throne room when a shriek hit his ears. Tagi ran in and threw her monkey at his feet, sobbing wretchedly. His guards flinched and lowered their spears. Talia appeared soon after, bowing and mumbling frantic apologies to Laki and the priests. The intimidating men of God still did not move.

Laki waved two fingers at the guards and knelt down next to the child. Her fists were balled over her eyes, and her wails split the stifling tension of the room. Wincing at the sound, so foreign to his ears, and not knowing how to comfort her whatsoever, Laki cleared his throat. "What's wrong, my Tagi?"

But it was clear to see what had happened. The monkey's crude seams had split over its chest, spilling the dried pomegranate seeds it had been stuffed with all over the marble. The scarlet seeds reminded him of clotted blood, and the monkey's limp stillness suddenly struck him as something awful.

"Monkey is dead! Heart is broken!" the child sobbed in a lisping voice. Her wails grew with every word, and great rivers of tears gushed down her chin where they dropped to her feet. "I want my mommy! Where's my mommy? Mommy fix my heart!"

Lei.

Where was Lei to fix his broken heart?

As the child freely expressed her sadness and rage, and as the monkey lay with spilled crimson at his feet, Laki felt all was truly lost.

Heat rose under his lower eyelids, and a prickling began at his nose. In panic, he reflexively stiffened, but remembering the sea of blood red standing in the corner waiting for him to cry, he let the first tears of two decades well up in his eyes. His arms trembled, chin quivering. Gasping in terror and sorrow, he reached for the child. Pulling her round, wet cheeks into his shoulder, he threw his arms around her and squeezed her as tightly as he dared, his hands shaking.

Two wet drops escaped his eyelids and slid down his own face. He reached up a hand and touched one. In wonderment, he felt the dampness on his fingertips, marveling at the fact that he could finally cry.

The priests all swarmed forward like a single mass, frightening the child deeper into his embrace. The sober men examined his eyes and touched his hand to feel the last traces of the tear.

And then, as one, they bowed with their faces to the ground, and in a rush of heavy fabric, left the palace. No one had spoken a word.

It was done.

Once the last reverberating thud of the heavy golden doors had faded, Laki realized the little girl had stopped crying. She stared up at him in amazement, her eyes as big as a cresting wave, still wet and glistening. She looked at him like her mother once had, full of awe and warm trust. In her mind, an adult had cried with her over her toy. He assumed she must be astonished. Still unsmiling, his heart thudded in his chest, like the tide pounding a rock. What catastrophe would befall them? How long would he have to wait? In the past, things had happened within the day.

Talia crouched and wrapped her arms around both of them. She trembled as well. "I will sew your monkey, precious child. Be sad no longer," she whispered. "You have done a great thing for the kingdom this day. You were aptly named 'tears.'"

The child still stared in confusion, her rosy mouth a round circle. "You fix monkey?"

"Yes," Talia reassured, her voice breaking, her own tears filling her eyes – the first tears Laki had ever seen her shed. "Come now, child. I'll sew your monkey while you eat your pineapple." Peeling the little girl out of Laki's arms, she left him staring mutely after them. His guards' heads bowed in reverence and discretion. Their fists clenched tightly over their chests showed their loyalty even in this terrible moment.

Laki wiped his face and stood. His knees knocked together and he almost fell, stumbling to his gold-covered bamboo seat. What destruction might begin outside his doors at this very moment? When would he receive the first piece of news about what he – and God – had done? He stared at the inlaid gold as if his eyes were the sun and they could melt it down to ash – to show him the truth of what lay beyond.

In only a few minutes the pounding began.

Fists hitting the door startled him out of his tense focus, making him leap out of his seat. It had begun so quickly. Who would be the first to bring him the bad news?

Laki had to lick his lips twice to make his voice form the words. "Open it," he said to his ready guards, their spears lowered, eyes trained on the front of the room. Whatever suffering and misery his people would face, he would be ready to stand with them.

Then the massive doors were thrown open, warm sunlight flooding the room, bringing with it the scent of the sea.

And in stumbled Lei.

New tears rose to Laki's eyes, far easier to produce this second time. His sister! Come to say her last goodbye?

She was thin and gaunt, her face pale and hair unkempt. Gone was the luster in her cheeks. Her arms and legs were sandy and filthy, her clothing ragged and torn.

But her eyes shone.

With a bright sparkle so like her daughter's, Laki's sister ran towards him with wild abandonment, and he forgot everything from the past four years. He forgave in an instant every pang of pain she had caused. He had never loved her more than he did in that moment.

Lei.

She threw herself at his feet, her face pressing the tile, grasping at his ankles with her slender fingers. And she wept, like her own father had done four years previously, when he had begged her to stay. She rained tears upon the tops of Laki's feet.

His guards fell to one knee to bow their own heads toward her, their weapons clattering to the ground.

Laki threw his arms around his sister and lifted her to her feet. "Lei!" he said over and over again. "Lei! How have you been? Do you know about the tears? Did you know I never stopped loving you?" The words flowed and crashed out of his mouth like storm waves throwing themselves in delight at his palace steps.

His sister was home. Had his tears done this?

When she calmed her weeping enough to speak, she lifted tear-stained eyes - round, beautiful eyes that looked so much like the young wet eyes he had just looked into only minutes before. "Laki, my dear brother, I have news!"

"Speak! Speak!" he begged, his eyes roving over her face as if memorizing every detail. He held his sister in his arms!

Fumbling in the ratty bag at her side, she pulled out a fistful of yellowed, aging scrolls. Ink was smudged and smeared in places, but Laki could see there were row after row of thousands of words - all neatly lined up on the pages. Paper was expensive, and the majority of it lay in the priest's hands.

"Do you know what this is?" she whispered. When he hurriedly shook his head, she grasped his arms, and her face split into an exuberant smile. "I have more of the sacred texts!" She shook the scrolls at him, her entire body quivering. "Saua and his men recently came across a new method of crushing the reed and rolling it in paper to smoke it. But these papers they found had writing on them! None of them knew how to read, and valued the precious paper only for smoking." She shuddered. "But one day, feeling miserable and like I wanted to die after a dangerously high dose of the reed, I grew sick of the life I was in. I held one of the pages and, instead of rolling a reed with it, began to read it instead."

Laki's heart raced.

"It is part of the sacred texts that the priests have always read to us... but there's more. Passages and sections we have never seen before!" She bounced, waving her hands over her head passionately. "I secretly found out where he uncovered the scrolls, and it was a day's journey. I left immediately. It's a cave on the far, uninhabited part of the island, forgotten by our people. There in bundles lay the texts, sprawled out and abandoned, some buried far under the sand in water-tight clay urns." She threw her arms around him and buried her face in his chest. "Laki, I sat and read many of them right then and there, and my heart was moved. My heart was changed toward our God." Tears flooded her eyelashes. "Did you know that He loves us, Laki? Did you know that our God loves both of us? Did you know our God has a one and only Son? And this Son of God already cleansed the world from evil once and for all?" Her words flew at him without a breath in between. "Did you know these things?"

His head was full of wind and the air was gone out of his lungs. He could not process all that she was saying. But a deep certainty filled his heart with peace. God *had* cleansed the island of evil after all using his tears. His tears had brought his stubborn, wild, and disobedient sister, repentant and changed. Praise God! There were more sacred texts!

Suddenly Lei shoved the texts back into her bag. "I will have to go back for... for someone..." she stammered.

"But I will return and then I can read this to you! I left Saua for good three days ago, and I want to get to know the rest of the truth about our God with you, my brother. Please forgive me for so much evil." Her eyes flew to the door.

"We must let the whole island know!" She spun away from him.

Laki grasped her arm and pulled her back into his embrace. Smiling broadly, he pulled her toward the far curtain. "I think I know who you are looking for, Lei. Come, and let us sit down to eat as a family. I want to hear everything you have to say, and I plan to listen for the next hundred years and never stop." New tears flowed unbidden and free. "I am so glad you're home."

Blessed are they who mourn
For they shall be comforted

RJ Conte

R J Conte, author of "The Tears of the Emperor," has kissed only one boy in her entire life - and she married him - inspiring her to write about sweet and powerful love stories ever since. She writes issue-driven fiction that explores human nature and the depths of the soul while pointing readers to their Creator.

She writes a blog on parenting, publishing, painting, and decorating at http://blonderj.wordpress.com/

The Meek Shall Inherit

The motorcycle chugged as I revved the engine, struggling to keep up with the van ahead.

Knew I should have changed out that spark plug, I thought, scowling briefly at the highway speeding by below my tires.

I drove between two semi-trucks, eliciting a horn blast from one. The booming sound made me jump, almost causing me to lose my grip on the handlebars. Despite my growing body of superheroic experience, saving the day and socking it to the bad guys, I still got jumpy once in awhile.

Throttling up, the engine howled as the van sped across Vanewind Bridge, the bridge that led out of the city. In my mind, they'd crossed an invisible barrier. I had let them escape town. I would still catch them— naturally— it just meant I owed Nightshade five bucks. When she'd given me the bounty, I had bet her they wouldn't set foot out of Empire City.

An open lane of lonely highway stretched ahead. The van sped up even faster, blazing around a slow-moving SUV. I reached the bridge, tall cables stretching into the night sky dizzyingly far above me.

Lifting one hand, I used my powers to swap places with the SUV, putting myself were they had been, and moving them back to the start of the bridge. In the span of a second, I put myself mere feet behind the van. My tires skidded for a moment, confused by the sudden change in location, but the asphalt here was as good as where I'd been, so I didn't wreck.

Someone leaned out of the passenger side of the van, black machine gun in hand. I pulled a quarter out of my pocket and swapped it for the weapon. The thug stared in shock at the coin in his hand.

"Lose something?" I laughed with glee, waggling the gun. The motion put me off balance though, and I dropped it. The weapon sparked as it skidded off the street near my wheels. "I didn't want to use that anyway," I muttered.

The evildoer threw the quarter at me and ducked inside the van. It plinked off my windshield, chipping the glass. "Hey!" the high wind pulled at my words. "Dang bad guys, breaking my stuff," I muttered.

We were about to clear the bridge. *Running out of time.* Once they got out there, it would be harder to safely stop the van. Swapped items kept most their momentum, so moving the van back would only get me so far.

I tossed a quarter into the river below. I would have rather thrown a dime— my chances of getting the money back were low— but I was all out of smaller change. The quarter plinked onto the road in front of me as I swapped it for the van.
Below, I heard the kidnappers' vehicle roar as the engine struggled through the murk and brush near the shore. As I'd hoped, the van had plopped into the shallows, then lost its speed plowing through the weeds and sand near the edge of the river. I slowed down. Now came the delicate work of getting the victim safely out of the van. Before I could do anything, the roof of the van exploded, the driver bursting right through.

"Ok, Nightshade did *not* tell me about that." I decided I might want the gun after all.

I tilted my motorcycle, as though bringing her down, then swapped it for the gun. Armed but hanging in midair, I swapped myself for the quarter ahead of me, not wanting to hit the ground at thirty miles an hour.

My motorcycle clattered, drawing a wince from me. I rolled as I landed on the ground, expending some momentum against the street.

I pointed the gun at the kidnapper. He'd been floating over the river, watching in confusion. Spotting my sprawled form, he rocketed toward me. I fired the gun, but the bullets just pinged off his chest. I huffed a sigh and threw the dented weapon away.

"One of those, huh?" I asked.

The burly fellow nodded and grinned. He had a big, square lantern jaw, a mop of dark, curly hair, and a long, red cape. Depending on how strong he was, this could get messy quick. There was always a chance of coming up against Invincibles, but they were rare enough to be worth the risk.

"Capes are never coming into fashion, bud," I scanned the bridge. Talking had become a defense mechanism for me. The longer I stalled, the better I could strategize. I needed to get the girl out of the van and away from there. Preferably without getting my handsome mug beat to a pulp.

"They are," the floating thug protested. He flapped the edge
of the cape, suddenly self-conscious. "I'm bringing them in."

What was an Invincible doing working as a common thug?

That didn't make any sense, unless—

Unless he had a big-time weakness he was hiding. "You're not super strong, are you?" I asked.

His smile collapsed. He didn't need to answer.

Bullet-protection and flight, but no super strength. He was afraid of me! I almost laughed, but decided that would be a *terrible* idea.

Gun, motorcycle, quarter. I also had a few quarters in my pocket. And the thug himself, though swapping with someone able to fly could be incredibly dangerous. If I swapped with him and he was too high, I could break my ankle. Or kill myself.

"You got any powers I should know about?" The thug cracked his knuckles.

I didn't, but I wasn't about to let onto the fact.

"Garden variety atomics," I said. "And I can fly, but I don't like to show off, so I drive a motorcycle," I added. Joking around was like a neon flashing sign over myself blinking NOPE NO MORE POWERS but sometimes when I opened the floodgates on my witty repartee it was hard to stop.

"Liar." The grin returned. And then he rushed me, moving at something like half the speed of light. I swapped our places on instinct, but I forgot to make sure he was facing away from me, so I was suddenly falling through the air *with the bad guy still flying right toward me.* I panicked and swapped with my motorcycle. The thug crashed through it, sending motorcycle parts flying everywhere.

"Oh..." I bit back a bad word. "Crud muffins. I liked that bike!"

I stumbled, having picked up some momentum falling through the air. Down below, I heard the van's engine roar as the second thug tried to get it out of the river. If I lost my bike and they still got away I was going to be *furious*.

I moved to swap the van and felt a tightness between my eyes. I was getting close to my limit. Swapping too many big things would wear me out.

Mr. Lantern Jaw's head swiveled as he searched for me. "You

got a real annoying power there, Porter."

"Not a Porter," I said quietly— a little insulted. "Not a teleporter. My powers are so much cooler than teleporting."

I swapped the van for the gun lying in the road, sending the weapon into the river, then swapped the front tires for motorcycle parts. I'd kept them from getting away. Now what? I needn't have worried too much on that count. With the front of the van pointed toward me, I spotted the second thug. He was unconscious somehow. Knocked out in one of the transitions? The flying thug moved to punch me. *Time to get creative*, I thought, though in truth I had no idea what I was going to do now. Moving the van again had been a big mistake. I was all

but tapped. I ran to the back doors of the vehicle.

They burst open. Lightning surged into the flying thug, dropping him to his knees.

A girl in a dirty hoodie and stained leggings stepped out. She wore a yellow domino mask over her eyes, hiding a youthful, perhaps twenty-something face.

"Ugh, you ruined everything, you idiot!" she shouted at me.

"What?" I asked.

"What?" the flying thug added, apparently as confused as I was.

"Shut up." The girl jolted him again. He fell flat on the asphalt this time, unconscious.

"Wait. You're Zap-Girl," I said, grinning with excitement. "I know you!"

"Then you should know you completely screwed up our operation. These two-bit morons were going to take me to their base of operations. We've been tracking their kidnapping ring for weeks!"

"So have I. I was, you know, rescuing you from said kidnapping.

"I was never in any danger." Zap-Girl smirked. "You, on the other hand, were about to get your face bashed in."

"No way, had him right where I wanted him."

"What's going on?" A man in a red and white costume dropped from the sky.

"Justice Lord?" I asked. "You're working with Zap-Girl?"

Justice Lord's cape flapped behind him as he landed hard enough to crack the asphalt. He lifted a foot and grimaced at a black pebble embedded in his shiny, red boots.

"Yes, of course. Justice Squad? Haven't you heard of us?" he asked.

"Of course, I just didn't know you picked up Zap-Girl," I said.

"Aren't you part of a team?" he asked. "Everyone's teaming up these days, ever since that Steel Fox kid and his buddies saved the world."

"I don't need a team," I replied. "I work better alone. And don't talk about the alien invasion. Nobody talks about the alien invasion." It was true though. With the Vigilante Prevention Act being passed a few years ago, lone wolves like me were a dying breed.

"What do you mean?" Zap-Girl asked. "Everyone talks about the alien invasion. All the time."

"Well, I don't." I had successfully made it several years avoiding talk of the Invasion, and I intended to keep it that way.

"Hey, aren't you Swap Master?" Justice Lord asked. "I thought it was Flip Man," Zap-Girl said.

"Switch Master," I said. "I tried Swap Master for a bit. Didn't like it."

"The media called him Flipper," Zap-Girl said to the Captain.

65

"What, like the dolphin?" Justice Lord looked me up and down and grinned.

I decided it was a good time to change subjects. "Now what?" I asked.

"You mean now that you ruined an op weeks in the making?" Justice Lord shrugged. "I guess we're playing it by ear now."

"We got two low-lifes we can question," Zap-Girl pointed out.

"Good idea," Justice Lord said.

I surveyed the destruction wrought by my battle. The ruined motorcycle, the van's shredded roof. I spotted something shiny near the rear wheel of the van. My quarter! *Guess I'm saving a little money after all.*

"'Scuse me," I said, brushing past Zap-Girl to pick up the quarter.

"Let's get these two down to the precinct then," Justice Lord said, giving me an odd look as I tucked away my lost pocket change.

"What? Tomorrow's Taco Tuesday."

"Tomorrow's Thursday." Zap-Girl spoke with mild disgust, and an appalling lack of taco respect.

"Every day's Taco Tuesday when all you can afford is Taco Bell," I told her. "Can I come? I need to come with so I can report on the bounty,"

"You mean…?"

"Yeah, I'm in the bounty program."

"You're a mercenary?" Justice Lord asked.

"I'm in the bounty program," I repeated. "Gotta eat somehow." The bounty program, part of the Vigilante Prevention Act, paid superheroes to take down bad guys. The money wasn't amazing, but getting paid to crack skulls wasn't so bad, even if it came hand in hand with my greatest arch-nemesis.

Paperwork.

"You could work a day job like the rest of us," Zap-Girl protested. Many supers didn't like the bounty program. A lot of regular people hated it too, since it meant handing out tax dollars to people like me.

"I do." I decided not to mention my financial situation. I don't want to call my spending habits 'out of control' but let's just say that if they were a freight train, it would be the runaway kind. "You can't come with us," Zap-Girl said. "Tell him he can't come with us."

"You can't come with us," Justice Lord agreed. "Unless you want to help."

"Help?" I asked, frowning. "Didn't you hear my inner monologue? I work alone."

"Well, if you want your bounty, you're going to have to scratch our backs."

"Try again," Zap-Girl said.

"I mean, we scratch your back, you scratch ours?" "Better," she told the Captain, "but we don't need him."

"We don't," Justice Lord agreed. "But his powers are pretty cool. I mean I got flight, invincibility, super-strength, and laser fists, but being able to swap stuff? Never heard of that one before."

"Big deal." She waved a dismissive hand toward me. "He's like a magic Lazy Susan."

"You want to make some money, kid?" Justice Lord asked, ignoring her.

"Pretty sure we're about the same age," I replied. "But yes. I think I've made my motivation clear."

"Alright, it's settled then. We'll take these men to the station. We can question them before we turn them over."

"Great!" I kicked at one of my motorcycle's ruined wheels. "Can I get a ride?"

Zap-Girl groaned. "It's going to be a long night, isn't it?"

* * *

A chaotic mixture of police and criminal, superpowered and normal, Precinct 89 had the air of a madhouse during a full moon. We moved through an open room cluttered with desks. All around us were criminals in chairs handcuffed to desks, detectives in cheap suits asking questions and making phone calls, here and there a man or woman in costume.

Justice Lord guided the Invincible thug. Zap-Girl kept a hand on the other criminal, who seemed to be a normie. Judging from the way he kept twitching, I guessed she was giving him a few volts on the DL. Both were restrained with Dillinger Cuffs, a new device meant to repress superpowers. The tech didn't work on all of us, though.

Spotting a vending machine, I stopped, scanning for Snickers. Sold out. I winced when I saw an IOU note trapped in the coils. "Hey, can I borrow some paper?" I asked Zap-Girl. My stomach rumbled, as though it knew what I was plotting.

"No. What for?" she asked, not turning.

"Never mind," I said. I patted the pockets of my leather coat until I found a gum wrapper. Grabbing a capless Bic ink pen from another pocket, I scrawled a hasty I-O-U in messy ink and swapped the note for a bag of peanuts.

Another jolt of guilt spiked through me when I spotted another IOU behind a package of frosted strawberry Pop-tarts. I shoved it down. "Nobody buys Pop-tarts from these things anyway," I muttered.

"Are you coming?" Zap-Girl asked. She held open the door to an interrogation room. Justice Lord and the normie thug were inside.

"Yep, yep," I said. I tore open the bag of peanuts. A woman in a pink and green costume bumped my shoulder, sending a few peanuts flying. I swapped them with paperclips in a coffee mug on a nearby desk.

The paperclips landed on the dirty tile floor with a metallic tinkling. The peanuts rolled to a stop in the mug.

The woman's eyes suddenly quadrupled in size. I felt a shudder run through my body. A Reader. Gross.

"You shouldn't steal what doesn't belong to you," she said.

"Grandma, what big eyes you have," I said. "I know perfectly well you can't read *my* mind, lady."

"I didn't need to," she said. "I saw you."

"Then put the high-beams away. You're creeping me out."

"Why can't I read you?" She sounded frustrated, a little wrinkle furrowing her brow.

"I'm an Immune." I couldn't resist giving my eyes a quick roll. Why else would her powers fail? She must not have run into one of us yet.

Immunity. A freak of nature in the land of freaks. Not technically considered a power, Immunity was a different kind of genetic anomaly. Even normies could be Immune.

"Flipper!" Zap-Girl called. "Come on!"

"Gotta go," I awkwardly reaching around the woman to grab the peanuts. I popped one in my mouth. Covered in dust. I smiled at the bug-eyed woman anyway. "Peanut?" I held them out, resisting the urge to blow the grit off first.

"Now!" Zap-Girl shouted, voice rising above the harried din of the police precinct to turn heads.

"Now's good," I hurried toward the interrogation room.

"Now's great. Sorry, I'm real hungry. Switching can take it out of me. And it's Flip Maestro."

"Terrible. What happened to Switch Master?"

"I'm trying Flip Maestro, but I see what you mean. Maybe Trade Maker? No, I can see it in your eyes. It's already a no. Let's go question the perp."

"Perp?" Zap-Girl asked with a laugh.

"It's short for perpetrator," I said with a dignified sniff.

"Stick close kid, you might learn something." I bumped into a chair near the door, making a loud clatter.

Justice Lord glanced at me, then waved toward the chair I'd just struck. Zap-Girl plopped into it before I could, though, grin wide beneath her yellow mask.

"I can stand," I said.

"What can you tell us about the Suit?" Justice asked. The normie licked his lips. "You serious? Full pardon?"

"If your info checks out. If not, you go into the system. Can't help you after that. I'm not a cop."

"Ok, well, you better put these jackals away, or I don't even want to be free." The normie licked his lips again, frowned, patted his knees with both hands, then cleared his throat.

"The Suit's running human trafficking out of the docks. They want chicas with superpowers, but they're not too picky."

Lightning crackled briefly in the air above Zap-Girl, drawing stares from everyone in the room.

"Go on," Justice urged. For his own part, he clenched the metal desk so hard it was warping beneath his fingertips.

These two *really* cared. It's not that I didn't... I was all for stomping trash that could do those kinds of things to another human being, but I couldn't swear to the same level of passion.

Apathy could creep up on you. I pictured the IOUs in the vending machine and winced again.

You're better than this, I told myself.

Shut up, me! I thought back, letting my pride squash the words. *We need to listen.*

"...it's not just people, though. They're running tech, too. Someone upgraded Dillinger's toys, and they're trying to weaponize it."

"Anti-superhero weaponry," Justice Lord said. "That could be a disaster."

"Where?" Zap-Girl asked. "Can you give us a location beyond 'the docks'?"

"No, but my partner can. I'm just a newbie." I swallowed. The caped thug.

"Well, thanks," Justice Lord said. "If this checks out and we make some busts, I'll make sure you get released. As long as you don't have any priors, I can keep them from booking you. Second chances don't come along very often. Use this one wisely."

He turned to stride out of the room. As soon as he opened the door, the noise from the outside room poured in like the buzzing of a beehive, a beehive of justice and law enforcement.

"We going to talk to the Invincible?" I asked.

"'Course we are." Justice Lord said the words over his shoulder, striding across the room with shoulders squared and back straight.

"But we can't offer *him* a pardon, can we?" I straightened my own posture for a moment, but slouching was *so* much more comfortable. "He's a living weapon!" I was iffy about letting the normie off, but that wasn't my call.

"No, but we can get the police to go easy on him," he replied.

Zap-Girl and I followed Justice Lord toward the holding cells on other side of the station.

"How'd it go, Thomas?" a voice called. I froze. Not many people knew my real name.

"Nightshade," I said, not turning around immediately. "Or should I say Mariella? You know we're not supposed to use real names."

Nightshade. The police-superhero liaison. They wouldn't hire supers, but they had to work with us, so Nightshade handed out the paid bounties for the area.

"How soon did you catch them?" she asked. Clad toe to head in solid black, Nightshade perpetually blended into the shadows. Even under the harsh light of the crowded room, she seemed as though she could disappear any second. "And don't lie—"

"I would never lie to you," I tried to surreptitiously put my last peanut in my mouth. "Vanewind Bridge."

"Which side?" she asked, a smirk already curling one lip.

"The wrong side."

"Is this necessary—" Justice Lord asked.

"It'll just take a minute." It just so happened I had five dollars. My emergency fund. I reached into one of my boots, fishing around in my sock till I was able to scrape out a few sweat-slick one dollar bills. I pulled two more from the other boot and held them out triumphantly to the woman.

Nightshade eyed the money. She made no move to grab it. "Buy me lunch tomorrow,' she said after a lengthy pause. "Extra mayonnaise. Don't forget this time."

"You got it," I said, putting the money away. "Quadruple mayo. I'm gonna bring you so much mayo, it's going to be like a white blob with bread in the middle. It'll make up for all the times I forgot. You'll love it.

"That is definitely not what I want."

"Flipper!" Zap-Girl called from across the room. "Coming!" I replied. "SwitchMan is coming!"

* * *

A row of jail cells lined one wall. They were filled with an interesting variety of ne'er-do-wells, which was my favorite words for bad guys, followed by miscreant, hoodlum, delinquent, and malfeasant.

"Malfeasant," I said aloud. "That's just fun to say." "What?" Justice Lord asked.

"He's being an idiot again." Zap-Girl shook her head.

The malfeasants watched us with baleful eyes as we strode down the corridor.

"Alright, let me at this guy," I said, mock-punching the air in little jabs.

"So," Justice Lord hesitated as we stopped in front of a cell near the end of the row. "This is going to take a great deal of tact. This man is deeper in the Suit's organization and must be handled carefully."

I nodded. "I got this." I cleared my throat. "I mean, we got this. You guys can help."

I glanced at the delinquents inside the cell. It wasn't hard to spot the Invincible. He was the only guy wearing a stupid cape. "Hey buddy." I gave him a little wave. "Ready for round two?"

Justice Lord pulled me to the far wall opposite the bars of the cage. He put a hand on my shoulder.

"You're a proud fellow," he said. "A little healthy pride is good for a man, but..." he sighed.

I stared at his hand. I wanted to say something, or swap him away, but I was keenly aware those fists could crush or vaporize me. Or both at once.

"Listen, son. I want to tell you something my dad used to say. 'The meek shall inherit the earth'. Ever heard that phrase?" Justice Lord smiled. "He was very fond of it, my father. Sometimes there is much to be gained in being a little quieter than——"

"Still the same age," I interrupted. "And I'm meek as a manatee. Just watch me meek it up." I knew I was blustering, but it was hard to back down now that I'd said something stupid, I felt like I had to keep up the act.

"It's ok to ask for help." Justice Lord faltered, clearly out of his depth with the whole heart-to-heart thing. "It's ok to need help, and…"

"I'm good," I interrupted. "We're good. Let's do this." I appreciated what he was trying to do, and he was probably right. I needed to shut up and listen once in a while. But it was just so *hard* to actually do sometimes.

"Let us take the lead, ok Flipper?" Justice Lord asked as we approached the bars again.

"It's Swap Man. I'm trying out Swap Man. Eh, eh? Pretty clever, right? Like *Swamp* Man?"

"That's not right," Zap-Girl said. "Pretty sure it's Swamp Thing."

"Is it? Oh crud."

"We'll stick with Flipper," she replied with a smirk.

Zap-Girl sent a jolt of electricity into the bars, driving a few of the incarcerated hoodlums back. One yelped.

"David Kripke," Justice Lord called.

The caped thug turned to glare at him. He shared a cell with five men.

"Yep, we know you, Kripke. Alias Megapunch."

I laughed. "Megapunch? That's gotta be the worst name I've heard since Stuffmaker, and he was like five."

"It's better than Flipper!" Megapunch laughed right back at me.

"See?" I asked Zap-Girl. "You're undermining my cred. My street cred."

"Tell us about your organization," Justice Lord said. "Give us some names, a location for your warehouse. We can help you out. Strong fellow like you, there's plenty of great jobs—"

"He's not superstrong," I said.

"Oh. Well, he can fly. He could deliver mail, or, like, medicine."

"Organs!" I shouted, louder than I'd intended. "He could totally deliver organs."

"Perfect!" Justice Lord snapped his fingers. "What do you say, Kripke? Let's get you out of this cell and into the organ business."

"Lawyer?" Megapunch asked.

"We're not bound by those laws," Zap-Girl said, rolling her eyes.

"Then I got two words for you," Megapunch said. "Government. Funding."

"What about it?" Justice Lord asked.

"Maybe 'budget cuts' would have been a better choice," Megapunch went on. "There's a crack in your Dillinger cage," the thug added with a grin.

Leaping into the air, he flew backward toward the bars where we stood, then rocketed forward, slamming a fist against a circle of worn stone where there was no metal. Lightning crackled across the surface of the wall, then the whole thing exploded outward. Six incredibly dangerous men were now free. Without looking back, they all bolted into the alley.

"He shorted out the cage somehow?" Zap-Girl shook her head. "Great."

"Get us to the other side!" Justice Lord said to me. The bars that had kept the bad guys in now held us back.

"Let's make it rain." I grabbed the three one dollar bills in my right boot and slid them through the bars, then swapped us to the other side of the ruined cell, first Justice, then Zap-Girl, then myself. Ever frugal, I caught the money before it hit the ground.

"How many can you get?" Justice asked.

"Two, maybe three?" I replied. I went straight to work.

I didn't have much to work with, so I swapped the malfeasants who had run to the left for the clothes of the hoodlums in the nearest cell.

"Hey!" one delinquent cried as his shoes were replaced by a miscreant laying on the ground. He fell backward, put off balance by the sudden change.

A pair of boots appeared in the alley, wobbled briefly, and fell.

"I've got Megapunch," Justice Lord said, leaping into the air. "You've got the other two?" he asked Zap-Girl.

"Yep."

Zap-Girl and I followed Justice out into the alley. Two long bolts of lightning struck two of the fleeing malfeasants, dropping them both. One staggered back to his feet and hurled a fireball at Zap-Girl.

I swapped Zap-Girl for one of the boots on the dirty street, moving her away from the path of the fireball. The superhot ball of plasma flew past the jail with a *whoosh* and slammed into a brick wall at the far end of the alley.

"Thanks," Zap-Girl said as I helped her up. She wiped at her yellow pants, which were now stained with miscellaneous alley filth. "Couldn't have swapped me to somewhere cleaner?"

"I was in a hurry saving your life," I replied.

Justice Lord dropped out of the sky with a thunderclap, slamming Megapunch into the asphalt so hard it cratered.

"A little help?" he asked me, waving a hand toward the downed villain.

I nodded, and swapped the man into one of the remaining cells. Since I couldn't see the cell from where I was, I grabbed blind and swapped him for someone's shirt.

"One got away," Zap-Girl said.

"This man?" Justice Lord asked. I'd failed to notice he had one hand wrapped around the face of the Fireball Guy. Somehow he'd caught him in midair while coming down with Megapunch. Geez.

I swapped Fireball Guy into a cell too, making a mental note to make sure Justice Lord hadn't broken his face or anything. The hero had a sterling reputation, but I'd never fully believed what I'd heard.

"Am I... free to go?" a new miscreant asked. I'd accidentally swapped Fireball Guy for a different prisoner. Whoops.

"Ugh, go away," I said, this time swapping the new prisoner for a shoe. I felt the familiar pressure between my eyes. Just about out of juice. I still hadn't fully recharged from the Vanewind Bridge battle.

We walked back into the police station. Megapunch lay on his back, limbs splayed. He didn't look hurt. Neither did Fireball Guy. Justice Lord supposedly had the finesse of a surgeon, and rarely— if ever— did his opponents serious harm.

"Ready to answer a few questions?" Justice Lord asked. Megapunch nodded.

"Who are these people, and what are they up to?" Justice asked.

"They're after the best Dillinger tech you've ever seen. Stuff so powerful it might even work on Immunes. Big shipment leaving the docks tonight. Couple hours."

"Why are they kidnapping superpowered girls?" Zap-Girl asked.

"Mind control. Got a dame who can control people with her mind, but her powers only work on other women. That's why we kidnapped you." He chuckled at our shocked looks and propped himself up on one elbow. "That's right, saw through your little ruse. We wanted the Lightning Queen herself to protect the tech we got shipping out."

"Where?" Justice Lord asked. "What warehouse?" "241 East Street, Dock 47."

"And the time?"

"Eh, about 2 A.M., if the ship arrives on time."

Zap-Girl checked her phone. "That's less than two hours away," she said.

"Well, this is escalating quickly," I replied, suddenly a little nervous. I wasn't sure I'd be fully recharged by then, if it came to another fight.

Justice Lord pointed a red-clad finger at Megapunch. "You're better than this. You should be on the side of the cage, helping us."

"Eh, it's too late for me," the downed villain replied.

"It's never too late to change." Justice Lord turned away as he spoke, putting an end to the conversation.

"We better get moving," he said to us, striding

toward the door, Zap-Girl on his heels.

Before following, I fished around in my pocket till I found my last peanut, then swapped it for Megapunch's red cape. I let the cape drop to the floor of the ruined cell, just out of reach. "I'm doing you a favor."

"I'm bringing them into style!" Megapunch bellowed as I left the holding area. "Everyone's gonna wear capes! You'll see!"

* * *

"The Justice-Mobile tore through the streets of Empire City," I said from the back seat. "Our heroes are on the prowl, ready to kick evil butt." We'd just left the drive-thru of a Burger King.

"What are you doing?" Zap-Girl asked. "Narrating?"

"Well, stop. This isn't the Justice-Mobile, anyway," Zap-Girl replied.

"What do you call it, then?" I popped my last french fry into my mouth, the remnants from a hasty meal at my side. Fast food isn't great before a battle, but it was better than nothing. "Crappy old van?"

Justice Lord flinched at this but said nothing. It wasn't the worst description. The mostly windowless commercial van had seen better days. Behind two rows of worn bench seats, an array of weapons, tech, body armor, and other miscellaneous equipment lined the walls in neat shelves. They clattered lightly at every bump and tremor of the road.

"Did you mean what you said?" I asked Justice Lord, then realized he had no idea what I was talking about. "You said Megapunch could change. He could be better. Did you really mean that?"

"Of course. It's like I was trying to tell you earlier," he cleared his throat, and I realized he wanted my permission to continue the story.

"Yeah," I said flatly.

"Well, my dad. He always said the meek would inherit the earth. Sometimes being gentle takes a lot of strength. Incredible strength. Those are the kind of people that rise to power. They inherit the Earth. Them and the people that follow them."

"That doesn't sound true," I said. "Most politicians seem like corrupt idiots."

"But what about the true leaders?" he asked. "The kind that inspire people, that change the world? Aren't they usually meek in some way?"

"Sometimes," I allowed. "I guess."

"Give it some thought," Justice Lord said. We lapsed into silence as he drove through city streets. Traffic had thinned, so we made good time.

Justice Lord cleared his throat. "This is going to be dangerous. These people don't mess around, and there's no time for backup."

"What about the rest of your team?" I asked.

"Shadowboxer and Fire Wolf are out of town," he replied. "Won't be able to get here in time. Do you know anyone?" he asked.

"Not really," I replied. "Well, we could ask Nightshade, I guess."

"Nightshade, the police liaison?" Justice Lord asked.

"Why didn't you bring her up when we were at the police station?" Zap-Girl asked.

I was beginning to think everything I said and did annoyed her.

"I was hungry. Saving the day is famishing work."

"What's the story, anyway?" Zap-Girl asked. "She seemed like she knew you."

"We went to school together. Kindergarten on up. She doesn't have special abilities, but she's faster and sneakier than a lot of supers I've run into."

Justice Lord put on his turn signal, sliding into a turn lane that would take us back to the police station.

"There were like eight or nine supers at the police station," I said when no one spoke. "Someone besides me could have thought of recruiting."

"A fair point," Justice Lord agreed. "We haven't got much time, but I don't want to be reckless. I know you two aren't bulletproof like me. We have to be careful."

I slurped up the last of my Dr. Pepper. Junk food or not, it *did* hit the spot. I leaned over and glanced into the greasy bag sitting between Justice and Zap-Girl.

"You gonna finish those onion rings?"

* * *

"I'll come."

"That was easy." I grinned in spite of my mixed feelings about having her along.

"Protecting my investment," Nightshade said. "I want lunch tomorrow."

"And I can't buy you lunch if I'm a bullet-riddled corpse!" I moved to pat her on the back, then remembered she could break my hand with her crazy judo skills. Thinking better of it, I turned the motion into an awkward thumbs up.

I was glad to have another superhero along, but I wished it could have been someone other than Nightshade. I didn't like the idea of my old friend being at risk. Better for her to be handing out bounties at the police station.

We'd asked around, but no other help came through. The other supers at the police station claimed to be busy. The police chief— a noted anti-vigilante— refused to help. He might have to hand out bounties, but he didn't have to help us. I could have done without the smug satisfaction on his face when he turned us down, though.

And so we drove across Empire City toward the docks. I drummed my fingers against the car door, finding the silence unbearable.

"Don't suppose we could listen to a little music?" I asked.

"Sure," Justice Lord said. He turned a knob on the dashboard, and classical music filled the van interior.

"Seriously?" Zap-Girl asked.

"What? Bach was a master!" Justice replied.

"I swear you were born seventy years old," she replied. She reached for the radio controls.

"Nah, leave it." I hummed with the music. After a moment, Justice Lord joined me.

"Oy vey," I heard Zap-Girl mutter.

We parked a several-minute walk from the port, in a seedy neighborhood of unkempt lawns.

"I gotta say, putting indoor furniture outside is a bold choice." I nodded toward a worn blue sofa sprawling across the nearest porch.

"Is this what you're always like on missions?" Nightshade asked.

"Mostly," I admitted.

"Huh."

"What?" I pressed.

"Well you usually catch the bad guys you go after. I just assumed you saved the banter for the precinct, and were actually serious when you went out and risked your life."

"Happy to defy expectations," I replied.

Justice Lord cleared his throat. "Can we focus, team?" "For sure," I said. "What's the plan, boss?"

"This is a surveillance mission first and foremost. I want to get in, see what we're dealing with, and verify that advanced anti-super tech is involved. If it is, we're gonna do our best to break up their operations. If not, we carefully slip out and go home."

"What about the kidnapping ring?" Zap-Girl asked.

"Yes, thank you, if we see any evidence or find any victims inside, we're going to do everything we can to free them." He clapped his gloved hands. "I hate to go in on a rush, but time is of the essence, and I think as long as we're quick, careful, and watch each other's backs, everything will be fine."

We left the neighborhood behind and crossed a patchy, poorly kept field, coming to a tall chain link fence.

Warehouses loomed on the other side in boxy rows. I couldn't see the oceanside docks from here, but I could smell the slight tang of brine on the air.

Justice Lord flew to the other side of the fence. Zap-Girl was right behind, shooting two shafts of electricity from her hands to propel herself up and over. Nightshade grabbed a fistful of metal and backflipped herself over, barely rattling the flexible metal.

"I thought you didn't have superpowers," Zap-Girl said.

"I don't." A hint of a smirk briefly flitted across Nightshade's face under her mask.

I swapped myself with Justice Lord. He flew back over the fence again, giving me a little frown.

Zap-Girl snorted. "Waste of your energy."

"Body swap. Transferring myself, for whatever reason, takes almost no energy if I'm close in size to whatever I swap with."

"Whatever works," Justice Lord said, shrugging. I stepped close to him and flexed.

"Not even close," Nightshade said. "You should work out more."

"It's not... I'm..."

"Mission?" Justice Lord hissed. "No unnecessary chatter from now on."

We nodded our agreement and slipped into the first row of warehouses, which butted up against Empire Bay. We crept through the shadows, checking the placards affixed to each building for the one we needed, dock 47.

At last, near the end of the row, we saw it. There were no guards visible, but the front door was conspicuously well-lit. And that wasn't the only problem. "There's two of them?" Zap-Girl asked. 47A and 47B.

"What now?" Nightshade asked.

"We split up," Justice Lord said. "I'll take Nightshade, Zap- Girl, you take Flipper."

"Switcheroo," I replied.

"Already taken," Zap-Girl said. "And ugh, have you seen the clown suit he wears? Also," she turned to Justice Lord. "Why him? Please don't make me take him."

"She has no superpowers, his powers are weakest. I'm splitting our strength as best as I can."

I frowned, held up a finger, then dropped it. "That's fair. It hurts, but it's fair."

"We'll take A," Justice said. "You two take B."

Justice Lord took to the air and Nightshade slipped into the shadows, intending to sneak around to the other side of the docks to approach warehouse A from the other side. In the depths of night, the docks seemed abandoned. Aside from low security lighting, the only glow came from the front of our target building.

Zap-Girl and I decided to sneak around to the dock side of the building to the right of 47B. We crept down a wide alley crowded with battered dumpsters and stacks of metal shipping containers.

"Nervous?" I asked, speaking at normal volume.

"Shhh, what the heck?" Zap-Girl held a finger to her lips.

"I can redirect nearby sound waves," I said. "No one further than a few feet away can hear us unless we yell."

"Really?" Zap-Girl sounded genuinely impressed. "You can do that?"

"Yeah, I taught myself years ago. Seemed easier than learning to shut up."

Zap-Girl let out a booming laugh, then clapped her hand to her mouth. We stopped and listened. When no alarms screamed or dogs barked, we kept walking.

"Why would I be nervous?" Zap-Girl asked. "Just making conversation."

"Are *you* nervous?" she replied.

"No." The lie came easily. I was embarrassingly good at lying.

Zap-Girl stopped and studied me for a moment. "Liar." She spun on her heel and continued on.

"How did you…?"

"Electrical signals. Your pulse changed when you lied."

"You can do that?" I asked.

"No. It was just a lucky guess. Why bring up nerves if you're not nervous? And I don't think you're as experienced as you'd have us believe. Back at the bridge, that Invincible could have killed you if he'd gotten ahold of you. I see right through your mask. The jokes. The bravado. You're not as tough as you act."

"You got me, ok?" My voice betrayed me, almost breaking.

We'd reached the end of the alley, but Zap-Girl didn't want to let it go just yet.

"Earlier you said you didn't want to talk about the invasion. Where were you during the Invasion?"

"Why? Where were you?" I knew deflection wouldn't work, but I tried anyway.

"Ninja-Girl's army, with everyone else. Why don't you like to talk about the Invasion?" she asked again.

"Because I hid!" I covered my mouth. We both stared at each other for a moment. I could see the whites of Zap-Girl's eyes through her mask.

"I hid," I said more softly after a quiet pause. "I didn't help fight the aliens. When it was over, I vowed I'd be less of a coward, but I'm still scared sometimes. You're right, joking helps. It's a mask, but…" I waved a hand at her face, then mine. "We all wear masks."

"With your powers you…?" Her voice trailed off.

I could hear the anger in the words. Maybe she had every right to be mad. I'd been angry with myself for years.

"I thought you were a hero." Zap-Girl delivered the words with firm finality, our conversation over.

The words hit me like a physical blow. I stopped in place, remembering the IOUs, the debt, all the mistakes I'd been making over the years. I always thought I'd do better next time, but it never seemed to happen.

It didn't matter that the words weren't fair. Paycheck or not, I was out here risking my life just the same as everyone else. The words still stung, though. Because she wasn't entirely wrong, either.

No longer speaking— which was good since I'd unconsciously dropped my sound redirection— we crept along the back of warehouse 48A toward our target. To our right, water lapped against the concrete walls and wooden pillars of the dock. There was already a boat docked ahead. "They're early," I said.

Zap-Girl nodded at the roof. "Can you get us up there? I think there's a skylight."

Still not ready to talk, I nodded, digging in my pocket for a quarter.

"Look, I'm sorry for what I said. I have no right to judge you for—"

"We should really focus on the mission," I said. "Imminent peril and all."

"Right," she replied.

This was where timing played a critical role. I had to swap us before the quarters landed— making noise— but not so soon that our boots hitting the roof could make even more noise. I tossed two of my three quarters onto the roof, then swapped them for us at what I judged was the right moment.

We landed quiet as church-mice. I spotted the pyramid of a glass window jutting from the roof. We peered inside the warehouse. The space was mostly open in the center, right below us. Two walls were obscured by dozens of crates. In the middle— almost dead center— stood a tall, glass cylinder.

Six women were chained to chairs in a circle around the strange tube. Three of them wore filthy superhero costumes.

"Now what?" I whispered. Justice Lord hadn't said what to do if we actually *saw* anything.

Or heard anything.

"This is ridiculous," a voice called from below. "Where are my men?"

"Well, I think a lot of them are sleeping," a sheepish male voice replied.

"So let me get this straight," the first voice thundered. "The most powerful tech of our lifetime ships out, and we've got *TWO* people guarding it? WAKE THEM UP. ALL OF THEM! NOW!"

"On it, sir," a new, female voice said.

"You don't *need* them when you've got me," the sheepish voice countered.

"Sure, if I want my merchandise blown to kingdom come!" The loud man's voice dropped, so I couldn't hear the rest of what he said.

Three figures came into view. A well-dressed man in an expensive looking suit, a woman in a tight black trench coat, and a man in a spangly blue and white superhero costume.

"Recognize any of them?" I asked, coming up blank.

"All of them," Zap-Girl whispered back, eyes wide with fear. "The woman in the trench coat is Pandora. The goon in the goofy costume is Atom Bomb. And the boss has to be the Suit, the guy we've been tracking."

"Wait... *the* Atom Bomb?"

Him I'd heard of. True to his name, Atom Bomb was capable of massive explosions. He had a lengthy cool down period, though. Almost two months, if the rumors could be believed. I tried to think back to the last time I'd heard about him blowing something up. How many weeks ago had it been?

"I'm calling Justice Lord," Zap-Girl told me. "We'll need all the help we can get."

"No kidding."

Zap-Girl stood, perhaps intending to walk away from the window to call Justice Lord. I never found out, because she put a hand against the glass to steady herself, and a loose pane fell to the floor below, shattering near the feet of one of the kidnapped women.

Three pairs of eyes shot toward us. "Kill them," the Suit said. Zap-Girl said a bad word, then "Guess we're going in."

"What, why? Shouldn't we wait for backup?"

Ignoring me, she tapped at her wrist. "Justice," she said into her mic. "We got trouble. Three supers, six friendlies. We're going in."

"Copy that. In a bit of trouble ourselves. Be there when we can." I heard Justice Lord's faint reply. When I used my powers to direct the sound closer, I heard a punch landing.

"Get us down there," Zap-Girl said.

"What's the plan?" I asked, heart pounding. I usually worked alone and created the plan as I went along, but that wouldn't fly on a team.

"Beat the bad guys, save those women! Come on!"

Nearly half a minute had passed. An eternity when there were people below your feet plotting to murder you.

"Step on the window," I said, throwing together a quick plan of my own.

To her credit, Zap-Girl didn't question me. We stepped out onto the sloping window together. Before it could crack, I swapped us for two of the crates below.

We stood atop a heap of wooden crates, suddenly ensconced in the musty, dim-lit interior of the warehouse.

"I could take care of this." Atom Bomb's voice echoed across the cavernous space.

"I've got this," Pandora said. "Try not to blow anything up." They stood where we'd last seen them. The Suit was gone.

The two crates smashed through the window above. While the bad guys' eyes were up, I swapped the villains for the airborne crates right before the boxes hit the ground. Before the crates landed, I swapped us with them. Now the villains were in the center of the room and well-lit, and the crates were thumping to rest across the room, so the baddies attention would be away from where we actually stood.

"Nicely done," Zap-Girl said with grudging respect, hands crackling with electricity.

"Cheap tricks," Pandora said, catching on quicker than I'd hoped.

Zap-Girl fired a thick bolt of lightning at the villains. Pandora made a graceful sweeping motion with both hands, and a dragon swept up to block the lightning. The monster exploded with a puff gray smoke. Pandora moved her hands again and more dragons appeared, springing from the air around the supervillain.

"I can take care of this," Atom Bomb repeated.

"For the last time, no! You want to help? Shoot one of them!" Pandora spoke distractedly, her thoughts probably focused on the dozens of dragon creatures she was filling the warehouse with.

"Fine."

Zap-Girl fired bolt after bolt of lightning into the dragon-monsters, but for every one she destroyed, two seemed to take its place. I swapped us from crate to crate, then to the middle of the room, then back again, but without fleeing outside, there was nowhere safe to go, nowhere was more than a few steps from a snapping, snarling dragon the sooty color of smog.

"I'm getting us out of here," I said. Our feet landed roughly on wooden crates as I brought us back where we'd started.

"Not yet," she replied. "We still need to rescue those women! Get them out of here while I distract everyone."

"Everyone? You're going to—" I paused. There was too little time to argue. There was only time to act.

I tried to picture something outside I could swap the women for, but came up blank. I cursed myself for failing to think ahead and leave some pocket change outside to swap with. I dropped from the pile of crates and ran toward the women. I tried to swap one with a nearby box, thinking she'd at least be free.

Nothing.

"What?" I stopped up short, flabbergasted. I'd never run up against something I couldn't swap. Aside from certain very large or well rooted objects, my powers usually worked on everything.

Dragons tore past, but they were focused on Zap-Girl, who kept up her attack on Pandora. I didn't see Atom Bomb.

"This is new," I said.

"It's Dillinger tech," One of the women— who wore a blue costume— told me.

"That stuff doesn't work on me," I said, frowning. I eyed the tall cylinder in the middle of the room. What was it for?

"Oh, you're right!" She rolled her eyes and rattled her chains. "My hero, thank you for saving us!"

"Oh, pipe down," I muttered, examining the chains of a closer woman.

"Look out," a woman in a floral dress warned.

"I'm not falling for that again," I said, then realized my mistake. "What? Why would I try to trick you?" the woman asked, incredulous.

"Who is this guy?" a woman in a dark red costume complained.

I swapped myself for whoever was behind me. Standing where I'd been a second ago, Atom Bomb fired a bullet into the cylinder. A tiny line of a crack appeared in the glass, like a chip in a windshield hit by a pebble on the highway. The bullet ricocheted into a nearby wall with a wild *bang*.

"Hey! Careful with the merchandise, you idiot!" Pandora called, creating three more dragons.

"Guns aren't nice," I said. I pulled a quarter from my pocket and swapped it for the gun. "On the ground!" I ordered. "Hands in the air!"

Atom Bomb laughed. "You can't kill me." He spread his arms wide, though. "I'll blow up! You'd murder everyone in this room!"

"Is that true?" I asked the kidnapped women.

They shrugged or shook their heads.

"You're no help."

"Wait," I said to Atom Bomb. "How in the holy guacamole would you know what happens when you die?"

Atom Bomb said a bad word, then began to glow bright yellow. "I'm going nuclear!" he cried.

"No, stupid!" Pandora cried. "Gah!"

Zap-Girl's head turned our way. Taking advantage of the distraction, a dragon knocked her down.

I pointed Atom Bomb's gun toward the ruined window above and fired a bullet into the night sky. The sound cracked the air, momentarily deafening me. When the bullet was at the height of its climb—almost out of my reach—I switched it with Atom Bomb.

The resulting explosion high in the air blew half the the roof off the warehouse. Debris rained down on as the other half fell. I swapped myself to the clearest spot in the room, under the window. Now standing near the mystery machine, I kicked off one of my shoes. I swapped it for Zap-Girl, the dragon's jaws clicking on empty air rather than her throat.

The middle of the room wasn't good enough. Sheer chunks of metal and glass fell toward us at high speed...

Only to be stopped by Pandora's dragons. They created a web, blocking the falling pieces of the roof.

I coughed, now filthy with dust and covered with tiny cuts from the bits of brick, glass, and metal that had fallen through Pandora's dragon net.

You're lucky we need that machine intact!" Pandora spat to the side, dirty and scratched up herself. The dragons shoved, sending the debris flying outside the building. I heard pieces clatter and splash as they landed on the ground and in the ocean.

"Enough." Zap-Girl levitated a foot into the air, growling with rage and crackling all over with hot blue lightning that melted the concrete near her feet.

"Get them out of here," she growled, eyes glowing blue.

"Come on, ladies." I tried again, and this time I found that with an extra *push* I didn't normally need, the women swapped across the room with a sort of *pop!*

Once they were free and bits of debris sat on the chairs in their place, I pushed them toward the door. "Go!" I said.

"I can help," one of the costumed women said, the first who had spoken to me.

"I think she's got it," I said. As I nodded at Zap-Girl, the superhero gave a lazy swipe at a dragon. It exploded into smoke. The room filled with static electricity, crackling against dust particles and making the hair on my arms stand on end. The women at last followed my advice and fled. Unable to bring myself to leave Zap-Girl, I ducked behind a tall sheet of metal from the roof.

I felt a terrible heat against my butt and yanked my phone out of my pocket. "Yowch!" I cried as it crackled in my hand. I hurled it as far as I could. The phone exploded in midair on the far side of the warehouse.

The dragons swirled around Zap-Girl. Every few seconds, one tested the blue barrier around her and exploded. Bolts of lightning flared from her body in a crackling, wing-like pattern, making her look like an avenging angel fallen from the sky. Her eyes moved from blue to white-hot, almost too bright to look at. Pandora's dragons tore at her from all sides, but she blasted them to oblivion with casual bolts of electricity.

Pandora was sweating, her eyes darting back and forth in fear. Her movements were erratic, her nerves shot. She had fewer and fewer dragons in the air, and had backed away, shaking her head. Soon there were only four dragons. Then three. Then two. Then…

Zap-Girl's wings stretched above her head and struck like lances into Pandora. The woman shrieked, skeleton momentarily visible. Pandora fell, unconscious.

I threw my last quarter at the floor nearby and swapped it for Pandora. Across the room, the quarter plinked and bounced as it fell in her place. I did my best to listen for it so I could find it later.

Zap-Girl hung in the air, unmoving. We locked eyes. Then the electricity went out. The room went still as Zap-Girl fell to her knees. I could still see the blinding afterimage of her eyes when I blinked. The room suddenly seemed too dark. I felt almost blinded.

"That was incredible," I said to Zap-Girl.

"It was stupid," she replied. "I'm spent."

"You're amazing," I said.

She gave me a tiny smile, then flopped onto her back. I'd barely had time to think *I got her to smile!* when a voice called out.

"Sorry we're late," Justice Lord said. "There were quite a few henchmen headed here. We fought them off while you kept the Suit's lieutenants busy. Made another mess, I see." Justice landed on top of the strange cylinder. Aside from the chip in the glass, it was undamaged.

"My specialty," I said. "I'm thinking of starting a demolition company, want to—"

I was cut off when the cylinder's lid opened, and Justice Lord fell inside. He tried to fly back out, but couldn't seem to get off the ground. The lid snapped shut above Justice Lord's head, trapping him.

"What is this thing?" he asked, voice muffled.

"I don't know," I said. "But it's what they came for."

"My powers aren't working!" He looked physically ill, his face gray and covered in a sheen of sweat.

"This is too good," the Suit said, stepping out from between two hulking pieces of metal from the roof, a hefty assault rifle held in both hands. "Justice Lord and Zap-Girl in the same day?"

Zap-Girl stood. She raised her hands, but could barely produce sparks from her fingertips.

"I don't know who you are," the Suit said to me, "but I'm looking forward to putting a bullet in your obnoxious face."

"You'll have to get in line." I felt the ache between my eyes.

Terrible timing. My powers were nearly spent.

Nightshade appeared from the shadows, seeming to pool from thin air into a silhouette. She swept the legs out from under the man, grabbing at his rifle as he fell. Resolute, the Suit held on, a few shots flying wildly into the wreckage of the warehouse.

I swapped him for a nearby chair. Nightshade stumbled over the chair, but caught herself without falling, coming up with gun in hand.

I took advantage of the Suit's momentary confusion at the shift and punched him as he stood. It was like hitting a brick. I felt bones in my hand break.

An invincible. Whoops.

"Ow," I said, the sudden shock of pain numbed by the adrenaline spiking through my system. Even better, I'd used up the last of my power. But I'd disarmed him, at least.

The Suit grinned. Zap-Girl approached. She pulled a small cylinder from her belt. When she shook it, the cylinder popped out into a fighting staff.

"Aw, girlie and her stick," the Suit laughed, rolling his eyes. "You got me shaking. I know you're out of juice, girlie."

With her free hand, Zap-Girl pulled a taser from her belt and shot the Suit in the chest. He fell toward her, twitching wildly as the prongs clung to his torso. She pushed him with her staff and he fell to his back with a heavy thump.

"I'm never out of juice," she said, smirking.

Groaning on the floor, the Suit should have been out of commission, but he reached for a remote control in the inner pocket of his suit coat, clicking a button. "At least I'll get one thing on my wish list," he grunted. "No more Justice Lord!"

A glow appeared from the bottom of the cylinder. Justice Lord began beating at the glass, but it was useless.

I pointed the pistol at the Suit, but he just threw back his head and laughed.

I turned back to Justice Lord. Trapped, he looked so helpless. Smaller somehow.

Body swaps don't take much energy.

Taking a deep breath, I swapped myself for Justice Lord.

The air was a little thin in the tiny chamber. Everyone watched me from outside, their faces distorted by the glass.

"Get out of there!" Zap-Girl shouted.

I tried to swap myself for the Suit, but felt the ache more strongly between my eyes. Trapped. I shook my head.

Justice Lord punched the glass near the bullet's crack. Nothing happened. There was no way out.

Zap-Girl tore her ruined mask away, revealing pretty Asian features, her olive skin marred by a long, jagged scar across one eye. Tears made tracks through the grime on her face.

Justice Lord wept too. He'd dropped to his knees, tearing his hands through his hair.

Nightshade shook her head. "You can't die. You still owe me a sandwich. Extra mayo." Her stoic facade cracked, her voice trembling briefly. "I'm not packing a lunch tomorrow, so you'd better deliver."

"Sorry," I replied, feeling a pang of sadness. "I guess that's one more promise I'll have to break."

I smiled at Zap-Girl. "I lived a good life. Take care of him," I nodded toward Justice. "He's going to take this hard."

"Why did you do that?" she asked, still crying. "Idiot." She forced a smile, the soft, sad expression on her face taking the sting from the word. *That's two smiles I got.*

"Haven't you heard?" I asked Zap-Girl. The machine seemed to be done charging. The glass cylinder rumbled. I could feel heat coming from below.

"The meek shall inherit—"

Blessed are the meek
For they shall inherit the Earth

J.L. Ender

J.L. Ender, author of "The Meek Shall Inherit," had his first published novel, Portal World come out last year. He has also released several short stories, including The Rocket Game. His next series, Steel Fox Investigations, is coming soon. Ender has worked as a dishwasher, a beef jerky labeler, a warehouse worker, a shelf stocker, a greeter, a traveling technician, a laser engraver, a package handler, a copywriter, a graphic designer, a librarian, an editor, a dispatcher, and a phone operator. He lives in Ohio with his dog Bear.

Cinema Bendiga

"Three more reports just came in."

The red folders landed on my desk and slewed across the surface. They just missed knocking over my tea. I glanced at the Lieutenant over my half glasses. That was going to be my only reaction, until I saw his face. He was worried. Enough to let it show. I sat up in my chair.

"Like the others?" I asked.

"Yes. And no." He dropped into the hard chair in front of my desk. The chair creaked under his weight. "All one-on-one events. All created a category 'B' public disturbance. All examples of self-thought."

I narrowed my eyes. "That's the 'yes.' What's the 'no?'"

The Lieutenant quirked one brow. I had the feeling he wasn't often questioned by his subordinates. But the flicker of faint amusement told me he hadn't minded.

"The 'no' is that unlike the first ones, these last three are in the neighboring district. We expect isolated flareups. That's why you're here. To track down any reversion to the old ways and report the violators for remediation. But these—"

The Lieutenant looked around the incident room, just a flick of the eyes to see if we were being watched, before he slipped a hand inside his tunic and pressed his midsection. He dropped his voice. "The squad is sure there's a group actively encouraging this behavior. And they're succeeding. The Council is concerned. And when they're concerned, I get a bellyache. You're the Overseer of that quadrant. What has your investigation turned up so far?"

I pulled off my glasses and polished the lenses to buy time. *Nothing.* That was what I had turned up so far. A series of seemingly unrelated but highly unusual events had taken place over the last month. They violated the strict codes of behavior that had been put into place when society had been reorganized after the Global Conflict. The events I was investigating had disturbed the populace, shaken its confidence in what we had been told was Right. The world had fought too hard, given up too much, to go back to the chaos of The Before Times. People were understandably spooked.

I was troubled by the events for a different reason. I stared down at the new files rather than allow the Lieutenant to read anything in my eyes.

The Lieutenant stretched out his long booted legs in front of him, crossed them at the ankles then slowly flexed the ankle on top. I knew that leg was the shorter one, the one that had been shattered in the final battle. It had healed wrong because there had been few doctors, fewer surgical instruments and no medicines by then. Nowadays the Lieutenant wore a wedge in his boot that, along with willpower and practice, nearly eliminated his limp. Between the talk of his aching belly and the display of his damaged leg, the Lieutenant was making a tacit admission of personal concern. Not at all the serene and certain, confident and correct Modern Citizen our new society relied upon to guide us and keep us from returning to the emotion-driven chaos of Before The Conflict.

Not at all the man I had expected. I resisted the urge to rub at the growing ache in my own gut.

The Lieutenant was the reason I had requested a transfer to this city and his command. He had been a decorated hero during the wars and one of the calmest voices and clearest minds during the reconstruction afterwards. Lately I had been growing restless. I had no reason to complain. In fact, my life and career were often cited as one of the success stories of the new era. An example of how the Doing The Right Thing was good for society, and good for the individual. Yet I had found myself yearning for something more. More than our safe and sanitized society offered. More than my tidy, untroubled life offered.

Something grittier. Riskier. Something—personal.

I kept having the same dream, the one that made me sit up in bed, sweating, heart pounding in my ears, unwinding tangled sheets that felt like shrouds. Was I reverting? Becoming self-serving? I still believed in Doing The Right Thing, didn't I? Could you do a right thing in a wrong way? I didn't know. I just knew I had transferred here looking for a leader who could inspire me with the confidence I once had. Who could reignite my belief.

Not infect me with his own concerns—and his ulcer.

I had been just a boy during the Conflict, orphaned at the age of six when my people died in the first riots. My memories centered around being hungry most of the time—bad; and being dirty all the time—not so bad, when you're six, and too busy playing and running wild with the other war orphans to worry about your growing personal herd of tiny livestock. Someone once told me, I can't remember who because it was during those last days, that 'saints are easy to admire but difficult to love.' But from my perspective now as an Overseer, they're also peace loving, God-fearing law abiders.

From my desk at HQ, I administered the law for an entire quadrant of the city, by myself. I could do that because there was no crime, no violence, no immorality, rarely even a raised voice. We all did what we were supposed to do, not by being compelled, but because it was The Right Thing. That's what the Council's leadership had brought us. Painful experience and the worldwide tutoring initiative had taught us to distrust every personal impulse, resist—no—fear any action that could feed the idol of self.

We had only to look back a few decades for the reason why. By the end of the 20th century as society finished burying the God it had already declared obsolete, it raised up The Self as a little god. That meant nine billion gods, each with a personal—and conflicting—definition of right and wrong. Society had imploded. Millions died then and in the ensuing Conflict, before people like the Lieutenant led us in a U-turn and rebuilt society. If life was a trifle more disconnected, a little less, well, joyful, it was also a paradise compared to how it had been before.

"When you look at the actual events, they're not self-serving."

My attention snapped back to the Lieutenant. Was he justifying—?

"At least, not if we judge by the spirit of the law. In that case, they were still Doing The Right Thing. Under the circumstances." He pointed with his chin. "Go ahead. Read them. See what you think."

I stared at him for a moment. Something flickered in his expression, something I hadn't noticed before. I didn't dare name it, even though I thought I recognized it. I fumbled my glasses back onto my nose and flipped open the uppermost file.

"Aloud. Refresh my memory," he said.

"Seventeen hundred hours, Ambrose Street, woman knocks on her widowed neighbor's door, asks the woman if she would like to come over for dinner." I shuffled that one to the bottom, opened the next. "Teenage boy in Marcus Road. That's, let's see," I closed my eyes to concentrate on geography that was still new to me, "five blocks from Ambrose Street?"

"More like three."

I glanced at the map on the wall.

"Not a criticism. You're catching on fast. But I fought in those streets," the Lieutenant said.

I bent to the file once again. "Boy seen buying diapers, then followed to a foster home facility where he entered and was observed—" the page crackled as I snatched at the corner, "playing and helping with the children." I released a breath.

"One more." With the ghost of a smile, the Lieutenant pushed the last file toward me.

"A married couple had started visiting a home for the elderly, and now are inviting residents who have no family to spend their holidays with the couple. In the couple's own home." I looked up, puzzled. "Why?"

"That's what I want you to find out. Each act is distinctly odd, out of character for the way we live now."

I nodded slowly. "There are systems in place to handle all these situations. Personal interaction by citizens is not necessary."

"That is what connects all of these." The Lieutenant nodded toward my desk, the gesture taking in the new files as well as the ones documenting my ongoing investigations. "Why have these people gotten involved? That's what the Council wants to know."

"As if each person took personal action, but that action wasn't self-serving?" I deliberately quoted the Lieutenant. "What if things had gone wrong?"

Instead of responding to my challenge, he pulled a sheet from his interior breast pocket. The light gleamed momentarily on a small metallic object, a button perhaps, on the underside of his lapel. "This came in just as Control gave me the files. Preliminary report. It's the strangest to date." He laid the single page on the desk, turning it in my direction but reading it aloud easily even though it was upside down. After he'd finished, he sat back. "The squad followed the individual back to the same place. That's where things seem to be centered. I'm taking you off your other cases until you can crack this."

I was lucky that was an order not requiring a reply. I stared at the Lieutenant's retreating figure while I shrugged into my coat. With all the questions and ideas revolving in my brain, I doubt I could have come up with anything that made sense, even to me.

* * *

The marquee of the Cinema Bendiga blazed out of the fog so brightly I had to shield my eyes with my hand. Electric lighting was rare nowadays, saved for facilities like hospitals, the steam plants supplying homes and hydroponic agroplants, churches, and a few other facilities considered essential for public health and welfare. High altitude NEMP weapons had taken out the power grid in the early days of the war, and society's first concerns after victory had been food and shelter, not televisions and cell phones. Later the survivors had taken a vote and decided to keep the clock of progress rewound a century or so. A slower, sweatier pace of life was considered a reasonable precaution against a repeat of the problems that had started the conflict.

From what I learned in school, the wattage in the marquee wasn't actually that high compared to the way things were before the Conflict. But we were all used to lantern light now, so the massed effect of even the tiny bulbs in the old sign seemed like a multihued star hanging just overhead, especially on this dank night.

Last year the Council issued a surprising directive, allowing a limited schedule of electricity to a few places they termed 'facilities for encouraging or amusing public gatherings or entertainments.' The Council's directive had not been an immediate success, and most of the ventures failed for lack of customers. Two decades after the conflict, it was difficult to unlearn the habit of keeping to yourself, of hurrying silently home after work and shutting yourself inside. The Cinema Bendiga had been one of the first of the 'entertainment facilities' to be approved, and was still a rare success, showing its small collection of cartoons, nature documentaries and ancient musicals in continual rotation on a patched screen to an ever-growing audience. In my first weeks in this city, before the weather cooled down, I had uncharitably chalked up the theater's success to its air conditioning. Now the facts pointed toward a more troubling reason.

I pushed through the double doors and paused just inside the lobby, enjoying the faded murals and chipped streamline ornamentation. Even battered and musty, the old movie palace invited me to step outside myself, be part of something new, different, exciting. Then I heard a rush of rubber wheels on carpet, and I remembered why I was there. I hoped—I didn't know what I hoped for. I wanted to do my duty well, perform my investigation successfully. That was The Right Thing. But what if The Right Thing meant closing down the Cinema Bendiga? Why was a part of me I didn't want to acknowledge whispering in my heart, urging me to find another solution?

The cinema's owner was rolling down the ramp from the theater auditorium's upper level. Her gleeful smile was equal parts welcome for me, and the thrill of the reckless speed of her wheelchair.

"Mrs. Elsey!" I jumped aside before she could run me down, and grabbed the handholds on the back of her chair. "You could break your neck doing that." The chair slewed as I dragged it in a diminishing circle to stop it, while her necklace flew out, the small gold pendant flashing in the oblique light.

"Already did. Twice in my life. I'm still here." Everything about her radiated freedom and joy. "Think the third time's a charm?"

"Not on my watch." My answer was clipped. She had frightened me and I didn't know what to do with the feeling of caring so much for someone who was nearly a stranger. That was what indulging personal impulses got you, I reminded myself. Spurious pride, momentary pleasure, then pain.

"Oh. I see." She grew serious, though that joy I had sensed did not depart, merely gathered itself, like a bird folding its wings when it comes to rest. "You've come about the latest incident. You want to know about us."

"'Us?' You're willing to talk about it? To me? Now?" I stammered.

"Of course. I've been praying for this day. We all have." She touched my hand. The weight of those thin, gnarled fingers didn't amount to more than a dry leaf brushing against my skin.

It was easy to forget how little of her there actually was. Yet the unexpected physical contact, the voluntary bridging of the gap between us, sent a trace of warmth up my arm.

I turned away to hide my reaction. She had as good as confessed. Yet it had been too easy. This was all too much. Too different. Too—winsome? I didn't want to care so deeply. Get so involved so easily. Without looking at her, I asked, "Is there somewhere private we can go?"

"Let's go up to the projection booth. We can talk while I get things ready for the next showing."

I took the handles of the chair and began pushing. It would be easier if I didn't to meet her eyes. "You'll explain everything about the violations?"

Mrs. Elsey craned her neck, looking at me half sideways and half upwards, birdlike. "Violations? Oh dear, I see you still have a ways to go before you understand. It's a good thing you've come tonight. I'll have help."

My heart sank. Sounded like we'd nab them all in this one visit. I'd need more help too. But at least it would be over. I swallowed down the lump in my throat so my voice would not betray me. "Before we start, I need to send a message. Is there someone who can take it to HQ?"

"To your Lieutenant?"

I stared at her.

"No, I'm not a spy or a psychic." Her eyes creased with her half smile. "But I'm old, and I've had time to make a lot of friends. Some that would surprise you. Here—" she gestured to a small desk in the corner. We'd made it up the ramp and into the projection booth. "Write your note and Daniel will take it for you.

There was a series of metallic clicks and clatters in the

background as Mrs. Elsey busied herself with the projectors while I wrote the note and gave the boy my instructions. As soon as the door closed, she wheeled herself to my side.

"Ask your questions."

There were so many. I stared at her, my mouth a little open, unable to begin. The questions were as much for me as for her.

Mrs. Elsey touched me again. "Don't be afraid, my dear. I can see this makes you uneasy. It is all so personal, isn't it? So different that what we're told is The Right Thing. The thirst rises up inside us, undeniable. We're called, each of us, though it takes some of us much longer to respond. But the longer we resist, the greater our confusion. I promise you, you'll have all the answers I can give you, then the only thing that will remain is for you to decide what is righteous."

Despite her telling me not to fear, my alarm was greater than ever. "You mean what is Doing the Right Thing?"

"Surely you know that we Do The Right Thing when we honor it in spirit, not just in letter." Mrs. Elsey patted my hand. "Why don't you bring out your files and we can go through the incidents in order?"

"Th-thank you. Yes. In order." Pulling out the files, arranging them, setting out my pad, checking the point of my pencil, they were soothing rituals. Mrs. Elsey waited patiently, her hands clasped in her lap over the clasp of her seatbelt. I wasn't quite sure, it was such a dim memory for me to compare it with, but I thought there was a trace of something motherly in her expression. Loving, I would almost call it.

I mentally shook myself. "The first one. The woman who invited her neighbor for dinner."

"Mrs. Lindsay."

"You admit you know her."

"Yes, she is one of ours. One of the first, actually."

I concentrated fiercely as I ticked the red boxes on the form. 'Subject admits...' 'Subject freely confesses...'

Mrs. Elsey broke the silence. "Would you like to know about it?"

I looked up. "I have the report here."

"Oh, the facts of the event, yes." The old woman nodded. "But you hunger to know the reason behind it."

"The Council wants to know."

"But you *need* to understand."

I shifted in my seat. The verbal fencing was feeding my anxiety.

"Have you ever heard that religion that pleases God is when we visit orphans and widows in their affliction?"

I shook my head. "There are the agencies. No one is afflicted anymore. Think what could have happened."

Her answer was quick. "Think what did happen. A widow was comforted. We used to call it the 'ministry of presence.' Simply by knowing someone else saw her, recognized her pain, and was willing to endure the discomfort of sharing it."

I grunted. There really wasn't anything actionable in it. I tapped my finger on the next file. "What about this one? The boy. Even you have to admit, a teenage boy buying a box of diapers is going to draw attention."

Mrs. Elsey smiled and looked down at her hands, as if enjoying a memory. "Micah. Yes. Such a heart for others. We told him he'd bring out the overseers, but he said he was acting righteously."

"By dropping off the diapers, perhaps. But he stayed. He was observed playing with the children. And there's a supplemental report. Handed to me just as I left the building." I pulled out

111

the half sheet. "One of the squads says he returns. Regularly."

"We're so proud of him."

I stared at her. There it was. That word. "The medical center treated him for pink eye, did you know? At cost to the public. And again, for—" I rifled through the paperwork. "—head lice. For pity's sake. Contagious diseases and tiny, er, pests. That is what comes from getting personally involved." I couldn't help myself. "That's why we raise orphans in the centers. Clean. Responsible. We Do What Is Right, without crossing the line!"

Mrs. Elsey rubbed the little pendant of her necklace between her fingers as she nodded. "Micah has crossed the line, I agree. He loves those children. Thrives on the time he spends with them. They're all handicapped in some way, did you know that?"

"There are schools for that. Perfectly adequate. Those children expect him now. He has obligated himself. He's entangled himself with them." I folded my left hand into my lap before she could touch it again, and make that winsome, healing warmth steal upwards to my heart.

"You were an orphan, weren't you?" I felt Mrs. Elsey's gaze touching me like a balm.

"How—?"

"Micah is acting as a father to the fatherless."

"That is God's job. We fought a world-wide war to prove that. It's what the Council stands for, what the education initiative teaches. We uphold it by Doing The Right Thing, not indulging selfish impulses for purely personal satisfaction."

"Is that would you call what Micah is doing? And Mrs. Lindsay? Seeking purely selfish satisfaction?"

"Well, they could have called the sector squads. We provide services to help those in need. It's why we've sacrificed so much. No discrimination, no personal considerations, everyone treated the same."

Mrs. Elsey nodded slowly. "Yes, we've become very good at taking care of people by providing services without prejudice. But do we provide enough love? Out of fear of violating the law of Doing Right, of indulging personal impulses, are we violating the spirit of Righteousness? That is what troubles you, isn't it?" The old woman's voice was nearly as gentle as the one I'd been hearing in my heart. And almost as frightening, for speaking it aloud. What if everyone had that kind of doubt?

My mouth was so dry I could barely get the words out. "That is how we nearly lost the world and everything in it. When you let people decide for themselves, their personal prejudices and selfishness corrupt everything." I flung my arms out.

Mrs. Elsey remained serene in spite of my outburst. "Sometimes, yes, we live down to our lowest impulses. That is the nature of man. We're fallen, mortal beings. But sometimes we rise above ourselves. When we yield to that still, small voice and risk becoming involved with others, risk loving them, then we are able to do God's will and work. And I do agree, that is most satisfying."

I slapped my hands down on the table and shot to my feet. I was so frustrated that it was filling me, burning inside me like a bomb ready to explode. Every one of her answers just added to my questions.

"You are at the center of this movement. Micah is one of yours. A child. You've brought a child into this."

"Oh yes. Micah hungers to do God's will. He started coming to our nature documentaries. Loves animals. That's what brought him, then he stayed to talk. I've found we have learned a great deal from him, as much or more as he's learned from us. Young people can have a very clear grasp of the essentials. Micah loves. Without fear and without reservation. 'Humbly' is what we used to call it."

My knees buckled. I collapsed back into the chair. With numb fingers I scratched a wobbly tick into the third red box. 'Subject clearly articulates doctrine...'

"'of agape...'" Mrs. Elsey read over my shoulder. She had rolled close without my hearing her. "Yes, our Micah is definitely guilty. He learned some methods from us and we encouraged him. But he came to us with a hunger for righteousness. He had seen, seen with his heart, not just his eyes, what our world is missing."

"Alright, alright. 'The right thing' versus 'righteousness.' This word play is giving me a headache." I rested my head in my hands. "Either way, you can't tell me what happened last night was either 'right' or 'righteous.'

The old woman's burst of laughter made me look up. "Oh, oh, poor dear Mrs. Agabashian," she managed, before she was off again. "That really was a mis—mis—it was all my fault!" She laughed until she cried. I had to wait until she started searching in her pockets.

I patted my tunic but I wasn't much better supplied. Finally I located the polishing cloth for my glasses. "Here."

She mopped her face, but I winced when she blew her nose heartily at the end. She handed the little wad back to me with a cheery, "Now that is loving another as yourself. Thank you!"

I plucked the cloth from her palm with two fingers. "You said the incident was your fault. I cannot see how that could be." I flicked my eyes downward to the wheels of her chair.

"Well, I did have *some* help."

"Have no fear naming your coconspirators. Each will be

located and interviewed for their version." I picked up my pencil, ready to write.

"Oh, they're in the theater now. Most of them, though one is still on his way. They'll all be happy to talk to you. No, what I meant is, it was my miscalculation of the effects of meeting together and encouraging each other that sparked Mrs. Agabashian's delightful effort to love that man as herself."

"'Delightful?' She seized the man by the arm and practically dragged him into the street. Nearly caused a collision, and backed up traffic for an hour while we overseers sorted things out."

"Oh, I'm off again!" Mrs. Elsey flapped her hands before her face, trying to dry the tears of laughter. "Wish I'd been there to see it. Rose is all of four foot nine, and the gentleman was what, six foot two?"

"Four, not that it makes a difference. Let us go back to your use of the words 'method' and 'susceptible.' Are you confessing you induced Mrs. Agabashian to assault the man?"

"No. Yes. Actually, some of each."

I rubbed my forehead and sighed. "Please, Mrs. Elsey."

"Oh, I am sorry, my child. You're being thrown in at the deep end, aren't you?" A lilt from her amusement lingered in her voice. "Mrs. Agabashian was assisting the man, not assaulting him."

I peered at her from under my hand. "She's eighty-seven and walks with a cane."

"She wants to be about the Lord's business until he calls her Home. Rose has a very bright spirit. She told me the fellow hesitated right on the edge of the curb after the walk sign lit. And Rose needs all the time she can get to cross. It's that crosswalk on J Street, right outside the theater." Mrs. Elsey pointed with her chin, as if I could see through the plaster and sheetrock to the busy street outside. "Naturally she offered help, as she sometimes needs it herself."

"The man says she wrestled with him."

"I believe they had an ongoing discussion about who was assisting whom. You see, Rose was already thirsting for a world that did more than quote The Right Thing. She was susceptible, as you call it, to being a doer of Righteousness. My 'method' is very simple, just a matter of a few verses of encouragement shared before each film. Rose was a dancer, did you know that? She's here for every showing of our musicals. Fifth row back on the right, second seat in. And between you and me, the three musicals I have aren't really very good. But the cumulative effect on an old saint like Rose Agabashian was electrifying."

"But why did she do it? Even if the man had actually needed help, the squads are always within call. She didn't need to get involved. It's just not prudent."

"Rose was born long before the conflict. She remembers when the world was at its darkest, but there were still people willing to reach out, extend themselves, risk their hearts to love others and not count the cost. God did not create us to live alone, untouched and untouching."

The pressure inside my chest and my head was pulsing. My investigation was concluded. Mrs. Elsey had practically written the finding for me. But what would my judicial recommendation be? What did I dare recommend? Everything I'd seen in the last month had fed it, all these events. Then the Lieutenant's visit to my desk tonight, and now this interview with Mrs. Elsey—it was all feeding something inside me, making my heart crack and swell painfully with the possibilities.

I slipped out the JR form. There was an open box at

the bottom of the form labeled 'Extraordinary Precedents, Proceedings and Recommendations.' I could argue for leniency. No. Not just leniency, but for the condoning of this new form of citizen-based action. I could make a case for letting these people follow the leadings of their hearts. Not selfish desires, but the promptings of that still, small voice, the spirit of Righteousness that we'd nearly succeeded in drowning out by idolizing Right.

I could even—I realized my breaths were coming short, my heart beating fast—I could even recommend Mrs. Elsey's group be officially sanctioned as Community Partners. Help this spread even further.

And the cost? So much for that perfect life and career that had made me the poster child of The Modern Citizen. What else would it cost me? I raised my voice. "But even with the right motivation, that kind of reckless love leads to messy entanglements. It means obligations and misunderstandings. Unhappiness."

"The point of this life is not happiness."

I slewed around. The Lieutenant stood in the open door.

"We know we will face tribulations," he said, stepping inside. In the hallway I caught a glimpse of others: a slender boy with a mop of blond hair, a full-figured woman, like dozens I passed every day, except all the lines in this woman's face were upward, as if she smiled from the inside out. And when the Lieutenant sat down, I could see a tiny old woman with a cane—and a dancer's upright carriage.

"But we can have joy," the Lieutenant went on. "Joy and freedom in serving God. Loving others as He first loved us. That is the point."

"Well, I already do that," I said, defensiveness raising its head again. "I Do The Right Thing. I bother no one. I do my duty. I pay my taxes so the agencies can supply any unmet needs. What else can anyone expect?" But even as the words escaped me, I could hear the selfishness behind them.

Mrs. Agabashian made an elegant snort. The little golden button on her collar gleamed. Even standing, she was not much taller than I was, sitting, which brought the little ornament to my eye level. It was engraved with a tiny golden cross. "A lot more! Including a brand new rubber tip to my cane and getting the scuffs polished out of my new pumps."

Everyone laughed—except the Lieutenant and me. He folded his arms across his chest as if to make himself take up a little less space in the crowded room. The little gold button gleamed on his tunic. I could see now it was a match to the ones worn by Mrs. Agabashian, Mrs. Elsey, and the others. "I know it's a big leap, from safety to vulnerability. It's why I told you about myself when this operation began. I could see you had the hunger, so you'd be the best prospect as my second in command in this movement. But I had to let you work it out for yourself and trust you would act righteously. Not just Do The Right Thing. We're changing lives here. It will take time, there are no guarantees, and we're fighting an uphill battle. Including against the Council. But it's The Right Thing."

The little group chuckled at that. Even the Lieutenant smiled. That flicker I had noticed from time to time in his eyes, was that joy, I realized now.

But I was still angry and embarrassed at being manipulated and so easily deceived. I concentrated at shoving the files back into order, working off my emotions by rapping them on the desk to line them up in an ordered pile. At last one impression remained. The Lieutenant, that perfect Modern Citizen, had taken an awful risk. What else could be so important? My head spun. I could have reported him to the Council and likely received his rank as reward. Yet he shared that same joy I sensed in all the others.

Mrs. Elsey wheeled forward. She had scant room to maneuver in the crowded space. I watched the Lieutenant stifle a sound when her wheel ran over the toe of his boot.

"What more could anyone ask? Besides steel-toed boots?" She threw a wink over her shoulder at the Lieutenant. Then she grew serious. She took my hands in hers. I felt the dry, brittle fingers wrap my own young, hard fingers around a small metal object. A little gold button incised with a cross.

And I let her.

"People around us are perishing," she said. "They are hungering and thirsting for righteousness, the righteousness that comes from God and following His way, not from just being right, which comes from following man's laws."

There could be no going back from this moment. I knew, once I let the joy in, I'd never be the same. I'd never want to be the same.

"And that's the point," Micah said with a nod that sent a shingle of blond bangs flopping over his eyes. He might just as well have been responding to the change in my heart as reacting to the older woman's statement.

The others laughed. As I fastened the little pin to my collar, the warmth of Mrs. Elsey's joy, and of the little group of friends, of their messy, intimate, vulnerable, dangerous, righteous love began to fill me.

And I let it.

Blessed are they that hunger and thirst for righteousness
For they shall be filled

Hillari DeSchane

Hillari DeSchane is author of "Cinema Bendiga" and a journalist and speaker. Her 'Fatally Fun' 2018 debut cozy novel *A Christmas Tail* received a Certificate of Excellence from the Cat Writers Association of America. Her next historical cozy, *When In Rome*, releases in July, 2019. Hillari lives in California with her 'FurRensics Team' Jocko the Black Lab and Ambrose the Siamese.

Blessed are the Merciful

On the planet of Talifar, island of Stone Shell, village of High Harbor
2,500 years after the crash

Sunrise stood among the villagers and watched the royals march past him, their red, coiled hair shining in the sunlight, their kilts the color of indigo, their skin a copper brown, their faces tattooed and proud. He brushed back his hair, crow black and straight as a waterfall, as they set up a pavilion in the middle of the podvine field, presumably because the crop had been harvested and the ground lay closest to the raised bamboo homes clustered like fingers of a hand. Cluckers under raised verandas squawked as drums were brought out and set up, seadogs bugled their excitement, and the women formed lines to dance and sing a welcome song to the king of all Stone Grove.

The king was here to settle an argument between two farmers that even the elders had been unable to resolve. The two feuding men stood near the pavilion, looking nervous as well they should, for the king was known for both his justice and his sternness. The men should have listened to the elders.

A tall boy the same age as Sunrise, ten, walked past, wearing an indigo kilt. Dad nudged Sunrise. "That's the presumed."

Sunrise brushed his hair back again. He did not envy the boy. Being presumed not only meant that it was presumed that he would be the next king, but also that he would someday need to fight and kill someone to prove he was worthy. What must it be like to grow up with that hanging over your head? Surely being My King's son should be enough. The only fate Sunrise faced was that of being a pig farmer all his life.

The royal guards set up the portable throne under the pavilion and braziers near the front two corners. The only commoner guard, NineToes, a young man from their village, poured fragrant oil into the braziers and sparked them into flame. Sunrise snickered. Did the royals really think that would cover the smell of pigs that pervaded the entire area?

JumpAlong gave Sunrise a friendly shove. Sunrise shoved him back. The shoves became wrestling and then they were racing around the field and other children were joining them. The presumed looked at them with longing on his face.

Why not? Sunrise jerked his chin in invitation. The presumed slipped away from where he had been watching the judgment and chased after Sunrise. They ran around the people sitting in the field and the pavilion. The presumed slapped him on the shoulder. They skidded on the dirt and reversed direction. Sunrise reached out, this close to catching him as they rounded the pavilion again.

The presumed tripped and fell flat on his stomach. Too close to stop, Sunrise tripped over him and crashed into the brazier which fell apart and slopped burning oil on his neck.

Sunrise screamed. Thought fled. He scrabbled in the dirt, trying to get away from the agony. People grabbed him, threw water on him, and pressed cloth against his burning flesh. He squirmed, unable to get away. Someone grabbed his head and turned it. The pain receded enough that he could catch his breath. And then all awareness faded to nothing.

123

* * *

"Son."

Sunrise opened his eyes a crack. In the dim light, Dad's golden-brown face blurred, almost indistinguishable from the leaf-mat ceiling. His hammock pressed against his back. Sunrise grabbed his Giver's Hand medallion. *Giver, help me.* He squirmed, still unable to escape the pain on his neck, his jaw, his shoulder. The noxious smells of salve invaded his nose.

"Son, can you hear me?"

Sunrise whispered, "Truth."

"You need to forgive the presumed."

Sunrise forced himself to think. Had the presumed plopped his face in the dirt deliberately to trip him? That made no sense. And what did it matter? "Why?" The royals would go back to the palace on the other side of the island, and none of them would return until it was time to buy a trained seadog or special pig for a feast. Thought dissipated as he closed his eyes.

"Son! Listen to me."

Sunrise mumbled, "I am."

"The presumed is moving in with us."

He was dreaming. "What?"

"My King judged his own son. He decreed that the presumed would live with us and do your chores until you're healed. You must forgive the presumed so he doesn't feel threatened."

His mind floated on a sea of pain and bewilderment. "Forgive him for what?"

"I don't forgive him!" little MoonGleam shrilled from somewhere near the hammock. "He hurt my brother!"

Dad heaved a sigh. "Stop it. You know what an accident is."

Sunrise whispered, "She should. She has enough of them."

A tiny fist hit his leg. Sunrise almost laughed, but he choked on pain instead.

"Both of you listen to me. This is important. My King's son is going to live with us. He must call us something, so we've arranged for him to call us mom and dad."

Dad said more, however the words ceased to have meaning and Sunrise fell asleep again.

* * *

Sunrise sprang up from where he had been hiding behind the redberry bush. "I saw you!"

BigStep dropped the pods he'd been filching from the field that belonged to Sunrise's family. The surprise on his face shifted to anger. "I only took a few."

Sunrise stepped onto the field of podvines. Was BigStep really going to lie to his face? "Not true. You've cleaned out a quarter of our field this week. You've never weeded here, but you think you can take our food."

BigStep jutted his chin and grumbled, "Could have been monkeys or bigfa birds."

He should have been named Bigfa, after the massive, dirty birds. Did he think everybody was as stupid as he was? "Monkeys don't leave boy footprints." Sunrise pointed with his elbow at a deep print in the volcanic soil.

BigStep hunched his shoulders. Flying mice cheeped overhead in the deepening dusk. The sun had disappeared behind the mountain but had not yet fallen beneath the ocean on the mountain's other side. BigStep hitched up his brown kilt and crossed his arms. Straight black hair draped across golden brown eyes and traces of a bruise around one of them. "Could be *your* footprints."

Sunrise puffed out his thin chest and crossed his arms as well. "I'm going to tell MightyArm you're stealing from us. We need those pods to feed our pigs."

BigStep dropped his arms and clutched the sides of his kilt. "Don't, please. My dad will beat me."

Both boys studied their bare feet entangled with the pod vines.

The first moon appeared in the darkening sky. The sound of the surf and songs of settling lizards filled the silence between the two boys. Lamplight glowed through the window of the nearest raised bamboo home two fields away. A cool breeze flowed from the bamboo grove and somewhere within the forest an eight-legged snake groaned.

The boys startled, for the groans reminded them that night could be dangerous on Stone Shell during snake-mating season. "It's not fair." BigStep frowned. "You have too many pigs and we don't have any."

Sunrise scratched his neck where the scars stretched his skin. The pain did not drop him to his knees. "Is it my fault your boar broke your pen and ran off to be killed?" Before it grew too dark to see them, Sunrise scooped up the dropped pods and stuffed them into his kilt pocket. The skin of his bare chest and back twitched a little in the gathering coolness.

"You don't really need them," BigStep muttered. He walked toward the path that would lead to the main lane of High Harbor.

Sunrise walked beside him. "You don't know anything."

"I know the presumed could bring enough baskets of pods to feed all the pigs and all the people for weeks."

He wasn't the only one who thought housing Bowmark the presumed was making his family rich. Ha. Sunrise hopped on one foot while untangling a vine wrapped around his ankle. "Of course he could, but he won't. All he brings is his labor and his guard."

"It's not fair a royal lives with you and does your chores."

Sunrise slapped a night biter on his forearm and then one on his cheek. "You want the presumed to move in with you? All you need to do is trip over him and burn off half your neck and shoulder. You go do that. I might even help throw some oil on you. I'll strike the flint."

"You're healed now. So it's not fair that he still comes to stay with you."

He didn't want a fistfight this close to the forest at night nor for his fresh skin to tear but anger tightened his hands into fists. Clenching his jaw stretched the still-tender skin. "We'll see how fair MightyArm is when he hears it's you stealing from us.

BigStep raised his clenched hand. "I thought you weren't going to tell on me. I told you my dad will beat me."

"I don't think so. The elders talked to him."

BigStep shook his head. "My dad isn't like your dad. He doesn't care what the elders say. He told me the next time I get in trouble, he'll throw me off the cliff. Don't make my dad do that to me."

Sunrise looked up at the second moon peeking over the shoulder of the mountain. BigStep's dad wouldn't really throw him off the cliff, would he? Truth, though, he might beat him. "Stop stealing our crops and I won't tell MightyArm."

"I pledge myself." BigStep gripped his Giver's Hand medallion necklace. "May Giver deal me disaster and death if I ever steal pods from you again."

Sunrise briefly touched the medallion on his own chest. "We

are reconciled." *I hope.*

They walked in silence past the rice field until they reached the lane.

"I won't forget this." BigStep sprinted off toward his home.

Sunrise strolled toward his, listening to families resting on their verandas singing songs about harvesting rice, fetching water, and why the third moon was so tiny. He pulled out a pod and bit into it. Sweet and savory flavor bloomed across his tongue.

A tiny figure thudded into him. MoonGleam shrilled, "Sunrise, you're safe! I was worried about you."

Ow! My shoulder. She had no idea how easily she could hurt him, and he wasn't about to let her know. "Oh, and because night is so dangerous for big brother, little sister thought she should run around looking for me."

"What if you were dead?"

"You finding me would fix that. Here." Sunrise groped in the dark until he found MoonGleam's hand and pressed a pod against her palm. "Eat this." As she crunched the pod they walked to their home and he gingerly hoisted her onto the veranda. Only a couple twinges reminded him that he wasn't supposed to lift things yet. One of the village seadogs must have smelled a snake for suddenly they all bugled, their notes swooping through the air, their back quills rattling against each other.

May a tearjaw eat his liver, he'd forgotten to tie their seadog's rope to the pig fence while he was lurking near the podvine field. All the weaner pigs they were preparing for next week's auction in Mid Village would be a tempting target for snakes. Dad had been breeding the fatty pig strain for all of Sunrise's life, and the sale of this year's litter would finally make them rich the way housing Bowmark had not. He dashed up the lane to do his forgotten chore.

Some time later, Sunrise crept into the house, hoping everybody was sleeping in their hammocks, but Dad sat on a grass mat with a tiny oil lamp shedding light and perfume into the air. Dad pinned Sunrise with his implacable gaze. "MoonGleam said you were right behind her. Where did you go?"

Sunrise ducked his head and sat in front of Dad. "I'm sorry. I remembered I needed to tie Chew to the pig fence, so that's where I went."

"I see. What did you find there?"

"That somebody had already tied Chew to the fence."

"Who do you suppose that somebody was?"

"You or Mom."

Dad studied Sunrise while Sunrise studied his knees. "You're letting the presumed make you lazy. When he's not here, you need to do your chores. Your family is counting on you."

"I know, Dad. I'm sorry."

From a dark corner, MoonGleam called, "When is Bowmark coming back? I miss him."

From another dark corner, Mom said, "Hush. *The presumed* left only yesterday."

Telling MoonGleam to hush and to call Bowmark by his proper title was like telling the surf to stay back. "But Bowmark left early."

Mom sighed. "Babies come when they come. After his brother or sister is born, My King might decide that the presumed should stay at the palace. Your brother is nearly healed. Since the presumed fulfilled My King's judgment, there's no reason for him to come back."

"But I miss him. He's a lot nicer than Sunrise."

He's a lot nicer than MoonGleam, too. Sunrise bit his lips to keep from smirking.

"Enough," rumbled Dad. He did not move as he continued his scrutiny of Sunrise.

What did Dad want? He had apologized. "I won't forget my chores again, Dad."

"That would be good." After a long moment, Dad asked, "Did you catch your thief?"

Sunrise stumbled over his words. "I, um, I—I think maybe—I think it might be monkeys." He lowered his gaze and rubbed the bridge of his nose.

After a pause, Dad placed his hands on his knees. His face stayed still. "You think so?" He rose.

Sunrise winced. Dad knew he had lied and yet he let the lie go. Maybe he knew what had happened on the field the way he seemed to know everything Sunrise did. Sunrise said nothing. After Dad blew out the lamp, both walked in the dark as easily as in the light for their feet knew every strand on the floor. Sunrise shook out his hammock, strung it up, and rolled in.

* * *

Sunrise tossed the last pod to the boar. "I can't wait until we roast you for the Wind Change feast."

The boar twitched one ear and kept its quills pressed to its back. Sunrise moved a pen over to watch the newly-weaned pigs lashing their long tails and shoving their noses through the slats trying to reach their mother. The sow lay on the mud as though she was too exhausted to ever move again. Nubbins on the piglet's backs showed where quills would soon grow. These fatty piggies had grown twice as fast as the neighbors' pigs and produced twice as much waste for Sunrise to muck out.

One piglet wandered over to Sunrise and snuffled his shin. He rubbed its moist nose. The shadow of a cloud darkened the pen. At the same time the ground shuddered. Sunrise widened his stance and grabbed hold of a post. As quick as the shaking had come, the quake left. Sunrise waited a few heartbeats before jogging down the lane to retrieve a bucket from under the house to fetch water. He reached home the same time a royal guard he did not recognize slung a basket from his back onto the veranda. "Ho, the house!" the guard called.

Since the walk from the palace to High Harbor took three hours, guards seldom visited the village. Something in the guard's facial expression frightened Sunrise. Villagers abandoned their work to drift close enough to hear his words.

Mom slid the door open and stepped onto the veranda, wearing the baby on her back wrapped in a tattered blanket. MoonGleam followed.

Everyone waited.

The guard said in a voice that broke. "My Queen has died during childbirth."

Sunrise took a step back. He had never met My Queen, but the way Bowmark talked about her, she stood next to the Giver.

Mom collapsed to her knees and then sat heavily on the veranda. She covered her mouth with her hands. "Ah, no."

The guard's red dreadlocks fell forward as he bent over the basket and lifted the lid to reveal white ribbons. "This is a gift from My King."

Many in the village, including Sunrise's family, could not afford the mourning ribbons and needed to settle for light-colored string. Enough ribbons lay coiled in the basket for his family and half the village.

Mom choked out, "I give you thanks. Ah, the poor presumed. I told him she would live. He'll never believe another word from me. Ah, My King. What will they do?"

Without another word, the guard turned away and worked his way through the silent villagers and then down the trail that led to Safe Harbor and the palace.

"No!" screamed MoonGleam. She clutched Mom. Many of the villagers keened, attracting more villagers to hear the bad news.

With his heart thudding in a hollowed-out chest, Sunrise needed to do something, needed to move. He ran to the stairs that had been carved in the harbor cliff and skittered down to the tiny beach that could hold six fishing canoes. He pounded broken lava chunks against smoother lava boulders until his fingers bled and his arms trembled with exhaustion. Only allowing his mind to focus on sensations, he lay back on the gritty sand and felt the warm surf brushing his feet and backing off.

Clouds bunched, darkened, and finally dumped rain on him. He rose and plodded back up the long stairs. White ribbons striped the veranda posts. Everyone in sight wore three white ribbons or light strings around their necks. Wordlessly, Mom tied three ribbons around Sunrise's neck. They would wear these for a week before taking them off to paint prayers on them and throw them into the sea.

That night, they ate only unseasoned rice.

* * *

Sunrise woke up slowly. His fingers hurt. Bright sunlight showed through the open door. What? Dad should have dumped him out of his hammock for sleeping in so late. He dashed out and nearly collided with Dad who was sitting on the edge of the veranda. "I'msorryDadI'llgatherthepodsnow"

Dad pointed with his elbow to the basket of pods. "Don't worry, son. Grief will make us slow and stupid for a while. Today all you need to do is take care of the pigs."

Sunrise nodded. Then he caught a whiff of roasted pig. No one roasted a pig unless it was a feast day, and then the meat was shared with everybody. Who would roast a pig on a day of mourning and unseasoned rice?

Sunrise trudged through sunlight and a cloud of buzzers to Pig Row, where most of the village's pigs were kept. The sheds and pens of Sunrise's family were the largest and best maintained. The backs of the sheds faced the village, and most pig owners affixed decorative wreaths on them. The shed of BigStep's family bore no wreath and was half-collapsed.

The family had not known or had not cared that the bamboo slats needed to be replaced on a regular basis and so they had lost the two breeders they had just purchased from Dad.

Sunrise passed the shed and turned to walk along the pen. Why weren't the pigs squealing for their food? Their seadog, Chew lay on the path with her tongue lolling out of her mouth and her eyes open and unblinking. Sunrise dropped his bucket and the pods bounced in every direction as he ran and knelt by the seadog's head. Blood soaked the dust under her neck. Chew was dead.

Sunrise could not move. His only thought was the one word, *How?*

Touch-me-not flowers littered the ground in front of the pen and inside. Someone had dusted Chew's muzzle with the sleep pollen from such flowers and then slit its throat. The pigs!

Sunrise dashed through the gate and peered into the piglet's shed. Only rice straw and manure. He vaulted over the fence to the sows' shed. Instead of the three sows in the shed, a pile of intestines and organs glistened. Flies covered the offal and blood puddled on the floor. He could not breathe for several moments.

He vaulted over the fence again into the piglets's pen, ran across the mud and vaulted into the boar's pen. Blood streaked the ground, making a trail to the gate and a short distance beyond.

Someone had made the pigs sleep with touch-me-not pollen so they could be butchered quietly. Where had the carcasses gone?

The roast pig he had smelled. Who had roasted a pig? He sprinted back home. "Mom! Dad! Somebody killed our pigs!"

Mom ran out of the house. Dad straightened up from where he had been pulling weeds in the yellowfruit field. Mom waved frantically at him to come home. Dad ran straight through the yellowfruits and someone else's podvine field. Unable to stand still, Sunrise wrapped his arms around himself and bounced.

Dad arrived, panting. "What's wrong?"

"Someone killed our pigs and stole the piglets!"

Dad gasped. "No. Maybe they broke out."

"Dad! They wouldn't leave their guts and blood behind. And I thought I smelled someone roasting a pig farther down the lane."

Dad used both hands to wipe down his face. He turned and strode along the house lane. Sunrise trotted after him.

The smell was strongest at BigStep's house. Dad stood in

front of the sliding door and called, "Ho, the house!" No one answered, though quick footsteps inside could be heard. Grim-faced, Dad hopped off the veranda and walked around the corner of the house to the cooking area behind. BigStep and his sister HideUnder were hastily shoveling soil into a pit. A stiff blanket soaked with blood and covered with bones lay nearby. Two smaller children huddled behind a palm tree. BigStep's dad EagleSoar and mom PickFruit—with grease on their faces—stepped out of the house and stopped between Sunrise and the pit.

PickFruit stared at the soil but EagleSoar crossed his arms and sneered. "It wasn't fair."

Sunrise leaped onto BigStep and pummeled him. Dad grabbed Sunrise, pulled him off, and carried him off despite all the yelling and kicking he did. Dad did not set him down until they reached their house.

"Dad! They ruined us!" Sunrise punched the air.

"They impoverished us because they were jealous. That's not quite the same thing."

Mom touched Dad's shoulder. "GoDown, I followed a trail of blood and drag marks to the seaside cliff. You need to see this." Sunrise and MoonGleam followed Mom and Dad to the cliff and looked over. On the far-below rocks their pigs lay smashed. Seagulls and lizards squabbled over the flesh.

Breath left Dad and Sunrise. Not only had EagleSoar's family stolen the fatty piggies and eaten all they could in a night, they had made sure that no one else ever enjoyed eating one of the pigs.

MoonGleam squealed. "They didn't even share! We should push them over the cliff!" She picked up a rock and threw it over the cliff. Sunrise couldn't speak.

Dad grabbed her arm, and then Sunrise's and pulled them to the house where he let go of them, dropped onto the veranda, placed his elbows on his knees, pressed his forehead against his clenched hands, and breathed heavily. The muscles of his jaw twitched. Mom sat beside him and wiped the tears on her face.

Sunrise could not stand the silence. "Dad! What are you going to do?"

Dad said through gritted teeth. "Nothing."

"Dad! How can we do nothing?" Sunrise pounded his fist on his palm. MoonGleam was right. They should be shoved off the cliff.

Dad pulled him close and hissed in his ear so the gathering neighbors could not hear what he said. "Stop. Hold your Giver's Hand. What does Giver require of us?"

To love our neighbor and reconcile whenever possible. Sunrise could not say the words.

"Maybe the words of the Holy Books aren't enough for you. Listen, after the presumed stops living with us, we still need to live in this village. You will not ask My King for justice. You will not allow the presumed to replace what EagleSoar stole from us."

"But Dad, BigStep promised he wouldn't forget, and now—" Sunrise slapped his hand over his mouth. They had reconciled, and now Sunrise was supposed to pretend BigStep had not been stealing from them. "It's not fair!"

Dad's eye's squeezed shut a moment. "That's what EagleSoar and his children say. Do you want to be like them?"

Before Sunrise could answer, MightyArm walked through the gathered neighbors. Sunlight sheened on his coconut-oiled and braided hair. His tattoos shifted over his muscles. "What happened?"

MoonGleam shouted, "EagleSoar stole and killed our pigs."

As the neighbors angrily exclaimed, Mom tugged on Moon-Gleam until his sister sat beside Mom.

MightyArm nodded slowly. "I'll gather the elders. We will require him to replace your pigs triple."

Dad rubbed his knees. "How can he? The means by which he could replace the fatty piggies lie at the base of a cliff being eaten by seabirds. No, MightyArm. I do not ask you nor My King for justice. I ask for nothing from him. I will not be responsible for that family losing everything and going hungry."

"Then my feet are tied," MightyArm said. He walked away.

Some of the women gathered around Mom to hug her and cry. Everyone else slowly returned to their chores. Sunrise slouched into the house to slump against a wall. He had pardoned BigStep's theft, and this was how he was repaid. The urge to tell MightyArm about BigStep's theft and to smash the liar's nose felt as strong as the urge to vomit. Bitterness coated his tongue.

* * *

They were sitting in their darkened house to feel sad together and to pray to Giver for peace for My King and the presumed and everyone else in the palace when the door slid open and sunlight spilled in. The presumed's escort and guard NineToes, stepped into the room. "Give me pardon," he murmured. "I want to prepare you for the presumed. He . . . is changed into an overstrung bow. He thinks he must exercise every moment of the day so that he can protect his baby brother. If you can find a way to help him unstring, My King will be most grateful."

Mom said, "My poor presumed. He always worries so much."

"This is past worry. He's obsessed. Now I'm the one who's worried. He won't rest."

Sunrise looked from one to the other. Mom had said that she didn't think Bowmark would ever come back. What did they mean?

Mom sighed. "Send him in." As soon as Bowmark came in Mom stood and shuffled over to him. "Everyone else, please go away. I need the presumed to help me."

Everyone else left the room and sat on the veranda. Dad slid the door shut. Soon they heard Bowmark wailing while Mom crooned at him about how wonderful My Queen had been.

Sunrise's lips trembled. Any moment now he would start crying. "Dad, let me pick the last of the pods."

MoonGleam jumped off the veranda. "I'll help." She meant she would be stepping on pods while racing to pick the fattest ones. Still, anything to get away from those heart-broken sobs.

Cleaning the fields of the last of the pods did not take long. Next thing would be to pull up the vines and feed them to the pigs. Sunrise stopped. They did not have pigs anymore. That hollow space inside opened the way it had the first time he saw the pigs on the rocks. He blinked rapidly and considered. The stone cutter SleepDeep had hurt his foot and was limping. Truth, tomorrow Sunrise would pile the vines in SleepDeep's pens. "Let's go, pest."

"I am not a pest." MoonGleam picked up the heaviest bucket, promptly tripped, and scattered the pods. Sunrise gathered her and pods up, and then they ambled back to the quiet house.

Their neighbor two houses down the lane, SeeHerGo, sat on the veranda cradling a baby monkey in her hands. "When he wakes up, I'm going to give this to the presumed."

A flash of jealousy throttled Sunrise, *She didn't offer me one, but the moment passed. I won't say it's not fair. He leaned over her hands and finger stroked the monkey's back. If Dad doesn't want revenge, then I don't want revenge. Except I do.*

BigStep and EagleSoar stepped out of their house eleven houses down the lane, saw Sunrise, and turned to take the longer way to their field of yellowfruit.

Sunrise watched them, trembling. *Giver, I want to smash his face. Why won't Dad let me?*

Every farmer they passed straightened from their task and yelled, "Pigfat!" at them. Father and son scurried down the path with their shoulders bent over.

Sunrise sat and rubbed his arms until his rage abated. He, MoonGleam, and SeeHerGo played with the monkey until Mom called from the rope grass field, "I'm sure he's awake now.

They rattled into the house and gave the monkey to Bowmark. In a few moments the monkey dangled around Bowmark's neck picking at the Giver's Hand medallion, one foot and its tail hanging onto Bowmark's hair. It tugged at the golden hand and squeaked. "Gimme gimme gimme mine!" They decided to name the creature SnatchFast.

MoonGleam took hold of the monkey, stroked SnatchFast, and cooed. "We should teach him warrior shouts too!"

Outside, the farmer CoolShadow shouted angrily, "Pigfat! Pigfat!" Then HeHelps shouted, "Pigfat!"

NineToes walked in. "Presumed, are you ready to eat?" When the children had seated themselves on the edge of the veranda, the guard handed all of them bowls of cold, unseasoned rice. Mom and Dad leaned on each other and refused the mourning rice.

MoonGleam set her bowl aside, pattered up to Bowmark,

giggled, and dropped SnatchFast on Bowmark's head..Then, abruptly, she jumped off the veranda and chased after Hideunder who had been sidling past their house "Pigfat!"

HideUnder covered her head with her arms and ran up the path. At every house she passed, someone shouted at her, "Pigfat."

Sunrise leaped off the veranda, grabbed MoonGleam, and dragged her back to the house. She didn't stop struggling until Dad rumbled, "Behave yourself. We can't help what other people do, but we are not taking revenge on that family. Do you hear me?"

Sunrise rubbed his arms again. Dad's commands had never before felt so hard to do. He swallowed the words he would like to say. "Truth." He would obey Dad.

Bowmark looked from face to face. "What did HideUnder do? Why is everybody yelling 'pigfat' at her?"

Sunrise tapped him on the shoulder. "Let's go up to the farrowing shed."

Bowmark followed Sunrise higher up the slope to the pen and shed. SnatchFast hung onto Bowmark's dreadlocks as they walked. Farmers standing in the lane between pens moved out of sight.

No grunting, no howling greeted them. No boar battered the fence. No piglets thrust their noses through the bamboo bars.

Bowmark looked from empty pen to empty pen. "Did you sell all of them?"

Sunrise slumped against a fence. "HideUnder's family has been jealous of my family for a long time. Their pigs stay skinny or die. Then you moved in with us."

"Why would they be jealous of me moving in with you?"

Sunrise took a deep breath. *Love your neighbor.* Too bad

140

EagleSoar hadn't obeyed that command. "It doesn't matter. The night before the market, they stole all the piglets, the sow, and the boar. They cooked and ate all they could. What they couldn't eat, they killed and threw over a cliff."

Bowmark gaped.

Sunrise held his fists close to his side. "Twelve years of breeding gone. Dad spent a lot of money buying the best pigs. Now we're ruined."

"No, I'll make Father—My King come and judge them."

Sunrise gripped Bowmark's arm. "You won't. Dad said we're not going to ask for judgment."

"Why? This isn't right!" He clenched his jaw.

"I don't know why. Dad says we still need to live here when you're not here. We've always lived here. I don't know what he's talking about." Sunrise slapped the top of the fence.

"I'll have My King send you new pigs."

Instead of shouting, "I agree!" Sunrise forced out the words, "Dad said you would say that. I'm supposed to tell you that you're not doing that either."

Bowmark pulled the monkey off his hair. "Why?"

"Dad told me to take you to Mount Fist and explore some of the lava tubes."

"I don't want to. I want to give you justice."

"Everybody hates HideUnder's family now. Dad said we need to accept that as justice enough. Mom agreed. We won't ruin them the way they ruined us."

Standing in the hot sun, surrounded by dust and silence, Bowmark absentmindedly stroked SnatchFast.

They needed to talk about something else. Ah, they had heard that during My Queen's funeral at sea one of the crab-like people from the sea had visited. "Bowmark? I heard you saw a shlak. I wish I could see a shlak."

Either Bowmark surrendered the argument or that was enough to divert him. Sunrise wiped away his unshed tears before Bowmark could see them. And so Sunrise obeyed Dad even though he saw no reason to.

* * *

A week later, Sunrise waved at Bowmark as the presumed walked behind NineToes toward the palace and Safe Harbor. When his friend disappeared into the jungle, Sunrise drew his legs up on the veranda and rested his chin on his knees. Would everyone in the village still believe that taking care of the presumed would make them rich?

Sunrise sighed. Somehow the bitterness had grown old and faded. Perhaps someday he wouldn't feel it at all. Dad trudged up from the lower field and sat beside him. Sunrise asked, "Dad, did we unstring him?"

"Unstring? Ah, what NineToes said. Maybe. I don't know."

They sat, resting, listening to the cluckers under the veranda, watching the seagulls circle, smelling the salt-laden air, enjoying the bit of shade over them.

Carrying a bundle of rice straw on his back, PokeTheFire approached Dad. PokeTheFire drew lines in the dust with his toe and watched the women three houses down pounding rice as he murmured. "My wife is having a baby soon. She's tired of caring for our sow and I don't want to do it either. Could you keep our sow in your pens for a year? She should farrow in the wind turn. Money is always hard to come by, so I'm hoping you will accept half the piglets as pay for their space and care."

Sunrise stared at the man. How could he afford such a

generous gift?

Dad took several breaths as PokeTheFire looked everywhere but at him. "Sunrise? Do you think you're healed enough to take care of his sow?"

Sunrise broke from his shock to stretch his shoulder and turn his head from side to side. "Truth. It still hurts but I can move without tearing anything."

Dad said, "We will be pleased to take care of your sow for a year. Sunrise will fetch it tomorrow morning."

"I give you thanks." The man moved off and stumped up the lane.

Next, ScentOfPlumeria approached, holding a seadog so young its quills had not started to develop. "Ho, the house. We have too many puppies. Would you mind taking one?"

She can't have too many puppies. The seadogs of ScentOfPlumeria were known over the entire island as excellent guards that stayed gentle around children. Even nobles came to buy her puppies. Sunrise clamped his lips together before he could say anything.

Dad said, "We would be pleased to take a puppy from you. Sunrise?"

Sunrise held out his arms and the woman laid her puppy on them. "I give you thanks."

The warm puppy snuggled against his chest. He rubbed behind its ears.

One of the elders tapped his way to them. When his cane touched Sunrise's leg, he stopped. "GoDown?"

"Over here," Dad said.

"I'm tired of dealing with a boar when I'm half-blind. If you would like to deal with him, I'd like to give him to you in exchange for a haunch when you roast him."

Dad made a noncommittal noise. "What would the stud fees be?"

The elder waved his cane. "All I want is the haunch, along with that special sauce you make."

Dad nodded. "Then I would like to deal with your boar. Sunrise will fetch him tomorrow afternoon."

"I give you thanks." The man tapped away.

The puppy yawned. "Dad? A boar? All by myself?"

Dad flipped a hand. "If his grandsons won't help, I will."

FoamDrift walked up with a gaggle of children behind her. "I hear the presumed eats a lot. May I share some eggs with you?" She extended a reed basket.

Dad said, "I would be happy to share eggs from you. Sunrise, take this inside." He said something to each of the children as Sunrise took the basket in. Mom would likely return it filled with riceballs.

Mom came out, sat with Dad, and together they greeted the villagers as they came by, one by one and offered fruit, a sickly piglet that maybe they could nurse to health, dried fish, dried pods, shredded coconut, a song bird in a cage, another piglet because pigs like to be in herds, a hammock in case the presumed wore his out, a new bucket that did not leak, a roll of cloth to make a tunic, a bundle of bamboo poles to renew the pig fences, a giant storage basket, a cup of redberry, a wreath of plumeria, some scented oils for their lamps, a clucker to roast because he was annoying, and more.

Was he dreaming? He'd never seen anything like this.

Mom invited everybody to the feast she would give tomorrow because their family could not eat all this alone.

The parade of gifts ended when the sun dove into the ocean. Dazed, Sunrise took the puppy to the garden behind the house and showed him the poop pit. He returned to the house filled with light, scents, and piles of food spread out on banana leaves. "Dad, did you know this was going to happen?"

"No, but I did hope people might remember they are Giver's hands once they saw that My King was not the Giver."

Sunrise gripped the Giver's Hand medallion on his chest, remembering the sentence in the First Holy Book: Mercy belongs to the merciful. Was this what that sentence meant?

Blessed are the merciful
For they shall obtain mercy

Lelia Rose Foreman

L elia Rose Foreman is author of "Blessed are the Merciful."

When she was in the fifth grade and working her way through the long row of Reader's Digest Condensed Books on her mother's shelf, she ran across A Fall of Moondust by Arthur C. Clarke. It was though a fuse had been lit and fireworks went off.

Next she read every speculative fiction book in her small town library. (There were a lot fewer then.)In high school she discovered J. R. R. Tolkien and fell in love with fantasy as well. As for horror, she's still working on appreciating the genre.

She obtained a B.S. in Medical Technology, raised and released five children, all of whom survived, and followed her husband in the U.S.A.F to bases in Japan, Texas, and Alaska. She is the author of A Shattered World and a number of short stories in anthologies. http://leliaroseforeman.blogspot.com/

The Heartstone

I don't consider myself to have a weak stomach, but I've never been around a dead body, much less try to bury one. I didn't know your body loses all its fluids and the smell I was not prepared for. I haven't been around anything that's dead. It is forbidden. At least for one person of every tribe.

Every year one person from every tribe must enter the temple. I am the youngest at fifteen years and the oldest anyone can be is twenty-one. The Ascension is where they are tested. If no one passes the tests, all twelve die as a sacrifice, buying my people another year. Only one needs to pass.

I stomp on the shovel, forcing it deeper into the damp ground. It cuts in the clay and scrapes loudly across a rock. I freeze. I know I shouldn't worry; no one would dare come here, and I'm not expected to be anywhere for at least another day. I stab at the ground, cleaving off another chunk of dirt and clay.

The visit was supposed to be a quick one. "What can I help you with, Grandpa?" "Need me to lift anything heavy, Grandpa?" I was hoping to get some of Grandpa's unshakable hope—could have used that right now. But I should have known better; nothing is ever simple or quick with him. I'm supposed be communing with nature, readying my mind and spirit for the Ascendance. I keep imagining what the maker looks like. That only happens if I pass all the tests earning the right to see Him and break the curse. Leaning on the shovel's handle I rest my arms. I could have used grandpa today. I wanted to ask him how you face death. I don't know if I'm ready to be a sacrifice.

I'm a long shot anyway. My tribe is not highly regarded. I shove the shovel down into the hole. It disappears, measuring the side wall at three mics in depth. Not enough to even come up to my knees. It's going to need to be deeper.

The Ascendance is why I came to see Grandpa in the first place. He isn't, I mean wasn't, like the other elders who refuse to talk about the first days. His stories were fantastic. He claimed we could command water and bend it to our will, heal sickness, and even replace whole limbs. Some could speak to animals and understand them. All this power flowed from a stone that was permanently planted in our sternums. The stones used to glow with brilliant light, each tribe a different color. Today, all the stones are a shade of lightless gray. Some have said in the early days you could listen carefully, and the stones would speak softly but clearly with the Maker's divine voice. Grandpa claimed he could still talk to the Maker, and from time to time his stone would glow a pure white. It was stories like these that brought about his banishment.

If I had not come today and discovered him dead, a pack of timber-dogs surely would have eaten his body and the blackrows would have picked him clean. Despite the danger, I really wish his stone would glow a little to help with the waning light. Blackrows don't fly at night but the darkness won't keep the timber-dogs away.

I hop down into the hole which now reaches my chest. Six mics, according to our law book, is the perfect depth to help a man through his transcendence. The scent of fresh dirt fills my throat, replacing for a brief but welcome moment the stench that covers my grandpa. I slip my hands under the stiff body. For a slender man, over a hundred years old, Grandpa is still solid. I can hear him right now as I struggle with his weight. "Son, use the young limbs you have. In my day I was pulling the family cart uphill by age ten."

I manage to lower him into the ground and lay him at my feet, carefully slipping each foot out from under his body. Gently, I position his hands just beneath his heartstone. "Grandpa, I would have loved to see your day."

From my back pocket I retrieve copy of the law book. I turn to the reading marked for transcendence. I divide the tiny black book with my thumb to hold my place. My other hand rests on his stone which, oddly, still feels warm to the touch. This ceremony is not for the banished— not for a novice to perform— but it will have to do.

"From the ground you came and to it your body will return.
May the Maker receive you.
May He find a clean and pure heart."

His stone seems to be getting warmer. I pause and stare at it, then shift my hand to my fingertips, hoping to dissipate the heat.

"May what we see faintly now be clear.
Receive your son as He received you."

Now my whole body is heating up. Sweat pools on my upper lip.

"So be it."

I withdraw my hand swiftly as soon as I finish, nursing the red skin with the cold night air. My stone has never warmed like that. I don't know a single person whose stone has. Even in death, Grandpa's life brings more questions than answers.

I boost myself up to the ridge of the hole. I stretch my hand, which is beginning to feel normal. Why was his stone so warm? Touching my own. I find a groove I've never felt before. It's so dark, I can't really see, running my finger the length of the stone. Please be small.

No, it runs the whole length of the stone! I fold to my knees, falling short of the hole. These stones are nearly indestructible; only another stone can make this kind of damage.

That's it. My stone must have hit Grandpa's when I picked him up.

It's one thing to hide that you've been moonlighting with a dead body; it's a completely different thing to attempt to hide a flawed stone. It's impossible. Tomorrow when I arrive at the Ascension, they will strike my stone with a harmonic resonator. It will pick up the smallest imperfection. My tribe chose me for this great honor. Now I'll bring shame to them all.

Who was I kidding anyway? Pushing up on the ground, I rise to my feet. I was coming here tonight so Grandpa could tell me I was wrong. He always had a way of seeing things I missed. Instead, I found him lying still and cold. I did the right thing by him, despite our law, and now my stone is scratched. I look up searching the stars for an answer.

I bury my head in my hands. "Thanks, Grandpa, for showing me I'm not worthy." I never was.

A distant light filters through my fingers and my heart sinks. They've found me. A scratched stone is now the least of my worries. I open my eyes. No one has found me. The light is coming from the hole. Grandpa's stone! I remember. He told me that it still did this but I had never seen it. I hop down, almost falling on top of Grandpa. The place I am is remote, but any light here is like a beacon. It's too dangerous; it will only bring unwelcome company.

"Take me." A haunting voice crawls out of the grave.

The stone flickers with each word.

I lay almost completely down, the top half of my body covering Grandpa's stone. The heat from it is still rising.

"Take me," commands the voice.

The thought takes root in my mind, making its way to my heart. I could switch the stones, mine for his. I can't keep both. He needs one to transcend to the Everlast. The Maker will weigh and gaze into it one day and decide if Grandpa will live again when our world is born a second time. If I take it, he could remain in the ground forever in darkness. I would never see him again.

"Trust me," The voice softens, almost soothing.

The stone goes cold and dark just as fast as it had illuminated. I use the wall to get to my feet. I can't shake the urge to take the stone.

"Grandpa, forgive me." I grab the stone and twist a quarter to the right, doing the same with my own stone. I stagger a moment as life drains from my limbs. I can't catch my breath. Between the seizing chest muscles my own stone slips out of my fingers. It falls to the ground. I reach for it to put it into Grandpa's chest. My own pain stops me. *He's dead, Ever. If you don't get his stone you'll join him.* I use my free hand to steady Grandpa's rock and with a twist it locks.

A wave of warmth and a flash of light shoot out from my chest, spreading through my whole body, using my veins like a highway. A strange peace overtakes me. It's getting darker, and I need to fill this hole and get out of here. The shovel has a mind of its own. It is the same dirt filling the same hole I dug but it takes half the time to fill it. I lift the final scoop waist high and let it sprinkle slowly like I'm watching the last of my grandpa's existence.

I look up past the dust of the settling dirt. A pair of yellow iridescent eyes greets me. Timber-dogs. My mind screams, *run,* but the message never reaches my limbs. Fear hijacks all my senses. I have taken too long, lingered where I should not have, and now I will reap what I've sown. I might have a fighting chance with my shovel against one timber-dog but not against several pairs of eyes that now appear around me. I take a step back. A snarl warms the back of my neck. A timber-dog has worked its way behind me, cutting off my last means of escape. My heart beat sounds the march of my impending doom. It was foolish to think I could break the Laws and not suffer. The Maker has sent them to clean up this mistake. My thoughts hang like lead weights in my mind and my knees comply. I close my eyes. I can't watch as the timber-dogs tighten their circle like a noose.

Maker. A sigh leaks from my slumped frame. No one has ever tried to talk directly to him. The royal class are the only ones that can speak with the Maker and even then, the Maker does not always answer.

My hands press against the warming stone. "I am not worthy of being heard, but if you heard my grandpa maybe you will hear me. If you wish for me to take my own life, then I will take it. But not in this way."

The stone pulls my chest out and up, causing my back to arch. The heat is unbearable. My hands and head fling back, as a wave of energy and light releases from the stone. The force causes my ears to pop and ring.

"It's not time," the stone commands.

Then it is quiet and pressure leaves my body. Hunching over

on all fours, my chest seizes and releases quickly, trying to replace the air I've just lost.

"Get up and go." The stone's voice cuts through the silence.

I look up. My heart stops. Inches from me is a timber-dog, mouth open wide. The moonlight dances across its formidable teeth. *Is it frozen?* I rise to my feet and cautiously poke at the beast. Nothing, not one sign of life. I whirl around to find all the dogs frozen in various states of attack. Fur weaves its way through my fingers. I never noticed the beauty of these creatures.

Whoa. The dog is still warm. I can still feel its heart beating.

"Go, they will not stay like this," the stone warns.

"Go where?" I ask, still not believing that I'm talking to my stone.

"To the Ascension. There, death awaits you," the stone replies.

"Wait, what?"

"Or stay here." At this, a low growl emanates from a timber-dog.

The stone fades back to an all-too-familiar yet frustrating gray.

I quickly turn south, hoping to make it to the Ascension before daylight.

* * *

The camp is quiet. There is no wind and even the nearby stream runs silent. In its center is the entrance to a cave. In a few short hours the Ascension will happen right here. I work my way down the tree-line just in case. My chamber is just down the trail, although I dare not take the path. If I'm caught, Grandpa's punishment will be nothing compared to what awaits me.

I was supposed to arrive with a clear mind and refreshed heart. Instead I'm covered in dirt, which will do nothing to help my loose alibi. We were supposed to arrive last night, each to our own chamber. The Laws state that no one is to see us arrive or have contact with us. Just in case one of the workers has brought something unclean like illness. In the early morning just before twilight, two guards are placed outside the living chambers. The chambers were nothing more than military tents at first, but now each tribe has endowed its own flavor to each. Mine is just a cottage with a living space, kitchen, and bathroom, very modest compared to the others. I slow my walk, becoming purposeful with every step. I can just make out the modest entrance. It's not like the tribes that have a mansion. Three's chamber is all glass and voice-activated and high tech. No guards. There's a window on the south side. It might be unlocked and I could slip into the living room unnoticed.

I stop mid-step. On the morning air two voices carry through the sleeping woods. I squat in the brush. It's high enough to hide me, standing, but I'm not taking any chances. *Please don't be my guards.* I dare not even move my head. The voices are coming up behind me. Two sets of green glowing eyes matching the cadence of its owner's step enter my peripheral. The glow is not overpowering but enough to make out a helmet, gun, and night vision goggles. *Breathe Ever, just breathe. They are not your guards.* But my heart sinks as they approach my chamber.

Great. No big deal. Just have to slip past guards with night vision.

I'm just to the south and far left of the guards. It's about three hundred mics to the chamber. Good, there's the brush pile I remember about half way. I can sneak along the rose bushes till I get to it. I navigate around the rose bushes and past the fence. Edging to the end of the brush pile, I peek around the side. I shift my weight. SNAP! How can the smallest stick have the loudest *crunch* I've ever heard? I hold my breath. Maybe they didn't hear it. A voice is thrown my direction along the front of the chamber. I need to reach the window before they round the corner. I break into a run.

"Maker, help me?" I didn't mean to say these words, but there they are. Surely the stone wouldn't bail me out a second time. The light nears the corner of the house.

"Come on, say something!" I cry in the most forceful whisper I can muster.

"Do you trust me?" The stone flashes briefly.

"Trust you? Do I have a choice?"

"Always."

The guards footsteps put them nearly rounding the corner.

"Okay, okay I trust you." Inside, I'm begging the stone to hurry and do what it did to the timber-dogs.

"Close your eyes and remain completely still. Only move when and where I tell you."

"Still? You want me to be still?"

"Now!"

My body goes rigid and my eyelids seal tightly. I brace myself for the angry voices of the guards and wailing of alarms. Instead, even with my eyes as tight as I can shut them, An intense light pushes past my closed eyelids filling the space between me and the guards. My chest is burning. It's not painful, but fierce.

"My eyes!" One the guards screams. Someone moans and equipment hits the ground.

"Step to the right one step. Three steps forward." The stone's voice is calm and clear.

My legs move with complete trust almost like an outside force is placing each step.

"Stop. Open your eyes."

The warmth in my chest lingers, and I obey. Two guards grope at the ground, blinded by the fading light of the stone.

I reach for the window. It's about waist high. I lift up with a clear and concise jerk. It doesn't move. I look along the glass inside. Locked.

I slam my hand against the window. It shakes. I notice the lock move, but how?

"It will comply far better if you speak to it," the rock chimes in.

"I did that?"

"If you call accidentally becoming angry doing something then yes. Speak to the lock in your mind. Push out all doubt."

I press my hands against the window and try to think only of opening the lock. The window moves ever so slightly as the lock moves against the old wood still not completely open. The rest of the camp is waking. A low hum of voices travels down the path. The royal will soon call my name.

"Ever, you can't do this yourself. The sooner you realize that truth is the moment you can," offers the stone.

Alright, I can't. I relax and simply place my hand on the glass. The warmth wells up from my chest into my arms and then into the glass. The lock shoots up. I'm relieved. I almost forget to move. I glance back at the guards still recovering from the light. Good, I'm in. Pushing the window up, I slip in feet first and close the window behind me. Before I can exhale…

"Where have you been?" In my surprise I nearly let the window slam shut. Syrililian sits on the sofa which faces the window of my not-so-stealthy entrance. Her dark violet hair is almost black like satin. We've been friends for years.

My heart beats out of my chest. "Syrililian what are you

doing? You know the law!"

"Ever. I asked you a question."

My face is flushed. I can feel warmth rising to my cheeks. "Well Syrililian— You see—" I stutter, leaning against the window sill.

She rises from the couch only a mic from me.

"I'm not letting you screw this up for me. Well, not this time Ever. I swear." Her hands on her hips and her death glare in her eyes said it all.

"I…"

"Save your breath and get in the shower. If a royal finds you like this the whole thing is off." Her eyes are like the blue part of a flame, beautifully alive, but dangerous. "They're already uncomfortable with you and your Grandfather's radical ideas." She pauses. A devilish grin pushes up her perfect cheeks. She closes the distance and leans into me searching my eyes. "You went to see him. Oh, this is too good." She is all too pleased with herself. "Well what are you staring at? Hit that shower. It's better to be late than unclean." She turns to the side, hand tangled in her silky hair.

"You're not going to tell anyone?"

"What good would that do me? The Ascension would be canceled, your tribe would endure more shame. Oh, and there's the little matter that we need all twelve, or we are not protected for another year." She turns to face me.

I draw in my first full breath since the field, but it is short lived.

"However, once we are in, all bets are off. If it is to my advantage, it might just slip. No hard feelings, right?" Her elegant finger taps my nose.

I linger a little, contemplating what she said.

"Ever! Shower. Now. If you screw this up for me, the royals will be the least of your problems." She turns me around and somehow with her slender frame pushes me in the direction of the shower. "But how will you get back to your chamber?" I call from the back hall.

"Well, the guards won't be a problem, thanks to you. You're full surprises, Ever! Good lu—"

The door slams and cuts off the end of her sentence.

* * *

The sound of that harmonic resonator is unnerving. It never bothered me much before, but to be fair, before I wasn't waiting with the fate of my race in the balance. And I wasn't harboring someone else's stone.

The smooth black marble of the floors seems to gather all the heat from the open air and spread it beneath my feet. Grandpa told me it was a temple where we worshipped our maker without fear of death. The columns are all that's left of what had been a crystal ceiling. A massive cave opening and its oak doors stand opposite of where I am. Cold damp air seeps from them and hangs in my nose. Light catches the gold trim about the doors shooting the sun back into my eyes.

All twelve of us stand shoulder to shoulder at the opposite end of the cave's great doors. There's Titus at the front of the line. He looks like someone carved him out a rock and is just as smart. I catch his side glance and his irritated eye roll in my direction. The others I only know by their tribe number except for Syrililian. She looks over with her eyes and motions to get my eyes forward. A nervous tension presses on my chest like I'm holding breath and can't release it.

I'm next and last in the line. I quickly wipe the sweat from my face. A royal not much taller than me points the crude apparatus at my— no, Grandpa's stone. I don't know how this won't end badly. The device in effect can tell if someone is lying or has been in the presence of death. I can only hope it's malfunctioning today. My mind is racing with how they will punish me. Maybe they will take my stone out right here and let the other eleven watch. The royal pulls the trigger and reads the display which is just out of my sight. He strains, pulling his chin out. His eyes narrow. Yup, that's it. I'm done.

"Sirrus take a look at this." He points to the gauge and turns it toward his companion.

Sirrus glides over with her long gait. Her narrow eyes scan the screen.

"What's the matter?" I force out.

Sirrus's glare silences my voice. She glances at my name tag. "Ever, I don't believe I addressed you."

I nod.

"Twelve, are you in the habit of addressing a royal without an invitation?" Her nose is nearly touching mine.

"No."

She lingers for another uncomfortable moment. Her eyes might as well be a resonator. I swear she is looking right through me.

"Scan him again. It's high, especially for his tribe." She resets the machine and directs the other royal to scan me again.

"The same. What should we do?" the other royal says without expression.

Is this where it ends? I can let go of this secret. I fear what might happen to me, but right now the weight of carrying all this could override the seal on my lips at any moment.

"I'll get the captain." She turns and speaks in the pocket com. The captain is not someone I want to meet. Grandpa and he were friends once. Not anymore. If you step out of line, break any of the Laws, he's the one you see.

"Yes, sir. No, sir." What is taking so long? Sirrus nods as she talks to the captain on the commutator.

I can't take much more of this. I'm about to burst with the truth. Anything to stop my mind from finding new ways to torture me with what might happen. Sirrus turns toward me and the other royal. She only has one expression: angry.

"We do nothing," she says to the royal. "Our job is to find imperfections. We will let the Maker sort whether the stone's host is worthy of it." The back-handedness of this comment is not lost. She's right. I am taking my own life into my hands.

The royals quicken their pace, making sure no stone or person is out of place. The sun crests over the doors to the cave and almost in line with the great circle. Two stone columns from the door extend past it and frame the circle. I keep looking for anything holding it in place. Nothing, it just floats above the door. This is the only day of the year it pivots in line with the sun. The Laws state the great circle is the origin of the first stones of my people. The circle gathers the high sun's rays and throws them three mics down. The reflection gathers to a single point on the door. The brighter it becomes, the stronger the breeze is from behind the door. I almost lose my feet as the ground shifts into a steady rumble beneath me. The sound of rocks splitting causes me to cover my ears. The massive doors give way. I stagger back, expecting the force to blow them right off their hinges. The only thing left to do now is hope one of us is pure enough to see the Maker.

The wind calms to a breeze. We tread slowly through the cave opening placing each step with caution. None of us are rushing into the ominous opening. I reach the threshold, crossing between the temple and cave. The massive doors close behind me, squeezing out the last bit of light in here. The breeze is gone like someone reached over and flipped a switch. The Cold steals the air in my lungs like I've just plunged into a freezing lake. It's pitch black. I cannot see a thing. I wring my shaking hands finally catching my breath.

"Any man may find his way in the light, but the man who listens to his heart will never be blind— even if he may lose his eyes." The voice echoes off the walls. "A word of caution: you may be tempted to light your way, but light will only blind you."

"Forget that! How are we supposed to see?" Titus from Tribe One strikes a match. A breeze buzzes my head and a shadow dances past the flickering flame. Before Titus can light his torch, the shadow covers his face.

"My eyes!" Titus's cries. My ears fill with painful cries and ripping of flesh. They echo and fall away from us. Feet shuffle with short steps that also fade away, ending in a large thud. Three more voices crying out fade into the distance, dropping below us. I dare not move.

There must be holes in the floor. A third of us are gone. How do I even see with my heart? I've spent my whole life training not to see things with it. The heart muddies things up. We were praised the more we denied our own desires for the sake of the common good

I look down in the direction of my stone, wishing it would tell me what to do. On the other hand, I don't want to be introduced to whatever those shadows are. Of course, the stone would choose this moment to be silent. The sound of my heart beating is so loud I can hardly think. I draw a deep breath and let it out slowly. And another. Closing my eyes, I put my hand on my stone and begin to listen. Stepping forward my heart slows as the stone warms. I lean to the left and it speeds up and cools. Moving forward again and it slows. It's almost like I can feel the ground. There's a path. It's smooth and firm, but when I leave that ground my heart beats faster. At first, I must really concentrate on my heart and feet to sense the path, but soon it feels more natural almost like I can see it in my heart.

I bump into a wall of moss. I push through it and feel an opening. Ducking down into it, I press through the damp curtain. The moss ends and I try to stand. Light hurts my eyes as they open. I can't tell whether it is because it is so bright or because where I came from is so dark. As my eyes adjust, four more blurry dark spots emerge from the small opening. Including myself, that means only five of us made it out of the pitch-black room.

"That's it?" questions the dark blob to my left.

"I'm Ryger from Four. You're from Twelve, right?"

I hold out my hand in his general direction.

"What's this? Just 'cause I know who you are doesn't mean I want to be friends. Just wanted to know who my competition is." Ryger turns away quickly as my eyes clear up.

"Good talk." starring down at my empty hand still extended.

"What did you say Twevle!" Ryger wheels eyes lit with fire.

"Ryger enough!" Syrililian slips between Ryger and I.

"Syrililian, you made it!" She and others are covered in scratches and blood stains.

"Barely, how did you manage not to get a scratch on you?" She's nursing a hefty cur on her forearm.

"I closed my eyes and listened to my heart. Isn't that how you got out?" I grab the moss from the cave wall and tease it apart. I begin chewing on it.

"I tried opening my eyes and those things attacked me. Nearly fell off the edge several times. Then a faint glow that didn't attract those things began to move. It looked like a stone and I followed it. It led me to this opening." Wincing in pain, she pulls her right forearm toward her body.

I remove the moss from my mouth and put my hand out for her arm. She rolls her eyes in disgust even as she complies. I look down at my stone. Could it have been my stone that glowed? If so, why didn't those things attack it?

"This is nightingale. It should help with the pain and keep it from getting infected." I rip a piece of my shirt and tighten the poultice down.

Over Syrililian's shoulder I see Ryger probing the moss.

"Ryger, I can make you one next."

He turns. "I don't need you to play doctor, Twelve. I was looking for a way out of this room to the next challenge. Besides, Twelve, she's a Three. You don't have a chance." He turns back to his search. I step towards Ryger clinching my fist down at my side. Syrillilian steps in front of me shoving her hand into the center of my chest. Her cheeks turn a shade of red before she whips her arm away.

"Got it!" Ryger pulls the moss aside to reveal a lever.

He pulls down on it and the floor shifts. I catch my balance breathing a sight of relief it only shifted a couple of inches. Then ground begins to lower slowly. After the pitch black nightmare even the slightest shift is unnerving me. Suddenly it drops six mics, putting most of the party, including myself, on our butts. Before I can regain my feet, the bottom drops out again. The fall threatens to separate me from the falling rock. The floor crumbles beneath my body, dumping me into the water. I frantically flail my arms so as not to drown. One of my arms touches the bottom. I gain my feet, finding the water is only knee-high. We fell right thorough the floor and landed in small cavern with a pool for a floor. It's greenish blue from the iridescent crystals that line the cave wall which meets the water at the far edge. It's shallow for a few mics before the water appears much darker. I walk up to the edge of the deep water. The opening of the cavern widens a little, yet I can almost reach the opposite wall by leaning out over the water.

Someone speaks. "My people know my voice and listen, for my words are life. All others lead to death. You must navigate the underwater catacombs listening only for my voice."

Five lights exit the water. The lights float a moment and then separate, each heading to a different person in our party. The lights push us into a back-peddle, pinning us against the wall. "By the maker what is that? Ryger's voice cracks. His eye are wide-open, swinging wildly at the light and missing. Syrillain is shaking against the wall, clutching her injured arm and turning her face as far from the light as the wall will allow her. Wall sharp edges dig into my back. My fear won't let me breathe. I'm learning quickly what you don't know can kill you.

My stone is warm for a second as the light enters my body. The rush of warmth releases panic's grip on my lungs and I exhale. The other four lights follow suit, entering the others' stones and then their bodies. Everyone relaxes and stares out into the water.

"This will give you ten minutes of air. The path should take eight minutes. You cannot delay. And be careful of the voices that tell you what you want to hear. Only one is true. Let those who have ears, hear." The sound fades into the cave walls.

A light appears about ten mics ahead in a notably deep part of the pool.

Ryger's pupils are wide and his eyes are unmoving. "Hey, are you ok?" I wave my hand in front of his face. He pushes past me, almost knocking me down. He wades into the water, sinking deeper with every step. I turn back to Syrililian and the others. Each is walking as if compelled by an unseen lure. The water is bubbling behind me. Turning, the water stirs near Ryger, who stands at the end of the shallow pool.

A hand covered with iridescent scales slips out of the water and runs up Ryger's arm. The head and shoulders of the creature break the surface of the water. Water runs down its beautiful auburn hair. I've never seen anything more beautiful. The creature from the waist up looks like woman, minus the scales. She guides Ryger into the pool, leaning into him as she speaks into his ear. "Come, Ryger. I can show you the way."

The creature turns and opens its mouth. A piercing sound fills the small cave. My hands flash to my ears and my knees give way as I attempt to drown out the noise. The creature's beautiful features are gone. The skin hangs on its bones like cobwebs draped over forgotten wood. Its eyes become pools of blackness. Razor-sharp teeth line its mouth. Words become clear amid the creatures screams. "We have come to steal, kill, and destroy. Come, come find all you have desired. Come, come! Tormented, and you shall sleep."

The twisted song drills into my head. I can't control my hands as they feel like lead, wanting to fall from my ears. From the pool rises a creature I know in my gut it is for me. I can feel my focus slipping as my eyes flutter, struggling not to fall into a waking sleep. I shake my head. I must rid myself of the fog that is rolling in. A numbness starts at the top of my head and falls down my cheeks and neck. *Maybe they do know the way.* I see my hand reach to take the creature's.

"Ever, Ever! Listen, listen only to me. These are singers, and they cannot be trusted." A calm voice cuts through the screaming, fights the fog. "Ever, you know my voice. I am your Maker. Do you trust me?" A warmth stirs in my stone and rides up my back and chest until it collides with the numbness around my lips. The creature moves behind me and sings softly.

"I can give you her. She will yield to you alone." Its voice slithers into my ear like honey as the creature points to Syrililian.

"Ever! You must say you trust me. Her songs promise many things, but all lead to death."

My lips are on fire. The muscles in my neck pull and my tongue moves.

"I— trust— you," pushes its way through my nearly numb lips.

The fog in my mind burns off instantly and the numbness fades. It leaving a slight headache in its wake. The Creature's arm around my chest is encased in stone. I push the arm away and it breaks at the elbow and turns to dust in my hands. I stand and the rest of the statue disintegrates, sifting and disappearing into the water.

I turn in time to see Syrililian's creature leading her by the hand and they disappear into the deep water.

"It's a trap!" But the words echo off the rippling water and empty cave.

"What troubles you, Ever?" the stone questions.

"Syrililian and the others just led astray like that. They had no chance," my voice pitches up suddenly.

"Ever, this is my greatest pain. When my sons and daughters

bow to things below them and become slaves. Nothing has happened to them that was not already in their hearts. The singers use things people covet and desire to prey upon them."

"There's got to be a way I can save her." I stare at the ground like the answer is going to come from the depths.

"There is a way but it is dangerous," the stone warns. "Go after her. I will give you the words. But Ever, remember you cannot place in her heart what is not there."

I wade out into the deep water.

"She must see the need for the stone and put her trust in it completely. It cannot be forced. I will lead the way with your stone's light. If you reach the purple algae you must turn back. You won't have enough air to make it."

I part the water and dive into the deep. The water opens up to a giant cave. There must be hundreds of passages leading in every direction. Just in time I see Syrililian slip into a catacomb to the far left. I kick and a burst of energy propels me through the water. The touch of the stone did more than give me air. My feet are webbed and so are my hands.

I'm thankful for the stone's light, which illuminates the otherwise black cavern. There she is, swimming just below me. She is not going to be able to hear anything with that song consuming her thoughts. How do I disrupt it? Ah, the red seaweed I can put it in her ears! I grab the seaweed from the wall of the cave and swim toward her.

I pull alongside her. Scales are already forming on her arms and down her body. Her eyes are cloudy. The creature hisses at me. I stuff some red seaweed into my ears in time not to hear its song. It swipes at me. I dodge it and swim beneath Syrililian, rolling one hundred eighty degrees to face her. I quickly stuff the seaweed into her ears. The creature screams, sending shock waves through the water. My stone warms and sends out a burst of light. The creature shields its eyes. I place my foot on the creatures chin extending my legs driving the creature away. It releases its prey. I turn with Syrililian in hand and duck into a side cave.

Bursts of song push through the water, impacting my body at points the vibration is unnerving. A pause and another burst of song moving around in a circle, as if seeking. The creature must be using sound waves to find us. We don't have long. Suspended in water, I put my hand on Syrililian's stone and hers on mine. Her hand offers little resistance as she stares past me. I can hear her thoughts. It is like dozens of voices talking at once. My lips move without provocation. In the mist of these voices I hear my own. *Syrililian, listen carefully. you must wake up. Whatever they have promised you, it will lead to death.* The voices grow louder, trying to drown me out.

A sonic wave crashes through us. We duck into another cavern. Just feet from us is the purple algae. The creature screams as it closes in on us. Syrillian's eyes begin to move.

Open your ears. Hear your stone. Trust the voice from your stone. I place my palm on her stone and hope the words will soak in.

The creature enters the opening. I push Syrililian protectively behind me. Somehow she and I are still connected even though I am not longer touching her stone. Her mind goes darker as the creature comes close. *Have I done the right thing? My mind drifts to the first time we met. She skinned her knee in front of my house. I might have let my feelings cloud my choices, but I can't leave her here to die.*

A blinding light shoots from my stone. My back arches and my head reels back.

The creature sends a pulse through the water.

I can't hold them off forever. Syrililian. Believe, just say it! Believe!

The creature swings wildly at me. Through the thrashing water and in my mind, I hear *I believe.* The creature's arm breaks against my arm as it turns to stone. My stone pulses, sending waves through the water, shattering the creature.

I turn frantically. Syrililian's eyes are clear. Suddenly I remember air. We need to get going. I grab her hand and start swimming. She kicks her feet doing her best to keep up. I feel we need to find a way out fast. The stone is on fire, and I seem to know these caves all of a sudden. My lungs burn for a breath and Syrililian is slowing down. She's been in the water longer than me.

We turn a corner and I see light bleeding down from the distant surface of the water. My lungs are losing steam. I know only one of us can make it. Pulling her up to me I put my mouth on hers and blow the last of my breath into her lungs. Her eyes pop open. I know that look, she is not happy with me. She tries to pull on me, but I know she can barely push herself through the water. She pauses, and I swear her blue eyes are grey. She reluctantly lets go of me and turns toward the light.

I am only able to take a few strokes before my lungs draw in the cold water. I shudder, trying to expel the foreign invader. My mind fights, filling my body with what's left of my adrenaline. It gives me one more kick, a false hope. Then my limbs stop responding. My lungs surrender. It's a double-edged sword, the cold water. On one hand it quenches the fire in my lungs, on the other it causes my muscles to jerk uncontrollably with pain. The cold overtakes my body and my nerves give up their fight. My throat is on fire and my lungs are seizing, causing every muscle in my chest to constrict. My eyelids are the last to surrender.

I hear a gurgling and my chest convulses again. My body rolls to one side and the smell of vomit burns my nose. A rush of water exits my nose and mouth, leaving a burning trail. I hack violently, like I might cough up my soul. My water-laced eyes make out a blurry but familiar face.

"You had me worried. Good to know there isn't any treasure at the bottom of the cavern."

Syrililian's wet hair tickles my nose nearly sending me into another coughing jag.

"I figured you'd leave me. If I'm honest, I was going to leave you. You don't know what this would mean for my tribe and my family." She looks down and pulls her hand from her chest. Her stone has the slightest glow. "But this voice told me to go back. This stone warms up your body and is very convincing." Her cheeks fill with a rosy red.

"So, it had nothing to do with me saving your life. Huh?"

Syrililian rises to her feet, pulling me up by my forearm, slugging me in the shoulder with her free hand. "Shut up, Ever. Shut up while you're ahead."

Upright, my toes sink into pure white sand. I rub my arms furiously, attempting to warm them up. The sand continues at a slight incline which is challenging for me as my limbs are still cold. We are still underground but the air is fresher so we must be closer to the surface. The ceiling is solid rock and covered with iridescent crystals. I think I hear water crashing on the rocks above my head. As I turn, a giant door stands before us, etched completely out of stone. Its details are too fine to be made by any human tool. Reaching out with one hand keeping the other in to preserve what body heat I have left. It's warm, not cold like I expected. I'm probably not a good judge of temperature after nearly drowning. Almost anything is going to feel warm right now.

A voice speaks from behind the door. "Speak truth and live. For a lie leads to destruction, but the truth will lead to a long life. Careful the words you speak for this room has no tolerance for those who speak evil. Speak truth and enter."

Syrililian looks down at the sand. "Ever, say 'alitheia.' It is the ancient's word for truth. It means to hide nothing. Say the word aloud and the door will open and let you through." She turns, unable to look at me.

"Me? We are doing this together. I am not going without you." I reach for her to take my hand.

She cups my hand and looks up at me. "Ever, I'm sure there are many things we will do together, but this is not one of them." She places her right hand on her stone. "I'm listening to my stone. It tells me I can go no further. Considering it is the only reason either of us is here, I don't feel like hedging my bets." She closes her hand around mine. "You're the only one who has really understood what this means. The rest of us have done it for pride, duty, but not you. You really want to see the Maker." Her eyes fill me with strength. There is a life in them that was not there before. "You may not believe in yourself, but you really believe we can see our Maker." She kisses my hand and tears slip out onto her high cheekbones.

I have a million things to say, but none of them reach my tongue. Only one word forms at my lips. "Alitheia."

I hear the doors open behind me. I can't bring myself to look away from Syrililian. What if this is the last time I see her this side of the Everlast. I backpedal through the doors several mics until the doors stand in front of me.

This was supposed to be a great moment. Look what I have

done for myself, my tribe, my people.

"It's hard to watch your brothers and sisters die. It seems unfair, doesn't it?"

It sounds like he is in the room with me.

"Yes, Ever, I'm here. Turn around."

Turning slowly, I'm met with a plain man. He isn't much taller or stronger than me. His long hair flows loosely down over his shoulders. Yet his presence that is striking, and he carries himself like a warrior. A quiet confidence adorns him like armor. His blue eyes are peaceful and yet his stone is on fire. White flames lick out from his chest.

"I am the Son of the Maker." He moves toward me and puts his arm around my shoulder. I'm close. I can taste it. I will see the Maker. "All of them rejected me and chose their vices over my virtues. As I said before, they were handed over to idols and the attitudes they set in their heart long ago."

We walk down a path lined with stones the color of gold, and ivory arches brace the rock ceiling. "If they had entered this room," he motions to the chamber looming before us, "with those things it would have brought eternal consequences."

He leaves me at the entrance and drifts into the room without effort. I hadn't noticed he wasn't walking. His robes turn pure white and flow as he floats. "They now wait with your grandfather for someone to see the Maker, making way for them to enter the Everlast."

I can't help but think of Syrililian. Did she make it back? Did she mean all those things she said?

"Oh, you're worried about Syrililian. She is alive." He turns to me and his eyes bring a strange peace. "Every word she spoke to you was true."

"I returned her to her tribe, unharmed. She did the greatest thing anyone can do for another. She risked her life for yours. Her heart is changing, but she was not ready to see the Maker." As he sits, the rocks from the floor slide up and form a chair for him.

"Didn't you say, through my stone, that you were the Maker?" I wonder how he could be the Son and the Maker.

"Call me Zion. If you prove worthy, all your questions will either have answers or will not matter."

I can hardly contain my joy. I'm not only looking at our Maker but having a conversation with the Supreme Being who designed everything.

"Now, the task at hand." Zion waves his hand over the ground.

I notice that there are holes all along the floor and a giant tablet rolls away from the back wall. A path is lit with lamps every two or three mics. Out of each hole, arises a pedestal with a stone on it. The stones are beautiful. Every color you could imagine. Some are inlaid with gold and silver and diamonds. The pedestals stop.

"This is the final test. We tested your ability to see in the dark and to hear. Now your ability to know and speak the truth. First question: are you worthy to see your maker?" Zion folds his hands together and presses them to his lips.

I look down at the floor. It could be yes, I mean I did pass every test. Wait, did I? No. I failed every test. If it wasn't for the stone and the guidance of Zion I would have failed. I thought back to the window. How the stone blinded the guards. I was only able to unlock that window because I listened to Zion. I want to say I am worthy, but the truth is I'm not.

Sorrow fills my feet and they become impossible to move. Tears fill my eyes and spill down my cheeks. I didn't know until this moment how much I wanted to see the Maker. I wanted to be the one worthy. Had I known that I would come this close, I would have lived differently. I watch sorrow fall from my cheeks and wet the stone at my feet…to be this close and not make it. My heart drops, and my shoulders sink. I have to admit this is not my stone. I must not hide anything. But it will likely cost me my life to admit it.

"Zion, I am not. Without my grandfather's stone and your help, I would be no different than the others who failed. I and my stone are flawed." My hands won't stop shaking, and my body braces for the wrath of the Maker and my rightful destruction.

By admitting it is not my stone, Zion will know— if he does not already— that I buried my grandfather. The countless Laws I've broken. At least my people will be pardoned another year for my life.

"You have answered truthfully." A smile breaks across Zion's face. "I know what you did for your grandfather." Zion leans in and touches my stone. A ripple of warmth and energy pulse through the stone. I nearly lose my balance. Zion steadies me with his other hand.

"As you have stated your stone is flawed. In this room is a stone that is not. You must trade your stone for the other." Zion points to my stone. "Do not worry. I will return your stone to your grandfather. If you choose incorrectly you will die. Your people will be covered for another year and will have another attempt to see the Maker."

There must be twenty stones, each beautiful but very different. *Why me*? This is not going to end well. I already told him I'm not worthy. What would the Maker think is clean?

I pass a gold one. Picking it up, the thing weighs a ton. I set it back down. Beyond that is a perfectly clear diamond one. It looks clean, but nothing has been as it seems today. My stone is flawed, my grandfather— the one who was closest to Zion and the Maker—even his stone unworthy. It hit me. What if all of my people's stones are flawed? If that is the case, then there is only one stone that is clean.

Only one stone is worthy of being in the presence of the Maker.

I turn to Zion. "I can pick any stone in this room?"

"Yes, it is as I have said." Zion bows slightly.

I hold out my hand. "I choose yours."

Zion quickly reaches across, twists, and dislodges my stone. I fall to my knees, struggling to catch my breath, as I slowly suffocate without the stone.

"Your grandfather will need this back." He holds the stone out and with a breath it vanishes. Zion, leans down putting his forehead to mine. "Ever, I'm not doing this to be cruel. Remember how this feels. How helpless you are to quench your burning lungs."

I can hear the empty heaves as my ribs struggle to drag air in.

"This is how the spirit of all your people feel without the Maker. This is the death that awaits them if they do not see Me."

Zion kneels, facing me, his strong arms holding me up. "We have longed for this day. When our beloved creation would walk with us again." His hand rests on his stone. My heart is beating faster, pushing blood to my starving limbs.

"Ever, now you will see your Maker. A way has been made for all to see." Zion twists his stone and places it into my chest. The air rushes into my starving lungs.

Zion's body now claws for air. He leans slowly unable to hold himself up. I steady him. From his stone, power courses through my veins. A veil is peeled away from my eyes. "The stones live again." Zion squeezes out before another coughing fit arrests him. Before me is a cloud of blinding white light. A figure brighter than any star stands within the cloud.

Zion shakes violently. "Father—"

All other feelings become pale and an indescribable joy fills my whole being. I am face to face with my Maker.

"A sacrifice has been made, once and for all. They need only to believe." His shallow breaths are more like hiccups.

My joy is interrupted by profound sadness as his light fades. "I'm sorry, Zion." My voice breaks and tears stream down wetting his face. "So sorry."

"Ever, don't be." Three short breaths divide his words. "For this I was born."

"Zion, if you go how will anyone see the Maker?"

With the little strength he has left Zion rises his hand and places it on my stone. "In you, Ever, and those would believe with you. In you…"

His body goes still and his full weight hits my arms.

"Zion they will see you. I promise. They will see you."

Blessed are the pure in heart
For they shall see God

Andrew Hamlet

ndrew Hamlet, author of "The Heartstone," is a gifted storyteller and teacher who uses his skills to further the truth of the gospel through his stories. He resides in Grand Rapids, Michigan with his wife and five children.

Andrew sang and told stories through 80 songs and countless stories as well as spoken word.

He wants to engage culture and influence change. He wants to ensure the marketplace is filled with strong stories that challenge people to seek out God, not just pleasure.

Andrew completed a 4-year degree at Cornerstone University with a Communication Arts major. He completed film school at Compass Arts Film Academy where he focused on creating compelling stories and characters.

The Door to Wishes

D etroit, Michigan
9th District Kulterian Morals Court
May 19, 2107

"I object!" Chanucer Dewright leapt up from his seat in the courtroom. "She's a liar!"

"Ms. Sautern, please restrain your client," Judge Markolo Quinn ordered with a narrowing of his eyes. "Before I hold him in contempt of court."

"Yes, Your Honor," Advocate Judith Sautern assured hastily, placing a restraining blue hand on Chanucer's shoulder. "Please understand my client is severely distressed about the—"

"I can appreciate your client's situation, Ms. Sautern, but he will respect this court and this office. Have I made myself clear?" Judge Quinn's eyebrow lifted in warning.

"Perfectly, Your Honor." Judith glared, her black pupil-less eyes hardened like chips of obsidian. "Chaz, sit."

"Anyanna's lying," he hissed, sending an incensed gaze in the direction of the witness stand to behold the Kulterian woman sitting in the box.

The woman's royal blue skin, with its patches of darker blue hexagonal scales along her neck and on the right side of her face, seemed almost garish among the warm, brown tones of the courtroom. Chaz snorted at the sight of the blue tears trickling down her cheeks from the same obsidian orbs as his advocate. It was all a show. A show to condemn him.

"She's trying to destroy me," he told Judith as he flopped back down into the chair. "You can see she's trying to destroy me!" He rubbed the back of his neck. "I'm surprised her father isn't here in court, gloating."

"I know that, but you have to control your emotions or people, human and Kulterian alike, are just going to assume you're lying."

Chaz dragged shaky fingers through his long dreadlocks, feeling the slight slickness of the jojoba oil he used to care for them, moisten his hand. His blessed oil that his sister, Gloria, had given him before she left to marry her Kulterian husband, the brother of his wife, and relocate to the distant world of Kulkutern.

"Use this whenever you're in doubt," Gloria had told him that day two years ago. "I've had it blessed…by Pastor Owen," she added, referring to the pastor who's church they had gone to for years. "It's not like it has special powers or properties, Chaz. Just a way of consecration and being obedient to whatever God's will is."

Was this farce, this great lie gripping his life with the acidic talons of a beast, a part of God's will?

"This is a delicate matter." Advocate Judith whispered. "It's already going to be difficult to prove you aren't the father when the DNA test states otherwise."

"I'm not," he gritted out. "I'm not."

"If you don't maintain your composure, this court will rule in her favor. There is too much at stake here. So, please, keep quiet no matter what she says."

Chaz's jaw tensed and he bit the inside of his cheek, tasting blood. He gave his advocate a curt nod and wiped his moist hands on his pants leg. Then dug his fingers into his knees, trying to use pain as an inhibitor to his outbursts.

"Shall I continue, Your Honor?"

The query came from the Kulterian-human hybrid man standing next to the witness box. He appeared mostly human with a delicate bluish tinge underneath his pale freckled skin. Clusters of hexagonal-shaped scales on his neck and right side of his face lacked the characteristic royal blue as a full-blooded Kulterian. As a hybrid with a Kulterian mother, the scales took on the skin of the father.

Chaz fought to keep his mouth from sneering. Anyanna had even gone out of the way to select a court advocate of mixed-races. All to validify her deceit so she could commit a greater crime.

Judge Quinn nodded. "You may continue, Mr. Wickman."

"Thank you, Your Honor." Advocate Huller Wickman rubbed his hands together in a greedy fashion, a shrewd look glinting from green pupils centered his otherwise black eyes.

"Now, Mrs. Dewright, you stated your husband had continued to have intimate relations with you until the day you announced your pregnancy. Is that correct?"

"Yes, Mr. Wickman," Anyanna lied, swiping at another blue tear.

Chaz's muscles along his stomach hardened like stone.

"When you told your husband about this rather happy occasion—"

Chaz growled but Judith had already stood to her feet. "Objection, Your Honor. Advocate Wickman is attempting to sway this court to suggest that my client should feel a certain emotion about Mrs. Dewright's pregnancy that he does not have. Indeed, if he did, we would not be here before you now."

"Sustained," Judge Quinn acceded. "Rephrase the question, Mr. Wickman."

"Very well, Your Honor. Mrs. Dewright, when you told your husband about your pregnancy, what was his reaction?"

Anyanna gave a great sniff. "He was furious," she answered, her voice wobbling.

Huller frowned. "Furious? Are you certain about that?"

"Yes, Mr. Wickman. My husband was furious." She took the brilliant white Kleenex in her hand and wiped at her face, staining it with her tears.

"Are you certain about that? Maybe he was only surprised or taken over by shock."

"No," Anyanna denied, bowing her head, until her blue and green braids shielded her face. "When I say he was furious, he was."

"What happened?"

I could tell you what happened, the derisive thought came. *I shook her. Shook her so hard her head whipped back and forth like a rag doll. I shook her because it was either that or hit her.*

A deep sob rang out in the court room. "He grabbed me by my shoulders and shook me so hard I thought my neck would snap."

"Shook you? You mean to tell me he...," Huller allowed his voice to trail off, as if he had difficulty comprehending that anyone would do such a horrible act.

It was all so orchestrated; couldn't the court see that?

Clearing his throat Huller continued, strain lacing every word, "He abused you? Hurt you?"

183

"Yes." Anyanna's voice broke. "He'd never done that before."

Her head dropped into her hands as her sobs echoed in the courtroom. The crowd seated in the spectator seats behind him murmured. Though he kept his back toward them, Chaz could imagine what he'd see if he turned around.

Faces of various opacities of human melanin and ethnicity mixing with the dominant blue of the Kulterian race. Interspersed with the hybrid individuals of both races. All different and unique in their own way and yet, if Chaz thought of meeting their gazes, he knew they would stare at him with one universal look.

Contempt.

"Do you need a recess, Mrs. Dewright?" Huller asked as a few seconds of letting the charade continue.

"No," Anyanna sniffed. "No. I'll be all right."

Of course she will. She's got too much riding on this.

"What happened after...after...Mr. Dewright shook you?"

Anyanna tucked a stray braid behind her ear. "I asked him why would he do that. I'd thought he'd be happy. Lord knows we've wanted a child for such a long time."

Of course I wanted a child. Chaz's lips compressed into a firm line. There would have been a time when discovering Anyanna bore his child would have sent waves of exultation through him. The odds had been against them but he'd loved her for herself, not for her fertility.

Now, the thought she carried their offspring only filled him with aversion.

"Did he say anything?"

A pensive look appeared on her face. Chaz knew that look well. Unlike all the other theatrics, Anyanna had to mix a bit of the truth with a lie. That same penned expression happened whenever she was uncomfortable about revealing a particular thing.

"He accused me of…cheating on him. That I had become impregnated by someone else."

"Why would he think that?' Huller asked.

"I'm not sure," Anyanna's lashes lowered over her eyes. They made a thick black arc against the high cheekbones. It was an incredibly sensual look, one that never failed to ignite him. In the past, before all of this had happened, she'd only had to affect that expression and he'd be willing putty in her hands.

Chaz's legs shifted in a restless manner as his scorn abated for a brief moment.

He'd once caressed and placed tiny kisses along those cheeks, luxuriating in the satiny smoothness of her blue skin. He remembered the wonder of seeing his dark thumb gently press her voluptuous blue lips against her white teeth. The blood pulsed underneath the pad of his thumb along with the steady rhythm of her heartbeat.

Sometimes, he'd tugged at her bottom lip to steal a peek of the flat, black mole in the right-hand corner. Colloquially called a black pearl by Kulterians, it was an extremely rare birthmark among their women. Those who bore the mark carried a higher risk of infertility. Medical professionals of both worlds had studied the anomaly for the past fifteen years but the answer for why eluded them.

"Do you have a history of infidelity with Mr. Dewright?"

Huller's words brought him out of his thoughts, shattering the softer emotions which had come with the tender recollection. No, he could not allow the romantic, rose-colored past to interfere with the gray, bitter present.

"No!" Anyanna denied vehemently. "No, I don't. I made a

vow before his God and mine that I would never do such a thing. There isn't a Kulterian on Earth or our own home world who would go against a vow that they made before God."

Chaz dug his fingers deeper into his knees. *Say nothing. Say nothing!*

"If that's the case, then why would Mr. Dewright accuse you of wavering from your vows?"

"I don't know, Mr. Wickman. I would have love to have created a family with my husband had he allowed it."

A family born of a lie, Anyanna.

"Although you may find this reprehensible, Mrs. Dewright, I do need to ask this question: are you lying before this court, Mrs. Dewright? Is the child truly Mr. Chanucer Dewright's child?"

She nodded in a curt manner. "Yes."

"Your Honor, I want to call to your attention Exhibit D." Huller went back over to his table and retrieved a document from a folder. "As you see, this is a DNA test concludes, Mr. Dewright is the father of the child Mrs. Dewright carries within her womb."

Chaz's fists clenched and unclenched as the blood pounded in his ears. Waves of blistering heat crashed against his body. How could she sit there, with those damnable blue tears of hers, and lie?

"She's lying!" He roared, leaping to his feet and flipping over the table. Papers, legal pad, and writing implements crashed the floor. Judith jumped up.

"Chaz! Stop it!"

Judith's voice came from somewhere behind him. She was saying more but he couldn't hear. Judge Quinn had taken the mallet and crashed it against the block but only a muted sound made to his ear drums.

All he could see was red as it misted his vision, honed in on the woman he'd once pledged his heart to.

"I haven't touched you in eight months!" He yelled at her. "There's no way that child is mine!"

Anyanna's pupil-less eyes widened, and she lay a protective hand over her swollen stomach. The sight of that maternal instinct, of seeing that fragile blue hand lay claim to the life in her womb, the child that should have been his, it made him snap.

"I'll get the truth out of you if it's the last thing I do!"

He lunged toward her but gruff hands captured his arms and yanked him back. Chaz snarled. "Let go of me!"

"Chanucer Dewright, you are in contempt of court," Judge Quinn announced with a dark glance. "Bailiff, get him out of here. Maybe a night in jail will cool him off."

"Tell them the truth, Anyanna!" Chaz struggled against the men holding him. "End this now."

Anyanna said nothing, just gazed at him as the bailiffs gained the upper hand and soon had him in handcuffs. The last he saw of her before he was dragged away was a single blue tear trailing from black, pitiless eyes.

* * *

Chaz's gaze remained fixed on the non-descript ceiling as the door to his cell opened. It clanged shut a few seconds later and silence reigned supreme. He lay as still as a statue. A deep, soul-wrenching sigh soon broke the quietness.

"If you aren't going to let me do my job, then fire me," Judith clipped out. "You can mount your own defense and then I can watch you get sentenced to twelve years of hard labor to an ice prison on the home world. You'd like that, wouldn't you?"

Chaz flung his arm over his eyes "No, that's not what I want," he admitted in a weary voice. "I just wish my life was what it was a year ago."

Judith mumbled something but he didn't catch what she said. "Huh?"

"A door for wishes," she answered. "It's a saying among my people. There's an old story that our children are told about Kulkutern. That our world is a wish."

"A wish?"

She nodded. "On Earth, a wish is limited to the understanding that it is a strong desire to do something, be something, claim something, etc. For us, a wish more than a desire. It is physical but unrealized. Tangible but unseen. And once you wish for something, it comes through a door."

Momentarily distracted he said, "So how would that make Kulkutern a wish?"

Judith said brusquely. "This isn't a time for children's stories."

"Tell me," he insisted. Anything to change the course of his thoughts

"This is ridiculous," Judith huffed. "The story goes that two worlds once lived side by side. Circling each other like two children at play. One world lush and green. The other world vibrant and blue. Due to their proximity, the inhabitants of both these worlds were able to visit each other by employing wishes. After thousands of years of peaceful community, something happened and a war broke out."

"What happened?"

"Who knows?" Judith retorted impatiently. "It's a child's bedtime story, nothing more. War broke out and the wishes that once created union now created disharmony. The inhabitants then used wishes to send ruin to each other's worlds. The wishes became more and more harmful. They threatened to destroy both worlds. So a door was created to block the wishes from coming through. And then, a final wish: the blue world was wished away from the green world. Far away where wishes could no longer enter. Yet, the further away the world went, the stranger it became. From a wish, Kulkutern became what it is today. A world of ice and snow."

Chaz mulled over her words. "Do you think Earth was the green world and the blue world Kulkutern? That we once lived side by side?"

"Maybe. Until we made contact with your world, I simply regulated the story to fantasy. After all, none of us were here at the beginning of the universe. A number of our mythical stories involve the community of the two worlds at the beginning of our history and then a separation.

"When we came here, we Kulterians immediately noticed how you humans used the word wish. For you, the word represents one side of the equation. The desire, the longing. For us, its physicality, its movement—the other half of the equation."

"But what about—"

"Enough of this," Judith cut him off. "You made a wish for things to be as they once were. Well, it can't be that way. Ever again. The door to wishes is closed."

Judith's harsh words brought with them a finality, one that forced him to accept the truth and the child-like fascination from the story she'd told receded.

He was no longer that blissful man.

No longer the besotted fool who had fallen in love with the Kulterian beauty at first sight three years ago. No longer the impatient would-be lover who proposed to her six months later when his desires for her threatened to supersede his belief that intimacy lay in the bonds of marriage. No longer the fiancé who stood in the face her father's fierce disapproval that his only daughter would unite herself to a man he found unworthy.

No longer the husband who thanked God every day for the gift of a wife who he loved more than anything else.

All that had changed.

"You're right," he replied dejectedly. "Of course, you're right."

Judith's heels clicked on the floor as she came over to where he laid. She removed his arm from his face. Her black eyes, pupil-less, but not soulless as Anyanna's, gazed compassionately into his own. "I know this is painful for you, Chaz. It's a disgrace for a Kulterian man or woman to behave with such a disregard for morals."

"I can't understand why she is insistent on making sure I claim this child as my own when she and I both know it's not."

"But you do know," Judith responded a slow, deliberate manner.

"Yeah," Chaz said after a breath of silence. "It's to save face with her father."

"Exactly. If she were any other Kulterian woman, we would not be in this situation now. Especially as the people of this planet have given us a chance for new life and whose ingenuity saved our own world."

Chaz pushed himself upright and swung his legs to the floor, dragging his fingers through his dreadlocks. He snorted in derision. "I just never thought she would do this at my expense."

His wife's father, Primary Lirt Bronad, held a position of great importance. He initiated first contact in the form of a planetary distress call when Kulkutern had sent out a message via a probe which had taken three years to reach the surface of Earth.

After every human picked their mouths off the floor after discovering they're weren't alone in the universe, they decoded the message to discover that Kulkutern had experienced a virulent viral outbreak among their people to which they had no cure. Though the disease had affected thousands of their citizens, the fatalities were low due to precautionary measures of isolating the sick from the healthy.

The probe contained all the medical information about the Kulterians, their DNA, blood, anatomical schematics and anything else they felt Earth would need to help develop a cure. The probe also contained Kulterian scans of the viral agent affecting its citizenry.

From what Chaz had always heard, the disease and its symptoms sounded very similar to a childhood ailment that used to plague the masses called 'measles'. Left untreated, it could be harmful. The medical and scientific communities banded together to send out the first interplanetary call for medical aid. After the three-year trip back to Kulkutern, space communications began and after twenty years, travel back and forth became commonplace.

Judith folded her arms. "True. Primary Bronad negotiated the treaty with our worlds fifty years ago. He's staked his life on the contents of that treaty. That neither race would ever try to subjugate the other although our debt to you is greater than anything we have to offer."

She paced up and down the narrow confines of the cell. "On the strength of that treaty, every Kulterian has been reminded of their obligation to bring only good to both our peoples. There isn't a year that goes by where I thank your God and mine that we have such rapport."

Chaz stared at his advocate. "Humans don't expect eternal gratitude."

"Perhaps. But if someone saves your life from certain destruction, aren't you obligated to do all you can for them? Shouldn't you give them everything you have?"

"That's what amazing about you Kulterians. You truly are an appreciative race," Chaz observed with something akin to shame although he wasn't quite sure why. Maybe it was the fact that humanity had a propensity to forget.

"Why shouldn't we be?" Judith countered. "You know, I've heard your thoughts mirrored by other humans. As if our constant memory of what your planet has done for us shouldn't have as much weight as it does."

"Well," Chaz hazarded to say something, tugging at the collar of his shirt. "It's just that—"

"But I digress," Judith interrupted and Chaz released an unconscious pent up breath. "We're here to discuss the present and our strategy for tomorrow."

"I'm aware of what the strategy is, Judith. We've gone over a dozen times."

"I've adjusted it."

Chaz blinked. "In what way?"

His advocate came and sat next to him on the narrow bed, opening the briefcase and withdrawing some papers. Mumbling as she sorted through the papers out, she said, "I do wish we carried your planet's legal system of allowing an accused person to remain silent throughout these proceedings. It does prevent one from incriminating one's self. But in our morals court, silence is the worst possible position for an accused."

She found the papers she was looking for and released a sound of satisfaction. "Here it is."

"What?"

Judith stuffed the rest of the papers back into the briefcase and shut it. Setting it aside and she leaned eagerly forward. "Because of your outburst, once court resumes tomorrow, Mrs. Dewright's argument will begin again. Fortunately, for you, Huller cannot ask any questions different from the ones that's been transcribed by the recorder. This works to our benefit due to this small thing."

She handed over the paper. It was a copy of the transcript typed in the pictorial glyphic language of Kulkutern but underneath was the English translation. Several lines had been highlighted along with notes she's scribbled in the margin.

Chaz read the notes aloud. "Confirm date of DNA testing through questioning." He glanced up from the paper. "I don't understand."

Judith's eyes gleamed like black marbles. "The date of the DNA test is going to confirm what I think happened."

"How so?"

"On Earth, one can receive a paternity test nine weeks after the child has been seeded. But on Kulkutern, the earliest a paternity test can occur is six weeks. Yet, all Kulterian women, even the hybrids, would know if they are carrying a child by week three after the seeding."

Judith took the paper from his nerveless fingers. "If there was any doubt about who the father of her child was, Mrs. Dewright would have had a paternity test done at the sixth week mark."

"If that is the case, why did she wait to tell me?"

Footsteps came from outside the jail cell. A guard appeared. "Time's up, Advocate Sautern."

"I'll be there." She opened her briefcase and pushed the single paper inside. "I won't tell you. I don't want you to worry about it. Get some rest. Pray to your God and mine that we will be successful."

Judith patted him on the shoulder in a maternal fashion and then left. The sound of the door closing echoed like the gong of a bell. The guard's and Judith's footsteps grew fainter until he could no longer hear them. Chaz sat alone, his head bowed as he unseeingly contemplated the variegated tile of the floor.

Anyanna, why?

He'd asked her that over seven months ago when she revealed her pregnancy. A pregnancy he had no part in because he couldn't bring himself to touch her. He'd discovered her infidelity almost a year ago. Purely by chance, he happened to drive by his house on a way to an appointment when he saw his wife kissing a strange Kulterian man in the doorway.

She'd never even seen him, so wrapped up in the passionate embrace.

Chaz felt something sting. He glanced down and saw his fingernails had carved deep grooves into the base of his palms. Were the same kind of marks embedded in his heart? No, not physically but spiritually?

He'd gone over everything in his mind for over the past two years of their marriage. What had he done? Why had she betrayed him? For what purpose? Hadn't they been happy?

Sighing, he lay back on the bed and stared once more at the ceiling. Coming home that night he discovered her betrayal, he stared as Anyanna went about the house, humming and singing as if nothing had happened. She'd even lifted her face to kiss him, but he'd stepped back, the rage within threatening his self-control to do harm.

"What's wrong, Chanucer?" Anyanna had asked in that

honeyed-accented Kulterian voice of hers. She was the only one whoever called him by his first name.

"I know what I saw today, Anyanna." How carefully had those words exited his mouth. Amazing that he hadn't acted on the violent impulses that wracked his body, desperate for release. "Please, don't play me for a fool."

Her black eyes had widened. "Chanucer, what are you talking about?"

She'd extended her hand to touch his face, as she had so many times before. Like a rabbit before a snake, he watched that delicate blue hand reached toward him. In their more passionate moments, he'd been set afire by her touch. Now, all he could see was that same hand caressing the body of some blue Kulterian.

"Don't!" He shoved himself away.

"What is it, Chanucer? What did I do? Why are you so angry with me? What happened?"

Her anxious questions flew at him like arrows. He could almost have believed the worry in her eyes, almost fall prey to the wounded expression which dominated her face. Almost. It seemed so genuine for the barest hint of a breath, he wondered if he could have mistaken what his eyes told him was true.

"How could you let another man touch you?"

"What? Chanucer, what are you talking about?"

"I saw you, Anyanna! You and that Kulterian male were kissing in the doorway this afternoon. You didn't even see me you were so…engaged."

Her mouth had dropped open in shock and she paused for a brief moment. The strangest expression had appeared on her face, as if a lightbulb had gone off.

"Now you remember?" he spat out. "Trying to come up with

a suitable lie? You can't tell me to deny what my eyes saw."

"Chanucer," she'd licked her lips nervously, "it's not what you think."

With a vicious twist of his head, he cut off the memory. He had to trust Judith. His advocate was one of the best in the Kulterian morals court system. Taking on a case of falsifying a paternity claim had never been disputed before, especially when results of the test showed he in fact indeed was the father.

How could the test have been fabricated? He and Anyanna both knew he wasn't the father of her child.

The image of her hand lying on her swollen belly sent a slice of pain through his middle that was so sharp, it almost carried a physical quality to it. How could she let another man look at her, much less touch her? What had he done to send her away?

He had no answer.

Over the course of the year, after he discovered her deceit. he wracked his brain but came up with no answer. They had been happy, blessed more than most. He knew it. Chanucer Dewright had married the daughter of the Kulterian who made first contact.

Many had envied his good fortune. Their marriage had rivaled that of Earth monarchy.

How could Anyanna throw all of it away? Why?

Chaz had asked himself those questions many times over of the year. He had no answer to them and he certainly wasn't going to come up with one now. Sleep. He needed to sleep.

Lying there in the quiet of the jail, surrounded by the semi-darkness, his tense muscles relaxed in slow degrees. The thundering of his heart slowed. His hands and feet grew limp. In a deliberate way, he suppressed his chaotic thoughts. He hammered down the emotions clamoring for recognition. On a whispered prayer, he begged God to give him rest for the night.

Soon, his eyes drifted shut and entered into sleep.

* * *

"Chanucer? Chanucer, please say you can hear me?"

Chaz turned over in the big canopy bed in the master bedroom of the home he shared with his wife. "Of course, I can hear you. You've woken me up, haven't you?" A tide of warmth spread through his body as he instinctively reached out to gather Anyanna closer in his arms. "Why did you wake me?"

Her eyes, those beautiful black wells he drowned in daily glistened with unshed tears. "You can hear me!" Anyanna exclaimed, her voice watery.

Chaz frowned. "Woman, what are you going on about?"

The blue tears made a horizontal tread across the bridge of her nose. "I can't believe it. After all this time...,"

"Anyanna, baby blue, why are you crying?"

Her mouth parted and she gasped, "Baby blue! Oh, you called me baby blue."

Without any warning, her slender arms reached up and dragged him even closer. She cradled his head against the space between her shoulder and neck. Awkwardly, Chaz patted her shoulder as sobs wracked her body. He didn't know why she was crying but something must be bothering her. Whatever it was, they would solve it together.

When her sobs relented, she pulled back and then cupped the sides of his face in her hands.

"Chanucer, I've tried to reach you for several months. I've screamed your name from the other side of the door until my voice was hoarse." Her fingers toyed with his locks in an almost reverent way. "It's been

so long since I've been able to—"

"The other side of the door? Baby blue, what are you talking about?"

She shook her head. "The door that separates you and me. I know you think I am there, in that courtroom, swollen with the child of another man. But I must tell you, that woman is not me."

Chaz felt his eyebrow perch into his hairline. Courtroom? Child? Another man? "Anyanna, are you feeling okay?"

"Oh Chaz," her lips wobbled. "I don't know how much of this you will remember but I hope something makes it through."

He sat up down, feeling the satin sheet slide down his chest. "Baby blue?"

"Humor me, Chaz," she sighed. "Just humor me. You're dreaming of me and at the same time, we're here in this place." She extended her arm to indicate the master bedroom. "In our home where we both have wanted to be."

Not understanding why her voice carried a wistful, sad tone, he nonetheless said, "Of course. I'm listening."

Anyanna's even white teeth bit into the flesh of her bottom lip. "What if I were to tell you of a door that existed between our two worlds?"

"The door to wishes," Chaz replied lazily as he stretched back out again. He trailed his fingers over the contours of his wife's face. Then suddenly he froze. How did he know that?

"You must have heard the story somehow," Anyanna replied to his unspoken question. "Yes, but the door to wishes is more than just a door. It's a portal that combines thoughts and actions. On your world, I've often heard humans say, 'If you want something bad enough you'll make it happen.' Well, the door to wishes makes it happen."

"So what does that mean?"

Her forehead creased. *"My father was against our marriage from the start. You know this?"*

Chaz scowled. *"Yes, I know. He took no issue when your brother married my sister. But me? Me he hated."*

"My father felt that my chances for fertility would be greater with the Kulterian male he'd selected for me because of the black pearl. Our inter-species relationships are still so new. We're only seeing the first generation of hybrids reach adulthood now.

"In any case, his anger toward me and you waxed hot. Perhaps in his anger he wished for our relationship to break apart. For Kulterians, wishes are physical, but unrealized. When he came to visit over a year ago, his wish came true. The wish that his daughter would find a Kulterian mate to love."

"Anyanna, I don't understand." Yet he felt as if he did. A warning, an awareness screamed in the dark recesses of his mind.

"I know you don't. That's because you and I are here in my wish," she emphasized the word with a note of bitterness. *"Where there is no past or future. Just an eternal present, locked in one single moment."*

Her pupil-less eyes shone like glistening stones. *"What do you see when you look at me, Chanucer?"*

Chaz caressed her face, lingering on the scales. *"Me. Looking at you."*

A powerful emotion worked over her features and she took his hand and pressed a kiss to the palm. *"My father's wish manifested into reality. I woke up from a strange dream of seeing my body being split apart. I saw myself above me and then, I went away."*

"Like a doppelgänger," Chaz breathed out.

"I guess but not quite. I pushed the strange dream behind me and more or less forgot about it until that day when you came home so angry. I knew then what had happened. My father's wish had come true. Finding my father's wish, the me that had fallen in love with a

Kulterian male, was the hard part."

Chaz wondered at the bevy of emotions wracking his mind. Awe at this strange story his wife was telling him. Along with it, was an underlying sensation of unease. "I have no idea what you are talking about Anyanna. I hear every word you're saying and yet, it seems as if it doesn't apply to me. But, then again, some part of me believes that it does."

"Just hear me out," Anyanna answered, pressing her finger against his lips. "Just listen."

"Well, if I have to just listen to you, I might as well be comfortable." He lay back down and placed her blue hand against his chest, right over his heart. "Go on."

His wife stared at the place where she touched him. "My father's wish and I cannot occupy the same place and time for long periods. It has to do with the door. Chanucer, if I can use the illustration you can only leave the door ajar for so long before it naturally slams shut.

"When I found her at last, it was in this house, in this room. In my bed." A look of disgust marred her pretty features.

Chaz's jaw tensed. "I'm glad I didn't see that." His hand contracted on hers.

"I dragged her and her Kulterian lover out of our bed. She and I started to argue about who had the right to exist and who didn't. It was an odd conversation. Then, in the middle of our argument, we felt a strong force begin to drag us toward it. I looked and saw the opening to the door. Before I could do more than react to that side of the gray portal, my father's wish shoved me into the opening and I was sucked into a vortex onto the other side."

A blue tear suddenly beaded in her black eyes. "What can I tell you of an existence trapped in a gray veil? Of being in this room and seeing my father's wish with her lover desecrate our bed? Of *seeing how she destroyed my marriage? Of screaming your name and begging your God and mine to hear my prayers, my pleas?*

"But I can't." She wiped at her cheeks. *"You may not even remember what I am telling you now. But I wanted to try because I just wanted you to know that I would never betray you. I love you more than words can say."*

* * *

"Chanucer Dewright, your presence is requested in court."

Chaz jerked awake, his eyes squinting at the bright light as well as the annoyance of the unfamiliar voice. For a moment, he felt disoriented, as if the jail cell were a dream and something else…something more familiar was the reality.

Whatever that meant.

Yet, becoming more alert and sitting up he up he called out to the guard, "Is my advocate here?"

The guard answered in the affirmative and Chaz stood up and stretched. He felt doubly relaxed and languid. Even a bit…satiated. As if he'd spent the night making love to his wife.

Impossible. He'd been in the jail cell the entire time. Nor would he touch her with a ten-foot pole. Yet, despite the fact he knew it wasn't possible that he'd been with his wife, misty images teased his mind. Not of long-ago reminiscences, but of recent amorous memories.

Of drowning in her black, passion-filled eyes. Of sipping the honey from those voluptuous lips with that hidden black pearl. Of shuddering as her hands sent lightning strokes along his nerve endings. Of shivering as long fingernails scraped his—

"Chaz?"

Violently he came out of his reverie. His advocate stood at

the entrance of the cell.

"Judith." He blinked and the images faded away.

"Where were you?" The guard opened the door and stood at attention as she entered with a new suit. "You looked a million miles away."

He gulped and tried to still the uneven beating of his heart. "I was."

Judith gave him an oblique black-eyed look but said nothing. "Here's your suit for today. And the jojoba oil for your dreadlocks."

Chaz took the offerings and followed the guard who stood watch as he showered and changed. All while he went through his ablutions, he kept thinking of the misty images of being with his wife. They had seemed so real. More than that, he was certain more than loving had taken place. If he didn't know any better, he almost believe he'd had a conversation with her.

"About what?" he muttered aloud as he slid on his shoe.

"Mr. Dewright?" the guard asked.

"Nothing." He stood and assessed his appearance in the long, slender mirror next to the sink. Satisfied, he reached for the jojoba oil to anoint himself as well as say a prayer for the proceedings.

But what should he pray for?

It stopped him. Something niggled his mind, something he knew was important but like a naughty child, it scampered back just as he thought he'd figure it out. It had to do with the baby in his wife's belly. He had to prove to the court that Anyanna had falsified the paternity report.

Or did he?

As if from a distance, he could see himself with Anyanna, lying in bed. She holding his face between her hands as she related something. The vision of his own reflection blurred away as he tried to focus. Her mouth, moving, saying, *Save the...*

"Are you ready, Mr. Dewright?"

The guard's voice knocked it out of his head again. Sighing, he drew the last of the jojoba oil through his hair and then closed the small container of oil.

"Yes, I'm ready."

* * *

"Why did you have a paternity test, Mrs. Dewright?" Huller stuffed his hands into his pockets.

"My husband didn't believe the child was his. I had to prove it to him."

Chaz watched his wife as she continued to lie. Though his fists kneaded his knees, the anger wasn't the same. What had happened?

"I submit again to the court the DNA test that identifies that Mr. Chanucer Dewright is the father of the child in Mrs. Dewright's womb."

Staring at the woman sitting in the witness stand, something about her seemed alien. The images from his dream in which he made love to his wife surged forward. In those frenzied moments the innate tenderness he'd come to expect from Anyanna exuded like rays of sunlight.

The woman in the witness stand lacked that quality.

What was he thinking? The woman in the witness stand *was* his wife. She had the same mannerisms, the same tears, but somehow, for the first time since his life had gone downhill, he sensed there was a difference from his wife he never noticed before.

203

"No further questions at this time, Your Honor. Advocacy for Mrs. Anyanna Dewright rests."

Judge Quinn nodded. "Very well. Advocacy for Mr. Chanucer Dewright is now in session."

Judith stood and then walked over to the witness stand. "Mrs. Dewright, how long was it until you decide to get a paternity test."

"It was about two and a half months," Anyanna replied in a careful tone.

"But you're Kulterian. Why did you wait so long?"

"I don't think I did. My husband distanced himself from me in every way." Anyanna released a long, shaky breath sure to elicit sympathy. "Because he was so insistent that the child wasn't his, it finally dawned on me that in order to prove the baby was his, I had to do it."

"But you waited almost three months to do this." Judith leaned forward. "Surely if you wanted your husband to believe he was the father, you would have thought of this sooner."

"Objection, Your Honor," Huller interjected. "Is there a question here or are we just killing time?"

"Sustained," Judge Quinn accepted.

"Isn't it true that a Kulterian woman knows when she has been seeded by her husband?"

Seeded! The sound of the interrogation muted in the background as Chaz for some reason latched onto the word. Why was that so important?

He saw Anyanna's face flushed violet from their lovemaking. He could feel her nimble fingers smooth the wrinkles from his brow as she said, "...seeded within her."

Why couldn't he remember the full statement? Why did that alarm ring in his head, louder than before? Too many questions and not enough answers.

"It doesn't matter when I performed the paternity test." Anyanna's voice infiltrated his musings and he turned his attention back to the trial. "It still proves my husband is the father."

"Then explain why you were found at the Perrison Fertility Clinic a week before the date of this test."

Anyanna's cheeks paled to a noticeable sky blue. "I've no idea what you're talking about."

"Allow me to show you then, Mrs. Dewright."

Judith returned to the table and retrieved a glossy picture. Huller Wickman stiffened. Unlike most legal jurisdictions on Earth, moral advocates in the Kulterian court did not require that evidence be shared.

Handing the picture over to Anyanna, Judith asked. "Mrs. Dewright, can you please describe what you see in this picture?"

"I see myself walking into the building."

"Isn't it true that Perrison Fertility clinic assists infertile couples?"

"Yes," came the soft reply.

"Isn't it also true that one of their services is surrogacy?"

Anyanna nodded in a slow robotic way.

"Please answer aloud for the court, Mrs. Dewright," Judge Quinn ordered.

"Yes." Chaz watched the way her Eve's tangerine, the Kulterian colloquial equivalent of Adam's apple, bobbed up and down.

"Why would a woman, who is already pregnant, go to an infertility clinic?"

The crowd murmured. Judge Quinn banged his mallet on the block to restore order.

"So why would you go to the clinic?"

Anyanna remained silent. The mumbling returned but Judge Quinn called for silence and then said, "Mrs. Dewright, please answer the question."

"I went there...to look in on a friend who was using their services."

"You have vowed before your God and mine that you are speaking the truth and yet you would lie?"

Before Huller could object, Judith asked. "Isn't it true that you went to see Dr. Lokun Granger, a Kulterian doctor who specializes in paternity surrogacy?"

"No!" Anyanna appeared frightened.

"Isn't it also true that Dr. Granger, with her surrogacy methods which are patented and proprietary to Earth standards, can manipulate a Kulterian embryo and essentially replace the DNA of the surrogate father with another?"

"Yes, but I didn't—"

Judith became relentless, shelling question after question to Anyanna because a morals court did not allow for the right to be silent. Chaz thought he'd be gratified to see his wife ripped apart under the pointed scourge of his advocate's cross examination. Yet, he knew something was wrong.

Once more, the image of his wife rose in his mind. He focused as hard as he could, knowing it was vital for him to remember the dream. He could see her but he couldn't remember the words. Why was it important to remember the words?

Dear God, help me, he prayed.

And then, his eyes drifted shut and the entire courtroom faded from sensory input. He was back in the dream, that place...where wishes come true.

"...my father's wish carries my wish, too." Anyanna spoke.

206

"I don't understand."

"When my father's wish came into being and separated from me, she took my wish with her."

"Your wish?"

"Yes, my wish. Or rather, my prayer," she whispered as her black eyes shone with an almost iridescent hue amidst the darkness. "She is carrying our child, Chanucer."

"Mr. Dewright!"

Judge Quinn's voice broke through his concentration. Chaz gulped, shaken to the core. Anyanna's voice, *his* Anyanna, echoed in an almost audible way. *"Save the child, Chanucer. Save our baby. No matter what."*

"Yes, Your Honor?"

"Are we keeping you from your sleep?"

A titter of laughter went around the courtroom. Chaz stood. "No, Your Honor, my apologies. I was…," he sent a frantic look to Judith. She had been glaring at him but swiftly she saw he needed to speak to her now.

With a deep frown, she said, "Your Honor, may I request a recess?"

"Duration?"

She glanced at Chaz and correctly interpreting his look, said, "A half hour, Your Honor."

"Recess granted."

Judge Quinn stood and everyone remained seated until he exited. Only then did the other occupants of the room moved.

"What in the world is going on?" Judith hissed.

"Judith, this is going to sound strange but…that's not my wife but she *is* carrying my child."

His advocate blinked and she rolled her eyes. "Chaz, have you slipped on ice?"

"No, really. Listen to me. Remember the childhood story you told me about yesterday. Well, I dreamed about Anyanna and she—"

"Dreamed?"

"Listen to me, Judith." He had to make her understood. As incredible as it sounded, and even now he didn't quite believe it, there was so much at stake.

"Listen to what?"

"The story of our worlds and the door to wishes?"

"What does a children's story have to do with any of this?"

"You said that the way Kulkutern views a wish is different from the way we view a wish. A wish is an unrealized physical element while for us it's a desire. No, wait. Don't interrupt me."

Judith's mouth closed.

"Well, if the creation story of our worlds is true, then with our 'being back together again' the door to wishes has been opened? Desire and reality working in tandem with each other. Anyanna's father never wanted me for his daughter and so, he made a wish that his daughter would fall in love with a man he deemed worthy. In this case, a Kulterian."

His shaky hands dragged through his locks. "Anyanna told me, in this dream, that she saw her father's wish, the daughter who should have given herself to a Kulterian male, separate from her. Like an evil twin or a doppelganger. Yet, when her father's wish, this imposter, separated from her, she took our child with her. Then she cast my wife to an existence on the other side of the wish."

Judith spluttered. "Do you expect me to—"

He grabbed her shoulders. "Judith, hear me out. Do you think I'm the kind of man to make this up? Do you?"

She stared at him, her black eyes pensive. "No," she answered finally. "You're not given to fantasy."

Rolling his shoulders, he went on. "The reason why this imposter, this wish, is so anxious to for this morals court to determine this child is mine is that, by the law, she would be able to destroy it."

"Destroy?"

"Yes."

"But why would she—"

"Think of it, Judith. My child is growing in her belly but…so is *her* child as if they were twins. The wish of Anyanna's father."

Anyanna's words from the dream came to mind. *"Chanucer, this is a battle. Her child is the product of a wish. But my child is an answer to prayer. I did more than wish, I prayed to your God and mine for my baby. My father's wish knows this. She knows that in order for my father's wish to come true, her child must live and mine must die."*

"If I am to take this at face value—I can't believe I'm saying this—then Anyanna's imposter needs you to be the father. That way, she can go to the doctors on earth and—"

"Yes. She'll destroy the child and my Anyanna would be trapped behind the door to wishes."

"I thought she'd gone to the Perrison clinic in order to manipulate the paternal DNA," Judith mumbled. "But…if what you're saying is true…" She bit her lower lip in thought. "If what you're saying is true, then she went to the clinic in order to confirm a test that would undoubtedly show you as the baby's father. And since you're the father, she would be able to terminate that child according to the legal standards of Earth."

His advocate paced back and forth in front of the table. "But how do I prove any of this? How?"

Chaz sighed. Would it be too difficult to convince a Kulterian that a wish had come true? Humans on the other hand are highly skeptical. How could he—

"The black pearl!" he exclaimed in a raised whisper.

Judith frowned. "What about it?"

"Most people know that Primary Bronad's daughter possesses the black pearl. I'm willing to bet that the imposter doesn't have it at all."

"Why is that?"

"Think about it: the imposter is the result of a wish. Wishes are never quite right. There's always some element missing. Sort of like that old human story about the monkey's paw. Each wish made caused catastrophe. Wishes come with consequences, while prayers come with conclusions."

"The catastrophe being?"

"This trial! The primary's daughter's name is being ruined. People, as least some people, suspect she is a woman of loose morals. She had stolen my child and has to keep the fact of her own child a secret. How is this a good thing?"

"You have a point. I'm also thinking that if she is carrying two children in her womb, that we need to be able to see that."

"How?"

"How, indeed," Judith echoed as Judge Quinn re-entered the courtroom. Swiftly, Judith reached into her briefcase and pulled out an electric tablet of a sort and started to browse through it.

A distinct movement caught Chaz's peripheral vision and he glanced over. The imposter Anyanna waddled back to the witness stand where she had been in conversation with Huller Wickman. Chaz gazed at the woman, seeing a thousand differences that he hadn't been able to see before.

What possessed him to think this woman had ever been his wife?

A pleased expression came over Judith as she paused in her scurrying and stared at the screen. "There you are," she said with satisfaction just as the judge sat down.

Judge Quinn nodded in their direction. "I take it the advocacy for Mr. Dewright will continue?"

"May I approach the bench, Your Honor?"

"Advocates, advance to the bench."

Huller scowled as he went up the bench but Judith ignored him as she began to talk in too low a voice to carry over the courtroom.

Chaz rubbed the back of his neck What would his advocate do? In order to save the children, he had to claim paternity, but by proclaiming it, he knew for certain it was doomed to die. A wish fulfilled and an answered prayer could not exist together.

Were they one in the same, simply a matter of semantics? Chaz glanced over at the imposter to see she was already staring at him. He held that gaze. Within those dark, pupil-less depths, he discovered the answer to his own question.

"Have you slipped on ice?" Huller's voice carried out, disbelief evident.

Chaz dragged his eyes away to see the huddle at the front. Huller's shiftiness as he balanced on one foot, then the other, showed his agitation.

Glancing at Judge Quinn, he looked as if he'd been hit by a ton of bricks.

"My client will submit to no such thing!" Huller declared, uncaring now if their voices were heard.

"She will," Judith denied. "This is a morals court, Mr. Wickman. If she has nothing to hide, then she will submit to an examination to prove her identity. Her refusal means then that the child she carries is not my client's."

"We've got a DNA test to prove that?"

"And the other?" Judith said pointedly.

Huller's fingers clenched. "Very well."

The huddle disbanded. Judge Quinn cleared his throat rather loudly, looking discomfited. "Mrs. Dewright, there has been speculation as to your identity. Mr. Dewright's advocate desires that you provide proof that you are who you say you are."

"I'm don't understand," she replied, her black eyes narrowed.

"Mrs. Dewright, can you provide proof that you are Anyanna Dewright?" Judge Quinn clasped his fingers together.

"In what way?"

"Show us the black pearl," Judith answered before the judge could speak. "That will be proof enough."

Anyanna's skin blanched to a sickly blue. "The black pearl?" Her voice was barely audible.

"Yes, like the one in this picture."

Judith turned the tablet over to show a goofy picture of Anyanna that Chaz had seen a few years ago. One where she pulled her lower lip down, revealing the black mole on the inside.

"Will you show us the black pearl?" Judith asked.

"NO! I won't be degraded in this fashion." The pale blue flushed dark. "I won't."

"I've said this before, Mrs. Dewright. Affront to my question is not an answer. Now, show us the black pearl."

The color of her face deepened. "No."

"Do you have something to hide, Mrs. Dewright? Or rather, do you have nothing to hide?"

Anyanna's hand fluttered to her stomach, a look of fright on her face. "No, I want my child. My baby. The other must die."

"No!" Chaz started to rise when a sharp retort from Judge Quinn stilled him. "The morals court is still in session, Mr. Dewright."

"Tell the court the truth, Mrs. Dewright. Tell them what you are."

"No, I'm real." She sent a pleading look to Chaz. "Tell them that I am your wife. And the child, the child is yours."

Chaz, despite everything recoiling inside, addressed the judge. "Judge Quinn, may I speak to the witness?"

Judge Quinn threw up his hands. "Everything else about this trial is unorthodox. Why bother with protocol anymore?" He waved Chaz to the witness stand.

Rising from his seat, he made his way to Anyanna, the imposter of his wife. "That is my child, but you are not its mother. Nor are you my wife." The words should have stung with accusation but instead, he softened them with an outstretched hand as he reached her. "It's time to end this."

"I look like her, don't I?" Her head lifted defiantly.

Chaz sighed and his hand dropped to his side. "No. Not anymore. You are the product of a wish gone awry. I want my wife back. I want my child."

"I am the one your father-in-law wanted. Me!"

"That may be true, but your father's wishes are futile. As are you."

Slowly, she began to fade. The entire courtroom erupted into bedlam at the sight. Electronic devices flashed and blinked as the onlookers took note of the event. As Anyanna, the imposter, began to fade, he saw a gray mist appear beside her. And though he had never seen it, Chaz knew instinctively that this was the door to wishes.

As the imposter continued to fade, another form began to

coalescence.

Anyanna, the real one. His wife.

"But what of my child?"

The imposter's voice was a mere breath of air. She appeared nebulous like a fine mist while his wife gained solidity. Chaz's heart began to beat hard in his chest. At long last, his wife had returned!

"I will keep them," his wife said, the words strong. She now stood before him.

Solid. Real.

He almost reached out to touch her but she shook her head as she went over to where the imposter sat, almost gone from sight. Anyanna sat down, her body completely overlaying the one fading away.

"Will you really?"

The imposter's shadowy form moved forward, her head down, while Anyanna's body sat back. "I was willing to kill your child so that mine could live. Can a wish and a prayer really co-exist? How do I know you will take care of my baby?"

Chaz saw a calmness fall over his wife. "By your God and mine. I will keep them and raise them as my own."

"I do not deserve your kindness, Anyanna." Then the imposter disappeared from sight. Then, the door also faded away.

Chaz leapt forward and clasped his wife in his arms. "Anyanna, it's really you."

"Chanucer," she said, her black eyes filled with blue tears. "You must be careful. The children."

He dropped his hands to gaze down at her stomach. It was swollen and she looked very pregnant. "Baby blue," he breathed.

"I never thought I could have one child and now I've been

given two."

Bedlam erupted in the courtroom. Judge Quinn's mallet striking the block did nothing to stop the applause and congratulations exploding from the on-lookers in the room.

Chaz lifted his wife's chin and spent the next few minutes enjoying the sweetness of her lips again. Certain, very certain now, it was real. Not a dream.

Nor a wish.

* * *

Four months later...

"They are both very beautiful," Primary Bronad stated as he gently rocked the cradle of his grandchildren.

"Of course, Primary," Chaz said with pride as he looked on. "We're very proud parents."

The wish and the prayer had given them a boy and a girl. They weren't twins in the normal sense of the word. Due to superfetation, his daughter was born three months later after her brother.

The brother, named Lirt after his grandfather, was the hybrid with his dark skin underlined by Kulterian blue and the dusky scales along his neck and face. His daughter was full-blooded Kulterian and her blue body was bright against the clear white sheets as she slept. Anyanna had given her a simple name, Wish.

"I hope you can truly forgive me," Primary Bronad said as he leaned back in his chair. "You are a man worthy of my daughter. I should have realized that."

Chaz said nothing but nodded, accepting his father-in-law's apology.

"The damage I caused was almost irreparable." The blue man's head bowed, his hair still dark blue but the scales showing white, a sign of old age among the Kulterians. "But, I look at them and I can still smile."

"Why is that?"

"Doesn't the book that your God and mine wrote through humanity's hand say, 'Blessed are the peacemakers for they shall be called the children of God?"

"It does," Chaz said.

"My daughter could have easily destroyed the grandchild of my wish but she didn't. Instead, she took the child of a wish and made it her own. Therefore, she will be called a child of God. Because her mother sought peace."

Chaz gently caressed his children's foreheads and then grinned. "I do believe you're right, Primary. I do believe you are."

Blessed are the peacemakers
For they shall be called the children of God

Parker J Cole

Parker J Cole, author of "The Door to Wishes," is an off and on recovering Mountain Dew and marshmallow addict, author, speaker, and radio show host with a fanatical obsession with the Lord, Star Trek, K-dramas, anime, romance books, old movies, speculative fiction, and knitting. She writes to fill the void the sugar left behind.

The Path of Mercy

The Twenty-Second of Fasna in the year 3766, by Kashtophim Reckoning

The mountain gods hunger for a sacrifice. The words echoed through Rillaph's mind as she quietly slipped into her room after finishing the day's work. Her hands shook so much she could barely latch the door. The Elevated One, high priest of the Order of the Mountain Gods, had assembled the heads of the noble families for dinner specifically to make that proclamation.

Resting her head against the doorframe, she tried to calm her pounding heart in the darkness. She didn't want to contemplate what the call for a sacrifice truly meant.

The last sacrifice occurred during her grandmother's time. One of her earliest memories was overhearing her grandmother relay the spectacle and horror of it all to Rillaph's father. She'd never revealed to her parents that she'd heard the conversation. It was the only reason she knew she should have had an uncle.

A single beam of moonlight fell through the window. Rillaph's eyes wandered over the sleeping lump of little boy in her bed. In many ways, Taphak was more like her son than her brother. He was only two years old when their parents died in the plague. Now he was nearly eight. She crossed the room and pressed her palm against his forehead to see if the fever still lingered. At the feel of cool skin, she sighed with relief.

The Sconnelans tended to pick their sacrifices, though rare, from the same family lines. Especially if a previous sacrifice had produced the desired effect. But she and Taphak were the last of their line after the plague. The Taph family crest felt heavy on her neck now. The crest was the only thing remaining of her old life—the only thing left to prove that noble blood ran in her veins, and she always wore it. She might never be Lady Taph, but she would *always* be Rillaph of Taph until the day she died.

Did I doom him, by clinging to that foolish pride? Rillaph's eyes filled with tears. Taphak rolled over, groaning in his sleep. Her hand fell away from his forehead. *I didn't even consider the possibility of a sacrifice... We could have vanished into the mountain mists if I'd been willing to throw away our name.*

Her throat tightened. A few tears escaped from her eyes. She pulled the blanket up a little higher over Taphak, brushing back the scraggly, dark hair from his brow before she crossed the room.

Rillaph's room was bare—not even a rug—except for the bed, hooks on the wall for their clothing, and the small wooden cabinet present in every woman's room. She stopped before the cabinet. The hinges creaked as she opened the doors. Cringing, she glanced back at Taphak. He hadn't stirred, thankfully.

Trembling, she brought herself to her knees, then bowed low before the statue of Aosca, the guardian of women. This likeness of Aosca had heard the pleas of at least four generations of Rillaph's ancestors. The goddess had never answered Rillaph's petitions—whether Aosca had ever answered *any*, she didn't know—but it was the only hope she had right now.

"Please," she softly pleaded. "Be merciful. Spare me. Spare my brother."

But Aosca, carved from a stalagmite, only looked out at the meager room with a stolid face and unseeing eyes.

The Twenty-Fifth of Fasna in the year 3766, by Kashtophim Reckoning

Rillaph was not a petitioner. The Elevated One had summoned her, which meant he wanted something. Recalling his words at dinner made her stomach twist into knots. She didn't dare think any further on the subject if she wanted to keep her mind sharp for any chance of survival.

Her footsteps echoed through the estate's hallway. She hadn't even had time to tie back her dark brown hair and put on her cap. Once, she had been accustomed to leaving her hair hanging loose, but no more. Now, the feel of it swishing against her back was discomfiting.

She paused, looking up and down the hall. It was strangely absent of... anyone. When had she last seen a guard? Or another maid? She turned to face the entrance of the audience hall. The doors already stood open. Had it always seemed like a gaping maw?

Rillaph took a deep breath and stepped inside, but the audience hall was empty except for a scribe, who seemed to have fallen asleep over his desk. Raucous laughter, both male and female, arose from the private chamber attached to the hall. The chamber door near the dais was ajar, but she didn't dare go any closer. The thought of what she might see in that room made her queasy.

The Elevated One didn't have a throne room, as a Highest

One—part of the monarchy—would have. He was just the religious figurehead. Yet the carved stone chair on the dais was cushioned with piles of exquisite furs, and a warming brazier had been moved nearby.

Long moments passed. Rillaph wondered if she'd misheard the other maid. *No*, she thought. *The maid definitely said the Elevated wanted to see me immediately*.

Laughter pealed out of the private chamber again. Rillaph's face tightened into a grimace as she stood in the center of the hall. She may have lost her noble rank, but she was still noble by blood, and in Sconnela, the Order did not rank above the nobility. The Elevated One had *summoned* her. Now he made her wait without even a cushion to sit on?

Enough was enough. She spun on her heel, crossed back to the entrance, and kicked the scribe's table. A bottle slipped off the edge, splattering ink across the floor and the hem of her dress as it shattered. The scribe shot upright in his seat, then paled when his eyes caught Rillaph's.

"Inform the Elevated One of my arrival," she ordered. The scribe scrambled to his feet, chair clattering to the floor. The laughter coming from behind the door finally faded away. Rillaph turned back to the dais. The Elevated One strode out the door just a moment later, and she raised a brow at the fine sheen of his silk tunic. Those sworn to the Order were supposed to dress modestly, but the tunic shone nearly as brightly as his bald head.

Rillaph heard the scribe righting his chair behind her. The Elevated One grinned. She suppressed a shudder at the sight of his rotting teeth. He seated himself, then motioned her forward. The dignity of her family had never left Rillaph, and she was grateful for that now. She might be garbed in a coarse woolen dress instead of fine silks, but she could still walk with a measured, graceful stride, and stand straight with her head raised. Even if it had been more than five years since she last *received* an audience rather than being summoned for one.

"You are the eldest of the Taph line, correct?" the Elevated One asked as she stopped at the foot of the dais.

"I am."

"The line of Taph that has offered up sacrifices through the generations?" he specified, fingers tapping away at the arm of the stone chair. Thankfully, the sound was muffled by a white fur.

Rillaph stilled, her gaze dropping to the floor. *It's an honor for a family to present the sacrifice*, she silently reminded herself. *No matter their status. Don't give away your dismay. Don't betray the family honor so soon.*

Gathering her courage, she looked back up at the Elevated One. "Yes."

"Who would you offer up?" the Elevated asked. "If you had to choose between you and your brother, who would you give for the sacrifice?"

"Is there to *be* a sacrifice?" Her voice trembled just a bit on the last word. Dinner the other night was the only place she'd heard anything about a sacrifice mentioned.

"Ah... yes." The Elevated rubbed a thumb along his lower lip. "I have discussed it with the nobles and the Highest Ones. They have agreed that the signs show the mountain gods are hungry."

Dizziness washed over Rillaph, but she did her best to not actually sway on her feet. The last time she'd felt like this was the moment she'd been informed of her parents' deaths. Her knees nearly gave out when she realized exactly *what* he'd said, though. *If. If* she had a choice, who would she offer? So did she have a choice, or not?

The Elevated One stood and descended the dais to slowly circle around her. "You, or your brother?"

Rillaph's heartbeat pounded in her ears for several moments. She would not be intimidated into submission so easily. For a second, she thought she felt the Elevated's fingers brush against her hair from behind her, but ignored the sensation despite her roiling stomach. She just needed to *think*. To figure out what response would be her best advantage.

If I offer myself up, Taphak will be left alone. Who's to say they won't call for another sacrifice a day later, and take him as well? Or... we try to escape. But how? When?

Or... "How could anyone decent make a decision like that?" Rillaph cringed as her voice carried around the room and out into the hallway. She hadn't meant to speak her thoughts aloud.

The Elevated One stopped circling and leaned close to her. "Perhaps I can help," he said, voice dripping with honey.

Rillaph met his gaze, not bothering to hide her scrutiny. She was *furious*, but she was a noble. She knew how to control her emotions, even when they were overwhelming. The Elevated's eyes shifted away from hers for just a moment, and a desperate hope jolted through her.

He wanted something more; something other than *just* the sacrifice. It almost certainly wasn't ethical, but the Order hadn't exactly been true to ethics for a while. Not since they stole the inheritance of nearly an entire generation of noble heirs after the plague, including hers. They were the ones who had made so many plague orphans dependent on their charity through a loophole. For most, the choice between hard labor or starvation had been a simple one to make.

"And how might that be?" She didn't bother to hide the

distress in her voice. It was better for the Elevated to think she was desperate. He hadn't been raised to consider every possible political machination the way she had. He used his status, not his wits, to manipulate.

The Elevated reached out and cupped Rillaph's chin in his hand. *Don't pull away*, she reproved herself. *Don't make him angry.*

"Become the mountain god's concubine." His gaze slid down her form. "Give up your brother for the sacrifice, become the concubine, and I will restore your family's lineage and wealth."

The proposed bargain was so ludicrous Rillaph's thoughts stalled as she tried to follow his reasoning. *Do... what?!*

His grip tightened on her chin, and she desperately cobbled together a response, something that would make him need to think for even a minute. "The mountain god hasn't taken a concubine in a hundred years," she gasped. "Not even the last sacrifice was that long ago. What have the gods shown you to suddenly demand such things?"

The Elevated gaped at her for a moment. She took advantage of his surprise and stepped back, pulling her chin out of his grip. How had he managed to scheme his way to the position of Elevated One when he couldn't even handle obvious questions?

What possible advantage can I gain in accepting his offer? She tried to pick apart his logic. *I don't have a choice in the sacrifice. For all the show made to the people, everyone knows that once the sacrifice is chosen, that's it. So based on that reasoning, Taphak has been selected. Possibly me as well, but the Elevated One wants me to think there is a choice.*

The Elevated shook off his confusion faster than she'd hoped. "There is no reason for our society to continue its decline. The plague nearly wiped us out, and now the Kashtophim press at our borders. We've seen many struggles since worship in accordance with the Old Ways waned. It's time for Sconnela to be revived."

Rillaph nearly bounced with glee at the Elevated's answer, if only Taphak's life—and hers—weren't on the line. The Kashtophim were preoccupied with ridding themselves of the Rishka; even nursing babes knew that. It would be many years before they would be able to try taking Sconnela, though the time *would* come, and Sconnela would have to be ready. But not yet.

The Elevated's true intent lay in the Old Ways. Back when the gods were higher than the law, and even the Highest Ones bowed their knees to the Order. When sacrifices happened nearly every season, and religion was used as the iron fist to control the masses. Then, even the simplest of decisions had been dictated by the whims of the gods.

What in the Nine Peaks did he tell the Highest Ones to get them to agree to a sacrifice? She wondered. *Do they know about his plan to take a concubine? Do they have any inkling of his interest in the Old Ways?*

The Elevated wasn't worried about the Kashtophim. He wanted the highest position in the land.

He needs a noble *concubine,* she realized. *He needs someone of power next to him, to fully legitimize his pursuit of the Old Ways. He's smarter than I gave him credit for, but he's inexperienced and clumsy.*

Being the mountain god's concubine wouldn't negate her lineage, or prevent her from passing on the Taph name and wealth to her offspring. But she wasn't about to side with a man who would sacrifice her brother to manipulate her, or side with an Order that abandoned the plague orphans when they had most needed genuine aid.

But now Rillaph knew how to use him.

"Perhaps the Old Ways do need to be revived," she feigned agreeance. "But I have some requests if I am to accept your proposition."

The Elevated One looked at her then—truly *looked*. Clearly, it hadn't occurred to him that she might want something *other* than her titles and wealth.

"O-of course," he stuttered. Rillaph's mouth twisted up with just the tiniest bit of satisfaction.

"I want my titles and wealth restored by the end of the day, including access to funds." She let the authority of the Taph lineage flow through her demeanor for the first time in five years. "I want my brother's title restored. He is to hear no news about the sacrifice or the concubinage."

The Elevated One stared at her, mouth gaping like a fish, as her demands filtered through his mind. His eyes looked empty for a moment, then he asked, "Why your brother's title?"

"The sacrifice of a noble heir will be far more prestigious than that of a penniless orphan, don't you think?" Rillaph nearly vomited as she spoke the sentence. Even if she didn't mean the words, they were revolting to say aloud. Nearly as revolting as the look of realization flickering over the Elevated's face.

Time, she told herself silently, trying to soothe her conscience. *You're just buying time.*

The Elevated's mouth stretched into a leer and he snapped his fingers at the scribe. "See to it *personally* that everything she requested is done by the end of the day!"

Rillaph almost felt pity for the scribe. The Elevated One clearly had no concept of the time something like this would take for a single person. But it wasn't her concern anymore.

There were other, more important things she had to figure out now.

* * *

For a bit longer, it was better to still be a serving girl than a restored noble.

Rillaph managed to snag the market trip for her final task of the night, though she'd barely had time to grab her cloak. She felt uneasy leaving the Order's estate without checking on Taphak, but the wagons were pulling out. If she walked to town, she wouldn't have time to make her preparations.

The ride into town was mostly silent. Rillaph's thoughts were only accompanied by the creaking of wooden wheels and the fleeting chirps of birds as they made their way to their nests. The tree-lined path grew dim from the mountain shadows, even though the sky was still bright overhead.

After the silence of the forest, the hum of voices beyond the town gates was too loud to miss. Once the guards waved them through, Rillaph thanked the driver, swung down from the wagon seat, and melted into the crowd. She should have at least a couple of hours before the market vendors began to close down for the night. Before they did, she needed to visit the treasurer.

Carefully, she pressed her hand to her chest, relaxing at the crinkle of paper under her palm. It was still there. She hadn't left the hall until she had written proof—signed by both the scribe and the Elevated One, and bearing the Order's seal—documenting her change in status and the restoration of the Taph family's wealth. Hopefully it would be sufficient for her to withdraw some funds.

* * *

Rillaph was stunned at the weight of the bag she left the treasurer's office with; various denominations of copper, silver, and even *gold* coinage filled the leather pouch nearly to bursting. The document from the Elevated One, combined with the Taph family crest, had proven more than sufficient. From there, she went and reserved a room at the inn, pretending to be a servant girl going ahead of a noble lady.

The cook had told her to return by curfew, but Rillaph wasn't returning as a serving girl.

Rillaph departed from the inn and hurriedly dropped off the various kitchen orders for the next morning, then went about acquiring clothing for herself and Taphak. What little clothing they had now was worn out, not befitting of their restored status. Her final purchase for herself was a nicer cloak to replace her threadbare one, but she didn't dare wear the silk-lined cashmere until she'd bathed.

Two hours passed by in a blur. Rillaph wasn't sure how she'd accomplished so much, so fast. When she finally took a moment to breathe, her knees buckled and she found herself leaning against an alley wall. Her plan was coming to fruition, and the relief overwhelmed her.

After a few minutes, Rillaph found her strength again and went to secure a horse. She would need it to return to the Order's manor this late. A stall filled with carved wooden toys caught her attention on the way to the stables. There was a smooth, carved horse that spanned across her two palms. Taphak always asked about learning to ride. She smiled.

Will I have a chance to teach him? Rillaph handed over a few silver coins to the merchant and asked him to deliver it to the

Lady Taph at the inn, then began her trek to the stables again.

"Rillaph!" a voice called above the crowd. At first, she ignored it, then remembered she was still dressed as a serving girl. It might be one of the group she had traveled into town with.

"It is you!" a man exclaimed. A hand grabbed her wrist just as she pivoted on her heel, and in an instant, she found herself face to face with her past.

Her betrothed.

No. The man who *had been* her betrothed, until Sconnelan law created a chasm between them when she was left without title and destitute.

Her voice was lost to her for several long moments, eyes latched to his face as she compared it to her memory. He was older now, but his blue eyes were still kind, and a rebellious blond curl still fell across his forehead. He smiled, and her heart still pattered at the sight.

He'd recognized her. Even dressed in dirty kitchen rags, with her hair tied back and hidden under a cap. Her once smooth, creamy skin was suntanned and freckled and he still recognized her.

"Lapik of Haka," she breathed, slightly awestruck by his presence.

He blinked, and she felt like she'd broken a spell as she broke the silence. The smile faded from his face as a quiet desperation took over. His hand moved down her wrist, fingers entwining with hers. He pulled her to the side of the street, into the shadows.

"I heard about the sacrifice," Lapik whispered.

She gawked at him. "Ho-"

"My guardian was there, at the dinner," he explained. "I'm a plague orphan, too, remember? I was just... fortunate enough to be a confirmed heir before…"

"Ah…" That's right. That's why she was in this nightmare to start with. Because she, and so many other plague orphans, had been days away from being presented and confirmed as heirs when the plague struck.

Lapik smoothed a loose lock of hair back behind her ear. "The sacrifice. Are you in danger?"

Rillaph shook her head. She'd tried not to think about *it* all day, but now tears threatened to spill from her eyes. She blinked them back furiously as she stared at the ground.

"My brother has been chosen," she choked out. The rest… wasn't important right now.

"Rillaph…" Lapik's arms slid around her and pulled her against him.

He's so much taller now, she realized through her heartache. *I'm glad he hasn't been hungry. His shoulders almost seem strong enough to share my burdens.*

She stilled as another thought occurred to her. *Why did Lapik appear now? Is it a trap? Is the Elevated One working with the noble families to destabilize the Highest Ones, and Taphak and I are just pawns?*

Then she recalled the foolish look on the Elevated's face when she'd made her demands. She'd also requested the market trip at the last minute. No, it was unlikely this was a trap. The Elevated couldn't think that many steps ahead.

"What do you want to do?" The sorrow in Lapik's voice was so deep it cut through her desperation. As she stood folded in the embrace of a man who might have been her husband now if life had turned out differently, she decided to trust him. The house of Haka had deep ties with Sconnela's trade infrastructure… with his help, her plan might actually succeed.

"I need to find a smuggler," she confessed.

* * *

When Rillaph reserved the room at the inn for Lady Taph, she'd also requested a hot bath and meal to be waiting. Unfortunately, both were cold by the time she returned, but she had to hurry through them both anyway. Her chance encounter with Lapik swirled through her mind. He'd agreed to meet her at the inn an hour after they parted.

She'd just finished dressing—*why, by the Nine Peaks, are there so many laces?* —and toweling her hair to dampness when a knock sounded at the door.

"Lady Taph?" a woman called. "You have a guest. Lord Haka is waiting in the private sitting room."

"Thank you!" Rillaph responded. "Please tell him I'll be down momentarily."

She rushed through combing and braiding her hair, rather than leaving it loose. She wasn't going to go down looking like she'd just come out of the bath, even if it was true. The final touch was a silk kerchief she draped over her hair and fastened in place with a long silver pin. Now she was the head of the Taph household.

Rillaph tucked the paper from the Order into a leather clutch which fastened to her bodice, made sure the Taph crest was secure around her neck, then headed downstairs.

The sitting room door was closed when she arrived, so she knocked lightly. Lapik opened it, smiled at her, and ushered her inside. He didn't show any surprise at her changed appearance, but she didn't miss the thorough inspection he gave the hall before he closed the door again. For a moment, she let her gaze linger. He filled out his woolen breeches and vest quite well, and she really wouldn't mind if he pulled her into his arms again.

Stop. Rillaph blushed at her thoughts. *If you leave Sconnela, you'll never see him again.*

She forced her attention away from Lapik and looked around the room. It wasn't large or well-lit, but the burning fireplace and the curtains against the opposite wall made it feel intimate and cozy. In the center of the room, a small table was set for tea. Lapik pulled out a chair for her, and she smoothed her skirts as she sat.

"I thought you were bringing someone?" she asked as Lapik seated himself across from her.

"He's here," Lapik answered, pouring a cup of tea for her, then himself.

"Where?" Rillaph asked incredulously, twisting around in her seat to look around the room again. Her gaze latched on the curtains.

"He'll reveal himself in time," Lapik said, sipping his tea. "Tell me about your situation. Everything, from the beginning."

Rillaph raised her cup of tea to her lips, took a sip to moisten her throat, then began. She told him about the dinner, the summoning… the Elevated One's proposition to restore her wealth and status, if she became the mountain god's concubine. Lapik's knuckles turned white around his teacup, and for a moment she worried it would shatter in his hands.

"Is that why you're dressed like this now?" Lapik asked. "Did you… accept his offer?"

"I didn't know what else to do," she confessed. "I was able to buy some time for myself and Taphak, though. The Elevated won't take me until… after the sacrifice."

Rillaph continued to speak, relaying the exact conditions the Elevated had agreed to, that she was able to withdraw funds at the treasury, and everything she'd done that evening before Lapik encountered her in the market.

By the time she finished and fell silent, Lapik had risen from his seat and was pacing across the room. He'd nearly run into the wall twice. The rage emanating from him was nearly palpable, and Rillaph tried not to let her heart wonder foolishly about *one day...*

No, she silently scolded herself. *If you leave, there is no 'one day.' And if you stay... it's at the cost of your brother's life.*

"I don't know what to do. Becoming Lady Taph again isn't worth Taphak's life," she said in a moment when Lapik's back was turned. She couldn't bear to see his face, not if he still felt so strongly about her to be this upset at the Elevated's proposition. Lapik paused in his pacing, and Rillaph watched his shoulders sag.

Lapik sighed. A moment later, a dull *thud* made her wince as his fist met the wall. He sighed again. Rillaph's gaze fell to her teacup. She swished the now-lukewarm liquid around, waiting for Lapik to regain his composure. The motion was soothing.

"What do you think?" Lapik spoke aloud so suddenly she jumped in her seat. "Can you help them? Does this situation meet the criteria your people have?"

Another voice replied from directly behind her. "I believe this is a case where we would offer refuge."

Rillaph almost screamed. She jumped up, pushing her chair backwards into the intruder.

She heard a grunt, and Lapik chuckled. Rillaph rounded the table with a huff, seeking the safety of Lapik's proximity. Lapik pushed away from the wall and turned to her, grasping her hand with a reassuring squeeze. She waited for the speaker to reveal himself.

A man stepped out of the shadows, pushing back the hood of his cloak. Rillaph caught a glimpse of sun-bleached hair and a face covered in more freckles than her own. Her eyes met his, and her lungs froze as her scalp prickled. There, standing before her, was one of the silver-eyed heathens she'd only ever heard about.

"I'm sorry I frightened you, Lady Taph. My name is Saral."

"You're a *Rishka*," she gasped. Rillaph couldn't tell what color his eyes were, but it was impossible to miss the ring of gleaming silver around his irises.

The Thirty-third of Fasna in the year 3766, by Kashtophim Reckoning

'Let truth kiss me on the path of mercy' was the passphrase the Rishka smuggler had given her. Rillaph had only dared to mutter the phrase in the deepest part of the night, when everyone slept, so she wouldn't forget it. Tonight, she waited to hear it.

Rillaph tried to keep the night's routine as normal as possible, for Taphak's sake. He was finally asleep, so she pulled out the single bag she'd packed days ago. The carved horse she'd purchased at the market was hidden at the bottom. It might be a good distraction as they traveled.

Traveling clothes were already set aside for Taphak. She quickly changed into simpler, sturdier garments herself, ones much less noticeable than true noblewomen's clothing. As she braided her hair, her fingers brushed against the leather cord holding the Taph crest around her neck. *Should I... discard it?*

235

She tied off her braid, then hesitantly removed the crest. The medallion glinted in the lamplight as she cupped it in her palms. The Taph insignia was a flying eagle carrying a quiver of arrows in its talons. Five years ago, Rillaph anxiously awaited the day she would begin training her own raptor. Now, she prepared to cast aside everything she knew, including her family name, to save her brother.

It's just a piece of metal, she thought. *I will always be Rillaph of Taph, even without it.*

Rillaph set it on the table and turned to walk away, then found she simply *couldn't*. With a sigh, she looped the cord back around her neck, tucked the crest into her collar, and pressed her hands to her face.

She was exhausted, having barely slept while keeping watch over Taphak the previous nights. But she didn't dare lie down and try to doze. Instead, she stood and paced across her newer, larger accommodations, fingers brushing over the polished stone walls and soft draperies. As a serving girl, she'd been too tired for anything besides work and sleep. The last ten days of physical leisure accompanied by emotional distress had her nerves in a jumble, and her old nervous habits had quickly resurfaced.

She checked the large window with each circuit.

When the moon rises above the 7th Peak, someone will come for you, Lapik said when they had made their plans at the inn. The 7th Peak was east of the Order's estate, but on the opposite side of the mountain pass.

She desperately hoped Lapik's connections would come through, because the sacrifice was set for the morning, before the new moon.

Rillaph's next loop away from the window brought her close

to the wooden cupboard relocated from her servant's quarters. The sight of it now made her shiver. She hadn't bowed before Aosca since the night before the Elevated summoned her. After that, she'd decided she needed no part of the gods that wanted to consume her brother. Removing the goddess' cupboard entirely would have brought her under other, perhaps more dangerous, suspicions, though. So she just tried to ignore it.

Maybe those suspicions would be justified… she was willing to turn herself and her brother over to a *Rishka* to escape, after all. And yet… as disconcerting as their eyes were—her stomach twisted at just the memory of them—she would rather chance survival with the Rishka than with the mountain gods' mercy.

Taphak groaned in his sleep. Rillaph turned away from the cupboard, suppressing a shiver once more, and crossed back to the bed. She extinguished the lamp on the bedside table. Taphak should get as much rest as possible.

She began pacing again. On her next turn around the room, she retrieved a spare blanket and draped it over Aosca's cupboard.

Rillaph lost count of how many times she looked out the window after sunset until, at last, just the edge of the waning moon crested over the 7th Peak. With the first glimmer of moonlight, Rillaph went to prepare Taphak for the journey.

She had just finished dressing him, ever grateful that her brother was a heavy sleeper, when there was a knock on the door. She laid him gently back on the bed before crossing the room. "Who is it?"

"Kama, from the kitchens, Lady Taph," a woman replied. "I have the tea you requested."

She hadn't sent for tea. Cautiously, Rillaph cracked the door open, observing the serving girl through narrowed eyes. Kama did indeed have a tray in her hands, and the girl pushed against the door, leaning in.

"Let truth kiss me on the path of mercy," Kama whispered. Rillaph's eyes widened. She stepped back, opening the door just enough for Kama to enter.

Rillaph refastened the latch as Kama set the tea tray on the table. When she turned around, the serving girl was setting a large leather satchel on the table as well, and her head tilted.

"Smoked meat and cheese, for you to eat on the way," Kama explained when she noticed Rillaph's curiosity. "Is your brother ready?"

"Yes." Rillaph ran her hands over her hair, trying to think of anything else she might want. She couldn't. She'd lost most of her prized possessions years ago, after all. Taphak was her priority now.

"We'll leave as soon as the guards change. If you can, try to get a swallow or two of the tea down your brother's throat before we go," Kama poured a cup as she spoke. "It will help him stay asleep as you escape."

Rillaph nodded instead of speaking, surprised at how dry and stiff her own throat felt. She went to prop Taphak up on the bed, and Kama followed with the tea. Rillaph's hand shook as she reached for the cup.

"Taphak," she whispered as his head fell against her shoulder. "Can you take a sip for me?"

"Why, Rilla?" Taphak groaned. "Not sick."

"I know," Rillaph soothed as she pressed the cup to his lips. "Just a sip."

Taphak blinked slowly, squinting against the light. His lips parted. Rillaph tipped the cup enough to pour a bit into his mouth. Taphak grimaced, but swallowed anyway. "Bitter."

"I'm sorry," Rillaph said. "Can you drink just a little more?"

Taphak's weight slumped against her, and she realized he had already slipped back into sleep. Rillaph returned the cup to Kama, then stood and pulled the covers back on the bed. She slipped Taphak's shoes on, and checked the bag one more time. Everything was ready.

"Is it almost time?" Rillaph asked.

Kama nodded. Rillaph handed the bag to her, then retrieved hers and Taphak's cloaks from the wardrobe. As she walked back to the bed, Kama spoke up. "Lady Taph."

Rillaph stopped and looked at the girl. Kama reached into her apron pocket, pulled out a folded letter affixed with a large wax seal, and pressed it into Rillaph's hand. "Lord Haka sent this for you."

Rillaph stared at the letter, wishing she had time to read it. But there was another knock at the door. Kama answered it as Rillaph tucked the letter deep into her skirt pocket.

"Elevated One!"

Rillaph froze, her vision going dark and ears stuffy for a second as she tried to figure out what to do now. The bag... their cloaks... Taphak lying in bed fully clothed, with shoes on. The Elevated One mustn't see any of that.

Kama's voice interrupted her panic. "Lady Taph was just preparing to visit the baths, Elevated One." Rillaph blinked rapidly, forcing the fog to clear from her vision. She heard the quiet *snick* of the door closing, and realized Kama had managed to keep the Elevated One out of the room. For now.

Why is he here? Rillaph wondered, frantically grabbed the traveling bag and cloaks, shoving them under the bed. She couldn't quite make out what the Elevated One was saying to Kama. *He's supposed to leave me alone until after the sacrifice.*

Rillaph's heart pounded. Kama would only be able to dissuade the Elevated One for so long. She glanced around the room again, desperate for any sort of solution, and her eyes fell on the pot of tea Kama had brought.

Quickly, she dashed back to the table, poured the tea from Taphak's cup back in the pot, and dried the cup as best she could with the edge of a bedsheet. "Thank you, Kama, for bringing a second cup," she muttered, setting the other cup quietly back on its saucer.

The door made a quiet *snick* again as it opened. Rillaph whirled around, wiping clammy palms against her skirt. Kama started to speak, but the Elevated One pushed his way inside the door.

"Rillaph of Taph!" The Elevated leered, wobbling toward her.

He's drunk! Rillaph realized, and darted forward to steady him. She cringed as he pawed at her back and waist, but fortunately she was able to settle him into a chair before he could knock both of them to the floor.

"To-tomorrow!" the Elevated chortled, leaning into her face. "Then you're mine."

Rillaph tried not to gag. "Tonight is not tomorrow, Elevated One." She carefully stepped back and took the other seat at the table, glancing back at Kama and motioning for her to shut the door. "But I'll have a cup of tea with you tonight. My brother fell asleep before he could share it with me."

The Elevated One scowled, planting his elbow on the table. "I suppose." He fixed his gaze on her, and she tried to keep her hands from trembling as she poured a cup of tea for each of them.

Please drink it quickly, Rillaph silently pleaded. *Please don't notice I'm not actually drinking mine.*

The Elevated One grinned, grabbing his cup. Rillaph winced as a good portion of it sloshed over the edge while he lifted it to his mouth, but she melted into her seat as he gulped it all down quickly.

The Elevated's eyes were still fastened on her. She lifted her own cup, and pretended to take a sip.

"It's not right," the Elevated mumbled. "You're too calm."

Rillaph stiffened.

"I- I thou…" The Elevated swayed in his seat. "Thought… you would be distraught… your brother…"

Had he come to… *comfort* her?

The Elevated grabbed the edge of the table and tried to pull himself up. Rillaph jumped up and stepped away, just as another knock sounded at the door, and she looked back at Kama.

"I'll have to answer it," Kama said. "We need to know who it is."

Rillaph nodded, swallowing hard as she turned back to the Elevated One. He had made it to his feet, but still held onto the table. His face was a blotchy red and sweat beaded across his scalp and forehead.

She heard Kama's voice behind her, but couldn't make out the words. The door groaned on its hinges a moment later.

"Y-you… drug-" The Elevated's voice broke as his knees crumbled, the table giving way beneath him. The teapot and cups slammed to the floor with a magnificent shatter. Groaning, he sank the rest of the way to the floor before falling limp, unconscious. Rillaph almost fell to her own knees in relief.

"Lady Taph, it's time," Kama said.

Rillaph turned her head to the door, then scrambled backward at the sight of a guard behind Kama. Her hands flew to her mouth, barely muffling a scream.

"Lady Taph!" Kama glanced back at the guard. "It's all right. He said the passphrase."

Rillaph barely held in a sob, and wondered why she couldn't *breathe*. Her knees finally did give way, and she barely caught herself with her hands. *Oh... my hands. That's why I couldn't breathe.*

"Did he really?" she gasped. "Did he really say it?"

Kama carefully approached Rillaph, and bent down to pull her back up. "He did, Lady Taph."

For just a moment, Rillaph let her eyes fall shut, and she leaned against Kama. When her heart slowed its frantic beating, she took a deep breath, and gathered her wits.

"How long will the tea keep him out?" she asked, gesturing at the Elevated One as Kama motioned the guard toward Taphak's sleeping form.

"Not long enough," Kama answered. "The dose was formulated for a child. It only knocked him out because he was already halfway there. But it's possible the alcohol might keep him out a little longer."

Rillaph groaned, then forced her legs to carry her back across the room. The guard threw back the covers to retrieve Taphak. Rillaph crouched down and pulled the bag and their cloaks back out from under the bed.

"I'll take the bag, and the guard will carry your brother," Kama said. "We'll lead you out of the estate."

* * *

Rillaph thought she knew every secret pathway on the Order's estate, but she apparently did not. Kama led them through winding halls and doors hidden behind tapestries, then through hedges and tree shadows until they reached the short rock wall bordering the Order's land.

The guard handed Taphak to Rillaph, then climbed the wall. It took both Rillaph and Kama to lift Taphak over the stones, then Rillaph scrambled over. Kama handed the leather satchel and Rillaph's bag across.

Rillaph extended her hand to help Kama over the wall, but Kama shook her head, then nodded toward the guard. "He will take you the rest of the way."

Rillaph stilled. "Oh…" She thought Kama would have been taking them all the way to the next meeting point.

"I will make sure any pursuers are delayed as much as they can be, since your escape will now be known long before dawn," she explained, then turned to the guard. "Get them to their escorts as quickly as you can. The woods are treacherous at night, and they'll need as much of a lead as possible."

Kama turned her back to the group and walked away. Rillaph felt impelled to watch as the girl's form faded into the darkness—their escape shouldn't have been known this early. How would Kama walk away unscathed? —but the guard pulled her attention away. "Lady Taph, we must go."

Rillaph pulled her gaze away from the estate, placed the satchel's strap across her shoulder and torso, then retrieved her bag. "I'm ready."

The three traveled as quickly as possible through rocky fields and sparse groves. Only once they reached the edge of the forest, and could no longer see the lighted windows of the now-distant manor, did the guard bring out a firestone torch to light their way. He handed it to Rillaph.

What invisible path the guard followed, Rillaph didn't know. He strode confidently through the trees, which were thankfully far apart from each other still, never pausing when he led her over or around fallen limbs and trunks. Time lost its meaning as she focused solely on not losing sight of the guard, and all sound vanished into the crunch of dead leaves and pine needles beneath her feet.

The forest was just becoming dense when the guard abruptly halted. Rillaph stepped to his side, then froze when she caught sight of two shadowed figures, and nearly dropped the torch. After a moment of quiet stillness, the two figures stepped forward into the light. She couldn't make out their features, but it was obviously two men. They wore animal skin garments, and thick fur hats. Both appeared to be shorter than her. One carried a length of rope looped over his shoulder.

Only one spoke, voice gruff and hoarse. "Let truth kiss me on the path of mercy."

"And love uphold your steps," the guard responded.

Rillaph looked at him curiously. She hadn't been informed of second part to the passphrase, but out of the corner of her eye, she saw the two hunters nod satisfactorily, and at this point there wasn't much she could do if this was a trap. They both stepped forward. The one with the rope held out a hand to Rillaph. She stared at it for a moment, confused, but when she looked up at the hunter, he looked pointedly down at the bag she carried in her arms.

"Ah," she murmured, and handed the bag over. The hunter set it aside and removed the rope from his shoulder. Rillaph stiffened as he stepped close and strung one end around her waist and tied it under the satchel's strap. He took the firestone torch, and for a brief moment, she noticed the other end of the rope was tied around the hunter's waist. There wasn't a lot of slack between them, but enough that it didn't tug at her when the hunter stepped over to the guard and handed back the torch.

"It's likely their escape will be known soon, if it isn't already," the guard said as he transferred Taphak to the other hunter's back. "I will cover our tracks as I return."

"We will cover our own tracks as we move," the hunter carrying Taphak answered. He said no more, just hefted Taphak a little higher, and then vanished into the shadows of the trees on silent footsteps.

Rillaph didn't get a chance to say another word before the second hunter picked up her bag, and tugged at her rope until she followed. She huffed lightly, but forced her irritation aside as the darkness of the forest swallowed them whole, and suddenly the rope made sense. Getting separated would be dangerous, and while the hunters clearly knew how to navigate the forest silently with essentially no moonlight, she did not.

It was the longest night of Rillaph's life as she struggled up the mountainside, in the dark. After the first hour, she lost count of how many times she stubbed her toes on a rock or a root. Eventually, she was just grateful she hadn't run face first into a tree. Most of the time, she had no idea where the hunter carrying Taphak was, but every so often the hunter accompanying her would grab the rope around her waist and bring her to a halt. She could never tell what their signal was, but a glowing firestone would be brought out from wherever they concealed it, and the hunters would trade roles. After too short of a rest, sometimes no more than a few minutes, they would start moving again.

The first sign of morning wasn't even the light suffusing the eastern horizon, as it was barely visible through the treetops. Rather, it was the chitter of birds and the soft snuffle of a squirrel.

But when the sky finally lightened overhead, Rillaph's strength faded away with the darkness. It was dawn. *We made it*, she realized, crumpling to the forest floor.

"The sacrifice will likely take place the dawning day of the new moon," Lapik said while at the inn. "The sacrifice always takes place in the morning. So as long as they are far enough away by dawn of that day, the boy will be safe."

"If we leave too soon, then, they could be easily tracked down and brought back with plenty of time for the sacrifice still take place," Saral murmured. "They'll have to leave the night before, and no sooner. Even if their escape becomes known, as long as they get far enough away, they'll be safe for that day."

Rillaph studied the map spread over the table while Saral and Lapik figured out the timing for their escape. She knew they couldn't go east. Even if going away from the Kashtophim Empire was wiser, it would take weeks instead of days to reach the Sconnelan border.

"Can we go west, to the coast?" Rillaph spoke up in a quiet moment. "We could take a ship out of the reach of both the Empire and Sconnela."

"The coast is too populated, and still too far. A messenger on a fast horse would have you and your brother's sketches to the ports before we even reached the next pass by foot." Saral shook his head. "We usually smuggle slaves out of the Kashtophim Empire. I've never taken a Sconnelan in. But with your status and the sacrifice situation, as soon as your disappearance is discovered, they will begin searching. We must get as far away as we can, as quickly as possible."

Rillaph traced the southern border of Sconnela on the map. Sconnela encompassed the upper heights of the southern edge of the mountain range, because the Kashtophim army had never been able to scale it. On paper, the distance between the Order's estate and the border seemed so short.

"The Elevated One won't try to follow us into Kashtophim territory, will he?" Rillaph asked. It was her one, lingering doubt.

Lapik shook his head. "Not once you're there. Even he knows our military has not recovered from the plague yet."

Rillaph anxiously twisted the Taph crest on its cord around her neck, and Saral gently laid a hand on her shoulder. "I will get you both there safely, Lady Taph. Do not fear."

Taphak groaned, and Rillaph blinked the weariness from her eyes just as the tree beside her... *moved.* Before she could gather breath to scream, she realized it was not bark on the tree, but tattered, dirt-caked cloth. A hand appeared before her face, and Saral's familiar voice greeted her. She hesitated a moment, his silver eyes still throwing her off guard, then grabbed his outstretched hand and let him pull her back to her feet.

"You are safe now, Rillaph," Saral said.

Rillaph groaned and let her head drop with relief. Saral chuckled. Wearily, she stood in place as the passphrase was exchanged again between the hunters and Saral, and the rope was untied from her waist. Her bag was returned, and Taphak was transferred to Saral's arms just as he began to stir from his assisted slumber. Through bleary vision, she saw the hunters say something more to Saral, then they faded into the forest so easily she wondered if they were spirits.

"Come, Rillaph," Saral said. "Just a little further, and then you can rest."

The First of Kishna in the year 3766, by Kashtophim Reckoning

Saral led them further up the mountain until they reached a

rocky clearing above the trees. Taphak had fully woken on the way, and despite the fatigue fogging her mind, Rillaph managed to explain that Saral was a friend, and he was helping them get away from something bad. Eventually, she would have to explain what exactly had happened, but for now, Taphak seemed happy enough to be exploring a new place.

It wasn't yet midday, but Rillaph thought she could sleep for hours despite the brightness of the sun. When Saral guided them to the entrance of a cave, she nearly wept with relief. Not only would she have a chance to rest, but perhaps in the cool darkness of the cave she would actually *sleep*.

As they moved deeper in, Rillaph was surprised to hear the murmur of voices. They rounded a bend, and a cavern opened up. Firelight reflected from the walls. Rillaph tried to see how many people were present as her eyes adjusted to the dim lighting, but her eyes fell on two more men with the same silver eyes as Saral. *More Rishka*, she thought, suppressing a shudder.

Saral led her to a quiet corner, and Taphak settled beside her. Saral began speaking with the others. Even as her eyes fell shut, she strained to hear his words, but exhaustion won.

* * *

Taphak's laughter roused Rillaph several hours later, and she scrambled up in panic. *The sacrifice! I must keep him safe!* Her thoughts swirled, and then she realized she wasn't in the Order's manor.

It was dim, and there were voices, and… *that's right. Saral brought us to a cave.*

Sighing, she rubbed the rest of the sleep from her eyes, and brushed back the tendrils of hair that had tangled in her sleep.

She looked around the cavern from the safety of her shadowed corner, but her stomach grumbled loudly and gave away her wakefulness as she realized she could smell *food*. Taphak ate enthusiastically near the fire.

She stepped out of the shadows, and Saral appeared at her side with a bowl of what appeared to be some sort of fried vegetable and chunks of meat. "Thank you," she whispered, then took the dish, checking the temperature with her fingers before she popped a piece of meat in her mouth.

"It's late afternoon," Saral said. "If we leave soon, we can make it through the caves and over the peak before dark. It would be best if we could make it to the timberline before nightfall. We won't be able to travel deeply into the trees, since we have no moonlight tonight. From there, we'll travel when it's safest—whether by daylight or moonlight."

Rillaph nodded as she swallowed her food, then asked, "Were we followed?"

"It doesn't appear so."

She didn't have words to express her relief, so she shoveled more food in her mouth.

"Come, I'll introduce you to the others."

The Fifth of Kishna in the year 3766, by Kashtophim Reckoning

On the fourth day, Saral announced that he, Rillaph, and Taphak would be separating from the main group. The other two Rishka had already headed in another direction that morning.

"My people will shelter you for a time," Saral explained to Rillaph. Lapik lit another lamp and brought it over, and the three seated themselves at the table in the sitting room. "If you wish, we will help you resettle into the Kashtophim Empire."

249

"Aren't they trying to kill you?" Rillaph asked, eyes wide. "How would you even do that?"

"Not all of our youth choose to remain among the Rishka," Saral said. "We don't cast them out with no chance of survival. There are those who help them become citizens. They will do the same for you and Taphak."

Rillaph slipped away from the group while Saral prepared an actual meal—the first since they'd been in the caves—after he stated that they were deep enough into the wilderness that no one would notice a small fire.

She walked far enough into the woods where she could still hear chattering voices, but not see the others. Taphak's laughter rang out loud and clear over them all, and she smiled gratefully. She had been so close to never hearing that laugh again…

A few paces ahead, she noticed a fallen tree. The trunk looked sturdy and easy to reach, and a few moments later she pulled herself up onto it. It was high enough off the ground that she could swing her feet, and she let them dangle as she finally retrieved Lapik's letter from her pocket.

The paper had become soft, almost crumpled, during travel. The corners were bent. One edge of the wax seal was crumbling. The letter wasn't thick, just one sheet of paper folded in on itself. She slid her fingers under the flap to break the seal.

"Rillaph?"

She yelped, twisting in her seat as she pressed a hand to her pounding heart. The letter slipped from her fingers and fluttered to the ground.

"I'm sorry, I didn't mean to frighten you," the intruder said. Rillaph recognized him as the one smuggler who had been rather aloof. She couldn't recall his name at all. His standoffishness hadn't bothered her before, but now there was a hard set to his face that made her pause. Suddenly, she wished she wasn't alone.

Quickly, she swung her legs back over the fallen tree, ready to hop down. The man continued to approach, and she clenched her skirts in her fists as she straightened her spine, sitting as tall as she could. He stepped closer, bent down to retrieve her letter, and handed it back with a flourish as he eyed the seal.

Rillaph's stomach twisted into a knot. She grabbed the letter from his hand, ignoring how it crumpled as she shoved it in her pocket again.

He scrutinized her face. His gaze fell lower, lips twisting into a condescending sneer. "Lady Taph."

A cold sweat broke out across the back of her neck. Her other hand flew to the collar of her dress, and the cool metal of her crest met her fingers. *Who is he? What does he want?*

"I'm not exactly a Sconnelan noble anymore, sir...?" Her voice was soft, but she was relieved it didn't falter.

He stepped closer, bumping her knees as he leaned in. "It doesn't really matter what you call me. What matters is that you listen to what I say."

Her hand wrapped around the Taph crest, the edges of the medallion biting at her palm.

"It doesn't really matter, either," he continued, "that you're *not exactly a Sconnelan noble anymore*. What matters is that you are *Sconnelan*, and you're about to cross into the territory of the Kashtophim Empire, accompanied by a *Rishka*."

Rillaph cringed as he hacked and spat at her feet. "Why does that matter to *you*?"

"Ah, that's because I'm a Kalan in service to the Empire."

Rillaph felt the blood drain from her head. Back before the plague, she'd studied some about the Kashtophim military, in preparation for her confirmation as an heir. The Sconnelan equivalent would be… a captain. He wasn't high-ranking, then, but still part of the chain of command, and probably looking for a promotion.

"It's my duty to cleanse the Empire of any filth that doesn't belong in our society," the Kalan said. "And you're going to help me, unless you want to see Lapik of Haka branded as a traitor to Sconnela."

Rillaph swayed where she sat. The Kalan grabbed her arms to keep her from sliding off the tree trunk, and she stiffened at his touch.

"Why should I believe your threat?" she whispered. "There's no proof that Lapik of Haka had anything to do with our escape."

The Kalan laughed. "Foolish woman. Do you truly think the Kashtophim don't have spies in the noble houses? Or even among the Order?"

Rillaph's mouth went dry. "You have someone close to Lord Haka," she whispered, horrified. That someone likely had evidence ready to plant.

"As close as we need," the Kalan confirmed. "We'll know if you try to warn him, too."

* * *

Rillaph was still trembling half an hour after the Kalan left her alone. When she tried to climb down from the tree, her knees gave out, and she crumpled into a heap on the forest floor.

When she finally found the strength to stand, she jerked the Taph crest over her head and threw it deep into the underbrush.

* * *

By the time Rillaph calmed herself enough to return, only one other smuggler besides the Kalan remained. It was obvious Saral and the other smugglers had traveled together several times before. Rillaph found the group to be fairly amiable, but she hadn't particularly cared to socialize with people she wouldn't even have the chance to know.

Rillaph's mouth twisted in disgust as she watched the Kalan chat with Saral, a deep camaraderie obvious in their mannerisms.

"Rilla!" Taphak dashed over to her and held up a piece of bark. "You missed breakfast. I saved you some."

She blinked, trying to clear her vision of a fog that wasn't real. After a minute, she realized the bark held berries, roasted bird eggs, and a couple slices of smoked sausage.

"Thanks, Taph," she reached out to ruffle his hair, but pulled her hand back when it wouldn't stop shaking. "Will you hang onto it for me for a bit?"

"Sure."

Rillaph crossed the small clearing to retrieve her cloak, then knelt and made sure their bags were securely shut. She glanced up to see Saral move over to the final smuggler. The Kalan's eyes met hers as he retrieved his own bags, and she heard his voice in her mind as she recalled his earlier words.

"You have until the new moon after the next to inform me of the location of the Rishka settlement. If I haven't received your letter by then, Lapik of Haka will be framed as a Kashtophim spy."

"Why can't you find the settlement yourself? Saral seems to like you."

The Kalan laughed. "The Rishka will never reveal their settlements to a Kashtophim citizen, no matter how friendly they might be. I've tried to get close for many years. But you... you and your brother have somehow been offered passage straight there."

Rillaph's breath grew erratic and her vision blurred. Had she really jumped from one nightmare right into another?

"Really, though," the Kalan continued, "I should thank the Order... and you. If they hadn't made your brother into a sacrifice, then who knows how long it would have been before we could find the Rishka. It's the only reason why only Lord Haka would be punished as a spy, and not you and your brother as well."

The Kalan's hands tightened around her arms, but the pain was barely noticeable. "Don't think I won't be able to find you after you've forged your citizenship," the Kalan hissed. "Your options now, as a Sconnelan refugee, are to become a Rishka and shelter among them—in which case your days are numbered anyway—or to join the Empire. But if you want Lord Haka to continue living well, then heed my words.

"The Kashtophim Empire may seem cruel, but the Sconnelan treatment of traitors is downright barbaric compared to what we do. Make sure you allow time for the letter to actually arrive at my post."

"Rilla!" Taphak's voice pulled her back to the present. She flinched. The Kalan smirked, then turned and started down another path that seemed like little more than a deer trail to her. "Rilla, I found a toad!"

"Did you?" Rillaph murmured. "And what did you do with it?"

"I left it where it was," Taphak pouted. "Even though I wanted to make you scream again."

Rillaph huffed and gave a weak smile, though her eyes were glued on the Kalan. When his back finally disappeared from view, she let out a sigh of relief. The last smuggler followed a moment later.

Paper crinkled in both her pockets as she stood again, and her smile quickly faded. The Kalan had given her the address for his post. She wished she had the courage to burn it without even reading it. And she hadn't dared to defile Lapik's letter by putting it in the same pocket.

Saral was smiling when he returned to Rillaph and Taphak. "Come," he said. "We've another week of travel ahead of us, at a much lighter pace. If we press hard, we can do it in five days, but by now, even if you were followed, they won't catch up to us, not in this terrain. There's no point in wearing you or the boy out needlessly."

"We appreciate the thought," Rillaph attempted to smile, but it felt more like a grimace. She watched as the Rishka man swung Taphak up onto his shoulders. Taphak was too heavy to stay up there for long, but his laughter rang through the forest, and for a moment Rillaph thought she was watching their father play with him.

Will you truly send this man to his death? Guilt prodded at her. She could... she could tell him everything. That a man he thought was a friend had demanded she betray him and his people. But her hand slid into her skirt pocket again, fingering Lapik's letter.

I can't turn Lapik into a traitor, though. Not since he was the one who made our safety possible.

* * *

For the remaining days of travel, Rillaph attempted to push the Kalan from her mind. She tried reading Lapik's letter, but

255

every time she brought it out, she was reminded of the Kalan's threat, and she would hide it away again.

The Rishka were the only other thing she could turn her mind to. The Sconnelans ridiculed them often, but mostly because they found them pitiful. The Rishka were pacifists. When they stood back and let the Kashtophim trample them, it seemed to the Sconnelans that there was nothing the Rishka valued about themselves. Nothing they deemed worthy of protection.

But her curiosity overcame her now, since she actually had the chance to converse with a Rishka. The fact that their people were willing to endanger themselves to protect someone else… she was grateful, but still not sure what to make of their intentions.

"Do you have a family?" she asked one morning as Saral guided them along the edge of a small stream. Taphak kept running into the current and splashing water back at them. Rillaph had long given up on trying to keep dry. At least the days were still above freezing, though they were cooling off quickly.

"I do," Saral answered. "My wife and I have been blessed with twin sons, about Taphak's age. We also have a two-year-old daughter."

"Twins?" Rillaph gasped. "Twins are almost unheard of in Sconnela. It's rare for them to survive till birth, let alone through their first year of life."

"As I said, we are blessed." The fondness in Saral's voice was nearly palpable. "Lita, my wife, almost died delivering them. The midwife said more children after them would be impossible, but Sachi surprised us all."

"Sachi is your daughter? What do you call your sons?"

Saral chuckled. "Nightmares."

Rillaph laughed.

"Their names are Sanich and Sanil."

* * *

"Why do you not defend yourselves against the Kashtophim?" Rillaph asked over supper the next night. It was a *hot* supper, even.

"We follow the Kveres' will," Saral answered as he carefully fished another *tonoga* root from the hot coals.

"Why do your people cling to the Kveres?" Rillaph blurted out. "They seem like powerless gods. Surely whatever favors they grant you is worth very little when compared to the lives of your people."

Even Taphak eyed her then, and she dropped her roasted *tonoga* in her lap as she ducked her head in embarrassment. Saral was silent for a few minutes. When Rillaph dared to look up again, she shivered at the sight of his silver eyes. She'd seen them glimmering in the moonlight before, but they didn't reflect the orange firelight like she expected them to. It was just a steady, silver light.

She'd met his gaze, fully, once before—that night in the inn. The shock of the mere *presence* of a Rishka had been tempered by Lapik's presence, but now… now it was her and Taphak and this man, alone in the wilderness. Where he could easily abandon them if she offended him.

Her heart raced. *If he abandons us, Lapik's fate is sealed.* "I'm sorry," she whispered. "Please don't take offense. The turmoil of the last couple weeks has made me forget my manners."

Saral's mouth tightened, but he glanced away. A sigh escaped her when his scrutiny ended. She retrieved the *tonoga* root she dropped earlier, and hesitantly started pulling the rough skin away from the soft flesh.

"If the Kveres is so powerless," Saral's voice was low and quiet with reverence, "how come the Kveres answered your pleas, instead of the mountain gods?"

Rillaph found herself speechless, then blushed a moment later when Taphak muttered under his breath, "You're in *fine* form tonight, Rilla."

"You're the one leading us to safety, not your strange gods," Rillaph mumbled before stuffing *tonoga* in her mouth. *Just stop talking. You're making a fool of yourself.*

"The Kveres is not *gods*," Saral's stare pinned her from across the fire again. "And everything I do represents the Kveres."

The *tonoga* seemed to turn dry in her mouth as she tried to chew and swallow it. Taphak's curiosity merged with her own, though, and he spoke up before she was able to. "Not gods?" her brother chimed in. "Then why do you say *the Kveres*? Wouldn't that *be* gods?"

"It is not our right to define the Kveres. The Kveres is revealed in the manner most suited to the individual."

Rillaph fell asleep that night with far more questions than she'd ever had before.

The Twelfth of Kishna in the year 3766, by Kashtophim Reckoning

"There." Saral pointed out flickering lights below them as dusk settled over the foothills after they'd found a spot to stop for the night. "We'll be home by suppertime tomorrow."

"Ah," Rillaph sighed, not sure what to feel at the moment. When the journey began, she had expected relief. Relief to be away from Sconnela, away from the risk of Taphak being sacrificed. There was still *some* relief... but it was muted by dread. *Can I... really do this?*

The settlement seemed surprisingly small, but Rillaph couldn't tell how high they were above it in the fading light. They were on a rock ledge that jutted out from the mountains. A portion of the cliff face curved in, but not deep enough to be called a cave. It was almost cozy.

"How many settlements are there?" Rillaph asked as she divided up the last of the smoked meat and cheese. It wasn't like she would singlehandedly wipe the Rishka out, after all. They'd survived for centuries... the Rishka would still be there long after she, Saral, and Taphak died from old age.

Saral was silent for so long she wondered if he hadn't heard her. Taphak was falling asleep where he sat next to her, and she nudged him with her elbow before handing him his food. "Eat this, then sleep," she whispered. She passed the third portion over to Saral. He was standing, leaning against the mountainside, eyes glued to the settlement below.

She was nibbling on a lump of stale cheese when Saral finally spoke, his tone grim. "Last year, there were at least five. Currently, I know of only two others besides mine."

Saral's shoulders rounded and his head drooped. Rillaph's hand fell from her mouth as she stilled. She didn't dare breathe. She didn't deserve to.

"We hadn't heard from one settlement in months when I left for this trip. It's too dangerous now for our people to assemble for the holy days. But the last time we could... there were less than a thousand of us."

Three settlements remain. You may very well wipe them out. Rillaph set aside her remaining food. She would save it for Taphak for breakfast. Her stomach was in knots, and her appetite was gone.

"What about the other Rishka who traveled with us?" she whispered.

"They were from one of the destroyed settlements," Saral answered. "Some of the only survivors. Once, we would have invited them to join the remaining groups, but the risk of being tracked by the Kashtophim is too high. Now, the survivors disperse."

* * *

The first snowflakes drifted through the trees the afternoon they approached the settlement, and winter established its hold on the foothills not long after.

Rillaph hadn't expected Saral and his family to welcome them under their roof, but they had, and she was grateful. The small, two-room hut—most of the Rishka homes were made of sticks and mud with thatch roofs—was humble and crowded, yet warm and peaceful. Taphak got along well with Saral's sons, and Lita welcomed a second set of hands in their home.

What struck her the most, though, was that the *children's* eyes were all like hers and Taphak's. *So they aren't born with silver eyes, after all.*

Rillaph easily fell into the rhythm of the Rishka's communal life, and for a time, she let herself completely forget the outside world. In some ways, it was similar to her life in the Order. The physical work occupied her senses and dulled her thoughts. Cooking, laundry, sewing; everything was done together from dawn to dusk, then each family returned to their own homes for the evening meal and to retire for the night.

There were less than a hundred families in the settlement.

Few enough that she knew nearly all of them by their family names within a week. One elderly woman in particular reminded Rillaph of her long-dead grandmother. Soon it was a morning habit for Rillaph to make sure grandmother had a hot breakfast and that she didn't fall on any icy patches as they visited from house to house.

"Rillaph?" Grandmother asked one morning, her hand wrapped around Rillaph's elbow as they walked together a few days after the full moon. "What weight is your soul carrying?"

The question caught her off guard. *Guilt. Dread at what I must do to save the man I love. To save myself and my brother.* She couldn't say that, though. Somehow, she managed to smile, but her voice wavered. "Just the cares of life, Grandmother."

Rillaph had pondered, many times now, if she dared to let Lapik die. It wasn't like she would see him again. They had no hope of a future together... and yet, even in Sconnela, when every living moment had been dark and weary as she adjusted to life as a penniless orphan, knowing that Lapik was alive and safe had brought her the strength and comfort she needed.

How would she live if his death had been something she could prevent?

Grandmother's steps slowed, and Rillaph matched her pace. The ground was frozen under their feet, though it was still early in the day. It would thaw, at least some, by afternoon.

"Rillaph." Grandmother's voice was firm, but Rillaph didn't want to look at her. If she looked her in the eye, who knew what she might confess.

She heard Grandmother sigh, and the woman's hand stroked her arm gently. "You can find peace here."

Rillaph twisted her head away, blinking back tears. "I don't think it's my fate to know peace of any sort."

* * *

Though Rillaph always refused, Saral and Lita invited her and Taphak to every worship ritual and spiritual gathering. The first time, Rillaph found herself a few moments to be truly alone while Taphak napped, and she finally pulled out Lapik's letter.

The once-crisp paper was now wrinkled and soft in her hands from weeks spent in her pocket. The wax seal had crumbled completely, leaving just a stain behind. Slowly, she unfolded the letter.

There was no salutation, no names. Not even hers. The wax seal would have been the only thing to identify the sender. She was relieved it was gone now… and unsure of why Lapik had put it on the letter in the first place. Perhaps from habit, or perhaps as a final reassurance, that last night, that Rillaph could trust him.

I have wanted to see your face again for so long. It saddens me that as soon as we are reunited, we must part again, most likely forever.

When our courtship began, I never dreamed our paths would diverge so much. I wish we could talk face to face and learn why our paths were brought back together, even for this brief moment.

May truth kiss you on the path of mercy, and love uphold your steps.

L.

Her hands began to shake. *Lapik of Haka, what are you? Why did you end the letter like this? Are you Rishka? But you can't be… your eyes weren't silver.*

The letter fell from her fingers. As she bent to pick it up, a second piece of paper—just as worn as Lapik's letter—fluttered to the floor.

The Kalan's threats, she remembered, her breath catching. She pressed her hands to her mouth to muffle her sudden sobs. *Don't wake Taphak,* she chanted silently. *Don't wake him.*

She heard the Kalan's words over and over in her sleep that night.

Don't think I won't be able to find you after you've forged your citizenship.

The Twelfth of Hagna in the year 3767, by Kashtophim Reckoning

"The citizenship papers are ready for you and Taphak," Saral said as they settled in for dinner on one of the coldest nights yet. "It's a few days' journey to the nearest town, and you and Taphak will need to go with me to verify them."

Rillaph's hands began to tremble. She quickly shoved them into her lap under the table. Hopefully, her voice wouldn't waver as she spoke. "When do we leave?"

"Can you be ready in the morning?" Saral asked.

"Yes."

Rillaph couldn't sleep that night. She and Saral had discussed what the next step would be for her and Taphak after their papers were ready. He had never told her they would not be welcome there, but if she was not going to convert, it made no sense for her and Taphak to remain. Not when the Rishka lived in hiding.

It hadn't taken long for her to pack up all their possessions. She'd made a point of not accumulating much of anything after their arrival. She didn't know if Rishka handiwork was significantly different from Kashtophim-crafted items, and there was no point in taking anything with them that might compromise their new identities. She had convinced Taphak to leave behind the toys he'd been gifted by Saral's children. The carved horse she'd bought in Sconnela was still hidden in their travel bag. She would console Taphak with it later.

They will have no use for those if they're all going to be dead soon, her heart whispered. *You're trading the lives of a hundred innocent families for Lapik. For your brother.*

"Lapik will be able to help more people if he's alive," she muttered into her pillow, trying to console her guilt. "He is worth it..."

The Thirteenth of Hagna in the year 3767, by Kashtophim Reckoning

Rillaph slipped back into the routine of covert travel far more easily than she expected, though it was more miserable with snow on the ground. On the first night of the journey, after a light supper of dried fish stew and Taphak was tucked into his blankets, Rillaph again asked the question that had lingered in her mind since she met Saral.

"Why do your people cling to the Kveres?"

Rillaph sat on the ground, knees pulled up to her chin, and a blanket wrapped around her. Saral watched her as he stoked the fire, his strange silver eyes glinting in the darkness. She should have been used to the sight, but still couldn't suppress a shiver.

"Do you truly wish to know?" His voice was low, solemn.

Her chest tightened as she met his gaze, and she wondered if... if she came to truly understand why the Rishka wouldn't give up the Kveres at any cost... she might not be able to save Lapik after all.

Don't sympathize, she silently steeled herself. *Just learn. They are just as human as you are, no matter what they believe. If you can give them up now to save Lapik, you can still give them up after you know more.*

"Yes," she leaned in. "Tell me."

"Your mountain gods—and your cave goddess, Aosca," Saral spoke quietly to avoid waking Taphak. "Have you ever encountered them? Walked and talked with them, face to face?"

"Of course not," she tilted her head. What sort of question was that? "They are gods. They are benevolent enough to look upon us occasionally. The Elevated, and others consecrated into the Order, are the mountain gods' voices to us."

She felt sick with how easily those words slipped off her tongue. She'd rarely prayed to them before, and had stopped entirely after the sacrifice incident. Why was she defending them as if she had ever truly believed?

Saral shifted, moving from a crouch to sit cross-legged at the far side of the fire. "Among the Rishka… when we come of age, we make a choice. Whether to serve the Kveres or not. Those who do not wish to are let go, most of them swearing allegiance to the Kashtophim Empire. Some move to Sconnela, since it's slightly easier to become a citizen there even if one has Rishka parents.

"For those who wish to remain, there is a ritual each individual completes. We call it the Naming, but not because our names change: rather, because we meet the Kveres face to face, and learn the Kveres name."

"The… *Kveres* isn't a name?" Rillaph pulled the blanket a little tighter around her shoulders as a breeze wafted through their campsite.

"Forgive the simple example," Saral answered, "But is your name Lady Taph?"

Well… in a sense it was, but she understood what he was

trying to explain. Rillaph may be Lady Taph, but her mother had also been Lady Taph, and her grandmother before that.

"So it's a title," she nodded decisively.

"Close enough," Saral chuckled. "The Naming is also when our eyes change."

"You won't tell me anymore about the Naming, will you?" she mumbled. She was tired, and the sound of the crackling fire was soothing, but she doubted she would sleep that night.

Saral raised his eyebrows. "Are you interested in converting?"

Rillaph quickly shook her head.

"Then no, I will not tell you more," Saral confirmed. "Not because the Naming is secret, but because of the reverence the ceremony demands."

Rillaph turned her gaze to the fire, unsure if she should ask any more questions. Her thoughts wandered back to her original curiosity. She gave a heavy sigh, still unsatisfied with Saral's answer. "Are the Kveres truly worth your life? Or the lives of your children?"

Saral was silent again. After long moments, Rillaph pulled her gaze away from the fire to check if he'd somehow fallen asleep where he sat. What she saw would stay engraved in her memory for the rest of her life.

Saral still sat, cross-legged, across the fire from her. His head was bowed, eyes closed, shoulders relaxed, and hands resting on his knees. He almost looked as if he were asleep, but she could see his lips forming silent words. A soft, silver glow radiated from him. Not from his eyes, but from *him*. Rillaph's eyes widened. She looked up to see if the clouds had dispersed, but she couldn't see the moon or stars.

He is praying, she realized. When she looked back at him, though, the glow had vanished, and he was watching her with a gentle look.

"You risked everything to get Taphak out of Sconnela because you love him, did you not?" Saral asked.

Rillaph's gaze strayed to where Taphak slept, safe and sound. "Yes," she whispered around the sudden lump in her throat. "I would give my life for him." Silently, she added, *I would forsake my conscience for him.*

"To know the Kveres is to love the Kveres," Saral stated simply. Rillaph looked back at Saral, and found herself speechless at the indescribable depth of emotion in his eyes.

As she silently pondered what she'd seen and learned, the fire burned low, fading into glowing coals.

"You love the Kveres so deeply that you would give up everything," Rillaph spoke much later. There was the barest tinge of bitterness to her voice. "Your homes and livelihood, your lives… even your families. But do the Kveres love you that much? Have they ever given up everything for the Rishka? For you?"

"How do you know the Kveres hasn't?"

The Fifteenth of Hagna in the year 3767, by Kashtophim Reckoning

Rillaph waited with Taphak by a fireplace in a house on the outskirts of the first Kashtophim town she'd ever seen, in the middle of the night. Saral looked over the documents on a nearby table. When he motioned her over, she whispered to Taphak, "Stay right here; don't move out of the light." Taphak nodded, and she went to see what Saral had to say.

"You can read Kash, correct?" Saral handed her two paper booklets and a small pouch of coins. Everything she and Taphak needed to start their new lives.

"Yes," she confirmed. "All the Sconnelan nobles are taught it. Our spoken languages are very similar as well, so we should be able to blend in as long as I can get Taphak to mimic the accents here."

Saral nodded. "Your names have been altered, both to keep you hidden from any Sconnelans who might try to find you, and to make them sound more like Kashtophim names."

Rillaph checked the papers. She was now Rillana, and Taphak had become Taxen. This might be the hardest part for her brother to understand, but she would make him do so. Somehow.

"Make sure you memorize all the information here," Saral said. "If you can, travel to the hometown listed for you, so you know something about it."

He continued to talk. Rillaph tried to store away as much of his advice in her mind as she could. She wouldn't get the opportunity to ask him again, no matter what happened.

How many more of Rishka youth will travel this path? she wondered. *How many more of their youth will there even be?*

When her attention returned to the present, Saral was silent. He watched her closely, and she wondered if he was waiting for a response, then realized he was looking back and forth between her and Taphak. There was a sheen to his eyes, unrelated to the silver glow.

"It has been a joy to shelter you and your brother," Saral said suddenly. "I hope, wherever your path leads next, you find peace."

Rillaph's eyes filled with tears as she thought of his wife and children back in the settlement, and the generosity they had shown her and Taphak.

"Yours as well," was all she managed to choke out, then

she called Taphak over. "Say goodbye, and thank you," she whispered and crossed the room. She didn't look back until Saral left. If she looked back, she would break. If she looked back... she would warn him about the Kalan, and she knew Saral well enough now to know that he wouldn't just save his family... he would try to save the whole settlement.

The Kalan would not spare Lapik for an abandoned settlement.

A serving girl, not too much older than Taphak, escorted them to a bedroom for the rest of the night.

The following morning, Rillana used three silver coins to pay a messenger to take a letter to the Kalan.

* * *

Diligent serving girls were apparently in demand no matter what country one lived in, and Rillana found employment and housing fairly quickly. While the first couple of estates where she applied weren't pleased she brought a child in tow, the third hadn't cared.

Settling into their new life had, so far, provided sufficient distraction from her guilt. Taphak—*Taxen*, she reminded herself. *His name is Taxen now, and I am Rillana.* —had asked after his Rishka playmates for the first several days, but that had ceased when... well...

"I don't want to do my lessons!" Taxen shrieked, as he had every night since they'd moved into this manor. "I want to play with Sanich and Sanil!"

A wave of heat washed over Rillana, so intense it felt like she stood next to a bonfire and the wind had suddenly shifted it her way, and then she found the heat traveling down her arm and into her hand. A part of her watched, horrified, as her palm connected with Taxen's cheek, his head twisting as the smack resounded through the room.

Taxen's eyes widened with shock and pain. "Rilla…" he gasped.

Briefly, she saw the red imprint of her hand on his face before he covered it with one of his own.

"Stop asking about them!" Rillana hissed as her stomach twisted, but she couldn't stop yet. He *had* to stop asking about the Rishka. It was too dangerous. "You won't see them again. By the *Nine,* I wish you'd forget that they ever existed!"

What have you done? her heart tormented her. She spun around, hanging her head in shame. "I'm sorry, Taxen."

The next morning, she gave him the carved horse.

The Thirty-First of Hagna in the year 3767, by Kashtophim Reckoning

One morning, the proclamation came for the public execution of the largest roundup of Rishka in a decade, and everyone in town was… *encouraged* to attend. Rillana managed to keep Taxen back at the house. He'd been running a slight fever again, and one of the elderly servants was allowed to stay back and tend to him.

Though it was still winter, the sun had come out a few days before and melted much of the snow. Rillana trailed behind the other servants, her stomach churning and threatening to revolt with every step.

It was the longest and shortest walk she'd ever taken.

She'd heard of Kashtophim executions, particularly the executions of the Rishka. In Sconnela, people often scoffed at the descriptions. Surely it was exaggerated, right? There was no need for them to go that far, especially against pacifists.

But when they reached the town square, she saw the throng of people waiting around the edges, and then the group of Rishka tied up in the center. She felt faint.

The crowd around her hummed with the frenzy of those hungry for blood. It was the same bloodlust she'd felt in the air that night in the Elevated One's dining hall, when he'd claimed the mountain gods hungered for a sacrifice.

Frantically, she scanned the faces of the Rishka. She'd given away their location, yes, but she knew that they took some precautions. They guarded themselves and posted patrols, even if they were pacifists.

There were only about twenty Rishka there, she realized. At first, she felt relief at not seeing Saral or his family. Then one face caught her eye.

Grandmother.

She couldn't stay. Rillana spun around, elbowing her way through the crowd, and tried to run. But when she broke away from the throng, she found herself face to face with the Kalan.

Several soldiers stood in file behind him, but the Kalan grabbed her elbow and pulled her aside before motioning for the soldiers to continue on. He waited for them to pass by before he leaned in close to her.

"Consider it another token of my gratitude that I will ignore your absence at the execution, Lady Taph," he whispered. "Since your information means I will be a Kazash after today."

Rillana paled, but found the strength to meet the Kalan's eyes. "You've mistaken me for someone else, Kalan," her voice was little more than a whisper, but in that moment, she was pleased to be speaking at all. "I've never heard of Lady Taph."

The Kalan snorted and let her have her worthless pride. "Begone, woman. No matter your name, you still have my gratitude."

The Kalan released her arm and strode into the crowd. Somehow, she found her feet, and began to run.

The screams started just as she made it out of town. Her legs crumpled, mouth and throat burning as she retched.

* * *

For the next month, guilt ate at Rillana's soul whenever her mind stilled. Even Taxen's antics couldn't bring a smile to her face. He started sleeping in the stables, so she wouldn't continually wake him with her nightmares.

Was it truly worth it? she pondered in the darkest hours of the night. *Would Lapik have wanted them to be sacrificed for his sake? Would Taxen hate me if he knew the playmates he adored might be dead because of my actions?*

But still… when she thought of Taxen being sacrificed for the mountain gods, instead of living, she found a little strength to persevere.

The First of Lishka in the year 3767, by Kashtophim Reckoning

On the first night of spring, Rillana woke with a jolt as the screams rang through her mind again. The worst dreams were the ones where Taxen was somehow trapped among the Rishka prisoners, and she couldn't reach him to save him.

She clutched her legs, trying to muffle her sobs against her knees. A shadow moved into the darkness of her room.

"Was it you?" Saral's voice shattered the silence, though he spoke softly. "Was it you who sent the Kashtophim?"

For a moment, Rillana wondered if she was dreaming or haunted by a ghost, but Saral stepped into the light cast by her fireplace and pushed the hood of his cloak back. His face was normal, human, and etched with a grief that seemed a thousand years old; not torn to shreds or dripping blood like the Rishka—or Taxen—in her dreams.

She could not find her voice to answer, dropping her head in shame.

"May truth kiss me on the path of mercy," Saral spoke. "Do you know what it means?'

She shook her head.

"We have another saying," he continued. "Truth is like a sword: will you learn from the flat of the blade, or the cutting edge?"

That one was easier to understand. She knew she'd, somehow, ended up on the harsh road. She would only learn truth now when it cut her to the bone.

"The truth is brutal, Rillaph. But the blow can be softened through love, when one desires to change. That is mercy."

She found her voice at last, but only enough to whisper. "Can it truly? Truth is still truth. A blow, whether soft or to kill, is still violence."

Saral didn't answer.

Rillana looked up to see if he was still there, and he was. He watched her closely. When their eyes met, she didn't look away, though the strange silver gleam of his eyes still made her shiver.

"I am sorry," she whispered.

"I know," he answered. "It's the only reason I'm here. I know you were threatened. It is not the first time we have watched those we helped betray us."

Bile burned in her throat, but she forced it back with a

273

swallow. *What have I done?*

"Is Taphak well?" Saral asked.

Rillana nodded. She didn't ask if Lita or the children had escaped. She didn't deserve to know. But... surely the Kashtophim wouldn't execute children, would they? Or an infant?

They would, her heart whispered. *It's not a sacrifice twice within a century. They are committing genocide.*

Saral stepped up next to her bed and rested his hand on her shoulder. "Do not let guilt destroy you," he said. "Repentance and atonement can only come after guilt, and only if you're still alive."

Rillana shook her head. "I do not deserve atonement."

"None of us do, but it is still offered."

"How can you even stand to look at me?" she gasped, twisting away from his hand and toppling out of bed at the action. "To talk to me?"

"Because there are two kinds of people who betray their friends," Saral answered as he circled around the bed and knelt beside her. "Those who were never truly a friend in the first place, and those who believe they have no other choice. I could not believe you were the former, and I am glad to know I was right."

Of course he is right, she realized as broken sobs escaped her. *It wouldn't hurt if I hadn't cared.*

"What does it matter when you will all die anyway?" she moaned brokenly, leaning her head against the side of the bed. "What does any of this matter if your people are destroyed?"

"That is not in our hands. It is not in *your* hands. It is up to the will of the Kveres."

"Why did you save us?" Rillana whispered later, as she drifted

274

back into sleep. "It would have been better for us to die in Sconnela."

Something—a hand? Blanket? —brushed against her shoulder. Silence settled over the room for a long moment.

Saral's voice was soft. "Because the Kveres told me to."

If she hadn't still been on the floor in the morning, she would have thought it was all a dream.

May your heart be at peace, Saral's voice whispered through her mind, a fragment of a memory from when she drifted in and out of slumber in the night. *We surrendered our fate to the Kveres long ago. Do not be so proud as to think that you alone are strong enough to change the path the Kveres has laid for us to walk.*

"I envy their peace," Rillana whispered to the empty room.

Blessed are they that are persecuted for righteousness' sake
For theirs is the kingdom of heaven

Rebekah Loper

R ebekah Loper, author of "The Path of Mercy," began creating fictional worlds and magical stories as a child and never stopped. Now she also helps inspire others to write their stories through her volunteer work as a NaNoWriMo Municipal Liaison, and with her workbook, The A-Zs of Worldbuilding: Building a Fictional World From Scratch.

Rebekah lives in Tulsa, Oklahoma with her husband, a dog, two formerly feral cats, a flock of chickens, and an extensive tea collection. She is often found battling the elements in an effort to create a productive, permaculture urban homestead on a shoestring budget.

She blogs about writing and urban homesteading at rebekahloper.com, and has been a contributing writer for Fantasy-Faction.com. You can follow her on Facebook (facebook.com/RebekahLoper), Instagram (rebekah.loper), and Twitter (rebekah_loper)

Hopefire

"*The mountain dreams of things to come, and I see the path ahead of you. Be careful, Airhead! Remember, I'm with you even through the flames...*"

"What's your name, pretty one?"

Airian rolled her eyes at the drunken ruffian who'd approached her table in the corner of the roadside inn. Couldn't she ever have a moment of quiet to herself? "None of your business."

The leathery-faced man, who she assumed was a hunter by his rustic vest and mottled green hood, clapped a meaty hand on her shoulder. "You wouldn't happen to be Airian of Aeflerwood, would you?"

She flinched and shoved his hand away. "Who? Nah, you must be thinking of someone else." She looked into her mug and sloshed the lukewarm tea inside, desperately trying to remain nonchalant even though her heart pounded. How did he know her name? She risked a glance up at his face, hoping to glean some clue about him.

His eyes instantly narrowed. Ah. Perhaps he wasn't as drunk as she'd first thought. "No, you are the one we're looking for!"

We? The door of the inn slammed open, and she peered around him to see seven more hunters pour into the rustic dining area. *Wurmpoop.*

She stood up and took a step toward the stairs.

Leatherface cut her off. "Where y'going, Airian?"

"Shut up," she murmured, keeping her eyes turned down. Maybe if these humans hadn't seen their telltale violet, she could get away without too much fuss. Her pointed ears were still hidden beneath her hood, as usual. Perhaps they had no knowledge of her true background. There was still a chance she could get out of this if she stayed quiet. She turned away from the hunter and found herself surrounded on three sides. The corner of the room was at her back. Great.

Leatherface sneered to his companions. "Airian the Airhead thinks she can hide!"

Hearing her brother's affectionate nickname come from this man's lips broke her resolve to keep her head down. She snapped her attention back to him. "I don't need to hide!" Her hand crept to the back of her belt to grip her knife.

"Oho!" The grizzled man's face creased into a gap-toothed grin. He leered closer to her, and she could smell the lakefish on his breath. "Then you choose to fight a losing battle. If your kind continue to rebel against the Darkspawn, you'll soon go the way of the dragons - hunted until extinct. What are you going do, elf-witch?"

So they did know. Airian struck at him with her knife, the deadly blade flashing in the light of the inn's hearth.

But the hunter merely stepped aside, apparently expecting her sudden attack. She stumbled forward. He grabbed her wrist and twisted hard. She winced, and the weapon clattered to the stone floor.

The man's companions crowded around her. She didn't like the look in their glittering black eyes from under their hoods.

279

She cursed her own stupidity, allowing herself to get riled up over some petty words.

"The Darkspawn don't take kindly to traitors," Leatherface said in a low tone. He nodded at his companions.

They parted to reveal a tall, hooded man in the back of the group. He raised his hands, showing his lifeless gray skin. A Darkspawn sorcerer! Shadows fell over the inn, the other patrons murmured nervously, and Airian recognized that she had indeed made a grave mistake. These were no ordinary huntsman. These were mercenaries working with the Darkspawn.

The blood drained from her face. "I meant no treason," she squeaked. They already knew she was an elf, but maybe she could still talk her way out of this.

"That's not true, Airian," the Darkspawn man said, stepping forward. "You knew exactly what you were doing." He pushed back his hood and Airian's heart sank even lower as she saw his stringy hair and familiar pale eyes. She even caught a whiff of decay.

"Zaurus," she said. "Always a displeasure." The skilled sorcerer had dogged her for the last month. She'd always managed to stay two steps ahead of him… until now.

Zaurus reached into his cloak and held up a poster to the dimmed light of the hearth.

The rough drawing of her brother's face blurred before her. She couldn't read the words beneath his image, but she knew them by heart. After all, she had written them. She closed her eyes as the tears finally spilled over, listening to the sorcerer read it in his harsh voice.

"Rylyn of Aeflerwood Forest, the Stoneseer for his people and all who follow the Creator, will one day put things to right, and turn darkness to light." Then came a ripping sound as Zaurus tore her handiwork in two. "Sounds like treason to me, Airian."

When she didn't answer, Leatherface shook her from behind. "We'll cut you to ribbons with your own knife for this! Or better yet, perhaps our friend here would like to have some fun of his own?"

To her surprise, Zaurus held up a hand. "Let's give her a chance to do the right thing first." He lifted her chin with a bony finger, and she stiffened at his clammy touch and acrid scent. "The Darkspawn are not an unreasonable people. We will absolve you of all charges if you agree to join us. I've heard how much influence you have over the other Elves of Aeflerwood. If you can convince them to serve us peacefully and cease these stubborn claims about the so-called Stoneseer, perhaps their deaths can be avoided."

At his threat, the shadows darkened further, so that even the hearth flame seemed to die out.

"So what do you say, Airian? Will you reconsider your position?"

Airian shivered. She glanced around the room at the frightened faces of the other patrons. They hunkered down, trying not to draw attention. None were Elves, of course, just humans who didn't dare to get involved in the conflict between Zaurus and his prey. Some of them would probably serve the Darkspawn whenever the sorcerers came to occupy this region in force.

Surely every one of these adults had heard rumors of the powers the Elves once held, how they kept the encroaching Darkspawn at bay for centuries. And yet she could see the doubt in their eyes. They wouldn't help her if this went sour. Perhaps they even blamed her for bringing this ruthless Darkspawn sorcerer to their sleepy little town.

She straightened as much as she could with one hand still twisted behind her back. "Never."

Leatherface shook her roughly, sending stabbing pain down her arm. "Well, Zaurus? She's made her choice."

Airian breathed in sharply and summoned her strength. She might never have learned to control the ancient Elven gift of Illumination as well as Rylyn, but she could still do something handy now and then. She stuck out her free hand and painfully drew the remaining light toward her, condensing it from the embers in the hearth and the dim oil lamps on the tables. Sweat beaded on her brow, dripping over her eyes, but she ignored it. Gritting her teeth, she managed to pull all the light in the room into her fist, where it grew brighter as it condensed into a tight, humming ball.

Zaurus cried out in fury as the fierce light seared his pale eyes. Airian knew she only had this one chance at escape. She yanked the trickle of light into her fist until the sphere blazed so bright and hot it nearly scorched her fingertips.

Then she threw it at the Darkspawn.

Zaurus fell back, covering his face in pain. With his magic grip on the shadows loosened, light exploded into the room again, blinding everyone. The other men shouted and surged forward, intending to grab her. But she slammed the heel of her boot on Leatherface's shin, and he let go of her. She dove under the dark shapes of the other men's bodies before they could see well enough to block her.

She reached the door and fled into the autumn evening.

* * *

For an Elven refugee, it was always smart to keep everything packed and ready to go at a moment's notice. For Airian, that meant a small pack of dried provisions and an extra waterskin tucked into a rolled-up bundle of clothes. Anything else she might have cared about had burned up long ago.

When she slipped into the mildew-rank basement she'd rented from a half-blind fisherman, she was relieved to find that her meager possessions had not been disturbed. She slung her bundle over one shoulder and readjusted her bow to be closer at hand. She'd lost her only knife in the scuffle, unfortunately.

She glanced at the small trestle table where her scraps of parchment and half-finished posters waited. She brushed her fingers over the shaky ink lines of her brother's face. She'd never been skilled at drawing, but she always added a small sketch to the posters that she left in every town, in the hope that someone would see his face and draw hope from his eyes, even if they couldn't read the words underneath. She'd found several of her scattered people by leaving such posters behind, guiding them on to the hidden refugee camps in the Southern Forest. She always came back to the mountain communities, though, drawn by the knowledge that more lost and frightened Elves might need her help.

She extinguished the one rusted lantern and shut the door behind her.

She drew her hood up again, hiding her distinctive ears and eyes, knowing that Zaurus would have his men looking for her as always.

It was definitely time to lay low in the woods for a few days, at least until all of this blew over. She would come back to civilization once she was sure that the Darkspawn had moved on.

But before she could slip off the main road into the trees, a horrible smell stopped her in her tracks. Smoke. Something was burning.

"No," she breathed. "No, no, no!" She turned back toward the village. To her horror, the roof of the tavern blazed orange in the night.

Images of another fire flared up in her mind, and she desperately tried to blink them away. She couldn't afford to let the past haunt her now, not while people's lives could be in danger. She ran toward the fire.

When she reached the edge of the town square, she gaped in confusion at the sight of the very same thugs who'd threatened her, now acting as a bucket brigade to help put out the inferno with water from the well. They were helping?

She hung back in the shadow of a nearby house, wishing she could run out there to assist. But she didn't dare.

Zaurus himself stood on top of the well and shouted over the townsfolk as they tried to put out the fire. "Attention, good folk! This fire was no accident! It was set by Airian of Aeflerwood, an elf-witch and malicious zealot. Several of you witnessed her throw arcane flames in the inn, and now look at what her magic has wrought!"

New fear rippled through the crowd, as the townsfolk voiced their questions and shock. They were actually believing Zaurus?

The Darkspawn raised his voice. "She is dangerous and not to be trusted. If you see her, you must apprehend her using whatever force necessary..."

Airian couldn't listen to another word. She backed away from the chaos in the square, her ears roaring with angry shouts and deadly flames. She'd helped so many of these people and now they'd believe her to be a monster.

She slid to the ground behind some dilapidated barrels and hugged her knees. She knew her little ball of magic light never could have caused a fire, but the humans wouldn't know that. The injustice of it stung, but there wasn't anything she could do to defend herself. Zaurus had all of those mercenaries on his side, not to mention his own twisted powers.

Could she still wait it out? After this, the townsfolk would certainly view her as a threat, whether they believed the Darkspawn's lies or not. Either way, she'd brought danger and destruction to their town.

"Who's there?" demanded a man's voice. She froze, silently cursing her flimsy hiding place. Someone approached with a lantern and held it up over her head. "You!" the man shouted. She recognized him as the enraged innkeeper. "You're the one! Stop! I found the witch!"

She leaped up and sprinted for the safety of the forest, even as she realized that running only made her look even more guilty.

* * *

Trees grabbed at her thick auburn braids, her cloak, her quiver. She didn't stop running through the thicket until the burn in her lungs threatened to overtake her whole chest. She collapsed against one of the smooth-barked aeflerwood trees, and huddled among the roots, gasping for air.

Where could she go now? She'd exhausted all possibilities in the towns around Rylyn's mountain. Ever since the Elven clans had fallen years ago, she'd tried to blend into the human towns, keeping her telltale violet eyes downcast and her pointed ears hidden. She'd worked secretly to find hidden pockets of other Elves and escort them to safety when their hiding places were compromised. She'd tried so hard to maintain the underground network of sympathizers among the humans. She'd painstakingly made those stupid posters and told stories of hope in quiet tones to anyone who would listen.

A lot of good all that did. Her efforts had only drawn the attention of the Darkspawn.

And her brother still hadn't returned.

Maybe it was time to leave the mountain and head south with the remaining Elves. She swallowed hard at the thought. Leaving felt like giving up. This was her home, even if everyone in her family was dead, missing, or taken captive. *Not everyone*, she thought firmly. She refused to let herself believe that Rylyn was gone. He said he would be back.

She wiped her eyes with her sleeve and looked up at the peak, glowing silver in the moonlight. Sure, she might be about to run away with her tail between her legs, but at least she could say goodbye.

* * *

The moon had set below the horizon by the time Airian finally reached the secret cave in the mountainside. She clambered up onto the ledge, remembering a time when she was too small to reach it on her own. Rylyn would reach down to pull her up beside him so they could look out at the vast forest that hugged the foothills.

"Someday I'll explore the other side of the forest, all the way to the sea," she'd confided in him once as they sat and watched the sunset. "I'm not meant to stay in one place like Dad."

Rylyn had glanced sidelong at her, his dark violet eyes

glinting with amusement. "I hope you won't forget us boring homebodies," he teased.

She stuck out her tongue at him. "I'll bring back maps for Dad, and seashells for Master Graylo, and enough rare scrolls to satisfy even your ridiculous appetite." She nudged Rylyn's ribs with her elbow.

"Or, I could go with you," he said, suddenly sounding serious.

She blinked. "You'd do that? I thought—"

"You thought I was duty-bound to stay here and protect our home, as Dad is?" He let out a puff of breath. "I suppose I am." Then his smile turned mischievous again. "You may be an Airhead at times, but you're still one of us, aren't you? Who will protect you out there except your big brother?" He wrapped an arm around her and vigorously rubbed the top of her head, messing up her hair.

The memory faded and Airian sighed, rubbing her hand over her scalp. She could almost remember the warmth of Rylyn's fingers. Now that she really was going to leave, it didn't feel right to set out without his blessing. She took a laborious moment to condense some starlight into a sphere to light her path, then stepped inside the suffocating darkness of the cave.

The familiar shape of her brother's lanky form emerged from the surrounding shadows.

"Hey Ry," she said softly. "How's the mountain treating you these days?"

She lifted the light higher, and it fell across his face - stone cold and gray as ever. She shuddered at his empty eyes, even though she knew to expect them. He didn't move. He never did anymore.

After all, he'd been the Stoneseer for decades now. He still looked exactly as he had the day she'd lost him to his destiny

- thin but steadfast and strong, with a determined set to his brows and mouth. She'd gone and grown up, but he remained perpetually young, unmarred by time.

She settled herself at his boots where they merged with the stone floor. She wrapped herself in her cloak to try to banish the chill of the cave air, but it couldn't hide the coldness of the statue's legs at her back.

"I came to say goodbye," she said.

Silence.

"I don't know if you can still hear me through the stone, but just in case, I wanted to let you know. I can't stay here anymore. It's too dangerous for Elves to be seen near the Darkspawn's domain these days, and besides," she ran a hand through her bangs, "I want to find more of our people beyond the mountain and tell them about you. About what you told me."

He didn't answer, but she imagined his mild voice repeating the last words he'd said to her.

It was years ago now, after he'd become living stone and mastered his unique powers. At that point he'd already saved their clan multiple times, and word had begun to spread to the other clans about the mysterious Stoneseer who could cause localized earthquakes and throw down glowing boulders to fend off the sorcerers. The Darkspawn took note, as they emerged from their deep underground caverns and focused more of their attacks on the mountain above, searching for Rylyn's hidden cave from which he operated.

Back then, she'd visited him every few days to let him know how their scattered people fared after losing their ancestral home to the flames. That particular time, however, he'd stopped her before she could give her report. "I have to go away for a while," he had said, not meeting her eyes. He turned his face away. "I mean, I'm not really going anywhere, but it'll seem like I'm gone."

She'd taken his heavy hand and rubbed her fingers over his coarse knuckles. When he was awake like this, his stone skin warmed like rocks in the summer sun, and she could almost forget about the weighty mantle he wore. "Stay," she pleaded. "I can't lose you more than I already have."

"It's important," he said. "I need to stop these Darkspawn once and for all, and to do that, it's going to take preparation. A lot of it." Finally he looked at her, his glowing purple eyes eerily sad in the dim cave. "Remember what Dad used to say about why Elves were given the gift of Illumination?"

She scuffed her feet. "It's a symbol. A 'faint flicker of a future kingdom of light,' as Dad called it."

"I'm going to bring that light with me when I come back. But I need you to do something for me while I'm gone."

"Anything!"

He put a heavy hand on her shoulder. "Things are going to get bad. The Darkspawn will try to wipe out all traces of our light. They know I'm an elf, so they'll take it out on all of you once I've disappeared."

"Okay...."

"I need you to keep our people from despair. Tell them that this suffering won't be forever. Keep teaching them the art of Illumination. Tell them I'm watching over them, even when the Darkspawn rule the day. Stay true, and know I'll bring the dawn when I return."

She swallowed hard. "I'll do my best."

He'd laughed. "Of course you will, Airhead. You've always spread hope and joy wherever you go. Well, chaos mostly, but also joy."

Now, curled up at her brother's lifeless feet, she wondered why he still hadn't come back. She pressed her eyes shut. "I don't know if you'll be able to watch over me once I leave the mountain, but I haven't given up hope yet. I'll be listening for any word that you've returned. Don't you dare leave us hanging!"

Silence.

She sighed and pushed herself up. She clasped one of his stiff hands in hers. "I won't forget anything you told me, brother. I'll... I'll make you proud." She gave his hand a squeeze and started to pull away. "I should go."

Her hand stuck to his.

She looked down. Their fingers were intertwined, and she could almost imagine that he'd squeezed back. But no, he hadn't moved.

"Hello, elf-witch."

She spun around. Out of the darkness deeper in the cave skulked at least five Darkspawn sorcerers, led by none other than Zaurus. How had they found her? This cave was supposed to be secret!

Zaurus' low chuckle echoed eerily around the cave. "Oh yes, we stumbled across this little hideout several days ago as we delved through the mountain." He gestured behind him. "Our tunneling crew found the smaller cave back there, and that finally led us here, to your precious Stoneseer."

She grabbed her shortbow and started to back up to gain space, but Rylyn's statue blocked her escape. "Get away from me!" she growled at them.

"I thought we might find you here after you eluded me in the inn, and sure enough, here you are! We won't make the mistake of underestimating you again." Zaurus raised his hands and the shadows deepened and spread.

Airian's little light didn't stand a chance against that many Darkspawn, especially with her so distracted. It flickered and snuffed out with a puff.

She couldn't aim in the dark at enemies she couldn't see. She tried to pull some more of the starlight from outside the cave to aid her, but it was too far away for her tenuous grip on the fabled Elven skill.

Something hard struck her from the side. She fell heavily to the stone floor, and before she realized what was happening, someone yanked her bow right out of her hands. A few grunts and efforts later, there was a terrible snapping sound. She blinked back sudden tears. Rylyn had made that bow.

"What do you want?" she shouted. "I don't have anything left to give!"

"Your loyalty, for one," Zaurus said. "And if you won't give that willingly, we'll just have to punish you instead."

She felt a whisper of air near her face, and she instinctively covered her head with her arms. Sure enough, the blunt weapon that had already bruised her ribs now collided with the back of her head, and she went sprawling. Her chin smacked against the floor. She blinked, dazed.

Sharp-clawed hands dug into her forearms. She tried to fight free, but the nails just sliced into her skin. She yelped and kicked, making contact with one of the Darkspawn, but there were too many of them. They wrenched her hands behind her back until the pain made her go rigid.

She panted, unable to move as they tied her hands with rough rope. She still couldn't see anything in the pitch blackness, but she turned her face toward where she thought Rylyn's statue stood. "Help!" she screamed. "Rylyn, please! I need you!"

One of the Darkspawn cuffed her ear. "Shut up, elf. He's dead."

"No, wait, let's see if the Stoneseer answers her," sneered Zaurus. She was dragged forward and thrown roughly against the statue's feet, where she had lain only minutes earlier. "Go on, girl," he said in a mocking voice. "Call for the mighty Stoneseer to save you, if he can!"

Hot tears streamed down her face now. She rested her forehead against his boots. "Rylyn, if you can hear me, please come back. I can't do this without you anymore." Her voice lowered to a whisper. "I don't want to believe you're actually gone for good."

Silence.

Airian hung her head.

Zaurus laughed, and his companions dragged her away, through their new tunnel at the back of the cave. She realized they were taking her away from the shallow, airy caves of the Elves' beloved mountain. Long ago the Darkspawn had emerged from a deeper labyrinth hidden well beneath the roots of the mountain, and she knew with a sinking feeling of dread that they were headed there now.

She didn't struggle. After all, if her brother was ever going to come back from his supposed slumber, surely that would have been the moment. Now, was there any point in fighting for hope?

"Don't give in, Airian. Stay strong, and don't listen to their lies! Their words are poisonous acid. Test the paving stones for the solid rock of truth before you're tempted to take a step down that road."

The Darkspawn pulled her through the endless maze of tunnels and caverns. She could barely keep her balance with her hands tied behind her back and unable to see her own feet. A few times, she saw faint bioluminescent fungus on the walls, but before she could gather her strength to condense the light, the Darkspawn skirted around it and plunged through darker caves beyond. Every once in a while, she heard water trickling somewhere nearby, and at one point, her feet splashed through a shallow stream.

They did not speak to her or to each other during the whole journey. She had no way of knowing how long or far they marched. Had the sun risen outside on the mountaintop? Was it afternoon already? She shivered, wishing she could absorb some warm golden rays.

Elves were not meant for deep cave-dwelling. She'd heard stories about a group of Elves who sought to mine precious gems but went mad for lack of sunlight when a cave-in trapped them in utter darkness for two days. How long before that happened to her?

The damp air affected her tired muscles, dampening her reflexes as they descended further into the earth. She stumbled more than once over her numb toes.

Finally, they came to a sudden halt. Unable to see, she took three more clumsy steps until the man who'd been prodding her from behind yanked on the rope that held her wrists. She lost her balance and fell hard on her tailbone. She barely had a chance to rest before they yanked her back to her feet and through a narrow door that brushed her elbows.

Instantly a foul smell reached her nostrils. She gagged, and tried not to breathe too deeply. The pungent air hinted that she'd been brought to a small cell that hadn't been cleaned in many moonturns. She heard a faint dribble of water somewhere off to the side.

One of the Darkspawn cut her bindings, nicking her skin in the process. Before she could sigh in relief, they clapped cold manacles on both wrists. She heard the jangling of chains, and then her arms were hoisted up above her head.

Panic rose up in her throat. "What are you going to do to me?"

A female Darkspawn spoke up. "Tell us something first: where are the others?"

Airian pressed her lips together.

She heard someone step closer. A knife blade traced her jawline, and she forced herself to stay still. She could smell the clammy sweat of her tormentor. It smelled like mildew and rotting swampwater. "Your precious Stoneseer is gone." That was Zaurus again. She should have known by his stench. "Face it, elf-witch. You're alone."

She spat blindly into the darkness. She was rewarded with a wet smacking sound as her spit collided with flesh.

"This is a wonderful learning opportunity," Zaurus hissed. "You see, if you resist, you will receive whatever I deem an appropriate punishment." Then the knife edge was back as he sliced a series of stinging cuts on her face and arms.

Tears sprang to her eyes, and she tried to flinch away. Zaurus only braced his other hand on her neck and kept making meandering little cuts, obviously toying with her. She shuddered when the knife retreated at last. Then Zaurus spat, and the pungent saliva splattered across her cut cheek. It burned.

"However, my earlier offer still stands," Zaurus said, sounding calmer. "Will you recant your claims about the Stoneseer and swear fealty to the Dark? We can end this at any time, you know. It's up to you."

Airian swallowed. Doubt and hope warred in her chest. Rylyn hadn't returned from his mystical quest to save her from this fate. Did that mean he'd failed? That he wasn't coming back?

"You know the truth, don't you?" That was the female voice, with an almost motherly tone. "You already know the Stoneseer is dead."

Airian tensed. "No! He said… he's coming back!"

Zaurus tsked his tongue. "Oh, Airian. I'm so glad I get to be the one to tell you. Your Stoneseer is not the first one to walk this earth. He's only the latest in a line of unfortunate souls cursed with this fate. Each has gradually faded away, only to be replaced with a new Stoneseer centuries later. By the looks of that statue in the cave we found, your friend died years ago. He isn't coming back."

Airian wanted to rage and rail against his words, but something stopped her. She knew Rylyn had not told her everything about being the Stoneseer. What if this was what he'd hidden from her? What if he knew he was dying, and he didn't want to hurt her?

But then why would he promise that he was coming back? "You're lying," she said at last.

Zaurus laughed. "Believe what you will, little elf. But know this: if you don't confess loyalty to our cause, we'll have no choice but to use you as bait to catch your annoying friends. After all, it worked so well on the dragons!"

She heard a faint hiss from the corner of the cell that she didn't understand.

"Now," said the woman. "Tell us. Where are the others?"

"If I knew," Airian said quietly, "I'd never tell you." Rylyn had made her promise to care for their people. Even if he never came back, she planned to do just that.

She heard the slosh of liquid in a bucket, and then she was drenched with a horrible, stinking wetness. It seeped into the bloody cuts on her arms, and suddenly she found she was screaming as it seared like fire in her wounds.

"And there's another punishment," scoffed Zaurus. "We'll leave you to think about your petty loyalty to a lie."

The two of them laughed and retreated, slamming the metal door behind them.

The acidic liquid continued to eat away at her damaged flesh after they'd gone. She writhed and screamed, desperate for relief, but it burned and burned, bringing to mind images of red-hot coals. Her last thought before she lost her tenuous grip on consciousness was simply, *Now what, brother?*

"Remember those who went before, and take courage. Look forward to the light to come, and there you'll find your joy again."

"…And now the rats just taste like sinew and bile. Bleh."

Airian groggily lifted her head, wincing as the movement pulled at her throbbing cuts. Who was talking?

The gravelly voice rambled on from somewhere to her left. "I used to roast them, but now that the fire's gone, there's nothing for it. Raw diet. Mmm. Good for the figure. Slims you down."

Airian groaned. Her throat felt sore and scratchy, and she remembered screaming. "Wh-who's there?" she managed to cough out.

The voice fell silent.

"I heard you talking, you know," she snapped. "Something about eating rats?"

"I thought you were dead," said the voice. "Too bad."

Airian huffed and twisted, though the complete darkness hid the speaker, of course. "Are you another Darkspawn sorcerer, come to question me some more?"

"Scales, no! What a horrid thing to say to a stranger! I am Tridian Falflight. Tridian the Disgraced." The voice cracked into a disturbed kind of laugh for a moment. Then it abruptly stopped.

Airian tried to pull at the chains that still held her arms out to the sides. She could hardly feel her fingers because of the tight manacles restraining her wrists. "Are you a prisoner here?"

"Am I a prisoner, she asks? Cruel, cruel." She assumed by the timbre of his voice that she was speaking to a relatively young man, though whether human or elf she couldn't tell. "I ate the last one who asked me that. At least, I think I did. Maybe I just ate his boot. It's hard to tell what's real, these days. Are you real?"

She was beginning to realize that her companion wasn't all there. Still, talking to a madman had to be better than going mad herself from the silent darkness. "My name's Airian," she said. "Formerly of Aeflerwood."

"An elf, are you?" She flinched, but didn't deny it. "Good, maybe I won't outlive you like everyone else."

"How long have you been down here?" She was almost afraid to ask.

"Skin it, girl, you think I know? Long enough to go blind, lose my fire, eat some rats… and some other things. I'm pretty sure I ate a fungus that made me puke rainbows once. Now *that* I almost miss."

Airian tugged again at her bonds, rattling the chains. "This is probably a stupid question, but have you tried escaping?"

There was a long silence, then, "What's the point? What does it matter even if I could get out of here? All of my people are dead. Soon yours will be, too."

"How dare you?" Airian snapped. "You may have lost all your hope, sitting here in the dark, but I won't give up mine so easily, not when my brother said— No, you know what? It's none of your business!"

"Fine, fine. No need to be beastly about it. That's my job." He chuckled bitterly.

She fell silent, thinking. If there was some way to slip out of her chains, maybe she and her strange companion could find a way to get out of the cell. And then what?

"You gonna eat that?" Tridian asked suddenly.

"Huh?"

"That's a lovely pile of leather you're standing on. Mind if I take a nibble?"

She coiled her toes. "You want to eat my boots? Sorry, but I'll need those when I escape."

"It's just—it's been so long since I've had leather." He sounded wistful.

"How about we get out of here and then you can eat all the leather you want?"

He growled.

"Fine, I'll escape, you stay here. I'm not going to sit around and rot when I have work to do."

"What on earth could be so important that you'd leave this dark paradise?"

She couldn't tell if he was being serious, and that worried her. "My—The Stoneseer asked me to take care of my people. And that's kind of hard to do from a cell. There must be a way out!"

Tridian scoffed loudly. "The Stoneseer, eh? It's because of that stupid legend that my family is dead."

She didn't know what to say to that. "Oh. Uh, I'm sorry."

They sat in silence for a long time. Airian's eyes dried out from straining to see, so she closed them.

Finally, she couldn't take it anymore. "What happened to them?"

She heard a cough from Tridian, and for a fleeting moment she thought she smelled stale smoke. Then he said in a scratchy voice, "My father believed the stories, silly as they are, even though there'd been no signs of stone magic for centuries. Then the Darkspawn came and infested our warm caves like rats." He smacked his lips. "Tasted better, though."

"You... ate them?"

He cleared his throat. "Beside the point. Then came the rumors about the Stoneseer arriving to the north, and the Darkspawn accused my father of stirring up trouble." He took a deep breath. "They sent dozens of sorcerers and made him watch as they killed our family before his eyes. He finally threw himself in front of the shadow arrows meant for me, but it was pointless. They just chased me down and took me captive after they killed him. Then they used me to lure in everyone else who remained. I'm the only one left of them all."

Airian winced. "So you blame the Stoneseer?"

"The Stoneseer doesn't exist, and if he does, he doesn't care. My father wouldn't have died for nothing like he did. Right up until the end, he was so confident that the Stoneseer would save us someday."

Airian pondered that. She hadn't ever thought that there were others who suffered because they believed that the Stoneseer would return. Her experience wasn't unique. The thought made her straighten a bit. "Your father was brave to stand up to the lies of the Darkspawn," she said softly. "I know it probably doesn't mean much, coming from me. But I've seen how their words can twist people against each other, rather than standing firm for what's right. Your father sounds like a good man."

Before Tridian could respond, the door to their cell banged open, and someone entered. The Darkspawn had come back to question her more. The pain in her wounds flared up at the memory of the knife and burning liquid.

"Well, Airian," came the sickly sweet voice of Zaurus, "Have you had time to think about what I said before?"

"I'm not going to fall for your lies," she said, surprising herself with how firm and confident she sounded. "So you should either let me go or kill me now."

"Don't you understand? It's simple. If you continue to refuse us, your stubbornness will be your doom. And if your people follow your example of treason, every last one will be destroyed for your pride."

"The Stoneseer would never let that happen."

"Oh, there you go with that superstitious drivel again. How boring you are! Let's make this a little more interesting, shall we? I've heard you made the acquaintance of your cellmate. How about a little demonstration? Recant, or I'll hurt him until he hates you."

"I've got a better idea," she said, thinking fast. She couldn't let him hurt Tridian. The poor guy had already been through so much. "How about you pick on someone who can actually fight back? Release me and we'll see who's stronger! You already have the advantage."

Her taunt seemed to work, because she was rewarded with a heavy punch to the gut that made her double over as much as the chains would let her, gagging breathlessly. "You're pitiful," Zaurus said. "You try so hard to fix things, and you just end up making everything worse for everyone."

Footsteps echoed in the chamber, and then Tridian yelped in pain.

She flinched. What was the Darkspawn doing to him? Unable to cover her ears, she was forced to keep listening to the shrieks and sobs that went on for half a minute.

"I'll have you know I've already captured several of your people before, Airian," Zaurus went on once Tridian's cries had quieted. "And by the end, all of them blamed you for their misfortunes. And for good reason, as you're the one who filled their head with false prophecies and saviors. No one came to rescue them from their eventual deaths, so why would anyone help you?"

She shook her head. "It's not true. Rylyn's coming back. He's watching even now, through these very stones around us."

Something clanked, and then the chains holding her up loosened. She collapsed on the floor, but before she could scramble away, Zaurus smashed the heel of his boot into her hand.

Bones and tendons crunched together, and shockwaves of agony lanced through her whole arm. She screeched. Her other hand clenched and unclenched, as if it could release the pressure on its twin.

Zaurus just ground her hand against the stone floor even harder, waiting out her screams until she could only whimper.

"This so-called Stoneseer is named Rylyn, huh? Obviously someone who was close to you. How fascinating. You've already started to lose your mind down here, thinking wishfully that someone you've lost will return with magic stone powers to save you. So poignant. I might even join you and shed a tear of my own."

She hadn't even realized she was crying. She blinked them away and tried to pull her crushed hand back.

Zaurus finally lifted his foot. "Pathetic. If your people saw you like this, they'd surely see your talk about the Stoneseer for what it really is—fables and children's tales."

She couldn't answer.

"Oh well, I suppose it's time to leave you again. If you're still belligerent in a few days, I'll have to get more creative." At that point, he must have kicked her in the head, because everything faded for a few seconds as her mind filled with the sensations of sharp pain and dizziness.

When she was able to push past the ringing sound in her ears, she realized that Zaurus had exited the cell, leaving her laying in a heap of bruised and scabbed limbs.

"Hey, hey elf-girl. Whatchamacallit. I forgot your name. You okay?"

She couldn't summon the energy to talk. The pain and distress caused by Zaurus' words had sapped her of the willingness even to move her tongue to respond to her cellmate.

"Did he hurt you? Are you dead?" After a moment, "Now can I eat your boots?"

After she didn't respond for awhile, he fell silent. She couldn't even tell him that he was welcome to eat her shoes. She just stared into the darkness and wished she could talk to Rylyn somehow.

But despite all her bravado, she was slipping toward despair. She knew it. She'd been bolstered by the story of Tridian's father, hopeful until the end, but Zaurus somehow twisted everything up in her head. She wasn't sure she could ever be that brave. Rylyn had told her to look forward to the future light. She still wanted to believe his words, but how could they help her now? She couldn't even use her small gift of Illumination.

It seemed she would die here. What purpose did that serve? A sob caught in her throat. She laid her head down on the cold stone and tried to picture the sun rising over the peak of the mountain somewhere far above. Nothing but darkness greeted her.

"Rylyn," she whispered. "Where are you?"

With her head pressed against the rock floor, she heard the moment the mountain shifted. It was so faint that she thought she'd imagined it at first, but then another vibration washed through her body, and the mountain actually spoke.

"I'm here."

Those two words filled her with awe. It hadn't been an audible sound, but a deep resonance through the stone that thrummed into her very heart. Still, she knew that voice.

"Rylyn?" she choked out. Reassurance and peace flowed over her, calming her racing heart. She breathed in deeply. Yes. He was watching over her in this light-forsaken place, just as he'd promised. She'd never felt this close to him before, even when he'd still been her flesh-and-blood elder brother.

She pressed her good hand closer to the stone, as if her fingertips could channel all her hope and love through the rock directly to him. "I know you'll bring the light someday."

The mountain rumbled softly.

She smiled. It felt odd to smile in this darkest pit in the bowels of the earth, where she couldn't even see her hand in front of her face. But somehow she'd found a piece of joy. It sparked like a tiny candle flame in her chest, a flicker of that future golden-glowing kingdom.

A faint echo of a laugh caught in her throat. Was that what

Rylyn had been trying to tell her? Even when all the light around her was swallowed by darkness, the spark from his promise stayed inside her.

Suddenly, something caught her attention at the corner of her vision. She blinked rapidly a few times, certain that she must have imagined it. Maybe she was losing her grip on reality. The dark-madness had already started to set in. But she wasn't as concerned about that as she probably should have been.

"I did it!" came Tridian's voice. "At least, I almost managed. Huh, and I thought I was blind. Did you see it? Please tell me you did!" After a moment, she saw it again. It looked like two tiny embers glowing in the ashes of an old firepit. Were those eyes?

The smell of smoke made her tense up. She was suddenly yanked back to those memories she'd tried so hard to tamp down, to the night when the Darkspawn had won their first true victory over the Elves.

Her people never expected the sorcerers of darkness to use fire to such effect, and it had been their downfall. She saw flames swallow old Master Graylo's cloak before he could shuffle to safety. She'd caught a last glimpse of her father entering the burning Elvenhall to get more people out, right before the beams collapsed around him. So many elders killed. Their records, history, and heritage, lost. All because they chose to follow the Stoneseer rather than embrace the Darkspawn.

After two more flarings of the strange ember-light, she forced back the memories and sat up. "Tridian?" she asked hesitantly. "What are you doing?"

"I'm trying," he puffed, as if he'd been running hard, "to rekindle my flame." He growled, and the two faint orange dots faded out again. "But... not working. Probably too hungry still.

That's how they doused it in the first place."

She smelled smoke again, and this time the answer jolted through her, slotting all the other puzzle pieces into place. Tridian had been used as bait by the Darkspawn so they could kill his whole family. He wasn't a human or an elf after all. Those glowing dots weren't his eyes, but his *nostrils.* "You're a dragon!"

He grunted. "Well I'm not a stupid elf like you, that's for sure."

By the tiny amount of light from his regular breaths, she could see now that he was indeed a dragon, though he had to be quite a small one. She blinked, trying to make out more, but his faint flames were far too weak to make out much more than his general location and shape every few seconds. She hugged herself with trembling arms, wincing as the chains clanked against her wrists. "I thought all the dragons were gone or extinct."

"Debatable," Tridian said. "Depends on whether or not you consider me a live specimen." He stopped to mutter something, that sounded a bit like, "Sometimes even I'm not sure."

Airian's heart clenched.

Then he went on, "The Darkspawn keep crowing about how they've successfully wiped out my people. And it's all thanks to me, Tridian the Disgraced."

Airian crawled closer to him, testing how far her loosened chains would let her move. "That's not true, and you need to stop thinking that way. You're alive, I'm here, and we're going to figure this out together. And if you can keep up that glowing breath, I might be able to brighten things up."

At Tridian's next breath, she reached her hand out and touched his face. She was surprised by the warmth of his scales. "Your flame goes out when you're hungry?" she asked.

He huffed. "Hunger, lack of sunlight, cold temperatures, loneliness, madness, you name it, it'll probably contribute to a weak flame, or in my case, douse out completely. I can't even breathe a solitary spark right now, let alone melt these skin-awful chains."

"I may be able to help with the hunger a bit. After all, I probably don't need my *whole* boot." She tugged at it thoughtfully. "But for now, this glow is enough, thank you." She patted his head and waited until he breathed another warm breath out, lighting up her hands orange.

She concentrated, remembering Rylyn's gentle instructions to her as a child, when she had struggled to even bend a candlelight toward her. He'd been so patient with her, even when she lost her temper and threw a glove at his face. "It's not about brute strength, silly," he'd said with an exasperated chuckle. "Though heaven knows you've got plenty of that! Just relax and concentrate on drawing the light. Remember, it's an ember of a future blaze."

As a youngster, that had made her more frustrated, but now, feeling the matching ember in her chest, she truly understood. She took a slow breath, and pulled on the faint glow. It moved to her open palm and hovered there, flickering faintly. She was pleased that the almost-flame didn't send her into another flashback. Then again, Tridian's fire wasn't destructive. It was constant and reassuring. And, if she added to it…

At the next breath, she repeated the process, pulling another little sheen of light to merge with the one she held. It grew brighter, and she kept up the rhythm every time the dragon breathed.

Eventually they both winced at the brightness of the light, but neither could bear to look away, tears streaming from their eyes from the beautiful pain.

Now she could see Tridian clearly. He was a small golden dragon, so thin she could see all his ribs through his tarnished flanks. His green eyes reflected the glow of the sphere in her hand. He seemed exhausted by his attempts to breathe flame, but even as he laid his head down on his forepaws, he continued to stare in wonder at their light.

She lifted it higher, looking around their cell. Other than the metal door that gated the only exit, it was all smooth stone walls and ceiling. She found the trickle of water that she'd heard earlier. It flowed from a fist-sized hole on one wall, and continued out the other wall. She started when she noticed glowing eyes in the deeper shadows on the edge of the room, then realized that those had to belong to rodents.

"Not much," Tridian said. "But hey, it's home. The rats are a nice touch, don't you agree?" Then his voice broke in a sob.

"Hey, listen to me," she said gently. She settled back against one wall with Tridian at her side, and put her injured hand on his scaled back. "I know it looks bleak. And… to be honest I'm not sure we're getting out of this alive." She swallowed hard, noting the patches of old blood on the stone floor. "But do you know what this is?" She held the light up to his nose.

"Ow, that hurts," he whined, squinting at the brightness. She pulled it back a little.

"It's a reminder," she said. "This isn't the end. There's a light about to dawn, just on the other side of everything. We'll see it someday."

Tridian blinked at her. "Who are you, really?"

She pondered her glowing hand as the bright feeling of hope still pulsed in her heart. She'd already found her joy despite the darkness. Now she had to help Tridian find it, too. "Let's try this again," she said in a teasing tone. "Since you forgot my name. I'm Airian, but my friends call me Airhead."

Tridian shifted restlessly. "How can you be so lighthearted about this? That rat-roasted sorcerer will be back eventually, and he certainly won't be happy about *that*." He nodded toward her glowing hand.

She caged her fingers around the light, casting long shadows against the walls. "Rylyn... My brother asked me to keep hope alive, so I'm going to do my best, even when those Darkspawn shout lies, and even when this little light goes out. The Stoneseer will be back someday. Maybe not today, or this year, but he will be back. And when he comes, he'll make things right. That's what I see, and that's why I can smile." She grinned at him.

Tridian hummed at that, apparently not convinced. It might take a while, but she'd work on him. Even separated from her people, she could still spread hope and joy, and right now, her troubled companion certainly had need of both.

She smiled and lifted the light a little higher.

"You did well, Airian. I'll see you again at the end of all things, when your trials and scars will become accolades and pearls of glory. That time isn't there yet, but take heart! The sun may be obscured, but that doesn't make it any less brilliant."

Blessed are you when they revile you and persecute you and say all kinds of evil against you falsely for my sake. Rejoice and be exceedingly glad, for great is your reward in heaven: for so they persecuted the prophets who were before you

Rachel Kimberly Hastings

R achel Kimberly Hastings is the author of "Hopefire."

She grew up on a farm in Minnesota, where her love of the fantastic was born through adventures in her grandpa's woods and reading far too many books. She penned her first novel as a teenager during National Novel Writing Month, and she loved the experience so much that she repeated it every year since.

She now resides in Burbank, California, and works in the TV animation industry. To survive city life, she often hikes in the mountains and imagines she's on a quest to save Middle-Earth.

Wondermind and the Almost King

Khaled could point out the stars straight through the blinding white sky. He heard them singing, thrumming into place and whirring on like tireless chimes in the windstorm of existence. And he was no longer afraid of death.

"Get out of the lake!" His mother had found him already. Her usually soft voice sounded hard as it echoed under water.

Khaled stopped paddling and let his feet drop to the bottom of the rocky pool. The lake shone green through his sun-blinded eyes and his mother was just a shadow with the early flames of sunset behind her. He'd been floating longer than he thought.

"Ten years old and you don't care a pinch about me." She slipped off her lengthy headscarf for him to dry in. "Khaled, you'll kill me still, the way you worry me."

But she'd already survived his death once. He looked up at her, dressed in rose, with lengths of black hair set free over her broad shoulders. He still remembered waking up in her arms, coming back from his dance in eternity, where he'd sunk to the floor of the lake. She'd drawn back the warmth in his blood and nursed him to wholeness again, but he'd never been quite the same. He realized that.

He sighed. It was impossible to make her understand. Still, he leaned into her chest and let her dry his hair. She smelled of

311

cardamom and sugar.

"I made luqaimat for after supper."

He smiled and breathed deeply. *I know.*

After a moment, she smoothed his hair and draped the violet paisley scarf over the crook of her arm. She held him at arm's length. "Is my home not good enough for you now?" A smile teased her lips. "You don't want to be my child, now that you have seen beyond?"

"It's not that." He smiled back. In fact, the thought of the syrupy dumplings made him nearly drool. He'd just not quite finished listening for the wisdom above the sun, the song of the stars. "I'm sorry, Mamtee, I will be better." At least he would act better. He could never actually be better. He was helplessly fascinated by the Wonder who had welcomed him to eternity for a moment. He sighed. But the Wonder had sent him home. *Siwa needs you still,* It'd said, before Mamtee had drawn him up.

He took her hand, and, like two brown birds on a white beach, they strolled home through the coarse grass, picking up stones that might fetch a qirsh or two at market. They used to collect long blades of grass here for Mother's baskets, but ever since the strange conqueror of the north had claimed Siwa for his own, the dusts of the Great Sand Sea had been slowly overtaking the once verdant oasis. History told this very story, time and again. For some reason, no man could claim the magic of Siwa, or it would vanish like pleasure itself.

"This won't last, will it?" Khaled had asked, the first time his mother wrapped a scarf about his face to keep the sand out of his nose when he went to feed Ruta, the donkey.

"No, babu, Siwa will restore itself when Cadmus is gone."

But he was still here, ruling with a heavier and heavier hand by the year. Now rumor had it he'd started calling on his viziers to seek out the dark magics that the oracles had worked so hard to hide.

The clay walls of the village rose in the distance. They burned red as the writhing sun bled its final rays through the ruptured horizon.

"What is it, Mamtee?" Khaled held out a small white stone with flecks of pale blue, but his mother wasn't looking. He tucked it in her pocket and followed her gaze back to the blazing city.

What was that?

Beyond the red wall, above the low thatch roofs of their village, where the white stone palace sat on the hills, a vine of sour-yellow smoke hovered. Even as they watched, it plumed suddenly and fingered down into the village, branching and winding its way through the streets.

Jashe. It had to be. The pick-pocket djinn who had grown far too greedy. The last oracle had made a specific proclamation before her death: *anyone who calls the yellow spirit up from its grave is the chief of idiots.* It may bring a man treasure, but with it came madness. That would be Cadmus— willing to risk his sanity for a few more treasures, a few more fading pleasures.

Khaled felt sorry for the man.

"The fool—" His mother gripped his hand. Her fingers were freezing. "The imposter has called the spirit of greed to ruin us all." Her voice broke.

"Jashe." Khaled nodded. He wasn't afraid.

"Do not say his name aloud, child." His mother fell to her knees and gripped his shoulders. "We must get to the house quickly, load Ruta's cart and—"

There was no way. They both watched as the smoke settled throughout the dusk-covered village, ending at the wall and gently billowing over.

Villagers, their neighbors and friends, began to pour out the gates, moaning and wailing, empty-handed. Mamtee pulled Khaled to meet them, to get the news. It was true. Jashe had claimed every treasure in Siwa with a curse: *every good thing belongs to the king.* They said their money and every item of value had suddenly acquired a yellow hue and become immovable. Cursed to remain stuck until some hand of this so-called king came to claim them. *The thief.*

Khaled's heart dropped. Their dumplings. "Mamtee, what about the luqaimat?" Instantly, he felt foolish. *Silly Khaled.* Like that mattered. But his stomach was growling and he'd been so excited.

"Is that what you're worried about?" Mamtee sank into the grass, inviting him to collapse there too. "Babu, he has taken everything. In a moment, our entire life has been robbed. Our silver. Grandpa's books." She looked up. Her eyes grew hard. "Babu, we have to leave."

"Leave?" *Just to collect more silver and books?* He understood what she was saying, but it troubled him. No matter where they lived, the heavens would still be unreachable, the star songs just out of hearing. Weren't they already accustomed to that sort of longing? A new home would change nothing. "We could live like dervishes—"

Mamtee's eyes scolded.

"Not the foreign ones who follow the mystic," he stuttered. She knew what he meant. "But our own dervishes who've taken the vow of poverty." He'd always loved them; homeless grandpas who roamed the hills, eating wild produce, sitting where the oracles had sat, and applying their minds to the study of what lay above the sun.

Husani, the coconut carver, had sidled up next to him. He gripped his shoulder. "You are a strange child." Khaled hated his cloying, woody smell. He pulled away before the man could knuckle his head.

Half a dozen neighbors had gathered around, too.

"Your mamtee is right." Sorma, their nearest neighbor, crouched between them and gripped Mamtee's hand. "There is nothing for us here. Even the dervishes will have to leave when the date palms die."

Big Husani nodded sagely and still managed to reach Khaled's head and give his hair a muffle. "Speaking of dervishes at your age—" He shook his head. "When Gamal was your age, he was concerned about nothing but dumplings and fig cakes. And that's what a sensible boy should be thinking about. Not the afterlife." He chuckled through his nose. "You leave those thoughts to the dead and dying."

"But sir, aren't we all dying?" Khaled answered, but the man had moved on, uninterested in an actual conversation.

Mamtee and Sorma made plans, Husani called his wife to find Gamal, and by the time the last hot cloud turned to cobalt, the general wailing of the assembly had become the quiet stoicism for which Siwans were known. It was in their blood to survive and thrive in drought and oppression. Apparently, it was also in their blood to abandon their homes without so much as a tear.

"We will head to Qara." Sorma shared her plans with the growing band. "They are like us, poor, but welcoming. We cannot stay there long, though, for they limit their population by decree." Her hard voice kept cutting into Khaled's thoughts, or rather, his sensing.

What was that strange guilt that kept snaking, nearer and

nearer, causing the hairs along his spine to rise? He put his hands over his ears to silence the distractions.

It wasn't guilt.

He turned back toward the city. In the deep blue of dusk, the village looked almost normal. The smoke had cleared, except for a wisp or two. He squinted. The more he focused, the stronger the terrible sense became.

He shuddered. *There.*

Fine tendrils of puffing and curling smoke sped through the grass.

"Mamtee!" He pointed. His voice had caught in his throat. He tried again. "Mamtee, look!"

His mother looked up, but Husani was pestering her with some complaint. Sorma held up a finger. "Shush, Khaled, not now."

The smoke found his ankles and wisped up his legs. He turned out his pockets quickly. "I've got nothing." But it didn't look in his pockets. It sped up his neck and twined into his course black hair. "Mamtee?" He didn't dare move.

"Khaled!" With a shriek, she finally fell to his side. "Someone help!"

"What's it doing with him?" Voices he didn't even recognize crowded his consciousness. "Don't touch him! It's cursing the boy!"

"He's my son!" Mamtee pleaded, but no one would help.

"How is Jashe claiming a human?"

"It's claiming him like it claimed my best urn." The voices were fading.

"He's no treasure, Madiha." That was Husani.

Khaled looked into his mother's eyes. "I'm not afraid." Nothing was unknown to the great Wonder, not even this.

"Heavens, help!" Mamtee's voice choked in his ear.

And a darkness he'd never known clamped over his thoughts—black irons shackling his mind, claiming it for the king.

* * *

Madiha gripped her son's weak form as he collapsed. "Oh, Babu, no!" She sank to the grass, holding his head against her chest. His star-bright eyes had turned dim, like clouds had climbed inside and hidden his light away from the world. *You cannot leave me again.*

"Possessed by the spirit of greed, he is." Husani, who always announced his thoughts as though he had researched them greatly, forced away the crowd. "Don't want that boy anywhere near you, I'll tell you that."

"You don't understand—" Hot tears smarted behind her eyes. She pulled Khaled closer, rocking him. But did it matter? Since he'd come back, no one had understood her boy.

"We understand plenty, Madiha." Husani grunted.

But Sorma bent to her side. "What do you think it is, friend? What's happened to Khaled?"

The tenderness of her neighbor released the tears she'd been holding back. She wanted to be strong for Khaled, but he was all she had. How could she be strong with her own life lying paralyzed in her arms? "He's a treasure, Sorma," she sobbed. "The king will come and collect him like he is collecting our money and our jewels."

"No, surely not." Sorma gripped her hand.

But she was right. Even as the crowd hushed at her words, the thundering of a palace chariot neared from the city gates.

They would rip Khaled from her arms. They would poke and prod at him and try to unlock what treasures he kept in his mind. Khaled may not be afraid, but he did not know Cadmus like she did. The man took treasures, used them, then threw them to the dogs.

"Help me!" she called to the crowd. Even though he was small for his age, her son was too heavy for her to run any great distance with. Gamal had brought his family's cart. "Hide him." Madiha stumbled toward Gamal and pushed her boy into his strong arms. "Go," she cried. "We need to run."

Gamal had a heart, unlike his father, but he paused. He paused just long enough for the chariot and several horsemen to surround the band.

"Hand over the treasure. Which of you is hiding it?"

"No treasure, here," dear Sorma tried.

Madiha felt through her pockets. "Rare stones for the emperor?" she choked, shielding Khaled from view. She felt Gamal turn slowly, carrying Khaled to the cart.

"You there, what is that?" A young man shoved Madiha aside.

"Nothing but a boy." Gamal stayed calm. "He's ill."

Madiha's heart sickened and slipped down to her feet. Khaled was marked. They hadn't noticed before, but he glowed an eerie yellow all about his hair and face.

"Yellow fever—" Gamal stuttered.

"Don't talk to us about yellow fever," the king's man laughed dryly, "we know it well and this isn't it."

"Take the boy." A guard with a regal scimitar at his side came forward. "And you—" He gripped Gamal's wrist. "You're coming too. King needs to know who's defying him."

Gamal's eyes widened. "I didn't. I—" He looked to Madiha.

"No, it was me." She pushed in. "I hid him. He's my son."

"This isn't a circus, you can't all come." But the captain eyed her. "What kind of a treasure is he?"

"He's not a treasure." She sounded like Husani. "Please, sir." She gripped the young man's arm. He scowled. "Sir, he's only a boy with a taste of death. He is not what the king desires."

The man pushed her off. "You know nothing of kings."

"I know enough." She stacked her courage as high as she could. Khaled was going nowhere without her. "Take me too."

The man was turning away, calling on the others to go.

She raised her voice. "Take me too or I will find you and your family. And tonight you will wish you had spared my son."

The man stiffened, but didn't turn back. He snapped his fingers. "Take her."

"Sir." Two of the king's men, barely more than children, left Gamal's side and gripped her by the arms. Madiha refused to cry out as the tight irons pinched her wrists.

"Take her to the stalls." The captain called to his men. "She's to be nowhere near the boy. And release the other one." He pointed to Gamal.

Husani had fumed just quietly enough to not make a scene, but clearly enough to probably worry the captain. The man was smart and must know that there was nothing as fierce as a father robbed of his child. Or a mother, for that matter.

* * *

"Can't put this one in the store rooms." Khaled woke to a blazing sun and a great hubbub of harsh voices.

"That one's to go directly in."

"Strange treasure if you ask me."

"Has to be a mistake."

319

Distant voices hollered, "shut up," and "get to work."

Khaled was on his back in an open carriage. His head hurt. Dusty coconut palms arched overhead and the constant clatter of wheels on stone proved he was somewhere within the palace grounds on the limestone roads.

"You going to walk, boy, or you going to make me carry you?" A large man shuffled up and stood over him, blocking out the sun.

Not a chance he'd be hoisted up like a sack of dates. Khaled sat up. The world tipped to the side at first, but soon stabilized. Had they hit him in the head, or was this the effect of Jashe's curse? Either way, his growling stomach proved he hadn't been too profoundly impacted.

"I'm hungry." He got to his feet. Suddenly the thought of Mamtee's cooking made his heart ache.

The man sneered. He took Khaled by the arm and pulled him past rows of wagons heaped with claimed tapestries, urns, and bags of every villager's life savings. They'd had a busy night.

Panic clawed up Khaled's throat. What was he really doing here? Did he compare to the heaps of treasures they'd stolen? He knew the Wonder had blessed him with wisdom, but what was that to a wealthy man?

The palace spread, ahead and to the left and right— a broad monstrosity of marble and gold.

"Make room." The shadow-like man pushed his way through a crowd, pulling his captive up a flight of hot white steps. The interior was paved with glistening blue and turquoise tiles. Dwarf palms in vases as large as well-fed grandpas rounded the edges of the first courtyard and high, carved archways led from one corridor to another until they came to a door.

Doors. Two of the highest, most ornate and colorful doors

Khaled had ever seen. And Siwa was a colorful place. Or, it *had* been.

"Enter."

The doors made no sound as his captor pressed them open.

Khaled gulped. This room seemed to have a thousand windows, every one of them draped in long white curtains that muted the sound of the wind. Tapestries of red and gold and the purple that only came from the far-away coast, stretched on the floor from wall to wall, and the king paced on them as though they were rugs.

"Ah, the boy." He stopped pacing, but took up ringing his hands. He was not what Khaled had expected. He was very trim and had the hard, tired jawline of a young laborer. He wasn't unattractive, but his fair skin was sweaty and he tugged at his stiff collar. It would probably help if he'd just exchange the constrictive apparel of his own country for the airy kameezes worn by locals.

When the doors closed, the young ruler relaxed. He scratched the light blond stubble that barely grew on his chin. "So, tell me, boy. Are you a genie—some kind of personification?"

"A—" Khaled didn't know either word. "Jeeni?"

The man snapped his fingers a few times, thinking. "Djinn. Are you a djinn?"

Khaled shook his head. Foreigners were strange.

The man approached. Khaled would have called his expression quizzical, except for the way his icy-blue eyes narrowed down and pinned him in place. He circled, coming back around to lift Khaled's chin, gaze at his teeth, and study the lines of his palms.

"What's your job here?" The man's thick accent returned an aura of harmlessness to him, and Khaled breathed again.

"I'm only ten, Sayidi. I don't have a job."

The man blew a gust of air into his hands and rubbed at his face. He turned another circle, almost going to the nearest window, but forced himself to return. He bent to a knee. "One of my genies went out last night—" He scratched his head. "And in all of the city he found no treasure so great as you. A boy of ten."

Little chills pricked up Khaled's arms and legs. "Really?"

Cadmus grunted. "Yes. So, tell me, what is it that you do?"

Khaled had never been one to lie. Not even before he'd touched the skies and felt the great honesty of things greater than him. But did the man really want to know that all the wisdom of the Wonder Itself was within Khaled's reach and that he was surer than sure that this man who claimed the throne of Siwa now would soon fall and wisp away like the very sands of the Great Sand Sea? Kings didn't like to hear such things, at least not straight up.

"Do you dance like the dervishes?" The man laughed coarsely, pressing. "Do you talk like a little monkey? Tell me."

"Sayidi, sir—" Khaled suddenly remembered the words of the oracle, *if you have to tell the truth, make it funny or people will kill you.* "Sayidi, I am a very strange wonder," he began, his heart rising to his throat. "You see, I am the oldest man you will ever meet, but I cannot even reach the stirrup of a camel's saddle." It was the first time he'd been grateful to whoever his father was, for giving him a shorter stature than his peers.

"Is that so?" A small smile lit the man's wary eyes.

"It's true. My mamtee says if I am not careful some sweet old grandma will come and sweep me off my feet."

Cadmus guffawed. "Does she now?"

Khaled nodded once.

The king set his hands on his hips. He grinned. "And what does your mamtee think about her little boy being so old?"

"Sir—" He thought. "Your highness, I'm afraid she is yet too young to understand."

The king's eyes widened, then filled with mirth as Khaled remained unmoved. "Oh, you will do marvelously." He turned and scratched his head, this time chuckling easily. "Say—" He stopped. "What great wisdom could I gain if my little old man were to sit at my right hand and eat dumplings with me tonight?" His eye twinkled. "Could you teach me how to make all the women love me and how to make a grape grow in this dratted desert?"

Khaled actually did know those things, so he shrugged. "Yes." He nodded. "If you'll listen," he added, with a thrill of impertinence. Because the man wouldn't listen.

But Cadmus loved it. "What a fun treasure. The boy who thinks he's a sage." He grinned. "You'll do. You'll do." He pushed him to the door. "Take him to the dressing rooms and suit him as a grandpa," he said to the waiting guard.

The king was still chuckling after the doors closed.

* * *

Madiha dabbed perspiration from her brow with the same scarf she'd given Khaled to dry with yesterday. A hot morning sun already slanted through the iron bars of her stall. Bars that were made to keep livestock from poking their heads into the street. The poor creatures. The air didn't move inside the stalls. No wonder their braying and neighing could be heard from as far as the village on nights when the heat didn't lift as it should.

But she had not made a sound. She'd listened. Talk of the

boy treasure—her boy treasure—had reassured her that, for the night, he was safe.

But the morning was a clamor of talk and trouble and, in the suffocating heat, panic grew from a seed to a full-grown cactus, pricking at her mind, calling her a fool for imprisoning herself. She would have been better off staying free.

She covered her ears. The clatter in the street was nonsense; two dialects and the imposter's language blurring together over the roar of wheels and clank of shod hooves. She felt like Khaled, how he always tried to quiet reality so he could listen to whatever it was that captivated his mind these days.

The afterlife, he always said. She sighed. It frightened her, how he no longer feared death. He would get himself killed. He would say things he shouldn't say. Especially to a king. Afterall, Cadmus was only seeking happiness, pleasure, and although Jashe may have found the pleasures of the afterlife in little Khaled's death-tainted mind, Khaled would have no words for it. He never did. And the king would kill him if he was not pleased.

"My lord, stop." She scrambled to her feet, seeing one of last night's young captors pass her stall. She could not continue to wait for news.

The man returned, a bit reluctantly, but she was glad she'd chosen him. He was the pruner's son, from her own village. A traitor, but at least they could speak clearly.

She brushed straw from her dress. "A word, Maleet—Sayidi," she corrected quickly.

He squared his jaw. "You are to be left without food or conversation, miss, until the king has judged that boy. You understand?" His words were much harder than his voice.

Madiha smiled. *Miss?* An idea started to bloom. It might be a cactus flower, but it was something. "Why do you call me miss, when you know I have a son?" She came to stand where the young man might see her face without the striped shadows contorting it.

"You are fair." He blushed.

Indeed? Many in the village would call her less, just because Khaled had come unexpectedly. Perhaps this was the single gift Cadmus had given her land: that women in the city were no longer blamed for the sins of men.

She chewed on that. "Tell your lord—" She touched the bars as the youth rubbed his neck, embarrassed. "Tell the king that a woman has finally been found, pleasing enough for his courts."

She'd gone too far. The man snorted. Not at her, but at the idea. "Plenty have been found pleasing enough, miss." He stopped laughing. "But none has been found who wishes to remain with him. He complains that they grow bored and do not truly love him."

Love? Was that why all the others had been cast out, sent back to their fathers with nothing but tear-stained cheeks? Because he wanted to be loved? Odd, for a king. Then again, she'd heard tell of the ways of the north; how marriages were neither arranged nor maintained by law. *Love.* She thought about it. Cadmus was very confused on the nature of that word, clearly.

She unknit her brow. "Here is an offer he cannot refuse: tell him I will give him my heart for as long as he is king." After all, in no time, he would abandon the oasis that he had ruined and she would be free again.

The youth studied her. "How could you love the man who stole your son?"

"Love is easy. Loss is what I cannot bear."

The man rubbed his nose. He checked the road in both

directions. "If this is a barter for the boy, don't." He drew nearer. "He may not relinquish him so easily."

"Oh, he will." She smiled. The youth meant well, but she knew better. The king would see Khaled as useless. It was an easy exchange. For where was the novelty in a child who did not fear death?

"Fair enough." The guard shrugged. "You know the boy's value best of all. I will take you there tonight, when the king is at ease over dinner."

She straightened her back. Nervous fireflies twisted in her stomach and she shivered despite the heat. Would she really bind herself to a man who had called on djinn long buried beneath the sands of her ancestors? What would Khaled say?

He would say it was better to die.

* * *

Khaled was happy to be clean again, and the promise of dumplings kept his stomach from giving up. But they wouldn't be Mamtee's dumplings. He rubbed his chest where his heart sat, sore and tired. *Oh, Mamtee.* They would be together again soon, but if he knew her, she would not be able to sleep or eat until then. What he wished she knew, though, was what the Wonder had made clear to him. He wiped a tear off his nose, reminding himself of this truth: every pleasure and every pain under the sun was but a passing breeze. The stars had not changed, the gold and blue starstreams and all their songs rang on, just above them, and there in their midst—the Wonder Itself.

He pulled back his shoulders. The tummy on his grandpa suit was heavy. *Siwa needs you still,* the Wonder had said. Never had he dreamed it meant he'd have a chance to influence the king.

He grinned. The *almost*-king.

The doors to the dining hall pulled open. "Welcome, my sage." Cadmus met him and took his hand. "Let us see this great wisdom of which you speak."

Khaled gulped. When he said "us" he didn't mean a few close friends. The king's entire entourage had showed up to dine with them. Long tables sat on either side of a broad isle, draped in gold cloths and set with jewel-colored plates and goblets of clear glass. Men in the foreign military dress outnumbered women ten to one. This was the same army he'd brought on his conquest five years ago. The king had not made many local companions, apparently.

A few whispers followed the two of them down the long walk to where a small throne had been constructed next to the king's.

"Dumplings, as promised," the almost-king whispered, pointing to a heaping plateful that rested by Khaled's throne. "And now—" He sat down with a flourish, suggesting Khaled do the same. He winked. "Entertain us with your wisdom."

Khaled munched into a gooey dumpling, just before hearing the king. Slowly, he peeled the remaining half dumpling off his lips. It wasn't luqaimat. There was no cardamom and the dough was too sticky. The crowd giggled. Tables full of grown men and women snickering. And him, hungry as a horse in summer.

"Eat, eat," the king said to the waiting crowd.

Khaled blessed him for that, but still didn't finish the dumpling. He set it back on the plate.

"Tell me, old man—" The king's voice rose above the clatter of flatware on plates. "Who is happier, the man with many wives or the man with a great host of friends?"

Khaled flushed. Nothing came to mind instantly. He looked at the crowd. Even though they ate, many of the men still stared up at him, eager. Who knew what they expected?

He wanted to run, but with a shudder remembered how Jashe had claimed him. Even now the hairs on his spine rose, reminding him that the djinn was near. Somehow it knew the treasures of his mind, and it would know if he did not speak the truth. He closed his eyes and listened past the clanking of dishes and the impatient breath of his ruler. Violet and gold streams of stardust danced into his vision, wrapping around the feet of the great Wonder. *That's right.* Whatever they did to him here, his consolation awaited above. Nothing could take that from him.

So, the truth it was. But gently.

"Sayidi—" He had it now. He allowed the present to return. "The answer is neither, for friends bring trouble and a wife brings grief."

The crowd chuckled. Some leaned back in their chairs, suddenly more interested than before.

The king scratched his chin. He scowled at first, but soon nodded. "I suppose that is true."

Khaled breathed.

"But, tell me—" Cadmus received a glass of wine, "what is the nature of contentment?" He sipped. "From where does it come?"

Khaled relaxed further. "You know this yourself, Sayidi." This answer was easy. "There is no true contentment under the sun."

The king laughed. "Try again, my sage." He raised his glass in salute. "For what you see before you is a contented man. Look—" He gestured to the long room, draped in white damask, cloudlike in its regality. "I have shade from the heat." He beamed. "I have fruit that is grown far away where there is plenty of rain. I have gold enough for a lifetime, now." He winked. "And not only do I have every comfort, but I have the very wisdom of the elderly at my right hand."

If you would only take advantage of it. Khaled rolled his eyes.

The king didn't notice. He winked again. "And neither do I have many wives or a great host of friends to detract from my contentment."

The crowd chuckled with him and he stretched. "Indeed, what you see is a man who has found every solace under the sun, as you say. But do tell me, wise one, where a sage like you might find contentment, if it is not in such fine things."

That was his first good question. "Death, Sayidi." Khaled remembered the happiest he'd ever been.

The man frowned. "Death?" He looked to the crowd and shrugged. "Death." Everyone laughed. "You are a sad old man."

Khaled sighed. "For now, perhaps, but not forever." He adjusted the collar of his suit where trickles of sweat gathered. He hoped this would be over soon.

Cadmus took a long drink of wine, then cleared his throat. "Well, answer this for me, since you promised: why is it that every wife I bring into my home, within a fortnight says she no longer wishes to stay. Why does no woman wish to be my wife, and will only be so if I command it?"

Khaled was confused. "But you do not want a wife."

A murmur of laughter moved through the crowd without the king's permission. He glared at Khaled. "Humor me."

Very well. He'd seen enough village men trample their wives to know this. "Sayidi, a wife is like your very throne, she does not wish to be sat upon." It sounded clever, and was resoundingly true.

The king snorted. "She does not wish to be—" But he stopped. "What are you saying about my throne?"

Khaled just looked at him. It was as he thought.

"Are you saying I am not fit for this throne? You know that's treason." He eyed Khaled as though this were some joke.

"Well—" Khaled decided to eat a dumpling while he spoke. It may ease the tension. "You see—" He munched, thinking. Yes, the man needed to know the truth. "You see, Sayidi," he ventured, letting his courage draw up his voice, "many things wish to have feet: the tree when you axe it, the fish when you leave it on shore, and the pride of Siwa when you put it on your head."

"Excuse me?" The king narrowed his eyes.

He understood. Khaled continued, fearless. "Yes, Sayidi." His voice rose, sharp and clear. The truth would stand, and die if he might, it would be worth it. "Siwa is not a treasure you can possess. Her glory will not return until you set her free."

A dragon could have entered the room and no one would have moved.

The king's jawline grew hard enough to crack in two. His eye pierced, but Khaled refused to look away.

"Actually, I was wrong." Anger gnawed up any remnant of reservation. For Mamtee, for the lake, for the trees. *For Cadmus himself.* "A tree and a fish *wish* they had feet, but Siwa does and she is running from you. Our land will only flourish when you let it go."

A knock at the giant doors broke the stare that had turned to ice.

"What is it?" the king ground through his teeth.

"Sir, we found this woman among your prisoners." A shy guard bowed into the room, cracking the door open only far enough to reveal himself.

"A prisoner, now?" Cadmus's face turned red as a pomegranate.

Khaled would not want to be that guard or that prisoner. He took the moment to close his eyes and think. When the king turned back, he may very well sentence him to death. He had said bold things. He had said things Mamtee would not want him to say. But what if these words could bring life back to Siwa? What if his words could somehow save the king?

The intruder did not back down easily. He spoke again and Khaled opened his eyes. "This woman claims she desires your hand. She is fair, my lord."

The king growled and rubbed his face. "Your timing could not be worse, Maleet." He shot a cold glance at Khaled and straightened his back. "But bring her in, if you must. I will see for myself."

This would buy Khaled time to consider his final words.

The doors swung open wide.

"Mamtee?" Khaled sprang to his feet.

She had shackles on her wrists. Why?

"Your mother?" The king sneered at Khaled. He sat back with a groan. "What crime is this woman guilty of?"

The guard would have answered, but Mamtee dragged the guard after her, rushing to the foot of the dais. "Sir, Khaled is mine. I got between him and one of your collectors. You would have done the same. It isn't right for a mother and child to be apart."

"This is true?"

The guard nodded, sheepish. "Sir."

The king stretched and rested the back of his head on clasped hands. "So, you've come to join your son in my court." His laugh was fake. "What is this, a family of traitors who calls themselves treasures?"

She should not have come. Not now. Not like this. Khaled found his nails digging into his palms.

"He is not the treasure you think." Mamtee glanced at him. Something stung, like her words were a bee burrowing into his chest. "I give you my heart and my devotion if you release him."

No. "Mamtee—"

The king leaned forward. He gripped the arms of his throne. "Woman, this child of yours has spoken treason to me. I cannot let him go so easily."

His mother tripped to her knees, nearly kissing the bottom step. "Treason, Sayidi?" Her voice broke. She looked up, pleading. "He is just a little boy with a taste of death. He needs a mother and a home, not a royal perch and a thousand listening ears."

No, he was more than that. Tears pricked at Khaled's nose. No, he knew that now. With the Wonder in him, he was so much more than she thought.

Cadmus laughed. "Take her to the dressing rooms. She is fair, but I will not trade her for the boy." He winked at Khaled. "I will have some fun with him yet."

"No, don't—" Khaled stared as they pulled her away. This wasn't happening. He glared back at the man who would never be king.

"You see?" The man lounged, mocking. "You see, old man, even entertainment comes to me at my beck and call. Perfectly for free. I am the most contented man."

Khaled opened his mouth to say whatever raw words would come, but the hairs on his neck rose, sharp as pins. Jashe was here.

"You know, that's not true," the king continued, unaware. He sipped his wine. "I need one more thing." He put the glass down and rubbed his hands.

Khaled couldn't actually be sure it was Jashe this time. The crowd felt it too. They murmured and set down their forks. A few stood. Maybe they would leave. The smells of spiced lamb and honeyed fruit lingered above the quiet room, as though contemplating running too.

The king turned and leaned on the arm of his throne. "You make a mockery of me, boy?" He got closer. "Then I will mock you." And he stood. "Sit down!" His voice rattled the room. Those who had stood resumed their seats slowly like young thieves returning their loot, hoping not to be slapped. "This child tells me my kingdom has up and run from me. Calls me a fool." He sneered. He was fingering a ring. Rubbing it secretly. "The boy calls himself wise," he continued, and he rubbed harder, "but I have the secret to all knowledge at my own fingertips."

Khaled gaped. *No.* His heart rose to his throat. The ring was turning blue. All the hairs on all his limbs spiked and a thrill of terror climbed up from his stomach.

It was Almarifi.

The king was calling the djinn of earthly knowledge, the demon who offered a single, limitless gift to any man willing to forfeit his afterlife and live forever under the sun.

"Sayidi, stop!" Khaled stood and pulled down Cadmus's hands. "Almarifi will destroy you."

The almost-king shoved Khaled away. He spoke, but his voice disappeared in a rush of dust-blue smoke.

"Who dares steal me from my studies?" The ancient voice yawned from within the cloud as it continued to plume and

333

grow throughout the room, searching.

It shied from Khaled's face and found Cadmus. "You again." And all the dust coalesced into a half-human form with a wisp of a tail, staring down at the king. "I told you—" the words rolled slowly, as though every syllable was a yawn, "I do nothing for the dying and as far as I can tell you are still marching straight to the grave, human." It sniffed.

The king still seethed, but his voice broke at his first word. "I—" He swallowed. "I am ready now." His voice grew. "I give you my death, my eternity in whatever rest awaits. I forfeit that." He gulped again and tensed his jaw and fists. "Now, return to me the magic of Siwa and make me king of it forever."

The djinn laughed, low and rolling. The smoke moved, mimicking his ongoing chuckles. "I said one thing. I can grant you one wish. And that is two."

Cadmus glanced at Khaled. His face hardened further and he snapped back at the djinn, "Fine. Return to me the magic of this oasis. Give me the verdant hills and the lake that overflows with rain. Give me a land that does not run from me."

And the djinn puffed out his chest, satisfied. It held out an unnatural hand with fingernails that curled up and twisted away into the air. "Your life ever after, from here to eternity—" He began the enchantment grandly.

Khaled knew it well. *Your life ever after, from here to eternity, will be on the earth, to the pit of insanity.* The curse of immortality. Cadmus would have all the pleasures below the sun, but he would never know the consolation of what lay above it, in death.

In the space of a second, Khaled saw the future unfold like a new tapestry, no thread of its story withheld from him. Even though Siwa would flourish again, even though they could stay and fish again, and all the trade routes would be restored, and Mamtee could earn back her silver and buy back grandpa's books— Khaled made fists— even though everything would be beautiful again, this man living his eternity here could not happen.

"Take mine!" he cried. "Give him the gift, but take my afterlife instead." Maybe this was what the Wonder had returned him for. He would save the king's only chance at eternal contentment.

The smoke hissed in surprise. "Yes?" It turned to him.

Khaled squared his gaze. "Yes."

Cadmus lurched toward him, across his throne. "Don't listen to the boy," he choked.

A guard stepped up to grab Khaled, but Almarifi blocked him.

"No. Leave him be." The spirit hovered near Khaled's face. "What might I find in your afterlife?"

"Wonders," Khaled said simply, although his breath came hard, pushing and pulling at the strange body of dust.

The spirit's dark eyes and bearded chin drew nearer still. "Once I enter your death, you know you will never see it again."

"Yes. Take my ability to die." He couldn't help that his small voice was only growing higher in his passion. "But do not rob this man of his only hope at contentment. Leave him mortal." He made fists and stared down the constantly wavering spirit.

"You would give your afterlife to save this man?" Almarifi scoffed, but his words were no longer tired. He twisted higher into the air, then jagged back down again. "Why?"

Khaled steadied his breath. "If I must live forever so that one more man might enter eternity and know what I know, so be it."

The djinn laughed warmly. "Then why aren't you the king instead of this fool?" He pointed. "You would not even need my gifts."

Khaled bit back a flood of shivers. What did he mean?

"What?" Cadmus grabbed Khaled's arm. "What did he say?"

The spirit pushed him back, scoffing. "If you'd made this child king, you never would have needed me. For don't you know that it is the heart of the one who rules this oasis that saves the magic? It is the heart of the ruler that is mirrored throughout the land. The whole land would be rich."

What? Khaled nearly lost his balance. He sat down hard. It made sense, but he'd never thought of it before. When the oracles had sat on their temple seats, Siwa had flourished. When no one ruled, in the year before Cadmus descended with his army, there had been storms and strange breezes from the west. The people and all their chaos had been the rulers at that time. If Siwa was a mirror of whoever had the highest seat— His heart thrilled. What would Siwa be if a little boy with all the stars and all the wisdom of the Wonder Itself inside his head took the seat?

He could do it, too. The tapestry of that future was larger and more beautiful than any before. This was his duty, from the Wonder Itself, to tend this land like the oracles had, to rule with wisdom and love. He glanced at the ring. He didn't need to surrender his afterlife.

"I changed my mind." He stood. "But I will take the throne."

The djinn chortled and pressed him in the face so that he almost tripped back. "However good a king you might have been, little one, I do *so* want to take your death and all the wisdom that awaits you. And since you offered—" It rushed into his mouth and ears. "I accept," it hissed, turning his vision black, his thoughts to chaos, and the starstreams of eternity to dust.

* * *

A child's cry pierced the hot night air. *Khaled.* The cry was raw— and cut short too soon. Madiha would have slumped to the floor, if her dressing maid wasn't pulling so hard at the ties about her waist. What had they done to him? She fought the tight-faced old woman who was dressing her.

"Are you a mother?" she beseeched. "Let me go to my son."

The woman didn't speak Siwi, but she seemed to understand. She let go.

Pulling up her awful gowns—layers of red and white meant to swirl like the dancing dervishes of the east— Madiha flew down the unguarded halls. The dressing rooms were on the opposite side of the palace from the dining halls, but nothing could have wearied her feet or exhausted her heart. She would find Khaled and she would take him home. If the Wonder that Khaled knew was kind at all, It would return her boy to life.

Just please, she prayed, *please don't let him cling to death.*

She burst through the two great doors. All the men who had been dining in regal mockery before now hid under the tables, covering their heads and crying. Cadmus lay motionless, crumpled on the dais steps. And Khaled—

She approached. He lay at the foot of his little throne, with his chin doubled over his body. His eyes were open and staring. Empty.

No.

"Khaled—" she choked, stumbling over the body of the king. They both looked as though they had been thrown by a mighty wind. "Babu—" She gripped his knee. "Come back." He was already growing cold. Who had done this?

She gathered his limp form into her arms, shaking. "You can't

337

leave me." *Not again. Not forever.*

But he did not stir. He did not try.

"Why?" She heard her own jagged cry as though it were far away. Why did he not fight to return to her? Why did this Wonder intrigue him and draw him away from this world? Cold, hard tears welled in her throat but she would not let them rain. The Wonder had made a desert of her.

* * *

Cadmus tried to clear his eyes, rubbing them fiercely and squinting through the darkness. Nothing.

Wait— He batted at a sparkling sort of fly that whizzed past his face. Then another. No, millions of them. He blinked hard. Waves of silver stars rose and fell on violet mists that interwove a great expanse of deep, unsearchable blue. He was surrounded by a weightless, incomprehensible space. He looked down.

For the love of—

He had no body.

"What are you doing here?" A voice, cold as a steel blade, sliced through the strange night.

Me? He looked around. He didn't even know where he was, let alone why.

"Not you." The voice warmed, then cooled again—hard as ice. "You."

A snake of pale mist crept from behind him, revealing itself to the voice.

Cadmus could finally detect a horizon of sorts. A slowly stretching, slowly yawning white light in the distance. From it came the voice. "Almarifi," it sighed, speaking to the faint spirit. "That is one of my names and you stole it."

"Wisdom," hissed the gray mist.

That was the genie—the djinn.

Cadmus tried to back away. But he was immovable, pinned to the scene as though tied. Was he inside Khaled's treasured afterlife?

No.

But he was. This was all wrong. He'd be blamed. He had let the child receive this spirit and now—He squirmed. The child was not here. The djinn had cursed the boy and taken his afterlife from him. Cadmus fought again, trying to look around. But why was he here, himself? Had he died in the fray?

"You, be still." The strangely flexible voice addressed him, then turned again to the djinn. The light grew ever nearer. "You called yourself wisdom." It was ice-like again. "You spurned my name for millennia and still you dare to come here and try to pillage and loot from those who are dead?" So he was dead.

"I was invited," the wisp bit back.

"I know." And sadness washed over the expanse like a physical wave. A grief wave.

The brilliance on the horizon doubled in size and out of it came what Cadmus could swear was a giant foot.

Yet another giant, sandaled foot. The two of them took massive strides. If Cadmus had had a choice, he'd have been a thousand kilometers underground by now. Each foot was the size of an entire universe and fear was not the word for what he felt as they grew ever nearer. It was shame. Shame like the weight of an army of oxen.

The smoky being felt it too. It sparked and sizzled, reeling and fleeing once again behind Cadmus. "Be gone," it shrieked. But, even hidden, it continued spitting and fizzing as water does when thrown against a fire. It seemed unable to withstand the voice's presence. "Be gone," it hissed again, frantic.

"That's my line." The feet strode one step nearer, and the genie crackled and fumed, spraying powder-blue mist in every direction until, with a final hiss, it dissipated.

Even without a body, Cadmus shivered. Now the gold of the feet, and the gold of the light pervaded everything. He was a dead man. Either already, or almost.

"Cadmus." The voice bent low and soothed the air.

Yes?

"I made you for more than the pleasures of life. Do not aim for satisfaction now—that is my job, but you have to wait for it." The voice slipped easily past all of Cadmus's fears and rebuttals. "Live for others and I will give you rest, in death. I promise."

The voice paused and Cadmus said nothing. His head was aching and all he could think was if he had a headache, he had a head, and if he had a head, he had a second chance.

The voice softened even further. "The mother misses her son. Will anyone miss you when you are gone?"

I know. The boy. Cadmus thought he said it aloud, but he couldn't be sure. *What have I done?* Would the child be immortal now, forever forbidden to enter his rest? Horror dawned as the light of the Wonder faded.

"My Khaled—" The stars spun on their purple scarves and the voice was—the voice was feminine.

* * *

Madiha sobbed. "My boy, my Khaled." She was tired. Tired of fighting, tired of longing, tired of waiting for him to breathe again. She lay with him in her arms, his eyes closed in rest, his lips dark with death. The room was still. The ages could come and go and she would not care.

A shift.

The child's limp arm recoiled.

A breath.

"Babu?" She gasped. "Khaled!" She pushed strands of his hair out of his blinking eyes.

"Mamtee." He stirred.

Bless the Wonder.

"Oh, bless the very Wonder!" She gripped him again and pulled him closer. He let her. He nuzzled into her neck and she pressed her cheek against the back of his head. He stroked her hair. She could feel him gaining strength.

When he looked up again, his smile was altered.

"Khaled—" She tried to keep him close, but he stood.

"Get Cadmus," he said, not pushing her away, but almost. He searched for the king. "Is he all right?"

"Why?" It was only him she was worried about. "My child, wait."

"Mamtee, I'm not waiting anymore." He looked back into her eyes. The mournful gaze she'd grown accustomed to was gone. But what was this—what was this strength he had now? He was changed.

"The king, Mamtee," he insisted, "get him up."

Anything for you, Babu. Confused, she bent to the young man's side and found him already stirring. His pale face was washed in the light of some knowledge she could not see.

He rubbed his neck as his eyes darted between memories or thoughts. Then his gaze latched onto her, and what little color he had drained from his face. "Forgive me." His eyes widened. "Forgive me," he said again, struggling to sit up. "Your son, he chose—" He choked. "He chose to take the curse of immortality."

"What?" Madiha's stomach rose to her throat. "Son?" She turned to him.

"No," Khaled laughed. "I'm not immortal." He bent to Cadmus. "You saw yourself. Almarifi is dead and Jashe has fled and everything they have done is undone."

Cadmus scrambled up to his knees, catching Khaled by the shoulders. "But you weren't there. I didn't see you."

Khaled laughed. "I was hidden in the Wonder. I was truly dead, for a little while. It was the only way." He glanced sadly at Mamtee, but quickly back to the king. "I knew that Almarifi would not be able to withstand the light of my afterlife, of the Wonder itself. I was not afraid."

"Then you truly are a wonder." Cadmus bowed.

Cadmus bowed. Madiha stared.

Men and women started to emerge from under tables and from behind curtains.

"Your highness, look!" several called at once. They pointed out the windows.

Rain. Madiha hadn't heard that sound these five long years.

"What is that?" Cadmus got to his feet. He listened.

"Rain, my friend." Khaled took the young man's hand and led him to the window. Madiha stayed back. What kind of a wonder was her son? What had he done? They would have to have a long chat about what she'd missed. A chat over dumplings, by their humble stove, listening to the rain.

She followed him and touched his back. "Time to go home, Babu."

He stayed watching the rain. It bounced off the gilded roofs of little gazebos in the courtyard below. Dwarf palms soaked up the long drink, their leaves bouncing and trembling in the playful torrent.

That smell. Fresh tears welled in her throat. "Come on, Babu," she insisted. "Ruta misses us. And maybe those dumplings are still good."

"No, Mamtee." He turned, the light in his eyes softened by the carefulness of his words. "We are home. Siwa is mine, and I have work to do."

Cadmus took a knee at Khaled's side, but he looked up at Madiha. "Siwa needs him, your highness. I give him my turban and my crown." He gripped Khaled's hands. "You took my foolish choice and made it your own. Why?"

Khaled shook his head. "Get up. You know why. You saw it yourself, didn't you? You saw what awaits. And it is worth more than all the wonders under the sun. Wouldn't you agree?"

"Yes." The almost-king stood. "In eternity, then? I hope by the will of the Wonder Itself, I may be granted the right to sit at your side."

After a deep bow toward Madiha, he called whoever wished to follow him. Two gathered what pride they had left and the three of them departed that very night. The rest fell to a knee, honoring Khaled, the king of Siwa.

Madiha's eyes filled with tears, warm like the rain. "Can I make the king some proper luqaimat?" She touched Khaled's chin. "You look famished."

And he was.

But woe unto you that are rich,
For you have received your consolation

343

Gen Gavel

Keen observer of life and humanity, Gen Gavel, author of "Wondermind and the Almost King," writes to make sense of her days in light of an incomprehensible God.

She edits for a similar reason: to make sense of authors' ramblings in light of the mighty Chicago Manual of Style.

When she's not moving words around on a page, she's either embarrassing her kids by badly belting Broadway beats, con- versing with her overly opinionated springer spaniel, Jessica, or catching a bus downtown to hang with her favorite kind of people: hipsters.

Rightfully Ours

03 March 2605
Sakana Star System

Dad brushed apple blossoms aside. "These could all be yours, someday, if you don't want command of your own starship."

"Why do I have to choose?" Achille walked beside his father, doing his best to match Corin Duval's long-legged stride. The artificial gravity aboard *Bienfaisance* seemed to lengthen it. Dad always had a bounce to his step when they left dock. "I could split my duties as captain and arborist."

Dad chuckled. "I bet you could, but then what would be left for your brother?"

Achille rolled his eyes. "That vac-head wouldn't know the difference between a graft and a shoot if I had the Tutor demo explain it with holograms."

Dad's raised eyebrow was enough to warn Achille from further commentary on his brother's intellect. "Kai is capable when it comes to the captain's chair, and his experience at the helm all but guarantees his ascendancy."

"Yes, but..." Achille blew out a breath as hard as an airlock expelling atmosphere. "Dad, you're the owner."

"Part owner. With your mother, and all of you." He winked. "There's five Duvals on the deed."

346

"Fine. Majority owner. Current captain."

They squeezed between the containers in which a stand of apple trees was secured. Achille squinted through the leaves at the soft yellow lighting streaming from the upper catwalks of *Bienfaisance*'s cargo bay. Even with hundreds packed together branch to branch, filling the main deck, the bay had a feel of a yawning cavern, albeit one made of reinforced alloys.

Not the pasty gray rock of their former home.

"Achille, I've been over this with you—I want all three of my children to play vital roles in the continuation of our legacy. Ariane chose Engineering, and if anyone thinks he'll pry her out of there with anything shy of a runaway reactor breach, he'd be a fool. Your mother's been training both Kai and Jiao on the comms. The two of them will make a fine pair to handle the bridge. They anticipate each other's commands well."

"They're disgustingly sweet," Achille muttered.

Dad nodded, his smile broadening. "Yes, newlyweds are like that. Give them time. They'll mellow—unless your mother and I still turn your stomach."

Achille reached for a broken branch. What could he do to convince Dad he didn't need Kai lording it over him? Working alongside his older brother was one thing. Taking orders from him, though... Only that thought made him sicker than imagining the young couple smooching in front of everyone on the bridge. It wasn't fair. He should have more time to decide, or to persuade Dad. But their departure had upped the timetable. "I wish we had stayed."

"That wasn't an option, sadly," Dad said. "I know it was hard for you to leave Garnet. Your mother and I understand. We were there at the beginning. We used handheld cutters to smooth the corners of our habitat from the asteroid's skin.

That place was our home away from *Bienfaisance*, meant to be a new Eden in a sterile corner of the galaxy."

"I don't understand why the colonists hated us." Achille clenched his fists. Anger at the betrayal only worsened his upset stomach. "It was our world, too. We could have shared it."

Dad grasped his shoulders. Achille kept his chin up, mimicking Dad's statuesque stance, but he was still too short, too scrawny. His face had the soft edges and Asian features of Mom's; Dad was to him a king with long, sharp nose and cheekbones. When he smiled, skin crinkled into a thousand canyons at the corners of brilliant blue eyes. "You have a good heart. It hurts me that you won't get the chance to help in the administrator's office, solving public problems like I did. We'd have made a good team. The best. But people can be cruel and greedy. They'll take what's rightfully ours if we're not vigilant."

Achille pondered this as Dad headed for the center marking on the cargo bay's deck plates. A post rose to waist height, lifting a control panel into Dad's reach. He entered a code. A long, broad hatch slid open, revealing a descending ramp. White lights flickered on, illuminating deep shadows.

Dad led him down to the next deck, Storage. Narrow aisles cut canyons through the maze of containers – gray, white, and black boxes arranged in checkerboard fashion. The manifest labels told Achille of the bounty enclosed in them, from coveted Liberty beef to Muhteremi spices and, of course, Duval apples. Dozens of the crates were marked, "Sold," the tag followed by an invoice number and shipping date.

"There's enough down here to keep us fed for years." Dad patted a black box. "And more than that already sold, as seed money for our new lives. Crews of every merchant ship and military vessel from the Twenty Territories to Earth itself will stock their stores with Duvals."

"You and Mom engineered them to be the best. Long-lasting, blight-resistant, rapid growth—"

"You're a born salesman," Dad said. "All the more reason for you to rise to orchard oversight instead of the bridge."

The comms unit on his wrist chirped, cutting off Achille's chance for rebuttal. No way he was going win the debate. Dad tapped the flat panel. "Go ahead, *mon Cherie*."

"I need you on the bridge, Corin." Mei Duval's voice was soft, like when she'd sung Achille lullabies in Mandarin—but had a titanium spine. "Traffic issues from the sundoor."

Sundoor. The colloquial term for tract shifts, the regions surrounding a star that were prime transit spots for all starships employing Raszewski drives. Achille knew *Bienfaisance* had made the shift into this remote star system hours ago, before embarking on a long, slow course that would bring it to a second sundoor on the other side of the star.

"On my way." Dad tousled Achille's hair. "Finish with the dodectites' diagnostics. Make sure Storage is sealed."

"You got it."

Dad was off, up the ramp and through the orchard to the lift at the back of the cargo bay. Achille triggered the Storage hatch, listening for the telltale hiss of pressurized seals and watching for the green lights on the control post.

Robot duty. He pulled a delver from his pocket and punched commands into the handheld device. Green-lined schematics of a slender robot with four arms and eight legs appeared. Maybe maintenance would take his mind off the succession issue, or at least give him time to come up with a new argument.

Bienfaisance carried sixteen dodectite robots to maintain the orchard. Every one glitched from time to time. They kept Achille busier than the trees themselves.

He found two of them in a head-butting contest, or maybe he should have said optical sensor module-butting. Both were as tall as his armpit, conical in shape, with four arms spaced equally around their ersatz torsos. Each arm could extend two meters, and the four appendages sported trimmers, graspers, and probes. Eight arched legs clattered on the deck as the bots battered each other.

"Easy, guys." Achille found their serial numbers: 10616 and 10622.

Of course, it was those two. They never missed a chance to target each other. He knew their operating systems weren't complex enough to allow them to engage in grudges, but he swore it happened regardless. Achille reset their parameters. The dodectites froze, retracted their arms, and scurried into the maze of trees. The sounds of their shears clipping dead branches filled the bay.

Achille ran diagnostics on the rest of the gang. Only one, 10613, was docked in a repair slot for a refit and so wasn't causing trouble. He'd have to tackle the hardware later. The rest were strolling the aisles, like tourists, occasionally bonking into each other and getting into ridiculous robot slap fights. He got them back in sync and put them back to work tending the orchard, plucking apples, checking for diseases, and tilling soil. Why they'd all chosen to glitch out at the same time was beyond Achille.

"Worse than the last time, when we picked up a digger that made them all spin in circles," he muttered.

The diagnostics for 10613 bounced back an error message. Some file clogging up the memory. Achille made a face. "That should've been cleaned out in the last update."

Deck plates trembled. Achille paused mid-step. He knelt and touched the nearest one. No, the tremor was gone. He'd have to ask Ariane if one the power conduits was loose.

The tantalizing aroma of apples in the cargo bay was so strong enough Achille snatched a discarded one from 10622's claw as it barreled past on its way to its next task. It was a spotted, lumpen fruit, one destined for the cider. Not fit for unblemished sale.

Achille bit into it, savoring the burst of fire that stung his mouth, instantly cooled by sweet juices.

Dad was right. They were going to make a fortune.

The entire cargo bay heaved with such violence he rolled into tree binds. He whacked his shin. His trousers tore. Blood welled from a cut visible inside the newborn rip.

His apple rolled out of sight.

Tremors rocked the compartment, one after the other. Everything seemed tilted. Achille struggled to regain his footing, the task made tougher by the trees swaying and apples careening along the deck. He finally got a handhold on one of the bigger trees. They weren't going anywhere, not with their containers anchored. Red lights flooded the compartment. A klaxon pierced the air.

Achille slapped his wrist comm. "Bridge! What's happening?"

"Achille! Get up here, now!" Dad's command was far from the friendly banter they'd had moments ago. "I'm sealing the bay!"

No time. Achille left the apples, left the bots, and sprinted for the emergency stairs. No lift. Not in an emergency.

He took the spiral steps two at a time, his footing sure even as the entire ship bucked around him. He didn't bother to read the yellow signs denoting the decks as he rose. It felt like he would never stop climbing, until he burst from the open hatch onto the broad corridor feeding into the bridge.

The compartment was an armored cylinder nestled in the fore section of *Bienfaisance*, a single level structure sporting a command chair in the center, a comms station to the right, plus a joint helm-sensor console ahead. An auxiliary console for sensor data and engineering stats was installed on the left, as were a few fold-down jump seats. A bowl five meters in diameter took up most of the front half of the bridge, a holographic projector that featured *Bienfaisance* in a blue-white miniature at its center.

Dad was in his seat, grasping the arms of the chair, as if he was going to rip them free. "Get us out of range!"

"Trying! We're leaking propellant and it's throwing off our course!" Kai Duval fought with the helm console's controls, goosing the main drives. He was tall like Dad, lithe, with the same icy blue eyes. Sweat dampened spiky black hair.

The deck shifted underfoot, and in the holographic plotter, the numbers indicating the ship's velocity spun up—slowly. Red images flashed on the auxiliary engineering screens. Kai wasn't kidding. The fuel tanks were draining.

Because it had taken critical damage.

"They're powering up!" Mom held a gray comms earpiece in place. She had black hair tied back in a ponytail, silver streaks aglow in the emergency lighting. "Intruding vessel, this is private cargo hauler *Bienfaisance* out of Garnet colony. Cease your attack! Authorities have been notified!"

"Only if the signal can push through their jamming," Kai muttered.

Jamming? Attack? Achille stumbled against Dad's chair. There was a red marker in the holo plotter, and an equally crimson line flashed between it and *Bienfaisance...*

The ship shuddered, the compensators straining to keep up with the stress of impact against the hull. At least they didn't quit while Kai was accelerating at the 28.9 gravities the readouts indicated, or they'd all be mashed flat.

"Kai!" The voice boomed through the ship's intercom—Ariane, Achille's oldest sibling. "I'm gonna have to shut down! The fuel tank's near empty. Not enough for the engines to maintain a burn."

"Yeah, well, if you haven't noticed, the guys shooting aren't having any trouble keeping up!" Kai snapped.

"They're not responding to our hails." Mom turned in her chair and her eyes went wide. "Achille! Strap in!"

Dad glanced at him, adding a nod to Mom's order.

"Storage is secure." Achille stumbled into one of the jump seats.

"Good work. Jiao, the lasers—"

"All turrets have enough charge stored in their capacitors for a single sustained shot." Jiao, Kai's wife, was shorter than everyone else in the family, with hair shaded lemon yellow. Her hands flew across the auxiliary engineering console. "I rerouted what I could, so I think it should be sufficient."

"I need certainty, not a guess."

"I'm sorry but that's all I can provide."

Dad slid open a panel on his chair. Three red switches protruded. He tapped a panel and all three glowed. "Turrets linked. Kai, line me up for a good shot."

"Working on it." Kai wiped sweat from the bridge of his nose and blew out a breath. He sent *Bienfaisance* into a spin.

Achille held on to his straps as the hull shuddered. A terrible moan echoed from far below.

"Structural integrity collapsing on the belowdecks!" Jiao said. "Venting atmosphere in compartments—!"

"Never mind that. Where are they?" Dad snapped.

"Sensors are cloudy. I can't make out—"

"*Coque cassee!*" Kai blurted. "They're right on top of us!"

The sensor images relayed to the holo projector showed the red diamond suddenly superimposed on *Bienfaisance*. A quick magnification revealed a 150-meter navastel cargo vessel so close to his family's ship Achille figured he could touch it.

Another alarm sounded.

"Killing the mains!" Ariane shouted through the intercom. "Kai, I can get you rockets and ions but that's—"

A tremendous shock banged Achille against his seat. Sparks showered Kai and Jiao. Smoke billowed from behind an access panel.

Every engine and reactor indicator went dead.

"Ariane. Ariane!" Mom's hands splayed on the comms board. "I've lost contact!"

Achille saw the results on the engineering console and his mouth went dry. "Dad... the aft quarter—"

The attacker's last shot had shear off a huge chunk of *Bienfaisance.* Water sprayed in a beautiful silver sheen as the engines, cooling vanes, and the twisted, blackened remnants of hull stringers spiraled onto a new course separate from the ship.

"Reactors are holding." He could barely hear Jiao's whisper over the clamor. "Raszewski sphere intact..."

Dad stared at Mom.

"Dad. Captain!" Kai pounded his console. "The attackers are pulling free of us. That impact? They cut Storage free of the ship! You get one shot in five seconds."

Achille was numb. Ariane. She was gone? Storage, stolen? What about the orchard?

"Captain!" Kai shouted.

Dad's hand slapped onto the firing buttons.

Three ruby lines stabbed from the *Bienfaisance* hologram, two spearing the attacking ship dead center, the other slicing into the aft hull where the engines were located. A brilliant flash lit up that section, and for a moment, Achille thought the whole ship had exploded.

He caught a glimpse of the attacking vessel, its image covered with damage readouts, before the power cut out and everything went black. His arms lifted free of his sides, of their own accord.

Even worse. No gravity.

Dad cleared his throat. His voice was thick with grief. "I'm … I'm going aft."

* * *

Achille gazed out into the cargo bay. There'd been an apple orchard here, not fifteen minutes ago. A violet forest speckled with crimson fruits.

Now, nothing

The entire compartment was open to space. Achille pressed his hands against the transparent emergency barrier extruding from the stairwell hatch. The hatch itself had been ripped clean off.

Jiao spun herself until she was oriented identically. Her hair was a starburst. Tears drifted free, past her eyes. "Gone. All of it. The trees blew out when the bay decompressed."

Achille nodded, everything numb. He didn't feel her fingers on his shoulder. All he could feel was the vacuum of space, greedy, on the other side of the barrier. The cargo bay was stripped bare. Beyond that, stars on a midnight curtain.

And still no word from Mom and Dad.

Kai floated down the stairwell, upside down to Achille. "They've cleared six more compartments. Reached Engineering. It wasn't open to space, but the decompression triggered lockdown barriers."

"Was she... there?"

"Dad said they haven't found a body. She could still be okay. Maybe she found a way out. Anything left here?"

Achille shook his head. "Storage is gone."

"I saw on the damage control board. Blown clean off the hull."

"No. Detached." Achille brought up the same specs on his delver's screen. "Here: they used their point defense laser to cut through the hull, then grappled the entire compartment free."

"Pirates." Kai scowled. "Probably thought they'd turn us into a derelict and take our cargo without a fight."

"The captain showed them," Jiao murmured.

"Blasted right he did. They're adrift. I'm tracking them from the bridge—Raszewski sphere is shattered, engines offline but they've got a good fuel reserve. At least we can get back what they took."

"It's not just storage." Achille accessed the last 24 hours of security vids. "Here."

The delver showed them 2D footage of the cargo bay, a monochrome reproduction of the orchard. Hulking bipedal robots—hefters, in spacer lingo—hauled trees down into storage. Achille winced as branches broke and apples smashed. They took as much as they could before the ramp sealed itself. Then, the hull ripped open, and Achille watched the family's future—his future—torn free into space.

"Our entire supply," Kai said. "Everything that wasn't in the galley. Gone."

"We had better take inventory," Jiao said. "With the engines down and Ariane gone, whatever's up there isn't going to last long."

Achille pushed the thoughts to the back of his head. Six—no, five of them. A thousand and a half calories a day. Two kilograms. Each. How many tons were in Storage? Enough for a couple of weeks. They'd been gone from Garnet only a handful of days. This wasn't intended to be a long voyage.

But with the anti-matter drives offline, and repairs looking uncertain…

Kai's comm unit crackled. "Corin! Corin, I have her!"

That was Mom. Ecstatic or anguished, Achille couldn't tell. His hands curled into fists.

"Mei, where are you? I'm in Access Tube Two-Nine."

"AT One-Eight. Junction Charlie. She has her EV suit on but it's punctured. Vitals are weak."

"Standby, I'm headed to your position."

Kai switched channels. "Captain, it's Kai. We're in the cargo bay. Orders?"

"Sickbay, and hurry. Jiao?"

"Understood, Captain." She kissed Kai on the cheek and shoved off up the stairwell, swirling up the steps with the ease of a dolphin in the sea—or at least, what Achille had seen on his delver screen.

"We're coming." Kai slapped Achille's shoulder and grinned. "Let's move. Ariane's alive."

* * *

They waited in the corridor outside sickbay while Jiao tended to Ariane. Dad and Mom clung to each other, free hands grasping brackets so they didn't float away. Their helmets drifted in the center, forgotten, as they whispered to each other. Pungent body odor wafted from the open extravehicular suits they wore.

Of course, Kai's body odor wasn't any better. He waited, his back to sickbay, arms crossed.

"Achille." Dad's voice was hoarse. "What did they take?"

"Everything. All of it." Why did he have to be the bearer of gloom?

"And their ship?"

"Adrift, a couple hundred klicks away from us," Kai said. "I used some of our remaining chemical rockets to put us on a parallel course to theirs. Not that either of us is going back toward the sundoors anytime soon."

"Get back up to the bridge and light up the ion engines. Route whatever fuel we have back to them." Dad kissed Mom on the forehead. "Go with him. See if you can restore comms."

"Any message we send could be intercepted."

"I know. We have to take the risk."

"We're four tract shifts off the nearest trade routes," Kai snapped. "The odds of anyone stumbling across two critically damaged ships is beyond tiny."

Dad raised an eyebrow. Uh-oh. To anyone in their family, the gesture was tantamount to a tirade. "Because we chose a long route to our new home, away from those who pursued us."

"Didn't work well, did it? We tried hiding and they found us. The same people who chased us off Garnet, aren't they? Now our whole crop is gone, *Bienfaisance* is wrecked, and Ariane is dying—"

"No one is dying. *We* are not beaten." Dad floated perpendicular to Kai, arms braced on the bulkhead to either side. "And if you want to sit in that chair upstairs, you'd better not panic. You're not allowed the luxury of panic. If you do, then everyone aboard *will* die, including you, and it will be your fault. Do I make myself clear?"

Kai glared at him. He glanced into the sickbay, where Ariane lay on an exam table surrounded by robot appendages and sensor posts. Jiao's hands performed an elaborate ballet with her instruments. "Yes."

"Yes…"

"Captain."

"I would have accepted 'Dad,' too." Dad grasped Kai's shoulders. "You'll be ready. You'll see."

A ghost of a smirk crossed Kai's lips.

I wouldn't have melted down, Achille thought. *I would have kept everyone confident.*

"Kai, with me." Mom touched his hand. Together they swooped down the corridor.

Achille felt Dad watching him. "Everything?" he asked.

"Everything."

Dad sighed.

"But if we can repair the engines, we can go get it all back," Achille insisted. "We could board *their* ship, take what's ours and some of their cargo—"

"We don't know their weapons capabilities. All we know is their ship is just as badly damaged as ours. Neither one of us is going anywhere, other than deeper into the star system. So, we have time." Dad watched Ariane through the sickbay windows. "We just have to see whether we can survive that time without starving."

* * *

Their inventory was bleak.

Dad gathered everyone in the galley a few hours later. Even Ariane, who drifted into the compartment behind Jiao.

"You should not be out of bed," he said.

"Like you could keep me there when *Bien* is hurting." Ariane was paler than her usual shade, freckles and all. Frizzy hair threatened to escape in a curly nova. "Jiao cleared me. Once the nanosurgeons finish their bone-knitting on my rib cage, I won't even hurt."

Dad shook his head, but Mom's well-placed touch in the crook of his arm stopped whatever argument he was formulating. "The priority is to get main power and gravity restored, in that order. The auxiliaries are holding steady. Any leaks are plugged."

"That's a small miracle." Ariane sighed, in perfect mimicry of Dad. "Mind if I borrow Achille? He won't be busy."

The realization stung Achille, but he didn't feel accused. The loss of the orchard was nothing he could have prevented.

"Focus on the present, everyone." Dad gestured at the containers squeezed into a single cabinet out of the rows of open, empty ones facing them. The galley was painted a pale green, with darker panels highlighting the edge of the ceiling and deck. Tiny beacons illuminated the open cabinets. "This is what we have."

It wasn't a lot of food. Some preserved meats, a few bundles of vegetables, vac-flashed fish, dried fruits and nuts. "How much?"

"Enough for each of us to maintain our strength for six days."

Six days.

"What's our current speed?" Mom asked.

360

Kai was staring at the containers. Jiao nudged him and whispered in his ears.

"Speed? 950 kilometers per second," Kai said. "In the wrong direction. Our course is taking us deeper in-system, and there's a whole lot of nothing—a couple gas giants, lots of frozen or volcanic moons. Nothing habitable. No settlements."

"Then we need to turn around, now," Ariane said.

"Gladly, *soeur*, but unless you can get the mains back and burning, any course correction could take us weeks to make with just thrusters."

"The mains are shot. Maybe you missed the part where half our drive nozzles were blown off the hull. What about the chemical rockets? I told you those—"

"Used up, maintaining our trajectory with our attackers."

Ariane frowned. "Why in blazes would you do that?"

"So we can retrieve supplies from Storage," Achille said. "It's the only way we'll have enough food to survive."

"After thirty days of no food, our bodies will react—poorly." Jiao fidgeted with her knuckles. "The strain of our situation won't help."

"We know," Mom said. "That's why we have to work as one. Achille, help your sister in Engineering. Power and gravity. Jiao and I will scrounge for whatever additional supplies we can find. Corin, you and Kai have—"

"I know what we have to do." Corin touched her shoulder. "First, we signal the attackers."

Achille made a face. Jiao's expression mirrored his. "Why? They won't help us."

"They'll have to if they want to make it out of here," Kai said. "They might have all the supplies and at least one working set of anti-matter drive nozzles, but their Raszewski drive is destroyed."

"They're trapped in the system." Ariane snorted. "They deserve it."

"If they hope to leave, we'll have to take them in tow, damaged or not."

Help the people who nearly killed his whole family? Achille would rather vent them all into space.

"This isn't up for debate," Dad said. "Get to your stations."

"Not up for debate?" Kai blurted. "Everything we do is up for debate. We all own a portion."

"You're upset about our departure from Garnet?"

"It's what got us into this disaster!"

Mom put her hands on her hips. Kai crossed his arms but he shut down his tirade. She'd given him the universal sign for "cease and desist."

"Better get out of here, Achille." Ariane tugged on his arm. "Before someone else punches a hole in the hull."

* * *

They squirmed through the tightest access tubes in Engineering, soldering broken connections, replacing circuits. Working in zero gravity meant getting through those bends and twists was as taxing as swimming—every muscle ached from constant adjustment to a new position. Achille's shoulders brushed both sides of a particularly narrow tube. He was sure he'd leave a permanent trail of sweat behind.

He'd finished swapping out a fried bundle of wiring when the lights blazed back on. "Ariane! We're good?"

"Yeah! Come on out of there." Her voice echoed from the Engineering compartment twenty meters aft. "I'm ready to switch on the gravity."

Achille shot feet-first through the tube, emerging into a brightly lit warren of catwalks, pipes, and spheres. The drive casings for the main engines protruded from the machinery, a dozen meters above and below the main catwalk. Ariane was hunched over a long, slanted console that contained three sets of drive controls—those for the main antimatter engines, the secondary ion drives, and the auxiliary chemical rockets. "Ready."

Ariane toggled the intercom. "All hands, stand by for gravity restoration."

A low rumble filtered through the overlapping sounds of the engine room. Achille held onto a brace and let the ship's field drag his feet slowly to the desk. His stomach gurgled. Could have been unsettled. He checked his wrist comm. No, it was well past lunch and he'd been too busy to eat a thing.

The image of their paltry food stores crammed into one cabinet haunted him. He'd wait until dinner.

"Nice work, Ariane." Dad's voice was tinny through the intercom's speakers. "Are the ion drives ready?"

"Ready and able as they can be. I have three of the five ports on-line. You'll get constant thrust for the next fifteen days before we run out of fuel, so tell Kai not to burn it all off at once."

"I think he's aware..." Dad trailed off as mutters filled the other end of the signal. "Hold. We've got a situation. The attacking ship—she's ignited her main drives."

Achille's guts twisted and knew the sensation had nothing to do with skipping a meal. "If they do a full burn with their anti-matter drives, we'll never keep pace."

"No kidding." Ariane gave him a shove. "Get down to the

rocket assembly on Deck Six! I'm gonna need you to trigger the manual override."

"Kai said they were all burnt out."

"As usual, he was wrong, because there's two rockets with enough fuel to adjust our trajectory. Move!"

Achille vaulted the handrail behind the console and landed a few meters below, on a diagonal crosswalk. He sprinted for a ladder and slid down it, boot ringing on the metal grating of Deck Six.

The manual overrides were a series of switches the size of Achille's arms. Four of the six were lined in red lights. Two were dark.

Achille heaved on the first one, his muscles burning. His face was flush. He stank of sweat. Finally, the first switch slammed into position. A green glow ringed it.

The second was stuck. Achille ran out of breath halfway through.

"Hey! I'm only showing one in the green. Hurry up!"

"I'm working on it!"

Kai's voice rang out from his wrist comm. "Achille, they're accelerating. I've got the ion drives pushing us but we can't match their rate unless you can give me both rockets."

"I said, I'm working on it!" Blasted thing wouldn't work. Why wouldn't those vac-heads get down here and help instead of yelling at him?

A shadow scuttled by. A hamster—one of the stubby, beetle-like robots rambling inside the engine room's tightest spaces. It was equipped with a plasma torch, whiskery sensors, a pair of grappling pincers.

Achille reached out, fingers brushing the curved metallic carapace. "Foxtrot! Get over here!"

The hamster skittered down a stanchion and rolled up the wall. It locked grapplers on the switch and pushed down, its tiny treads whirring. Heat washed over Achille as Foxtrot's miniature power source worked to its maximum.

The switch slammed down. More green lights.

"That's it!" he cried.

Ariane's hands clapped, echoing throughout Engineering. "*Fantastique!* Kai, ready to light!"

"Do it!"

The rocket's throaty rumble sent a tremor throughout Deck Six, building into a harsh roar. Achille scrambled back up the main catwalk, where Ariane had a hologram of the navigation readout suspended in the air over her console. The attacking ship scooted ahead on a flare of light, its velocity clicking upward. *Bienfaisance* bent its course, the green line turning yellow as the ship's computers recalculated the new trajectory. It, too, gained speed.

The two lines crossed after ten thousand kilometers.

"Uh, Bridge?" Ariane touched her fingers to her lips. "We're on an intercept."

"Yes, I can see that."

"Dad, what's the plan for when we meet up?"

Silence. Red text danced along the bottom of the hologram: **Collision probable.**

"Dad? Captain!"

"Stand by your stations." Dad's tone didn't wave. Achille wanted to see him in action, see the stoic confidence that would carry not just his ship but his family through the crisis.

I could do that. I could learn it. If he'd let me.

Collision likelihood increasing.

"Stand by grapples," Dad said. "Ariane…?"

365

"Laser primed. The interlinks were fried when the power went down. You've got Turrets One and Two."

"Those will have to work."

"Unidentified ship." Mom's voice could have belonged to a king's herald. "Repeat, relinquish your cargo or we will be forced to open fire. You can't escape the star system without your Raszewski drive. Ours is operational. Surrender and we will take you in tow."

"Blast it," Kai snapped. "They're boosting beyond their max gees."

"Thirty-one point six gravities and accelerating," Jiao said. "They could sustain damage to their drive nozzles if they go any faster."

"Lasers primed." Achille could hear Dad's fingers drumming on the arm of his chair. "Stand by…"

Overlapping cries of "Power surge!" and "They're firing!" and "Evasive!" flooded the intercom. Achille had time to hook an arm around Ariane's waist and grasp the railing when *Bienfaisance* bucked.

Alarms battered his ears, until she shut them down. "Bridge, what's happened? We took hits to the forward ventral hull."

"We're off course," Dad said. "The hits altered our trajectory. Rockets?"

"Burned out. Gone." Ariane brushed free of Achille's hold. "You've got the ions, for the next couple of weeks, and that's it."

Achille wanted an answer from someone, anyone, on the bridge, but the silence suffocated him. "Our intercept—"

"We missed," Kai said. "Their ship opened up the throttle and there's no catching them. New course has them returning to the sundoors in a few days."

"Where we need to be, to escape," Achille said.

366

"Flip us on our axis, Kai," Dad said. "Bring us into a parabolic course that will return us to the sundoors, too."

"We won't make it in time."

Achille didn't want to acknowledge what Kai meant by that.

* * *

One Week Later

Ariane hadn't emerged from Engineering for 48 hours. Achille found her with her legs sticking out of a crawlspace beneath the Number Four anti-matter drive nozzle. It was one of the two nozzles was still attached.

"Here." Achille nudged her boot. "You'd better have some."

She slid out, the upper part of her jumpsuit and most of her face covered with a greasy film. She swiped a sleeve across her mouth and nose. "That smells amazing."

"Jerky, from the Liberty ranches." The last of the package. Of all of them. Achille smiled as he handed her the meat, trying to focus on her happiness instead of the gnawing sensation inside him.

Ariane took a bite. She paused mid-chew. "Did you get any?"

He patted a pouch on his jumpsuit. "Dried apples."

"Oh. Is that…?"

"Yeah."

They sat cross-legged, nestled deep in Engineering. The reactor's reassuring hum meant they wouldn't go cold, or without gravity. The accompanying vibrations from the ion drive moved them ever nearer to the star system's sundoors.

But there'd been no indication anyone had received their distress signals. And though Kai commanded the nav computer to predict the attacking ship's vector, they'd lost sight of the ship itself.

Ariane slowed her chewing. After just two more bites, she tucked the jerky into a pocket and crawled back to work.

Achille couldn't blame her. He took one apple slice. That was it.

* * *

Two Weeks Later

Achille was inside his EV suit, using the microjets to maneuver across the barren cargo bay. He cushioned his arrival on the opposite bulkhead with his boots. A jolt of pain shot up his leg.

He'd misjudged his speed. And he'd reacted too slowly. That happened more often than not.

His stomach wouldn't leave him alone. Did he have anything left? An apple slice. Or two. Maybe. They'd stretched all the food supplies as far as they could go.

Achille sipped water from a tube. They had a fair supply, still. Recycling what they had from waste into something drinkable wasn't pleasant, but it would suffice. There was no way to manufacture more rations, though. Nowhere to find additional supplies.

Kai was in sickbay. He'd eaten less than anyone else. His body punished him for that generosity. Whether he'd get up again would depend upon how quickly the ship could get to the sundoors and how promptly help arrived. Jiao had thought she'd spotted something on the sensors a few days ago, but as damaged as they were, the range was limited.

Achille concentrated on his task—getting extra help. They'd developed leaks in the hull. Ariane had hamster bots working round the clock to find and seal them, but they were still losing oxygen. Slowly. Dodectite 10613 was their only bot left. It was still strapped into the repair socket, dented but otherwise untouched. Indicator lights showed its powerplant was in good shape.

He ran a reboot sequence. There was that same error message. Blocked memory. Achille opened an access panel and initiated a new connection between the bot and his delver. Like he'd thought… someone hadn't cleared out old memory files. The resultant overfill was impeding 10613's ability to restart.

* * *

The file was cumbersome, but not encrypted. In fact, it bore none of the standard Duval storage criteria. Achille extracted it, transferred it to his delver. Video, with scan data embedded. It was recorded just a few weeks ago.

Dad was in the first image that came up.

Dad and Mom. They stood at the entrance to the cargo bay, which was opened to a broad airlock lined with rock and framed with support beams. Hefters trundled in and out, bringing trees from the orchard and departing emptyhanded to get more. They lined the tree containers in the same neat rows Achille had seen a month ago.

But Mom and Dad weren't alone. There were people in front of them—eight men and women. Couples? Yeah. Achille saw the Oberfelds, the Huangs, and the Carons. He didn't recognize the others. Mrs. Caron had taught his younger elementary training sessions.

Mom shoved Mrs. Caron. Hard. It wasn't the shove of old neighbors.

Achille watched the replay through the grimy surface of his EV suit visor. He couldn't bring himself to activate the sound. Not yet.

He had to speak to the man in the captain's chair.

* * *

An hour later, he staggered up the stairwell. His head swam with every turn. How could this happen? How could Dad ruin everything?

He felt like he was heading up a funeral procession of one.

Dad was on the bridge, alone. He spun his chair, slowly, the gimbals squeaking every eighth of a turn to the right. All the stations were dark, save for comms and sensors. He stared into the holo display, flexing his right hand. There was nothing in the hologram except for the blue mark representing *Bienfaisance* and the glowing line indicating her trajectory,

"Everyone else is resting." He didn't look up. Achille figured he heard the approaching bootsteps. "Conserving their energy. Which, incidentally, is something the ship herself doesn't have to worry about. She'll keep running for a couple years after we're all gone."

"Dad…"

"I'm sorry, Achille." Dad faced him. His eyes were bloodshot, the circles beneath as dark as empty exhaust ports. "Your legacy is gone. Yours, Ariane's, Kai's… there's nothing left to give you. I'd hoped the orchard could give us all new lives—"

"Why did you steal it?" Achille was surprised by the anger in his tone.

Dad stared at him. "Steal—the orchard?"

"I found the recording. You forgot to clear out 10613. I mean,

I'm not surprised. You always leave the bot maintenance to me."

"Because you're the best at it. It must have slipped my memory."

"You—you're admitting?"

"We took the orchard to keep it out of the hand of people who'd destroy our livelihood. I told you, Achille, when greed and cruelty take over, people are capable of any misdeed. Look what they wound up doing to our orchard! They tracked us across star systems and ripped it from our home."

He wasn't listening. Nor was he confessing. Achille triggered the vid playback on his delver. The screen shone brilliant in the dim bridge lighting.

There were Mom and Dad, again. Mom slammed into Mrs. Caron, again.

Mr. Caron reached for Dad, but Dad drew a gun, a heavy pistol geared to fire magnetically-accelerated projectiles. Mom, too, was armed.

"Stand clear while we depart," Dad said. "We don't want anyone to come to harm."

"Harm?" Mr. Caron spit on the deck plates. "Scélérat! What are we to do without the trees? You promised them as the lifeblood of this colony. Our colony! We worked for you, year after year, tending them, breaking our backs on machines and over plasma torches to build Garnet. Now you take them from us?"

"It was our family who brought them here!" Mom's aim never wavered. "Our ingenuity that made them as resilient as they are. So, we are the ones who keep the genetic trademark. You've received your pay."

"Our pay will not feed us. You have our only ship!" Mrs. Huang was in tears. "Our supplies are low. The last trader is late."

"You'll have to stretch what you can." Meanwhile, the hefters brought in the last of the trees. Mr. Caron lunged for Dad.

Guns went off.

Mr. Caron was on the floor, cradling his arm. Mr. Huang's leg was soaked in blood.

"Stay away from us, and stay away from our family." Dad brandished the gun. He slapped the hatch controls.

It shut out the desperate colonists.

Tears stained Achille's cheeks.

"You don't understand the situation." Dad's smile was still as firm as the Garnet colony tunnels. "They would have ruined us. Ruined all our work. You and your siblings would have gone poor, had we let them claim the genetic trademark for the entire colony."

"But, Dad—you took all of what they had. Their food."

Dad rotated the chair, so he was gazing once again into the hologram. "Delete it."

Achille grabbed his shoulder. "Look at me and tell me the truth!"

Dad raised an eyebrow. He considered Achille's hand like it was an intruding starship, no better than the one that had attacked them. "Delete the file and go to your cabin. Now."

"No."

"This isn't a parental request, Achille. I'm still your captain."

A warning light flashed from the sensor console. Achille spun, too fast. His knees buckled.

Dad caught him. "Proximity alert. A ship decelerating, coming out of the sundoor. It's three light-seconds away."

Only 900,000 kilometers? How had it snuck so close? Were the sensors that badly damaged? Achille's head wouldn't stop whirling, even though he couldn't move with Dad anchoring him in place.

Comms beeped.

Dad's eyes were wide. "Unidentified ship, this is private cargo hauler *Bienfaisance*."

"*Bienfaisance*, this is Rescue Operations, *HMRC Weskeag*." The greeting was announced in a loud, lilting female voice. "Stand by and prepare to match course. We have you on our sensors. Medical teams standing by."

Achille thought he was hearing things.

Dad grabbed him by the shoulders. "Get everyone. Get them to the bridge. They've come for us, you see? We're saved!"

* * *

The boarding party consisted of six Rescue Ops personnel in white jackets but wasn't limited to only medical staff. Six more men and women in black vests and blue shirts arrived, armed with scramblers, stubby devices that looked like overfed guns. Achille knew their sole purpose was as stun weapons.

His heart trip-hammered when a thirteenth man stepped to the front of the entourage. He was tall, fit, with close-cropped red hair and a smattering of freckles on his face. The shirt underneath his vest was white.

"Lieutenant Commander Brian Gaudette, captain, *HRMC Weskeag*, Rescue Operations." Achille placed the accent—Levesque. Freeholding world of Tiaozhan. The same place the Duvals left years ago, when they struck out for new lives. "You're Captain Duval?"

"Corin Duval, and my wife, Mei." Dad offered his hand. "You have no idea how thankful we are to see you, Captain."

Gaudette didn't return the gesture. Didn't blink. When

He spoke, though, to Achille he sounded tired and maybe a tinge sad. "Captain Duval, I hereby remand you to the custody of the Crown Marshals Service, under authority of His Majesty King Andrew II of the Realm of Five. You may remain silent if you so choose. What statements you do choose to make will be used as evidence of your collusion of the crime for which you stand accused."

"Wait." Dad didn't struggle as two of the Rescue Ops crewmen put binders on him—and Mom, too. "Wait! For what crime?"

"Theft of a starship," Gaudette said. "Theft of public property. Willful endangerment of a colony's life support, namely Garnet Colony, chartered to a compact of fourteen families from Levesque in 2598. The ones you left without adequate supplies when you took the orchard."

"There's been a mistake!" Mom pulled against her restraints. "Those people attacked *us*! They could have killed our family!"

"We found them. Don't worry, they're facing charges of their own—piracy chief among them." Gaudette shook his head. "But the story they tell is that they were desperate to take what belonged them."

"This is insane!" Ariane was there, at Dad's shoulder, with Jiao holding her arm. "They tried to kill us all!"

"Miss, I'll need you to stand down." Gaudette held out his hand, which made one of the crewmen lower his scrambler—the same scrambler, Achille realized, that had been aimed at his sister. "Captain, is there anyone else aboard?"

"My oldest son, Kai. In his cabin, on Deck Three. He's … not well."

Gaudette glanced at a woman with toffee skin and spiky black hair, one of the medics. "Lucinda?"

"I'm on it, prayers and all. Bayliss, Hsu, you're with me."

They hurried down the corridor. Jiao followed, whispering to them.

"Your crew are to be detained, Captain Duval, but they're not charged with anything." Gaudette locked his gaze on Achille, who found the Rescue Ops captain's eyes unnervingly similar to Dad's—bold and blue. "One's listed as a minor."

"These accusations will never stand," Dad snapped. Achille had never heard him take a condescending, vile tone with anyone before, especially not someone in a position of authority. "It's their word against ours, and they're the ones with our stolen livelihood crammed into their ship!"

Achille was between the two groups, and off to the side. He kept eye contact with Gaudette, until the other said, "Give us a moment, Chief."

The crewmen herded Dad and Mom into one of the side corridors, Ariane arguing with the chief the whole way. That left Achille with Captain Gaudette.

"You look like a young man with something to say," he murmured. "Or at least, nothing you wanted everyone else to hear. What I said about you being a minor—that's true enough. None of the colonists are holding you accountable. So, if you know anything pertinent to the investigation, I'd have to relay it to the Crown Marshals."

Would they give him back the orchard? With Dad and Mom in custody, they really could lose everything. That left Achille with no legacy. No chance to follow in the family footsteps.

He found himself wondering what doing so would cost him—and whether it was worth it.

"Captain." Achille's throat was dry. He needed something to eat, before vertigo overtook him. Anything. But he wasn't the only one. "There's something you should see."

He held out his delver.

Woe to you that are full
For you shall hunger

Steve Rzasa

Steve Rzasa is the author of "Rightfully Ours." He is also the author of several novels of science-fiction, steampunk, and fantasy—with a bunch more in progress.

His third novel, Broken Sight, received the 2012 Award for Speculative Fiction from the American Christian Fiction Writers. The Word Reclaimed was a finalist for that award. The Word Endangered and Man Behind the Wheel were also finalists for the Realm Award. He's been a journalist and librarian, father and husband.

Something in the Water

BEGIN TRANSMISSION

They laughed when I said there was something in the water.

This is Dr. Steven Palowski, mission biologist on board the Saturn Alpha Space Station. Day 530. Christmas Day back home.

Station records will show we completed the third of our mission objectives before the Incident.

Objective One: Set up colony and workstations; Begin Hydroponic farming.

Objective Two: Begin water mining inside Saturn's D Ring.

Objective Three: Harvest and purify potable water.

* * *

The record will show we achieved Objective Three. The record is wrong.

Complications, human and computer errors in calculation set us behind on Objective Two, mining for water. By the time we were ready to send the first of the Collection crews into the Ring, our water stores were at dangerously low levels and we were forced to ration what remained among the 200 souls aboard Saturn Alpha.

We did our best, all of us, to follow all procedures, to study the incoming samples from the first of the collected ice chunks thoroughly and with accuracy. But always, we kept one eye on the remaining water stores. We tried to take our time to ensure the safety of everyone aboard. But our time was limited.

In the end, with Station Command demanding daily reports and riding us for results, we—I'm ashamed to say it—we cut some corners. We made assumptions, educated guesses, where we should have proceeded with extreme caution. Yes, we had cleansed the water of oxidizing radiation. We tested what was left and, within our limited knowledge, had declared the water safe for consumption.

Then, we believed we had succeeded in the nick of time. With a single week's worth of our water stores remaining, and barely enough in Agricultural storage to keep the plants flourishing, we thought we were ready to finally head into Objective Four.

Until I spotted the fungus.

* * *

According to the official record, the Sα Project discovered interstellar life on Day 365. One year to the day of our arrival on board the station and the start of our mission here. That is the day I told Dr. Kinzie Stoyvich about what I'd seen.

The eukaryotic cell structure left little doubt that we were, indeed, looking at a kind of extraterrestrial fungus. There was life in the rings of Saturn. It was organic. It was a type of mycoplankton. And, despite the cold, despite the lack of nutrients or soil, despite the solar radiation, it was alive. The fungus, Stoyvich insisted we name it Palowski Saturna—she always was generous when it came to her team—seemed to exist in a kind of stasis within the ice. It was also extremely small; though in many cases it existed in complex form, the individual cells were nearly too minute to be seen even with our strongest microscopes.

If we hadn't been in such a hurry, I feel certain that either Stoyvich, another team member, or myself would have considered these facts before we assumed our purification and filtration efforts had effectively eradicated it within legally acceptable levels from the new drinking supply. As it was, it appeared by all accounts that our efforts to clean the water of the fungi had worked, save the samples I'd collected for future study. On Mission Day 391, Objective Three was declared a success.

Captain Johnson, the mission commander, called for a celebration—and there was, after all, much to celebrate. So we thought. Not only had we replenished our water stores and completed another major milestone in both our mission and in humanity's ultimate goal of deep space travel, but we'd discovered extraterrestrial life! We had made all kinds of history, and our names would be revered for generations alongside those of the Wright Brothers, Yuri Gagarin, and Neil Armstrong.

The water flowed freely among the crew and colonists of Saturn Alpha, pure as the diminishing spring water back home. Raucous laughter filled the common areas. I sat alone brooding and avoided the water. Maybe it was irrational. Maybe it was simply that paranoia that follows success. It wasn't anything I could put my finger on exactly, but something in the back of my mind would not let me celebrate.

I found Commander Johnson and Dr. Stoyvich talking in the corner and interrupted as politely as I could. Johnson greeted me with a smile and congratulated me again on my find as Stoyvich beamed up at me. I waved off the felicitations.

"Commander," I said. "Dr. Stoyvich."

"Steven," said Johnson happily. "Why aren't you celebrating?"

"I will," I assured them. "Just thinking. "Kinzi, we still don't know how that organism will react with humans."

"Is that something we need to know," Johnson asked. "I thought we killed it."

"We did," said Dr. Stoyvich.

"We filtered it from the water as best as possible," I amended. "The water does conform to legal standards, but—."

"But," said Dr. Stoyvich, "we did eliminate all traces of the fungus according to the purification sensors. They were designed to detect contaminants harmful to human life, even if they don't sample every single molecule of water in the master cylinder."

Commander Johnson chuckled. "Just like a scientist," he said. "Always chasing perfection. It'll be fine, Dr. Kowalski." He clapped me on the shoulder. "You should be proud, man! The things your team has accomplished!" He shook his head, still laughing. "Enjoy the party!"

He nodded at us both and went off, probably searching for more optimistic company.

I felt a warm hand softly grip my own and turned to see Kinzi smiling at me.

"You really should be proud, you know," she said. "I know there's still work to do, but believe me; it can wait until tomorrow. Come with me."

We found a quiet corner, and I admit this new side to Dr.

Stoyvich put my doubts out of my mind. She opened a bottle of wine and offered me a glass. We toasted our success and finished one bottle together before she left me with another. She kissed my lips before she walked back to the party and I wondered, chuckling at the thought, whether the drink had simply rendered her less inhibited or if there had been an invitation in that kiss.

It isn't as though, of course, the thought of Kinzie and I had never crossed my mind; of course it had. But as the warmth of the wine spread from my belly to my cheeks and I sat wondering what a future might hold for the two of us, I couldn't help but wonder, too, if that same future might hold some new headaches or unforseen nightmares. We simply needed know more about Palowski Saturna and, as much as I wanted to return to Kinzie and explore what else she may have had in mind by way of celebration, I knew I wouldn't be able to concentrate on anything as long as my fears were nagging at me.

I also knew, as the alcohol began its work on my mind, that I would get nowhere that night. I prayed that the few hours before the rest of the station went lights out wouldn't do anyone any harm, if there was indeed harm to be done. I returned to my quarters, but did not sleep well.

* * *

I began DNA genome testing the next morning, carefully lining up samples from what we'd collected. The DNA was familiar in that it shared the same basic nucleotide makeup of terrestrial DNA, but was triple-stranded. The sequences that resulted were in many cases unlike anything I'd ever seen before.

My first task was to find and highlight familiar sequences. If I could begin to work with this lifeform in terms I could already understand, it might help me make sense of the new information. After hours of study, of parsing the makeup of the code, I found the plankton shared certain genetic features with terrestrial fungi. This was a place to start. Fungus produces spores and survives by breaking down and consuming organic matter.

By itself, this discovery was no great cause for alarm: it's rare for a fungus to begin decomposing living material. I searched for other clues: How was it able to survive frozen inside a radiation field? What specific organic matter supplied its food, assuming it was specific at all? How did the spores spread, and on what would they thrive?

My days of research are detailed comprehensively in the attached reports, but these data are by now academic at best: the practical effects were soon easy enough to spot without a microscope.

* * *

It is difficult to pinpoint a Patient Zero in the infection that began spreading throughout the station just days after we introduced the Cronian water. The first crew member to seek medical attention, however, was Selburn St. John. He presented in sick bay with signs of anemia: shortness of breath, heart palpitations, and his already pale complexion was now nearly translucent. Dr. Thomas Reed, the satellite's Chief Medical Officer, quickly diagnosed an iron deficiency and set to the task of discovering the reason for it. St. John had no history of anemia, and everyone on board added iron to a daily regimen of vitamins and minerals as a matter of course. The First Officer checked into sick bay with similar symptoms the next day, and was quickly followed by another three crew members.

Dr. Reed quickly put out a general alert to all station personnel that anyone experiencing symptoms of Iron Deficiency Anemia should stop by Sick Bay at their earliest convenience.

In the meantime, I had resisted drinking the water from Saturn and had begun anew my insistence that all personnel go back to rationing from our original stores until we could conclude our study of this organism. Commander Johnson again laughed off my concerns at first, though I had at least convinced Dr. Stoyvich to take precautions. She had, of course, already consumed some of the Saturnian water, but we hoped that limiting further exposure would mitigate any risk.

Dr. Stoyvich worked by my side as we sequenced genome after genome, searching for answers and finding only more questions. It was she who first theoretically connected the cases of anemia with our water sample. As we compared notes with Dr. Reed, the truth became clear: the organism was, indeed, thriving—even growing—inside the blood cells of the patients; there was an obvious correlation between the growth and number of this organism with the presentation of anemia. We could only conclude the organism was feeding off the iron in the red blood cells.

We three presented our findings to Commander Johnson, who finally decided in light of the evidence to restrict consumption of Saturnian water and to ration our original water stores until a solution could be found.

* * *

For a time, this solution seemed to work: Thirty station personnel had become anemic, and we were able to transfuse blood between the merely infected and the uninfected to cleanse those we could of the organism. Unfortunately, by this time, twenty of the thirty anemic patients were beyond help.

It was during the final days of those twenty patients that we began to discover how resourceful this new organism really is. A nurse, Eve Achebe, began to present with signs of anemia, despite successful transfusions and a clean blood reading days before. A second nurse and a doctor soon followed and with further research, we found the common link between them: In each case, one of the terminal patients had coughed on the caregiver.

The spores which had earlier survived in water had, in the hospitable environment of warm bodies, become airborne.

* * *

We quickly quarantined all known patients into one of the larger storage bays and took every precaution to avoid the further spread of Palowski Saturna. By then there were 75 infected and, with the fungus now taking root in the lungs before spreading into the bloodstream, simple transfusions were no longer enough. Doctors Stoyvich, Reed, and myself began studying the organism anew, searching for a way to kill it, but knowing time would run out for our patients before we found a solution.

Dr. Reed visited each patient in quarantine, making them comfortable where he was able and taking notes as their conditions progressed.

The growth of the organism was unprecedented. Cells combined and divided, growing first into colonies and then into merging into a single larger organism. As the fungus grew, it continued to drain away the nutrients of the host bodies. The lucky ones suffocated for lack of oxygenated blood cells. The rest simply starved to death.

* * *

It was in death that we finally realized the full, horrible potential of this new alien species. For the fungus had already reached the heart, the brain. When the body stopped producing the electrical signals required to continue pumping blood, the organism took over.

Dr. Reed was the first to discover this development, and ultimately lost his life as a consequence. Selburn St. John had been the first to die. The process was slower for him and the other victims of the waterborne spores, but the fungus eventually won out. Dr. Reed ventured into quarantine to collect the body and check on the other patients. He noted that St. John had begun sprouting what appeared to be mushrooms growing out of his ears and even tiny fungal heads sprouting through the pores of his arms and legs. As he bent to examine further, St. John suddenly sat up and the dead man's arm shot out and grabbed Dr. Reed by the shirt. St. John opened his mouth to reveal porous gills growing down his throat. As Reed struggled against what can only be described now as a revenant, his mask fell from his face and the body of St. John released a cloud of spores which Dr. Reed had no choice but to inhale. As he lay in shock, St. John's body rose and walked out the cargo bay door, into the station.

Dr. Reed reported the incident from inside the cargo bay, sealed once more, and begged us to find a way to destroy every patient remaining inside.

The Fungus-St. John hybrid walked through the station.

There is a fungus on Earth, *Ophiocordyceps*, which enslaves ants. These ants are compelled by the fungus, which overtakes the insect's nervous system, to climb to the end of a branch or leaf and bite down. At this point, the fungus kills the host as it sprouts out of the creature's body and releases spores. Palowski Saturna acts in a similar fashion upon a more complex host and this is why, perhaps, it kills before taking over the body.

Unlike *Ophiocordyceps*, however, this fungus appears able to sense the presence of a habitable space and thus introduce spores more directly. Is this a kind of intelligence, or merely an adapted, advanced product of what could, for lack of a better term, be called instinct?

I don't know. The organism's ability to adapt to a human host, despite its extraterrestrial origins, poses its own sort of questions. Had it evolved among similar species to our own—proving, at the very least, the existence of humanoid extraterrestrials? Was it simply adapting and responding to our electrical signals, using the very mechanics of our own bodies against us? Again, I hesitate to guess.

What I do know is that this fungus, as it animated the late Selburn St. John, sought out people and, just as it did with Dr. Reed, restrained them and introduced its spores. I don't know how many victims were infected before the body of St. John was brought down. It probably doesn't matter. Security personnel made every attempt to subdue the hybrid creature through traditional means: stunners, blunt weapons, even a Spike Pistol. It was with this last that a security officer was able to at least stop the creature's progress, pinning it to a station wall. Careful not to breathe in the struggling creature's spores, they finally doused the thing in an accelerant and lit it on fire.

I can't say for sure if it was the frenzied motion of the burning creature that disturbed me to my core. Perhaps—no, definitely—more horrifying than its thrashing was the fact that even as it writhed and squirmed within the flame, it did so in utter silence.

* * *

After the initial panic had subsided and station authorities brought the situation under control, the station settled into a strained calm for a time. The deaths on board had extended our water supply somewhat as Dr. Stoyvich and I continued to search for a means of killing the parasitic fungus that threatened our water supply, our mission, and our very lives.

In the cargo bay, the hybrid dead wandered aimlessly for a time, searching for new hosts, but eventually stood in place, motionless. Dormant. Though we knew our best hope of studying the organism lay in securing a complex sample, nobody dared enter quarantine for fear of letting loose another creature. We had radioed the nearest ships and stations for help, but despaired of their arriving before the water ran out.

As Commander Johnson, Dr. Stoyvich and I discussed our options, we knew our time was growing far too short.

"What about oxygen," Johnson asked. "If these creatures are using a human host, don't they need oxygen as well?"

"Maybe," I conceded. "But does that help us?"

Kinzie started to smile slowly. "I think it does," she said. "The creatures are in the cargo bay. If we cracked open the airlock and bled the oxygen out, we may be able to essentially starve the organism."

I caught on. "That eliminates the immediate threat, and then we just send a team in to recover a sample."

Kinzie nodded enthusiastically and we agreed: It could work. It *must* work.

* * *

Less than an hour later, we watched as the airlock slowly opened six inches. The reaction was immediate and violent: every body was thrust toward the vacuum of space by escaping atmosphere, along with any piece of cargo not secured. There was a sound like screaming over the intercom as the hybrid creatures were pulled against the doors and the air rushed from the room. Whether it was pain or rage, we didn't know, but we watched until the sensors told us there was no air left in the bay, and every single body stopped moving.

Then we waited. And watched.

We watched for hours, looking for the least sign of movement, of life. There was nothing. It appeared our gambit had been successful. Captain Johnson ordered a recovery team to collect one of the bodies.

Kinzie held my hand tight as we waited in the lab for the first sample. I looked her in the eyes and smiled. I wanted to assure her that we would be okay. And that the deaths of so many had not been our fault. But I couldn't even convince myself.

* * *

The claxon blared above us, sounding a red alert that shook us both out of our silence and a frantic security officer ran into the lab to report what had happened. After re-pressurizing the cargo bay, a three-man team entered to recover one of the bodies still prone next to the airlock. When they reached the pile of dead, they snapped suddenly to life and easily overwhelmed two of the men. The security officer managed to reach the cargo bay doors and attempted to get them closed, but the throng had simply moved too quickly.

The bottom line was seventy-five former comrades, their decaying bodies now overrun by an organism bent on survival and replication, out in force and loose in the station.

The panicked screams of men and women fleeing and fighting for their lives echoed through the metallic passages of Saturn Alpha, and Dr. Stoyvich and I knew there would be no getting these creatures under control. There would be no quarantine capable of holding everyone who was now, or would soon be, infected.

The station and her personnel were lost.

* * *

We hid in the lab, our medical masks secured over our faces as I watched the camera feeds, comparing what I saw with the station schematic. Our only hope would be the airlock, and the long-range shuttle that lay within. As quickly and as quietly as I could, I stocked clean water, praying there would be emergency stores still aboard the ship. At least enough for a few weeks. When it finally seemed all was clear, we unlocked the lab and sprinted up three decks to the waiting airlock.

I should have known when we encountered no resistance that it was too good to be true. I should have known to be more cautious as we approached the final corner before the airlock door. I was too relieved. Too optimistic.

A creature—it had once been Nurse Achebe—was standing between us and the airlock hatch. Neither of us saw it until we'd turned the corner. Dr. Stoyvich, her legs longer than my own, turned first and the creature clawed at her face, ripping her mask from her nose and mouth before blowing a cloud of spores at her. I grabbed the Achebe-fungus and threw it to the side, pulling Dr. Stoyvich into the airlock and slamming my hand on the lock button.

After we caught our breath, we went into the shuttle and waited for the oxygen and pressure to regulate. Dr. Stoyvich—Kinzie—grabbed my hand and looked into my eyes. There was a sadness in her own, blue and brimming with tears.

"You know I can't come with you," she said.

I protested. We were so close to a cure. I could give her a transfusion in flight.

"I could kill you," she answered. She brought her fingertips to my face. "I want you to live."

"I want us both to live," I said. I looked frantically around for some way, any way, to change her mind, when I saw the cryochambers.

She must have seen my smile. "What is it?"

I explained my plan, and finally she acquiesced. It's not a perfect plan, and it may not work. I pray to God it does.

After we launched the shuttle and I laid in the coordinates for the autopilot, I grabbed the emergency kit from the rear cargo hold and gave her a transfusion. In a few days, I will give her another. In the meantime, and after that, she will sleep. We don't know yet how to kill this thing, this wretched parasite that, in a moment of optimism and what I now recognize to have been love, Dr. Syoyvich named after me. But we do know it's dormant in the cold. We believe that with a surgeon on-hand and with enough supplies to pull it off, we just may be able to eradicate the parasite from her lungs and flush the rest out with another transfusion. There is always hope, and hope is what I have left to cling to.

My last pleasant memory of my friends and crewmates aboard Saturn Alpha is of laughter and celebration. I try to hold onto these memories as the names and faces of 298 men and women drift into my mind, accusing me in their silence of my negligence. If I had found the organism sooner. If I'd asked the right questions in time. If I hadn't been so worried about deadlines...

The nearest station is orbiting Mars, and we will spend roughly eighteen months in cryosleep, saving our supplies and keeping the fungus at bay. I will survive this, and God willing Kinzie and I will reach the Martian outpost in time to save her life.

But I may never laugh again.

END TRANSMISSION

Woe to you that laugh now,
For you shall mourn and weep

Randy Streu

Randy Streu is the author of "Something in the Water." When he isn't writing, he is voice acting, producing podcasts, fending off his cat, or enjoying his loving wife and four children.

As the Prophecy Foretold

A stranger with a white beard and an equally pale face approached on a horse-drawn wagon. It was curious to see a stranger in that nook of the kingdom. It was even more curious to see them stop in front of your family's cottage.

Robert, an under-stuffed scarecrow of a lad, was struggling to haul slop to the pig sty. He set down the pail and watched from a distance as the old man knocked on his home's front door. It opened, and Aunt Edelyn welcomed him.

"Here, pigs," Robert called.

Bracing against the fence, he managed to empty the pail into the trough. Eight piglets rushed out of the barn and crowded around the turbid breakfast. One piglet caught the last clump of slop with its ear.

Shouts leaked from the house. They were clear enough for Robert to know his aunt was angry, but he could not tell what she was saying.

The rear door to the cottage opened. Aunt Edelyn stuck out her head. "Robert, come inside. You have a guest."

"Coming, ma'am." Robert hung the pail on a fence post and jogged toward the house. Why had she said "guest" that way as if it were an insult? Who was this man come to see him? He was eleven. The only resident of Ashbend who visited him regularly was his friend Donnel.

How do I greet a guest? He brushed off his hands and patted down his straw-colored hair, which he could feel sticking up like quills. When he reached the cottage door, he paused long enough to consider whether he should rinse off his boots.

"Just come inside and take them off," Aunty Edelyn said, ushering him into the smoke kitchen. She had that pursed, exasperated look she made whenever Robert forgot to finish his chores. "Go on, child. He's in the sitting room."

Robert slipped off his boots and tiptoed to the next room. He froze when he saw the stranger. The man was tall, only a head shorter than the ceiling beams. Everything about the man flowed, from the shape of his long robe and beard to the smooth, gentle way he spread his hands. His wide smile gave a peek of his teeth.

"Welcome, boy. Are you Robert, Son of Warren?"

His father's name. That was almost as unfamiliar as this old man.

He was unsure how to respond. Aunt Edelyn answered for him.

"He is Robert. My husband and I have cared for him as if he were our own, thanks to you."

The stranger chuckled in spite of Edelyn's obvious annoyance. "You certainly have. You feed him well. He's grown much since I last saw him."

Robert's eyes jerked to his aunt, then back to the stranger. What was this secret between them?

The man had a large satchel, which he propped up in the corner. He then picked up a small chest that was at his feet. "I'm sure you have many questions. I will answer the first one. My name is Harabor of Autumnhill. I come bearing remarkable news."

A detail from Aunt Edelyn's stories sparked in Robert's memory. "Are you the man who brought me here when I was a babe?" he asked in a rush. He cringed at himself. Had he sounded rude?

"I am." Harabor said slowly. Everything he said was too slow, too finely pronounced, for Robert's eager curiosity.

"Do you know what became of Father and Mother?"

Harabor gave a nod that was more of a long blink than a tip of the head. "I do."

A pause in the conversation invited further inquiry. "Will you tell me?" Robert asked.

"Yes, but for you to understand, there is something I must show you."

He placed the small chest he was holding onto Aunt Edelyn's sewing table.

* * *

Warren's wife, Tula, stood in the way of their home's open door. She held their baby in her arms, using him as a barrier.

"I beg you, don't do this. What of me? What of Robert?"

Warren kissed their baby on the forehead, then kissed Tula on the cheek. She pulled away from him, but not before he had wetted his lips with her tears.

"I am doing this for you and Robert—"

"No, you're not." There was fear in her reddened eyes. "You're doing this because you can't stand the life of a farmer. You've always been a dreamer, and you want to abandon us so you can chase some flittering dream."

"It's not some dream, Tula. It's a prophecy, and one proven

to be true. That's not the same thing."

"And what are we supposed to eat while you're gone, hmm? I can't tend the whole farm on my own, especially not when I've got to care for Robert."

Warren sighed, calming himself. He ran his fingers through his mess of blond hair—hair that Robert had inherited, if the pale tufts atop his baby's scalp were any indication. "I promise you'll have help. And the journey is only one week out, one week to return. I'll come back before harvest season."

"If you come back at all." Tula's eyes narrowed. Hardened. "That's the problem. You can't assure me you'll be back. A little practice with a sword does not make you ready to be a hero. I could be a widow by next week."

This argument had been circling for months, and the constant prodding was beginning to bruise. To blister. To callous. How could she act like this now, in his moment of departure? Where was his concerned send-off?

Warren clamped his hands around his wife's elbows. "I'm needed. Our countrymen's lives are at stake, and it's my help they need. Do their lives mean nothing to you?"

"Not as much as I care about our son having a father."

Robert stirred. Their rising voices were waking him.

"He needs you," Tula snapped, "not some legend whose bones lie in the dung heap of a wyrm. He cares about you, but you don't care about him. All you've cared about for two years is that wretched prophecy."

That broke him. The stab of Tula's nagging reached his nerves. Heat rose to his face.

Warren snapped, "I do care, woman! I care enough to risk my life for him. I care enough to want him to have a better inheritance than I had, this bog-cursed farm and its sickly crops.

Robert will live like a king because of me."

Tula turned her back on him and sobbed. The conversation was through. It had been through for some time now. All they had left between them was resentment and a fight that had endured for a season.

Warren snatched his bag from the floor. He said, "I'll be back with a caravan of gold," to the back of Tula's head, then walked outside. The door slammed shut behind him. Robert wailed inside the house.

The prophet Harabor was waiting for him, seated on his one-horse wagon. Their provisions for the journey, as well as a few of Warren's belongings, were lying in the wagon bed.

"I do apologize for that," Harabor said. His bushy, white brows furrowed. "It was not my intention to bring such distress to your home."

"Stubborn woman," Warren grumbled. He shoved his bag onto the wagon, then climbed onto the seat beside Harabor.

"Would she feel better if she came to Autumnhill with us?" Harabor asked. "She and Robert are welcome to stay in my home."

"I would prefer they stay here where they're safe. If Tula came with us in this mood, she'd scare away the wyrm before I could slay it."

That comment stirred a snicker from Harabor. Warren managed the same.

The prophet tugged the reins and called his horse. The wagon rolled up the muddy trail toward the craggy hills in the north.

* * *

Robert sat beside his aunt, hands clasped on his lap.

"Have you ever heard the name 'Boyenor?'" Harabor asked. Robert nodded.

"We told him," Aunt Edelyn confirmed.

"It's my father's family," Robert said. "He was a Boyenor, as am I."

"The Boyenors are more than a family name." Harabor pointed skyward, as if gesturing to the heavens. "They are a storied line dating back centuries, to the foundations of this kingdom. People still tell the story of Boyenor the Brave, and his blood has been passed down through the generations."

The prophet lowered his hand until his finger was pointed at Robert. The boy felt a tickle of wonder in his spine. What greatness was there in him? He was just a farmer, or rather a farmhand, as he did not have his own land.

Harabor made a circling gesture over the small chest, causing the lid to open on its own. Robert gasped.

"You're a wizard?"

"In simple terms, yes. This is little more than a trick. The magic is in the box, even though it appears quite plain. I can conjure flames without flint and do other small acts like that. My true title is prophet. I preserve the wisdom of the past and interpret things that are yet to come."

Robert saw Harabor anew. There was depth to his eyes. The shadows in his pupils seemed to have no bottom.

His aunt leaned forward to peek inside the box. He did the same. Harabor pulled out the round, bronze disk that was inside. Even in the dim light of that sitting room, it glistened and shone like a star. It depicted a gray serpent's body and its severed head, which was nothing more than a fanged skull. Sticking up from the gaping wound was a blue sword. White rays of light projected from the blade, and written in the same brilliant white were the words *SLAYER OF KRAWG*.

"This is your family crest," Harabor explained. "Krawg was a fearsome, fire-breathing beast that killed hundreds. Boyenor the Brave chased him into his lair and slew the beast, restoring peace and protection for everyone across the land. The king honored Boyenor with great wealth and some of his prized land. The land and much of that treasure was shared down through the generations, from fathers to their sons and daughters."

Robert glanced at the cottage's worn wooden floor, its broken shutters and soot-stained walls. The home was humble even by the standards of their remote village.

Harabor guessed at his thoughts. "That was a long time ago, and the wealth was divided between many, many descendants. The shared portion has run dry, but there is another portion that is stored away, and it rightly belongs to any Boyenor who would claim it. There is enough treasure to make any commoner a king."

The excitement in Harabor's voice transferred to Robert.

"Where is it?" he asked.

Harabor handed him the crest. It was cool to the touch, and the smooth metal felt valuable. "It's guarded by Krawg."

"I thought Boyenor killed Krawg."

"He did, but a new Krawg has risen. The son of the beast. This was expected, though. Our ancestors wrote about it."

Harabor reached into the box and produced a thin, leather-bound book. He set it on the table and opened it to a page marked with a piece of golden thread. The parchment was freckled and yellow, the handwriting faded in some places."

"Do you know how to read?" he asked.

"A little," Robert answered. "I recognize most of these words."

"It's a passage that warns about the offspring of Krawg

inhabiting the world and inflicting calamity on its people, just like his father before. The Boyenor shadow still stretches over Krawg, however. It was written that a humble descendant of Boyenor would slay Krawg's offspring, ending the terror."

A warm grin showed through Harabor's thick beard. Wrinkles piled up at his temples. "You were the one they wrote about long ago, many generations before your father. You were born to save us from Krawg and claim the treasure that belongs to you."

A quaking excitement stirred inside Robert. Images of adventure, of distant lands and heaps of gold, flashed in his imagination. There were cheering townspeople, and a gleaming helmet, and sunsets as red as the blood of a slain dragon … but also black lairs and fangs emerging from the darkness. Powerful emotions, both exhilarating and terrifying, were growing too big for his body.

Aunt Edelyn wedged herself into the conversation. "He's only a boy," she protested. "He's not fit to kill a wyrm. Where're the king's soldiers."

"Many of them dead from trying to fight, I'm afraid," Harabor said. "Do not misinterpret me. I know he's not fit to fight yet. I would train him, and I would help him face this foe, as would the powers of the ancients. A son of Boyenor is no common man, and he will be needed to accomplish what others cannot."

"You said nothing of this when you brought him here," Edelyn protested. "And I'm still awaiting my explanation for why you abandoned him the way you did. You swoop into our home in the middle of the night like some lost bat, declaring that his parents were in grave danger, and you leave the boy in my arms. I was beside myself, worried for my sister, and you rode off, never to be heard from until now."

His parents. Robert had lost his focus on them in the talk of dragons and treasure. Now his attention clenched around them … around the question that had burdened him for all his life.

What became of them?

Harabor touched a hand to his heart. "Forgive me, ma'am. I had not realized … the letter never arrived? Time was of the essence that night, but I sent word to you by messenger later. I did not realize it never reached you."

No more delay.

"Please tell me," Robert pleaded. "Are my parents dead?"

Harabor's head sunk forward under the weight of a solemn expression. It was a wordless but loud confirmation of Robert's fear.

"How did they …?" He could not finish the question. Hot tears boiled behind his eyelids.

"I approached your father just as I approach you now," Harabor said. "He was older than you at the time because finding Boyenor descendants is a difficult task, especially nowadays. I thought he was the one to fulfill the prophecy, but the plan went awry. His concern for you and your mother was too great. It turned him away from his destiny."

Robert's hope had always been a frail, withered thing, but he had clung to it like the last brown leaf on an autumn tree. Now … he let go, and the leaf crashed to the ground. The worst had been confirmed. Was the relief to his mind, of finally knowing, worth the new pain in his heart?

He scraped tears off his cheeks with his knuckles. He felt an urge to go outside and finish his chores, anything so he could be away from his aunt and this man who had delivered such a heavy blow.

Harabor shuffled toward the door—or rather toward the

satchel near the door. He untied its clasp.

"I am hopeful that you, Robert Boyenor, will fulfill the prophecy that your father abandoned. The people await their hero."

He reached into the bag and withdrew a gleaming sword.

Robert's eyes widened at the sight of the blue steel blade. It was magnificent, as was the hilt, which ended in a gilded snake head.

"My stars," Aunt Edelyn whispered. "Whose sword is that?"

"The boy's," Harabor said, "and here's the proof."

He stepped toward Robert and held out the sword in both hands, offering it to him. As Robert reached for the grip, his fingers began to glow.

* * *

Warren knew the village of Autumnhill had been attacked, but he was still grieved when confronted with its desolation for the first time. Most of the homes were now charred heaps being overrun by brambles and ferns. Those that had been spared the flames looked like they would succumb to the elements within a few years' time. An overturned statue of a sword-wielding man lay in the center of the mess.

The only structure that looked capable of surviving for another generation was Harabor's manor house. The stone walls stood strong, but they were marred with numerous black scorch marks. The same flames that had decimated the village had tried to burn their way into the grand house.

Encroaching forest.

Untilled farm fields.

Roads that were little more than muddy ruts through grass.

Warren would have taken Autumnhill for a town abandoned, yet there were peasants here and there, toiling over various tasks. One man hammered boards loose from a barrel. Three women knelt beside the road, plucking grass blades as if they were weeds. Another woman shook a pine tree branch, but for what purpose, Warren could not tell.

The whole display surprised him, and the more he took in the people's behavior, the more unnerved he became. Fifteen men and women working, and none of them spoke with one another. Their labors were bizarre. No one was building new homes to replace those that were lost. No one was offering food or wares for sale. No one worked to reclaim the fields from nature.

Just as surprising were the things that were missing. No children ran about. No animals grazed. No one laughed or glanced over their shoulders in embarrassment at their own strangeness. It was if this land had been stricken with madness. Harabor, who was riding beside Warren, guessed at his thoughts. "Now you see the effect that Krawg has on those whom he attacks. This was a proud village, but Krawg burned it and poisoned the people with fear. You see the desolation out here, but there is desolation in here as well." He pointed to his head as he said this, then raised his chin toward the people he was describing.

There had been moments of intense fear during Warren's preparations to slay Krawg. His dreams had been especially capable of scaring him. Krawg would appear in various forms and colors, and more often than not, it got the better of him. But in seeing this destruction, Warren experienced a new form of terror, one of foreboding and hopelessness. Cool sweat bled from his brow, neck, and chest.

"What if I'm not ready for this?" he asked hastily. "What if my wife was right? I am no knight."

"If you were an ordinary man, I would agree," Harabor said, "but you were born with greatness that ordinary men lack. You are a Boyenor, and the monster will fear you and the power that flows through your veins."

At first, none of the villagers gave even a cursory glance to Warren or Harabor. The prophet brought the wagon to a halt in the center of the desolation and called out, "Your champion has arrived."

All fifteen pairs of eyes turned to them. The men and women halted their tasks and trudged toward Warren. Their dirty faces and even dirtier garments gathered around the wagon. They stopped within an arm's reach, staring at him, saying nothing.

"Greetings?" Warren said, more as a question than a declaration. If a commanding tone was any measure of greatness, he was already a failed hero.

Harabor lifted the blanket in the back of the wagon. "Show them this," he said as he handed over the blue Sword of Boyenor, the one that had proven Warren's powerful lineage in their first meeting.

Warren stood and raised the blade to the side of his face. Every part of his body that was close to the steel, from his hands and arms up to his head, glowed. His blood, the blood of a Boyenor descendant, shined white through his skin.

A rainbow of wondrous reactions appeared on the peasants' gray faces. All of them drew in long breaths.

"It's him, the son of Boyenor!" one man exclaimed.

"He's here!" a woman said excitedly.

The people crowded closer to the wagon and looked up expectantly, like goats pressing against a fence for straw.

Warren raised the sword above his head. The responses so far had disturbed him, though he was uncertain why. The people had seemed hollow, their souls shrunken and too small for their bodies. When he held up the blade, however, something inside them awakened. To these people, he was rain on parched soil, a breath of air to someone who had almost drowned.

He had not yet faced the wyrm. What could have made these people so desperate that they would see him as a savior? What kind of burden was he taking on, and could he bear it?

"Save us from Krawg," a half-starved man chanted. "Slay him. Save us from Krawg."

"Beware Krawg," said a woman with a severe overbite. Others joined her chant.

"Beware Krawg. Beware Krawg."

Krawg grew larger and more fearsome in Warren's imagination.

"You can save us," others mumbled. "You've come. Save us. Save us from the serpent."

"Enough!" Harabor growled more harshly than Warren thought possible from the genial old prophet. "No more of that begging. This is no way to greet an honorable guest. Go to my house and prepare supper for him."

The peasants shrunk back from the wagon as their attention snapped to Harabor. They bowed in apology and asked for Warren's forgiveness.

"Forgive us, sir," said one.

"My humblest apologies," said another.

"I regret myself, sir, but I'm pleased you've come."

The woman with the overbite stared long at Harabor, then at Warren. She opened her mouth as if to speak, but gave up. Had she been angry at the prophet? It had seemed that way judging by her darkened eyes.

Harabor returned her glare, and with it he herded the peasants up the steps to the manor. They disappeared inside.

Warren's mind was a stage for dancing questions. Were these people servants of Harabor? They had responded submissively to his commands as if they were puppets tied to his voice. Did they obey him out of respect, or out of fear?

How nightmarish must Krawg be for the wyrm to have this kind of effect on people?

Harabor ran a hand over his face, smoothing out the wrinkles between his knitted brows. "Now do you see how dire the people's need is for a hero? I grieve for their broken minds. No one survived the wyrm's attack with all of their spirit intact. You can change that, however. They can recover once the threat is vanquished."

Warren handed the sword to Harabor, then hopped down from the wagon. He peered at the toppled statue. There was a name carved into its base, showing through the vines and weeds. The letters were framed by two halves of a severed serpent.

"Boyenor?" Warren asked. His attention went to the statue's strong, proud face. "This is a statue of Boyenor the Brave?"

"Yes," Harabor answered. "It commemorates his fight with Krawg's father. That battle took place near here, in the same cave we shall soon explore. This manor house used to belong to him. This land was his reward."

Warren knelt and ran his fingers over the statue's sword. It looked precisely like his own, down to shape of the hilt and the depth of the fuller. "We rode together for six days, and not once did you mention this. Why?"

Harabor pondered the question for a moment, his gaze

meandering. "I thought I had." A smirk started to form, then vanished. "Perhaps I was mistaken."

"Then is the house part of my inheritance as one of Boyenor's heirs?"

Harabor sheathed the sword and tucked it under one arm. He grabbed a bag from the wagon. "No, this I purchased and own. It was sold out of the family generations ago."

He trudged toward the manor house, leaving Warren alone with the fallen replica of his ancestor. He felt a nagging suspicion that the prophet was not confessing everything. Harabor had shown nothing but kindness and wisdom in the years that Warren had known him, but he had hinted at other emotions in their few minutes at Autumnhill. He had revealed a deeply buried temper and forgetfulness that undercut his otherwise impressive memory for details.

Harabor had rattled off so much of the region's history during their ride, and not once had Warren's familial connection to the manor been mentioned.

A peasant threw open shutters on the first floor of the house. Warren felt a pang of disappointment. Those desperate people had cheered his arrival, but it had not been the triumphant moment he had envisioned. Instead, it felt wrong, like entering a room and seeing gossipers fall silent at the sight of you. Something was being hushed up, a secret buried in those grounds, beneath the untamed weeds, overgrown brush, and scorched debris.

Warren longed to hold his son, Robert, and to be held by his wife, Tula. It wasn't the first time he had felt that longing since leaving them behind, but it was by far the strongest.

* * *

Time melted to nothing as Robert held the sword of Boyenor. He stared at his hands until Harabor took the weapon back, at which point the white light that flowed through his veins faded. There had been no sensations from the light, neither heat nor cold, nor pain or pleasure. Nonetheless, now that it was gone, he felt like an awakened part of himself had just been forced back to sleep.

"Oy there!" Aunt Edelyn exclaimed. "He was glowing! How'd you do that?"

"It's nothing by my hand," Harabor said. "The power is in his blood. He was destined to be the next Boyenor the Brave. The sword is bringing out the greatness that was in him all along. This boy is special."

Unlike the light, Robert could feel the prophet's praise. He flushed, and eagerness to face the world beyond his village began to swell inside of him. Dragons, ogres, invading armies—these were things he had always fought in his imagination but never would have done so in his real life. Simple farm boys did not fight such dangers, not unless they wanted a swift end to their lives.

But he was no simple farm boy, was he? The sword had proved it.

Aunt Edelyn crossed her arms in that way she did when haggling for better prices at market. "The light proves nothing. You expect the boy to just practice swinging a sword and rely on his blood to help him slay a monster. He'll be killed. I'll not have it. You brought him to us unannounced, but you'll have to go through me and my husband if you plan to take him away."

"That won't be necessary." Harabor shoved the sword into its scabbard. The cross-guard clapped against the wood. "He's a boy now, but he'll grow strong, and he'll be ready. Today was just a test to prove his importance. His destiny must wait, even if the world is awaiting him. It has been longing for a hero since his father failed."

Again, the sadness of learning his parents' fate squeezed Robert's chest. "How did he fail, sir? Did the wyrm kill him?"

"No," Harabor said. "It was sickness for home that did him in—that, and the thieves. We never even reached Autumnhill. Every day and every night, he lamented being away from you and your mother. A few days before reached we Krawg's lair, he left in the middle of the night. I found a note from Warren in the morning. He asked forgiveness for abandoning the quest."

Aunt Edelyn cut into the conversation with a raised finger. "That's no explanation for why you rushed into my house with baby Robert in your arms?"

Frustration flashed in Harabor's eyes—anger for having been interrupted. Something else had flashed, too. Had that been a spark that jumped from the prophet's fingers? Or had it been a momentary lick of flame? Whatever it was, it startled Robert.

The prophet wiped away his annoyance with a double blink, but his smile did not feel as warm when it returned. "I followed Warren back to his home because he had the sword with him. I needed it so I could deliver it to another Boyenor. It was going to be a long search, as descendants are hard to find these days."

His head turned slowly like a rusted weather vane toward Robert. "When I arrived, I found men riding away with plunder. Their plunder included your parents, who were bound in ropes. You were left inside the house, which had been set aflame. I could hear you crying. The thieves chose to burn you alive rather than take you with them. Fortunately, I managed to get you out in time."

Harabor reached into his satchel and pulled out a wooden

replica of the Boyenor sword. He placed it on the table before Robert. "Forgive me for the way I delivered the boy, but I was in a hurry to pursue the thieves. I found Robert's parents, but they had already been murdered and left beside the road. I buried them, and I later I caught up with the ones responsible for the crime."

He sighed. "They tried to murder me, too, but this old prophet has a few tricks up his sleeves. I'll spare you details except to say I avenged your parents and recovered the sword."

There was a long span of silence between them, a long-overdue moment of respect for the dead. Eventually, Robert picked up the wooden sword. Based upon the way Harabor had placed it, he guessed it was for him.

"Take that one," the prophet said. "Train every day with it. In the meantime, I will keep the real sword. You'll be safer for it. I would be beside myself if I left it in your charge and thieves struck again. In the meantime, I shall travel far and wide, seeing if I can find another Boyenor more suited for this fight."

Robert considered the wooden weapon. It felt good in his hand.

"Feed the boy well," Harabor said to Aunt Edelyn as he picked up his satchel. "He needs to grow into a strong man."

* * *

Warren stared into the darkness of the wyrm's lair. It was difficult to tell if the quaking he felt was from the beast's thunderous steps or from his own nerves.

"Kill Krawg now," one of the people from Autumnhill shouted. "He's not … not …"

"The serpent's a deceiver," yelled Ana, the woman with the

overbite. "He's tricked others."

There was a pall of grief draped over her, as if she were already attending Warren's funeral.

Harabor turned to the survivors of Autumnhill. "Silence. You'll wake the beast."

No one said another word. Their jaws clenched.

The lair looked more like an oversized burrow than a cave. The hole opened into the hillside, and roots from trees further up the slope protruded through the cave's ceiling. The entrance was tall enough for Warren to ride a horse through it—not that he had a horse. Or armor. Just his sword and the blood of the kingdom's greatest hero.

The air outside the cave was replaced with fumes from brimstone and rotting carcasses. A half-eaten deer lay beside the hole. Several crows were eying the feast, but none dared approach it.

This is madness, protested the saner parts of Warren's mind.

"Courage, now," Harabor said. "I'll be with you."

Warren marched across the gravel and dead grass, his sword held in both hands. The light from his body was faint in the daylight, but as he stepped into the darkness, the fullness of its glow was revealed. Night became day. The bones, rocks, and moss that lined the tunnel emerged from the shadows.

The woman named Ana choked out a cry, "Krawg is behind you!"

Warren snapped around, weapon at the ready, heart drumming. He saw only Harabor and the entrance of the cave. He released his breath. How long had he been holding it?

The prophet muttered something to himself. "Pay them no mind. They're skittish. Focus on the task ahead. After today, you will be praised in song far across the land. Your boy will grow up a prince."

A prince. Warren liked the idea of a song in his honor, but even greater was the thought of Tula robed like a queen and Robert living like a prince. The people of Autumnhill would be free from fear, and Robert would inherit a fortune.

That was worth a risk.

Warren pressed deeper into the cave. Harabor pulled out a torch from his belt and, whispering a spell, caused it to ignite. They came to a manmade timber platform. A rope was tied to it. To reach the next chamber of the cave, he would have to climb down.

"Keep going," Harabor said. "I've been in this cave before. The wyrm cannot be far."

Warren moved to the edge of the platform. He knelt to grab the rope, then stopped. A clutter of white shapes on the floor below caught his eye.

They were bones. Hundreds of them. Judging by the skulls and the garments tangled among the skeletons, some were from humans.

Warren almost cursed at the ghastly sight, but he never got the chance. Harabor planted his foot in Warren's ribs and shoved him off the platform. He plunged, and his heart lurched so hard that it felt like he had left it behind.

He crashed to the floor, the bone pile worsening the impact rather than softening it. His vision swam to-and-fro as if he had been tossed into a stormy sea. Thrumming pain reverberated through his back and head. It consumed all of his senses until he became slowly aware of another hurt, a stabbing sensation in his ribs.

Warren reached to grab the spot. He felt bone. It was not his own. His fingers came away hot and wet. A fragment from one of the skeletons had pierced his side.

Blood, but it was white rather than red. He still had his sword in his left hand, so his blood, both internal and external, was glowing. The floor around him was illuminated as well, painted with more glowing blood.

A low chuckle came from the platform above. Harabor peered down at him. Warren wanted to yell at him, to demand answers for what he had done, but he struggled to breath.

"Another Boyenor for the collection," the prophet said between laughs.

Were these Boyenor bones? Was that why everything around him shined?

Warren rose to his elbows. The pain expanded. "Wh—" A gulp of air. "Why?"

"I'm fulfilling a promise. I swore vengeance on Boyenor the Braggart's descendants, from the first generation to the last, because he killed my father. I'm a man of my word."

Warren dug through the pain in his head, trying to come to some understanding. "He killed your father? I thought he killed the wyrm, Krawg."

"My father was Krawg. They called him a serpent." Harabor spat. His mask of kindness was gone. Anger carved deep wrinkles into his face. "He was the finest wizard this kingdom had ever known. The people feared him for his talent, so they tried again and again to kill him. Your ancestor succeeded, not just against my father, but my sisters as well. He took our lineage, so I take his."

"Like this? Like a coward?"

"Boyenor was anything but brave. He tricked my father before he murdered him."

Warren should have felt fury toward the prophet, but he was

too overwhelmed with confusion. "If you're the son of Krawg, then you're the one the prophecy said I would kill."

"Prophecy?" Harabor laughed. "I wrote that book a long, long time ago. Much of this has been a game, and you've been a delightful player. I have many games I play with you people, but this is by far my favorite."

"The wyrm was a deception, too?"

A cruel smirk curled on Harabor's lips. "No, what fun would there be in that? There is a wyrm, and I keep it fed."

Harabor gave a shrill whistle, and a skull the size of a hay cart rose from the cave floor.

* * *

Robert was no longer the child working on his aunt and uncle's farm. He was a strong lad of fifteen, one eager to fulfill his destiny. He had practiced his swordsmanship for years, and he took comfort in knowing Harabor was with him. Nonetheless, the darkness of the cave ahead of him, and the reek of brimstone and damp earth that seeped out of it, caused him to tremble.

The wyrm was in there, waiting for him.

"Press on, boy ," Harabor said. "Krawg's reign of terror ends today."

Robert glanced back at the six remaining people of Autumn-hill. All of them were old, their life and joy drained out of them. Ana, the woman with a large overbite, had such pity in her eyes. She opened her mouth, as if choking on the words she wanted to say, and pointed at him—or was she pointing at Harabor?

"Be swift," the prophet said. "Caution will only make the fight harder to win."

The cave tunnel slanted down into the earth. The light from

Robert's body reflected off the walls, as did the sound of his footfalls. Ahead, the stone ground changed to timber beams.

"Don't look back now," Harabor said. "You're almost to the beast."

As Robert approached the wooden platform, he noticed a faint glow on the ground.

* * *

Warren dove. The wyrm's jaws streaked past, following by the rest of the creature. Its dark, scaly body was segmented by white bones. The spine, ribs, and skull protruded through its hide, partially exposed. It was as much skeleton as it was dragon.

The wyrm had numerous legs along its body, each with a clawed foot. Warren tried to slash one of them but missed. The beast stampeded out of reach.

Harabor roared with laughter. "Boyenor passed on his blood but no intellect. Three-hundred-forty-eight of your kin have I fooled in my lifetime, and more than eighty are in here. It serves all of you right. They called my father a serpent and a trickster before they beheaded him. They made him a snake on your family crest. Well, here is your serpent."

The wyrm weaved through the bone field, kicking up skulls and femurs. Warren got to his feet, bracing for the next attack. The wound in his ribs burned. He could feel blood running down to his hip.

Harabor—or rather Krawg—gave a sharp whistle, causing the wyrm to round on Warren. "Eat him, Varrosa. Gorge yourself." Another whistle. "This has been great fun, Warren Boyenor. Take pleasure in knowing your wife will die next. The boy will live for a while. I'll need someone else to play this game."

The fear and despair that weighed Warren down burned up in a flare of rage. *Not Tula and Robert. That madman can't have my family.*

He had to kill the prophet Krawg, but first he had to escape the wyrm.

The beast charged him, jaws flashing side-to-side as it neared.

Warren stepped left, then dove right, thrusting the sword upward as he fell. The blade was knocked aside by the beast's exposed jawbone. Warren rolled to avoid the feet rushing by him on either side, but he was too slow. One of the claws sliced his shoulder.

He cried out in pain, which caused the prophet to laugh. "You can't kill it," he said. "It's life is bound to mine. I control it, even more than I control those simpletons from the village."

Warren slipped on bones as he got to his knees. Twice more the wyrm tried to snatch him in its jaws, and twice more the blade slid off its hide. On the last pass, it slammed him aside with its head.

The prophet's laughs went to a higher, more maniacal pitch. "Don't dull the blade. I'll have to pay to have it sharpened."

Krawg whistled again. Warren gathered himself like pieces of a shattered plate. He got to his feet in spite of his pain, just in time to see the jaws of the beast spreading around him. The thought of his wife and son gave him just enough strength and anger to extend his sword into the wyrm's throat.

He was thrown by the impact of a massive, wet tongue, but not out of the beast's reach. The jaws snapped around him. His body illuminated the inside of the wyrm's mouth. He was shaken about, smashing his head against the inside of the fangs, until all went dark.

He awoke later, a battered husk of himself. Even the act of opening his eyes was exhausting. His garments were soaked. Hot, sulfurous air blew over his body in waves.

Not air. Breaths.

Sharp terror cut through the haze of his confusion. He was still in the wyrm's mouth! His sword was stuck in its throat, keeping him from being swallowed.

The wyrm lifted him up and tilted its head. The jaws opened. Warren grabbed the sword hilt in order to steady himself, but the blade slid free of the dragon's flesh. He fell, clutching the sword.

Warren landed on his already injured back. A white, reptilian skull stared down at him with vacant eyes. He tried to scramble out of its vacant glare, knowing it was a fool's effort. Bones shifted under him like loose gravel, thwarting his escape.

He still held his sword, but what good was it? It was by luck that it had saved him from getting swallowed, but such luck would not strike again. He was no more than an insect before this monster.

The wyrm continued to stare ... and stare. It did not draw closer, nor did it lash out with its fangs. Its foul breaths washed over the ground.

What had Krawg called it? Varrosa? Warren crawled away from it, keeping his gaze on the fiend, but the attack never resumed. Its exposed bones seemed to float in the air. It was content to merely watch him. Or was it waiting for a command? Krawg was no longer laughing or commanding it with whistles.

The dragon's pale, rigid face hovered in the darkness. Waited. Waited.

Warren slid the sword under his belt, then climbed the rope he had tried to descend earlier. His terror gave him strength to make it halfway, but only half. The rest of the ascent was torment. Every thread of strength was frayed, every muscle gasping on its death bead. The wounds on his side and shoulder stretched, spilling out more and more of his life.

His body begged to let go of the rope, but his hope refused. He would see Tula again.

Warren found the strength to reach one more time.

He had made a promised Robert that he would return.

Warren moved his hand higher.

His rage toward Krawg, at the thought of him killing his family, clasped Warren's fingers around the edge of the timber platform.

He dragged himself onto the beams, recovering his breath, screaming at himself to get up. The edges of his vision darkened.

Krawg might be riding to his house at that moment.

I need to get up.

He only made it a few paces before he collapsed on the stone ground. The core of his body felt cold. The blood on his skin felt warm. He craved sleep.

Warren rolled to his side, causing his blade to clink against the ground. The spilled blood on his tunic and hands were daylight in the darkness. From somewhere in his mind, amidst the storm of pain and fear for his family, an idea sparked.

He drew a line of blood on the ground. It was white beside the sword of Boyenor. Warren touched his side and drew another line. Then another. He wrote out his message while his legs recouped some strength. Once finished, he forced himself to make his way to the cave entrance.

Sleep was leaning against him with all of its weight. It forced him to one knee. He braced himself against the sword to keep from falling over.

The sunlight was too bright. It made him dizzy, made his head feel like a hammered nail. His vision was turning utterly white, but before it did, he spotted the prophet hurrying toward him. He heard Krawg shouting something, but the words blurred. His ears were numb.

The white light swallowed Warren, separating him from the world. He saw Tula's beautiful face in that veil, and Robert, and all the things Robert would do as he grew into a man. He wanted to reach out to them, to touch them, but could not.

He could, however, weep over his broken promise.

I'm sorry I won't be coming home.

* * *

Because the lines were white instead of red, it took Robert several seconds to realize the marks on the ground were Boyenor blood.

He was hit by a thunderclap of shock and then a rumble of anger and grief. So many things that had seemed odd over the years, like the prophet's shifting recollections about his father, suddenly made sense. Harabor had blamed his aging mind, but now Robert understood the truth.

The message at the tip of his sword read, "Harabor is Krawg. Kill him. –Warren."

The lines were crooked. Messy. Scrawled by someone in distress.

"Why have you stopped, boy?" Harabor asked.

The flames of Robert's anger climbed his body, warming his muscles.

"Tell me, how do you know the wyrm is close?" he asked.

"Have you been in this cave before?" He snapped his head around. "How about my father? Has he been here?"

Harabor leaned to one side to get a clear view of the message. Robert studied him, looking for proof of the blood message's claim. He wanted it to be false, wanted the prophet to explain it away, but all of the wrong emotions crystallized on Harabor's face. He looked guilty. Outraged. Defiant.

Robert raised the blade toward his mentor's heart.

"You said thieves killed him. The number of thieves changed, the location of his death changed, but you always insisted he never reached the cave. Why is his name written here?"

Harabor, or rather Krawg, snarled. "That wretched cur."

The prophet had many kinds of magic at his disposal. Robert had always been intrigued by his powers, but now he feared them. As soon as Krawg raised a hand, Robert lunged at him, but a blast of fire drove him aside.

Robert scurried up from the ground, shielding himself with one arm in case more flames shot from Krawg's fingers. He wore no protection other than his tunic. He would have to strike quickly.

However, instead of launching flames, the prophet let out a shrill whistle. The cave shook.

Robert charged his mentor, screaming for vengeance. Krawg countered by shouting a strange word, one that seemed to bore into Robert's head. The direction of the tunnel shifted, not under his feet but in his mind. A rogue thought snuck into his head. *Maybe I'm mistaken. Maybe Harabor is innocent. Maybe I should lay down my sword and apologize.*

Robert shook his head. The thoughts weren't his own. They were a trick from the prophet. He clung to his grief over his parents' deaths, fighting off the deception.

He came to his senses just in time to see Krawg fleeing out of the tunnel. Then he turned to the rumble behind him.

The wyrm was racing toward him, jaws open.

Robert sprinted after the prophet. His young legs helped him close the gap on his enemy, but the wyrm was faster still. Its brimstone breaths flooded the tunnel. The stampede was deafening.

He could feel the massive teeth bearing down on his back. Robert feared for his life, but he also feared his chance for revenge had escaped. Krawg had reached the cave's entrance.

Rather than flee, the prophet turned and raised his hands. Robert recognized the gesture and dove. He felt a flash of warmth as Krawg's fireball hurtled over him. He also felt the tip of his sword cut through flesh.

The wyrm's massive bulk crashed into him. Robert was thrown by the beast's jaws. He slid across the ground, gravel tearing at his limbs.

His scrapped knees felt raw, but there was no time to nurse wounds. Robert scrambled to his feet and meant to raise his sword against the creature, but his hand was empty.

Krawg had his blade. It was buried in his gut. The prophet was lying on his back, horror-filled eyes staring upward, his right leg pinned beneath the wyrm. His fingers were wrapped around his wound, but blood continued to spread.

The massive wyrm breathed but remained otherwise motionless. Krawg was dying, and so, too, was his monstrous pet.

Villagers from Autumnhill approached cautiously. The woman named Ana was the first to reach Robert. She embraced him, her tears soaking his tunic.

"Thank you," she said, sniffling. "Thank you, sir."

It was over. When the wyrm tackled him, Robert had

managed to stab his enemy.

Robert cried as well, but not in celebration. His tears were for the parents he had never known. They were for his father, who had used his own blood to save him. His parents had been given justice, leaving Robert with nothing else but the chance to truly, fully grieve his loss for the first time.

> *Woe unto you, when all men speak well of you,*
> *For so did their fathers to the false prophets*

C.W. Briar

C W Briar is the author of the dark fantasy novel *Whispers From The Depths*. His stories gravitate toward suspenseful, bittersweet, and humorous. He resides in Upstate New York with his family and their pack of corgis.

Bear Publications

Bear Publications is a Christian publisher of speculative short story anthologies, novels, and non-fiction that relates to science fiction and fantasy. Learn more at: www.bearpublications.com

Made in the USA
Columbia, SC
05 August 2019